The Year of Lost and Found

Felicity Hayes-McCoy, author of the bestselling Finfarran series, was born in Dublin, Ireland. She studied literature at UCD before moving to England in the 1970s to train as an actress. Her work as a writer ranges from TV and radio drama and documentary, to screenplays, music theatre, memoir and children's books. Her Finfarran novels are widely read on both sides of the Atlantic, and in Australia, and have been translated into six languages.

She and her husband, opera director Wilf Judd, live in the West Kerry Gaeltacht and in Bermondsey, London. She blogs about life in both places on her website (www.felicityhayesmccoy.co.uk) and you can follow her on Twitter @fhayesmccoy and on Facebook at Felicity Hayes-McCoy Author.

ALSO BY FELICITY HAYES-MCCOY
The Finfarran series
The Library at the Edge of the World
Summer at the Garden Café
The Mistletoe Matchmaker
The Month of Borrowed Dreams
The Transatlantic Book Club
The Heart of Summer

Non-fiction
The House on an Irish Hillside
Enough is Plenty: The Year on Dingle Peninsula
A Woven Silence: Memory, History & Remembrance
Dingle and Its Hinterland: People, Places & Heritage

Felicity
Hayes-McCoy

The Year of
Lost
and
Found

HACHETTE
BOOKS
IRELAND

First published in Ireland in 2021 by
HACHETTE BOOKS IRELAND

1

Cataloguing in Publication Data is available from the British Library

ISBN 9781529361056

Typeset in Arno Pro by Bookends Publishing Services, Dublin

Printed and bound in Great Britain by Clays, Elcograf S.p.A

Hachette Books Ireland policy is to use papers that are natural, renewable
and recyclable products and made from wood grown in sustainable forests.
The logging and manufacturing processes are expected to conform to the environmental
regulations of the country of origin.

Hachette Books Ireland
8 Castlecourt Centre
Castleknock
Dublin 15, Ireland

A division of Hachette UK Ltd
Carmelite House, 50 Victoria Embankment, EC4Y 0DZ

www.hachettebooksireland.ie

For the ordinary people in extraordinary

times whose stories are seldom told

Visitors to the west coast of Ireland won't find Finfarran. The peninsula, its inhabitants and those of Hanna Casey's London exist only in the author's imagination.

Prologue

A hawk drifted lazily over Finfarran, carried by currents of air and the strength of her outspread wings. Far below, a library van stood outside the county-council building in Carrick, where figures emerging from offices were moving with the purposeful energy of workers making for home. Sloping and spiralling, the hawk flew westward. To her right was a compact market town and long, golden beaches backed by sand dunes starred with wildflowers. To the left, rolling hills rose above a forest to become a majestic mountain range that guarded the end of the tapering peninsula. Beyond the distant mountains was a little fishing port, which, since the advent of a road that ran in a straight line from Carrick, boasted luxury spa hotels and a sparkling marina beside which visitors sipped spritzers and wondered whether to choose steak frites or go for the catch of the day.

It was late afternoon at the start of summer. As the bird flew on, the landscape below became increasingly rugged, and the turquoise white-crested waves hurled themselves against higher cliffs. Losing height, she sheered away over farmland, where barns were readied for harvests that were still growing in fields. Beneath her, spilling out onto a road that led to a farmyard gate, were rows of parked cars. Foreshortened to a manikin from the hawk's lofty viewpoint, a girl got out of one and, balancing a plate against a hip, slammed and locked the car door.

Here the roads were narrow and the ditches that lined them were topped with heather and furze. The hawk circled deliberately. This was her hunting ground. The land above which she hovered was bounded by dry-stone walls, and her prey lived between them on lush pasture grazed by cattle and sheep. Wings whirring, she held her position, her talons outstretched and her bright yellow eye seeking movement. In the cropped grass a small creature stirred and darted towards a wall on which patches of lichen gleamed like silver coins. The hawk dropped instantly, but too late. Reaching shelter, the creature scurried behind an outcrop of brambles and found safety by grey stone between flowers and thorns.

As the bird whirled and regained height, a flight feather fell from her wing. A kaleidoscope of black, brown and grey, it spun gently, skimmed fields and ditches, and came to rest by a stream. She flew on and the feather was held in a tangle of fluttering grasses, the point of its quill dipped deep in rust-coloured mud. High above, the hawk stretched her wings, and made steadily for the mountains, which for centuries had offered safety to shadowy groups who lit secret fires and dreamed of a new day.

Chapter One

The farm kitchen was full of sunlight, subdued chatter and plates of ham sandwiches. Aideen had put the baby monitor on the work surface next to the kettle so she could lean in and hear Ronan's breathing. When she moved away, carrying cups or a steaming glass smelling of cloves and brown sugar, the soft snuffles from upstairs would give way to the sounds around her – murmured condolences, family reminiscences and the renewed acquaintance of neighbours who had long left Finfarran. Conor, Joe and Una were sitting side by side on upright chairs. Aideen knew Conor was longing to come and help her, but he and Joe couldn't leave their mother to shake all those hands alone. As each group entered, carrying tins of homemade buns or platters covered with tea-towels, some neighbour already installed with a drink would relieve them of their burdens, allowing them to join the queue passing the three kitchen chairs. The door was open, giving a view of ginger cats asleep on a sun-warmed flagstone, then a glimpse of the corner of the cowshed and the orchard beyond the yard. It was early summer and the trees had shed their white petals, leaving knots of green apples swelling on branches stippled with grey lichen.

Someone arrived with a Tupperware box and, as Aideen looked for somewhere to put it, her cousin Bríd held out a hand. 'Give it here to me. Will I stick it in the fridge?'

'There's no room.'

Bríd rolled her eyes. 'Wouldn't you think they'd know we'd be all right for the catering? I mean, duh, we do run a deli.'

'I know, but it's—'

'Don't tell me. Tradition.'

'Well, yeah. And kind. I mean, most people don't know how else to show sympathy.'

'Well, I don't know who'll be comforted by a box of cocktail sausages.' Seeing Aideen's face, Bríd's voice changed. 'Look, are you okay? Don't you want to sit with Conor?'

'I'm happier being useful.'

'Why not take a cup of tea and go up and check on Ronan?'

'Well ...'

'Go on. I'll serve drinks, and half the parish is stacking the dishwasher. Take a breather. You've been on your feet since we came back from the graveyard.'

Conor was shaking hands with Hanna Casey, Ronan's godmother, and hugging Hanna's daughter, Jazz, who'd been at school with Bríd and Aideen. He'd gone to the same school, as had Dan, Bríd's boyfriend. Aideen watched, thinking it was strange that she who, at twenty-two, was the youngest of the four girls, should be the one who was married with a baby. These days, the few years between them didn't appear to mean much to the others, but to her they still mattered. Though she liked Jazz, and Bríd had always been like a big sister, Aideen was shy and always felt happiest in the background – even today, when she was what the priest had called a 'chief mourner'. The words felt too big for her, yet the priest was right. Her father-in-law's death meant that Conor would now be farming alone with the help of the hired labourer. Although Joe was the elder brother, he had no interest in farming: he was married and working in Cork, and tomorrow, when he and his wife, Eileen, had gone, Aideen, Conor and Una would be left to cope with the aftermath of death.

The thought of life without Paddy's presence made Aideen's eyes fill with tears. Bríd gave her a gentle push. 'Go on upstairs and have a lie-down.' She poured a mug of tea and folded a biscuit in a napkin. 'That's one of my professional proper chocolate-chip cookies. Two euro fifty a throw in the deli, so mind you appreciate it. You'll be eating your own profits.'

At the mention of the deli, Aideen looked concerned. 'Listen, I'll be in to work tomorrow. It's one of my days.'

'You will not. Pavel will take your shift.'

'But he's not rostered.'

'Ah, for feck's sake, Ade, would you have a bit of sense? We own the place, you and me. The staff does what it's told.' Seeing Aideen's face, Bríd's voice softened again. 'Don't look like that.

Pavel will be fine. He sent his condolences. Now, will you take your tea and go and have a rest?'

Ronan was sleeping deeply. The window was half open and the sound of sheep calling to lambs drifted down from a hill field. Aideen lay on the bed holding her mug and propped up by pillows. Though Bríd's baking was delicious, she'd set aside the cookie and was gulping the scalding tea, thinking how weird it was that bereavement, which seemed to throw up the oddest random memories, also made you thirsty all the time. A gurgle from the cot made her turn to Ronan, who'd woken and kicked off his blanket. As she swung her legs from the bed and reached down to lift him, the door opened and Conor looked into the bedroom. 'How's the little guy?'

'Grand. He was fast asleep till just now.'

Conor came and sat on the bed beside her, taking Ronan and bouncing him on his knee. 'I'll have to see to the cows.'

'Are there still crowds below?'

'It's emptying out a bit.'

'Una must be exhausted.'

'I know. It cuts both ways, though, doesn't it? It's great to see the big turnout.'

Aideen put out her hand. Conor's sun-bleached hair felt as soft as the fair, fuzzy down on Ronan's head. She wished he didn't have to change his clothes and go up to the shed for the milking but, as he'd said that morning, cows took no account of burials. Ruffling his hair, she said, 'You can put your feet up when you're done.'

'No, I'll shower and get back into the suit. There'll probably be another crowd through this evening when people have finished work.'

'Paddy was really respected. Listen, I'll change this fella and come downstairs in a minute. You go on up to the cows.'

'Right so.' Conor stood up and kissed her. 'It's really something, isn't it? I mean, Paddy hadn't been to the mart for years, or even down the pub. He was practically a recluse. But I'd say the best part of Finfarran has come to give him a good send-off.'

By the time Aideen came down to the kitchen, Joe and his wife had said their goodbyes and driven off in their new Range Rover, and Una had moved to an easy chair by the range. Jazz and her mum were helping Bríd to clear plates and dishes, and Hanna's mother, Mary Casey, was ensconced opposite Una with a hot whiskey toddy and a plate of butterfly buns. Aideen went to join Bríd, holding Ronan against her shoulder. Hanna, to whom she hadn't had a chance to speak earlier, smiled and said she was sorry for her trouble. Aideen smiled back. 'Thanks, that's kind of you. You really don't need to be doing this.'

Hanna handed a casserole dish to Bríd. 'I'm just giving Mary a while with Una. I'll take her away shortly.'

Aideen hastily assured her that Mary was very welcome, and Hanna acknowledged the form of words with a grin. 'Well, she wanted to come and pay her respects, so I gave her a lift over. But no one knows better than I do that my mother can be wearing.'

Bríd was packing cutlery into a box. 'We'll be off too when Dan's ready. If people come by this evening, I'd say you'll have enough plates and cutlery yourself.'

'We'll be fine. We often feed a dozen when the silage contractors are here.' Aideen looked round. 'Where's Dan gone?'

'Up to help Conor. Mind you, Dan wouldn't know one end of a cow from the other unless she came with sails or an outboard engine. Still, I guess he'll be able to hose things down. He brought boots.'

The baby was straining sideways, having caught sight of Una. Aideen carried him over and Una took him on her lap. Mary Casey was a large-bosomed, good-looking widow in her seventies, wearing an outfit chosen to be suitable for a funeral yet smart enough to cut a dash at the gathering back at the farm. 'I've been telling Una I'm sorry for your trouble. Paddy McCarthy was a good man. Strange in his ways latterly, mind, but that was the medication. Time and again I've said to my neighbour you'd have to forgive the poor man for being surly. For all you'd be miffed when he wouldn't so much as salute you on the road.'

Aideen flushed. 'He wasn't surly.'

Mary pursed her lips judicially. 'No, fair play, you're right there, he wasn't. He was … What'll I call it? Distant. But a good man. And a fine farmer, by all accounts, before he had that fall. But, God, wasn't it terrible soon you lost him? He couldn't have been more than fifty-six or -seven.' This statement of the obvious made Aideen wince, but Una, with more experience of the ritual of funerals, replied that Paddy had indeed been young. Mary's attention switched abruptly to the baby. 'Do you know what it is? That child hasn't put up an ounce since I last saw him. He must be past eight months now, is he, Aideen?'

Una laughed. 'The clinic is perfectly happy with him, Mary. He takes after Conor, who takes after me, the way Joe takes after Paddy.'

Sparring being the only form of conversation Mary knew, she nodded with the air of one conceding a hard-fought point. 'And, to give Conor his due, Una, he got your looks as well as the slim cut of you. You did well to catch him, Aideen. No, I'm saying nothing, only that the child will never be the size of Paddy. But, with any luck, he won't have poor Paddy's ill-health either. Is it true, Una, it was a stroke that took him?'

'Yes.'

'But he hadn't been right for years.'

'No, but, like you said, that was the fall. He was in a lot of pain from his back and he missed working on the farm.'

'They tell me he got depression?'

'Yes. And you're right, there was a lot of medication. It pulled him down.'

Mary flicked a crumb from her blouse and refocused on Ronan. 'And that poor scrap will be growing up now without having a granddad on either side. Isn't that the way of the world, though?

One generation's folly falls on another.' Apparently unaware of the surge of colour to Aideen's face, Mary reached complacently for her glass. At that moment, an elderly man appeared at the door to the yard and, with a flick of her eyes, Una suggested that Aideen should go and greet him.

As she crossed the kitchen, Aideen was aware she'd been given a chance to escape. It was silly, she thought, to get annoyed, and shaming that Una, who'd just lost her husband, should have coped with Mary Casey's pinpricks so much better than she had. And what else could you expect from Mary? Even in her kindest moments, she could never resist a hit. Pulling herself together, Aideen smiled at Fury O'Shea, who was standing in the doorway. 'It's good of you to come by, Fury. Let me get you a drink. Where's The Divil?'

'Outside in the van. It wouldn't be proper to bring him in today.'

Unlike Mary, Fury hadn't dressed for the occasion. His cracked boots, ingrained with cement dust, were clearly those of a builder and his hands were thrust into the pockets of his torn waxed jacket. A lanky man who'd spent much of his life on construction sites in England, he wore corduroy trousers tucked into his socks and the eyes above his beaky nose were shrewd under an ancient woolly hat. Beyond his shoulder, Aideen could see the battered red van parked next to the cowshed, and Fury's Jack Russell terrier, with his front paws on the dashboard, peering through the windscreen.

'You could keep him under your arm.'

'Not at all. He'll settle and have a sleep for himself. Anyway, if I let him out he'd only be chasing after your cats.' It was unheard of for The Divil to misbehave while with his master, but Aideen nodded, touched by Fury's sense of propriety. Having shaken her hand, he crossed the room to Una, leaving a series of powdery footprints behind him, and, removing his hat, began what appeared to be a formal speech. Aideen became aware of the evening light slanting across the yard. Ronan was happy in Una's arms, and everyone else seemed content to be chatting or clearing up. So she stepped over the threshold and, with the breeze lifting her red-gold curls, walked up to the orchard above the house.

There'd been a brief shower as they'd driven home from the graveyard, and the unmown grass at the foot of the trees still glittered with fallen raindrops. Only a week earlier, as protection from hungry birds, Paddy had spread old net curtains over the gooseberry bushes. The green globes had yet to swell on the long, prickly branches but, like the apples, they were already full of the promise of summer. The oldest trees in the McCarthys' orchard had stood for three generations. A Bramley and a crab-apple planted by Conor's great-grandmother had still been producing fruit when Joe was little, but the Bramley had fallen in a storm in the week that Conor was born. When Una brought him home to the farm from the hospital, she set a replacement tree that they always called Conor's and, hearing the story, Aideen had decided to do the same for Ronan. They'd planted it under Paddy's instruction on a day when the blue air had rung with birdsong and, before Conor spread the root ball and lowered it into the hole, Aideen had dropped a silver coin into the dark earth. All three had spat on the roots, to bring good luck to the tree, then Conor and Paddy had trampled it in and replaced the turned-back sods of grass around it. It stood there now in gallant leaf, sheltered by a gnarled damson tree that was low-growing and resistant to the wind.

Aideen closed her hand around the little tree's slender trunk. She'd felt overwhelmed when Conor had first introduced her to his family and, though she'd done her best, had been at a loss to know how to converse. Paddy had noticed and, despite his dislike of company, had joined them for tea in the kitchen and been kind to her. With her council-house upbringing, she had known little about the land, but Paddy had sensed her deep affinity with it. A quiet, often inarticulate, friendship had grown up between them and, while Una was equally welcoming and Aideen had come to love her, time spent with Paddy had always felt precious. His depression was a subject never spoken of in the house but, here in the garden or on walks by the river, he'd talked to Aideen about it. 'It comes out of nowhere for no reason, that's the awful part. I feel I might lose my grip and disappear into the dark. But you know what keeps me anchored? You do.'

'Me?'

'You and Conor and Ronan. And Una. Ordinary life going

on. Seeds planted and crops growing, lambs being born and kept warm by the range.'

'But they die, don't they? The lambs. We raise sheep for slaughter.'

'Everything dies, girl. Lambs and flowers and grain that's cut down to make bread. Whatever lives dies eventually. That's Nature's way.'

Grasping the smooth trunk of Ronan's tree, Aideen closed her eyes. Paddy hadn't seemed to think of death as darkness. What he'd hated was the depression that had made his life so hard. Not that you'd want him gone, but at least that was over now. And he wasn't really gone. Una had said so this morning. He was still here in the land, and in Conor and the baby. Ronan would grow up knowing all about him. He'd learn things from Conor, as Conor had learned from Paddy, and as Paddy had learned from Conor's granddad before him. He'd know where he belonged, and where he came from. Only someone like me could understand how important this is, thought Aideen. Only someone who hadn't known her own father at all.

Chapter Two

Carrick, Finfarran's sprawling county town, had grown up in the shadow of a medieval castle. Between it and the little fishing port, with its luxury marina, was the market town of Lissbeg, where Aideen and Bríd had opened their deli and Hanna Casey was the local librarian.

Woken by a bird chirping outside her window, Hanna stretched and felt her usual rush of astonished contentment. Resting her chin on her up-drawn knees, she considered the lofty room with its floor-to-ceiling windows and the stunning view down the Hag's Glen to chequered farmland and a strip of dark forest. Far beyond the trees, visible from the first-floor bedroom, the turquoise ocean glinted under a cloudless sky. Here I am, she thought, living in this beautiful place designed by the man I love, with a bad divorce behind me and a job I enjoy to get up for. Beside her, Brian stirred and rolled over. 'Sleep well?'

'Perfectly. I've hardly been awake five minutes.'

'You're looking very smug, what are you thinking?'

'Smug? Don't be beastly. I was thinking how happy you make me.'

'That's nice.' Brian propped himself on his elbow and reached up to kiss her. 'What time is it?'

'Time we were both getting ready for work.' Hanna threw back the duvet and, ignoring his protest, rolled out of bed. There was a buzz from her phone, which she'd left on the dressing-table, and, shrugging on her kimono, she went to check it.

'What is it?'

'A text from my mother.' Hanna held out the phone and Brian read the text. YOU CAN DROP ME IN SOME SQUIRTYP CREQAM ON YOLUR WAY INTO WORK. Immediately a second message appeared on the screen. AND GLOVES IM DOING AN APPLETA RT.

Brian assumed a poker face. 'I'm saying nothing.'

With a reluctant laugh, Hanna subsided on the edge of the bed. 'The garage shop always has cans of cream.'

'And the gloves?'

'You know that's not what she meant.'

'I certainly do. I've had Mary's apple tart. Three cloves to a slice.'

'I doubt if the garage keeps whole cloves. There's a packet of ground ones here in the kitchen, though.'

'They won't be right.'

'Of course they won't. Nothing ever is with Mary.' Hanna stood up. 'I'll take our cloves and, if the garage doesn't have whole ones, she'll just have to settle for what she gets. We've been summoned to a county library meeting, which means I've a whole day's admin to get through this morning.'

'What's the meeting?'

'God knows.' Hanna laughed. 'It was one of Tim's pompous emails, shrouded in secrecy and signed "T. Slattery, Finfarran County Librarian", as if we were all going to scratch our heads and wonder who sent it.'

'I'll be working in the office. Do you fancy dinner in Carrick?'

Brian's office in Carrick was in the same complex as the county library and, as Finfarran's county architect, his position in the council's hierarchy was precisely equal to Tim's in terms of prestige. But, in appearance, character and attitude to their work, they couldn't have been more different. Brian, who was tall, wore his dark hair short and dressed in jeans and T-shirts, or linen shirts, and unstructured jackets. He bought the best clothes he could afford, wore them for years and replaced them without much thought, his mind always on the next scheme he was building. Tim was a short, middle-aged man with a brush of iron-grey hair and a predilection for three-piece suits, snakeskin shoes and silk handkerchiefs. His focus on his own importance, rather than his job, irritated Hanna and he was sharp enough to see and resent her efforts to conceal it.

She smiled across at Brian. 'Dinner would be great.'

'Give me a call when you're done and I'll come and collect you.'

'It'll be something to look forward to. Actually, the thought of it may just keep me sane. I'd prepared myself to put up with

Tim but I hadn't planned to start the day running errands for my mother.'

'I could try to find whole cloves somewhere further afield and drop them round.'

'No, it's fine. She's my problem, not yours.' Though Hanna spoke lightly, there was an undertone of tension that wasn't lost on Brian. Getting up, he drew her to the window. 'In that case, all I can offer is brilliant design and location. See?' Swinging open the tall window, he indicated the view. 'Living here puts everything into perspective.' As they stood looking down the glen, he could feel her shoulders relax, so he tried again. 'It's no trouble to go foraging for Mary. I've got time today, and you haven't.'

Hanna grinned. 'And I suppose you're going to say you enjoy her company.'

He grinned back, making a show of choosing his words carefully. 'She can be amusing.'

'So people tell me.' Hanna slipped from his arm and made for the shower. 'People who haven't had to put up with her as long as I have!'

Hanna's library was housed in the Old Convent Centre, in what had been Lissbeg's former convent school's assembly hall. The buildings were now home to a mix of council amenities, and a café stood in what had once been the nuns' private garden. Recently, it had been leased by Bríd and Aideen, as an extension of their deli on the opposite side of the street. Having skipped breakfast to make time for Mary's errands, Hanna stopped off at the café on her way into work. When she tapped on the glass door, Dan Cafferky, Bríd's boyfriend, opened it. 'How's it going, Miss Casey?'

'Grand, thanks, Dan. I'm sorry to come knocking.'

'No bother, I was about to open anyway. I told Bríd I'd do the morning shift. We're a bit short-handed this week with Aideen off.'

'I just wanted coffee and a croissant to take away.'

'Sure thing.' A pile of boxes on the counter contained wraps and sandwiches made that morning at the deli. As Hanna perched on a stool awaiting her coffee, Dan transferred them to a cooler unit, and arranged cakes and pastries under glass covers. She asked him how Aideen was and received the conventional answer. 'As well as can be expected. They're all a bit shook at the farm.'

'It was very sudden.'

'Bríd says Aideen's determined not to let it affect the business. Which is good. I mean, we're at a dodgy point, having taken on the café.'

How interesting, thought Hanna, that he'd twice used the pronoun 'we'. As far as she knew, Dan made his living by taking tourists out in his fishing boat, and only helped at the café occasionally. She wondered if he'd become an associate in the cousins' business, like Conor who, since marrying Aideen, was growing produce for the deli. Or if, having moved in with Bríd, he'd begun to feel proprietorial. If that's so, she told herself, there's sure to be squalls ahead. Though she hardly knew Dan, she was fond of Conor, who'd once worked as her part-time assistant, and for a moment she considered asking more questions. But professional instinct made her wary of gossip so, taking her coffee and the warm golden croissant, she set off across the nuns' garden to wrestle with her admin.

For a branch library in a small town, Hanna's workplace punched well above its weight. It had recently been extended to showcase a medieval psalter, a permanent loan made to the nation on the sole condition that it be exhibited in Lissbeg. The extension designed to house the exquisite book of psalms had been funded by its donor, Charles Aukin, an American who'd married the heir to Carrick's medieval castle. He was a retired banker whose eccentricity matched Tim Slattery's – but while Tim's was cultivated to suggest importance, Charles appeared to indulge in his simply for amusement. Drinking her coffee in the staff kitchenette, Hanna smiled at the thought of how the psalter had changed her life. When Charles had approached the authorities there had been plans to close Lissbeg Library, which were hastily dropped when the council was informed of the terms of his offer. The reversal had given Hanna far more than just job security or even the joy of having such a treasure in her care. Brian had been tasked with designing the psalter's state-of-the-art exhibition space, and it was then that they'd fallen in love.

By 2.30 p.m. the county library's staff room in Carrick was full of people who had no idea why they'd been summoned. Tim made a habit of arriving late to meetings and, in his absence, everyone was either chatting or scrolling through emails. Beside Hanna was her colleague Owen, an unassuming man in his early thirties. There wasn't much scope in Lissbeg's library for his specialist skill as an archivist, but he'd taken the job to be near friends and family. Such a different career path from mine, thought Hanna, idly. When I started out, I was desperate to get as far as I could from Finfarran. With no desire to check her phone and discover more texts from Mary, she let her thoughts drift into the past.

Having gone to London, she'd fallen in love, become Mrs Malcolm Turner, and abandoned a lifelong dream of being an art librarian. Then, after twenty years of marriage, she'd discovered her husband was a serial cheater. Furious and heartbroken, she'd returned to Ireland, reluctantly accepted a home for Jazz and herself with her mother and, having reverted to her maiden name, taken the Lissbeg job to pay her bills. But all that was what Jazz referred to as ancient history. Look at me now, thought Hanna, so fulfilled and so contented, and not just because I met Brian. I honestly believe I'm happier than I would have been in some glamorous art gallery. Maybe I needed to go away to rediscover my roots.

The door opened and Tim arrived, carrying a folder containing the meeting's agenda. 'I'm sorry if you feel you've been kept in the dark, but it seemed wisest not to circulate this in advance.' Hanna suspected that no one had been bothered, but a few of Tim's cronies played along, handling the pages he passed around with as much care as if they'd been live grenades. When Hanna's reached her, she saw it consisted of a single item next to a stamp saying 'IMPORTANCE' with a tick in a box marked 'HIGH'. The item simply read 'Local History Archive' so, none the wiser, everyone looked at Tim. He wore a gold hunter attached by a chain to his waistcoat, reminding Hanna of the White Rabbit's watch in *Alice in Wonderland*.

'So here's the thing and it's pretty damned exciting.' Pausing for effect, Tim joined the tips of his fingers. 'What you see before you is a golden opportunity, which, I assure you, won't come our way again. Nothing less than a chance to position Finfarran's library system front and centre on the national stage.' There was a pause in which the younger members of his staff looked excited, and Hanna and her contemporaries avoided each other's eyes. Assuming that Tim's announcement was true, one thing was certain. You'll be the one on stage, thought Hanna wryly. You'll be front and centre, beaming at the cameras, and we'll be kept in the background. Probably staggering under the weight of extra, unwelcome work.

Three hours later they all surged into the corridor, where Hanna found Brian leaning against the wall. He waved and approached, nodding at Tim. 'Are you done?'

Tim clapped him on the shoulder. 'We got through some serious planning, and now I'd say it's definitely gin o'clock.'

There was general consensus that a drink would be good and Brian turned to Hanna. 'What do you think?' Before she could answer, Tim announced that only the Royal Victoria Hotel served halfway drinkable gin. As the prices there were far higher than in the nearest pub, several people sloped away, saying they ought to get home, but two or three agreed with Tim and began to stride towards the lift. In the bustle, Brian drew Hanna aside, his eyes dancing. 'You may not want to hear this.'

'What?'

'I was going to book dinner in the Royal Victoria's grill.'

'No! We'll be dragged into the bar and I've had quite enough of Tim.'

'Shall we just go home?'

'Yes. Or – no, let's not. Let's go to the beach and have burgers. Huge ones, and proper bags of chips.' She took his arm and guided him towards the staircase. 'There's a guy on the road to Trawncarriga beach who sells burgers from a van. Quick, though. He'll be gone if we don't get a move on.'

The turn-off for Trawncarriga was a few miles outside Carrick, a one-track road where the tarmac was covered with sand blown from the dunes. They reached the van just as the man who owned it was closing up. 'I can do you doubles, if you like. I've a few left over.'

Hanna looked up at him, brushing her hair from her eyes. 'Go for it.'

'Right so, and you might as well have the rest of the chips in the tray.'

They carried their paper parcels into the sand dunes, to a point from which they could see the incoming tide. Hanna sat down next to a spiky clump of marram grass. 'This is so what I need after three hours of Tim's empire-building.' She shifted to lean against Brian's shoulder, took a deep breath and relaxed. 'Sea air, salty chips and a double cheeseburger.'

'Don't blame me if you keel over with a heart attack.'

'I won't. I'll die happy. Look at that sky.'

The expanse of blue was dotted with scudding clouds, mirroring the white crests of the rolling waves on the beach below. Brian unwrapped his chips, which were dripping with vinegar. 'Chances are that you'll die of thirst by the time we've eaten this lot.'

'We can stop for a drink in a pub on our way home.'

'Gin?'

'Anything but!' She bit into her burger. 'How was your day?'

'Uneventful. Tell me what Tim is planning.'

'It's quite interesting, actually. Owen is pleased. You know there's a local-history collection in Carrick?' Hanna dug in her bag for a tissue to spread on her knee. 'Back in 2016, Tim did a local-radio appeal for material relating to the Easter Rising. For the centenary commemorations. But he had no proper plan, and there was no funding. Essentially, it was Tim wanting his fifteen minutes of fame.'

'So what's happened now?'

Hanna snorted. 'A bigger and better chance of media coverage.'

'For Tim?'

'Yep. This time it's the War of Independence commemorations. The difference is that there's funding for a nationwide initiative. Open up libraries' local-history archives. Set up display boards in rural branches. That sort of thing.'

'When does it kick off?'

'Local displays are supposed to be organised by the winter. Then there's a national launch. The idea is to cover the Civil War too.'

'That's a serious chunk of history.'

'I suppose you can't explain things otherwise. After all, one led to the other. The War of Independence, 1919 to 1921, then a year or so of civil war about the terms of the treaty made with Britain. Officially the fighting was over by May 1923.'

Brian screwed up his chip paper and anchored it with his foot. 'So, what do you think?'

'That it's going to be a heap of hard work. But Owen's right. It should be fascinating. Like a treasure hunt.' A gust of wind whipped foam from the waves and sand, sharp as tiny needles, swept across the dunes. Suddenly Hanna shivered. 'It's getting chilly, isn't it?'

Brian frowned. 'Do you think so? I don't. Here, have my jacket.'

Licking her fingers, she smiled across at him. 'No, I'm fine. Really. Just a ghost walking over my grave.'

Chapter Three

Mary Casey stood at the bus stop across the road from her bright pink bungalow. A stream of traffic was bowling towards Carrick, hurling muddy splashes onto the pavement. It was 9 a.m. In half an hour the rain would have cleared and the rush-hour would be over, but neither time nor tide ever changed Mary's arrangements. She liked to be up and doing of a morning and disapproved of lolling about in a dressing-gown over your eggs. What was needed, in her view, was an organised schedule for the day's proceedings, starting with a whip around with a soapy mop. There was no point in starting the dishwasher till the evening. Not when you lived alone and the price of electric had gone through the roof. Still, she liked the place to be decent in case anybody came by. A neighbour, say, dropping in for a chat or, for that matter, the postman. You wouldn't want people telling each other you kept an untidy house.

Glancing at her watch, Mary observed that the bus was running late. She was clicking her tongue impatiently when a car drew into the kerb, and her granddaughter Jazz called through the window: 'Hi, there! Do you need a lift to Lissbeg?'

As Mary prepared to get in, Jazz leaned over and moved a briefcase from the passenger seat. She was smartly dressed in a tailored suit and her shirt was crisply ironed. Mary gave her a covert glance of approval. Whatever you might say about Hanna's cheating ex-husband, you had to admit that Jazz had turned out well. Loving, clever, and a credit to her mother, though it didn't do to tell Hanna so, and sassy enough to hold her own if it came to a war of words. Controlled irritation always annoyed Mary, who liked nothing better than what she called 'a good, clean row'. Jazz enjoyed standing up to her and they shared a wayward sense of humour, which meant that their fiercest spats often ended in laughter. Besides, Jazz was deeply fond of her gran, whose home had provided comfort and stability when she'd found herself living there after her parents' bitter divorce. A Jasmine among a classful of Ciaras, Kians, Patricks and Saoirses, even her name had made life in her new school difficult, and Mary's unwavering partisanship had supported her at a time when she'd felt she'd never find her feet.

Drawing her seatbelt across her ample bosom, Mary remarked that she needed a jar of cloves. 'Your mam gave me ground ones last week and, my God, they're wojeous.'

'If you don't like Mum's, why not buy your own?'

'What do you think I was doing standing there by the road in the rain? I'm well able to do my own shopping, and if the damn bus had been on time I wouldn't be sitting here taking cheek from you, miss!'

The mandatory initial skirmish over, Mary sat back, delighted to see that Jazz looked both pretty and happy. Her glossy black hair was stylishly cut and her smile was open and warm, unlike the tense, aggressive expression she'd worn as a teenager. 'How are things going at work?'

'Fine. We're expanding all the time.'

'There's a big market in smelly soaps, then?'

'I'm not going through this again, Nan. We don't make smelly soaps. We make cosmetic products from locally sourced organic ingredients. And you needn't pretend you didn't love that conditioner I gave you. I bet you've used it down to the last drop.'

'I haven't opened it.'

'Well, you should. Tell me what you think of it and I'll let you try another. Or a marigold face mask. What d'you reckon? Or a dandelion rinse.'

'I was mashing dandelions for hairwash long before you were born or thought of. What I want, these days, is something properly made in a sterile lab.'

'Our manufacturing conditions are impeccable.' Jazz glanced in the mirror and changed lanes before taking the turn-off for Lissbeg. 'Did you genuinely make dandelion hairwash?'

'I did. And it was the same recipe my grandmother used to cure bedwetting.'

'No!'

'I'm telling you. She dosed you late in the afternoon so you'd nothing left to piss out when you got to bed.'

'I never knew you were a bedwetter.'

With immense dignity, Mary replied that her grandmother had treated the neighbours' children. 'So you can take that look off your face right now, and not go round spreading tales.'

'We'll call it insider knowledge. I'll sign an NDA if you like.'

'I've no notion what that is, and I don't want to be told.' Feeling she'd let her guard down, Mary went into attack: 'I suppose you're still delighted with your bockety old shed on the side of the cliff.'

Jazz grinned. 'We're not going through this again, either. I love living in Maggie's place, and if you weren't trying to pick a fight you'd admit you were happy for me.'

'I never said I wasn't.'

'Good. Because I adore the house and I can't believe how lucky I am that Mum let me rent it when she moved in with Brian.'

'Lucky to live in Maggie's place? There's times you're as daft as your mother.'

For once, Jazz took time before she replied. She knew that life in the bungalow had been exhausting for her mum. Though Mary had taken them in without hesitation, she'd repeatedly announced that only a fool would have married Malcolm Turner. 'He might be a high-flying barrister but he's a pup and, in my day, women were better judges of character.' Much of Mary's aggression had been prompted by real concern but, by the time Jazz had finished school, Hanna had been desperate to move to a place of her own. But this, thought Jazz, was between her mum and her gran, and no business of hers so, with her eyes on the road, she avoided discussion of Hanna. 'It's not a bockety old shed now, Gran. Have you really not seen it?'

'I got Hanna to drive me over when she had Fury O'Shea working there. A pile of stones in a muddy field and me with my good shoes on. I saw all I needed to see from the side of the road.'

'You'll have to come round for tea sometime. I'll make you an apple tart.'

'If I come I'll bring my own apple tart, I promise you. I want nothing thrown together with ground cloves.'

'Actually, I use cinnamon.'

'Organic, I dare say.'

'Yes.'

Jazz's attention was on the traffic as she turned into Broad Street. Assuming an air of polite interest, Mary swooped in for the kill. 'And where, precisely, do you "source" organic cinnamon hereabouts?'

'I never said ... I was talking about ...' Jazz burst out laughing. 'That is *such* a low shot, and it doesn't even make sense!'

Triumphantly, Mary reached to open her seatbelt. 'Ay, well,

you would say that, wouldn't you? You never admit when you're floored. Right, you can let me out here by the horse trough. I'm going into the deli to source me cloves.'

The deli was opposite the entrance to the Old Convent Centre, next to a shop where a clock, surmounted by a seed merchant's sign, hung permanently stopped with its hands at a quarter to three. At the street's broadest point, which had once been the town's cattle market, a stone horse trough was planted with geraniums. Throughout the day, traffic flowed by on each side of it, isolating the flower-filled trough and a couple of wooden benches where schoolkids hung out and tourists drank coffee, checking their maps.

Bríd and Aideen had opened the deli in a premises that had once been the town's haberdasher's, perfectly sited to catch passing trade. Aideen, the daughter of a single mum who'd died giving birth to her, had been raised by elderly relatives who'd left her their small savings and the ex-council house she'd grown up in. As Bríd had done a course in culinary science, they'd decided to share the house and use the money to start the business. Then, when Aideen married, Dan had moved in with Bríd – an arrangement that troubled Aideen a little, since Bríd and Dan had broken up more times than Lissbeg could remember. Still, they'd seemed more committed since agreeing to live together and, as much of Aideen's time was taken up with baby Ronan, she was glad Dan was there to lend a hand now the business was taking off. When Mary surged in, swinging her oilcloth shopping bag, Aideen had just come in to work and was hanging up her coat. Having received renewed condolences, she retreated into the kitchen while Bríd sold Mary the cloves. The transaction included an outraged speech on what Mary referred to as fancy modern condiments. 'The size of the jars and the cheek of the prices you charge for them! Holy God Almighty, you could lick sea salt off a rock!'

'Our salt is Cornish.'

'Another example of locally sourced products. You're as bad as Jazz!'

When the old-fashioned shop bell tinkled as the door closed behind Mary, Bríd put her head around the kitchen door. 'She's gone. You're safe to come out.' Aideen emerged, wearing her apron, to find Bríd tipping olives into bowls. 'I wasn't hiding.'

'I wouldn't blame you if you were. God help poor Jazz with an oul one like that for a granny!'

Tucking her hair under a scarf, Aideen went behind the counter. 'She's not all bad. She was awfully nice to Una after the funeral. Or she meant to be.'

Bríd carried the bowls to the window, shifting jars of sun-dried tomatoes to squeeze the olives into the display. Despite its prime location in Broad Street, the deli's shopfront was narrow and there was no room for seating. This was why they'd expanded their business by taking on the lease of the Garden Café. The deli, which they'd called HabberDashery, had already supplied the café with cakes so, when the café's lease had come up for renewal, Bríd had been eager to grab it. Always more cautious than her cousin, Aideen had been less certain. She'd talked it through with Conor one evening in the orchard, Ronan on her lap and her chin on his fuzzy head. 'You don't think it'd be overreaching ourselves?'

'Well, it's only a year's lease, so it might be worth having a go. You can always choose not to renew if things don't go to plan.'

Aideen had wondered if everything in her life hadn't happened too quickly. The business, her marriage, and then the baby, who hadn't been planned and had taken them all by surprise. Then there'd been the decision to grow produce for the deli, and supply local guesthouses with the surplus. That was a new departure they were still getting used to. And now this. Taking Ronan in his arms, Conor had tossed him into the air. 'It's up to yourself. I'll support whatever decision you come to. Take your time and, if it feels like a step too far, just say no to Bríd.'

After that, Aideen had made up her mind easily, as always happened when she had time to think. She had good sense despite her lack of confidence and, as Paddy had once said of her, when she took a notion into her head she saw it through to the end. Having talked to Conor, she'd reviewed the figures with a calculator. The expansion would mean a higher wage bill to eat into their profits but, if she and Bríd took less for a while, and with Dan to lend a hand, the long-term prospect looked good for the business. It was Bríd who'd said that Dan would provide a stopgap in emergencies. 'His dad can keep an eye on the boat, if he has to. And with Pavel, who's completely reliable, and a couple of summer staff, it should work out fine.' It was Dan's reliability, not Pavel's, which bothered Aideen, and the likelihood of his falling out with Bríd. Nevertheless, the risk had seemed small, so she'd signed the lease happily, unaware that, only a few months later, Paddy's death would trigger their first emergency.

Now she looked anxiously at Bríd. 'I wish I didn't have to take off more time this week. I've got to drive Una to see the solicitor with all of Paddy's papers. Conor's up to his eyes with work on the farm.'

'I've told you it doesn't matter. We'll be fine. Dan's playing a blinder over at the café. He's even impressing me.'

'But he shouldn't have to be spending so much time there.'

'He's grand. Honestly, Ade, don't worry about it.'

'It's just that I wouldn't like Una to have to go to this meeting alone.'

'Of course not.' Bríd went back behind the counter and started constructing avocado wraps. 'You're really fond of Una, aren't you? It's like you found your mother when you married Conor.'

'I know. She's lovely. I'm lucky to have her.' Having said this, Aideen flushed. 'I mean, your mum's always been nice to me, Bríd, I'm not saying a word against her.'

'Of course not, dork. No one said you were. But it's different with Una. She's Conor's mum and Ronan's granny. It's what they call immediate family, isn't it? Makes a difference. Mind you, there are grannies and grannies. Look at Mary Casey.'

Aideen grinned. 'You went mental when I first told you I'd be living with Conor's parents.'

'I did not!'

'You so did! You said I saw farm life through rose-coloured spectacles, and you lectured me on the danger of living with in-laws. Blood on the hearthstone and everyone fighting like mad cats and dogs.'

'Okay, maybe I'd been reading too much John McGahern. Or do I mean John B. Keane?'

'Don't ask me. Conor's the one who was the library assistant.'

'Well, you know what I'm on about. Family sagas with all sorts of dark secrets in the past.'

Aideen gave her a cheerful push and began buttering bread rolls. 'The trouble with you is you enjoy living in a melodrama.'

'That is so not true.'

'Oh, please! Look at you and Dan.'

'Yeah, well, these days we're practically Darby and Joan.'

They continued their work in silence for a moment before Aideen spoke again. 'There's nothing wrong with being Darby and Joan, you know. You might learn to like it.'

'Is that how you see yourself and Conor?'

'Maybe. And I don't care if it's boring. To me it feels safe.'

Chapter Four

An arched gateway connected the nuns' garden to a courtyard outside the library, and although her quickest way in was through the main entrance from Broad Street, Hanna enjoyed using this side gate. In her schooldays the garden's trees and flowers had been a glimpsed paradise, inaccessible to anyone but the nuns. Now it was thronged with people passing through or lingering on benches. Behind formal rows of conifers, the perimeter walls were clad in Virginia creeper, and flowering herbs softened the lines of beds laid out between raked gravelled walks. In the centre, in a wide granite basin, a statue of St Francis stood on a plinth with stone arms extended and water rising from carved flowers at its feet. The herb beds radiated from the statue, which faced the former refectory where pointed stained-glass windows made bright streaks in the grey walls. Though the high wall that had once enclosed all this had been breached by the council, the visual rhythms of the garden retained a sense of cloistered calm. Each morning one of the volunteers who tended the herb beds waded across to pour birdseed into the statue's cupped hands. This ritual, begun by the nuns, had become embedded in the birds' communal memory, and flights of goldcrests constantly swooped from the creeper to the fountain, pecking and snatching for food. As their wings whirred, their gold and olive plumage echoed the colours of the stained-glass. This morning, enchanted by the light and movement, Hanna paused for a moment, thinking it would be hard to imagine a lovelier way to begin a day's work.

She arrived at the library just ahead of Owen, and as she unlocked the door and turned off the alarm, they were joined by a couple of tourists wanting to see the psalter. Hanna explained that tours of the exhibition took place every half-hour.

'We can't just go in?'

'Not unaccompanied, I'm afraid. It's a precious manuscript. Why not get a coffee and come back at ten? A guide will be here then.'

One of the girls looked inclined to object but her friend tugged her arm. 'Come on, let's have that coffee. I've got a leaflet. We can read up about the psalter while we wait.'

As they bounded away, Owen rolled his eyes. 'The opening hours are on the front of the leaflet. In a massive box outlined in red.'

'True, but that's the public for you.' Hanna led the way through the lobby into the library. 'It's great that the psalter's such a draw, though, isn't it?'

'It was an extraordinary donation.'

'Charles Aukin is a pretty extraordinary man. You might say he married into the psalter. That and everything else in Castle Lancy. When Lady Isobel died he was left to cope with centuries of stuff.'

'I've never been inside the castle.'

'Well, it's still a private residence. I'd say Charles finds it a huge responsibility. I suppose giving the psalter to the state was one weight off his mind.'

Hanna went to hang her jacket in the kitchenette. The library's public collection stood in parallel rows on open-access shelves, while the oak-panelled walls were lined with glazed cases containing an assortment of books left by the nuns. Morning sunlight flooded the steel shelving and glinted on the gilded, leather-bound books behind the glazing. Brian's extension had introduced windows at roof level, radically changing the dark hall where generations of girls had yawned through school assemblies. Hanna's reception desk now stood with its back to a glass wall dividing the library from the state-of-the-art exhibition space, and a new soundproof reading room had been equipped for talks and films. In her first year as librarian, when Conor had been her part-time assistant, much of Hanna's time had been spent reconciling the demands of toddlers' groups and pensioners' computer classes with those of people who simply wanted to sit and read a book. As she'd said to Brian, the difference made by the reading room was spectacular. He'd laughed. 'I don't know why that surprises you. Assessing the client's needs is a basic part of an architect's job.'

'Yes, but practically no one on the council had a clue about libraries.'

'Ah, but we also gently explain to the client what he *actually* needs. As opposed to what he thinks he wants or half remembers he's seen on some TV makeover show.'

'That would have been Tim.'

'It was. He never stopped sending emails. Fortunately, I persuaded the council to give me access to you.'

'Are you telling me all those meetings weren't necessary?'

'Of course they weren't. I knew what was required on the first day I assessed the scheme. I also knew that you and I needed time to get to know each other.'

'That's disgraceful!'

'Not at all. It was a matter of killing several birds with one stone.' Brian had cheerfully counted them off on his fingers. 'Lissbeg got the library it needed. The council got exactly what Charles Aukin was willing to pay for. And I, my beloved, got you.' Suddenly, he'd held her tightly. 'Sometimes I can't believe that happened. I wake up at night thinking it was a dream.'

Smiling at the memory, Hanna went to her desk. Owen was in the reading room, setting out chairs for a book club. Hanna was about to open her emails when a woman clutching a carrier bag peered around the door. Hanna smiled. 'Hi. Can I help you?'

The woman hesitated. 'I haven't been here before.'

'Well, you're very welcome. Would you like to register for a library card? Or I could show you round so you get a feel of what's on offer?'

Like a conjuror producing a rabbit from a hat, the woman took something from her bag. It was an album, bound in scuffed cloth with a synthetic leather spine. 'O'Carroll's my name. I had this from my granddad. He lived back in Ballyfin.' Placing the album on the desk, she folded her hands at her waist. Her grey hair was pulled back at the temples by plastic slides, and her clothes suggested a countrywoman dressed in her best for a trip into town. Accustomed to members of the public arriving with tattered books they thought were rare or valuable, Hanna was seeking a gentle response when the woman spoke again. 'Material relating to the War of Independence. That's what they said you wanted.'

Hanna blinked. 'I'm sorry? Who said that?'

'My husband heard it in the pub.'

Damn, thought Hanna. I should have expected this. Though Tim had ended last week's meeting with a promise to produce what he called his 'Communication Strategy', it seemed the Finfarran grapevine had beaten him to the mark. 'So what are these? Family photos?'

'My granddad took them when he was a lad. He had family out in America. They sent him a fancy camera and he set it up in a shed.'

As Hanna reached to open the album, the woman bent forward. 'Mind it there. The back is split, but the photos are all grand. It must have been a wild expensive camera. Telescopic lenses, my husband reckons. Something like that. And all taken through a chink in the wall. God knows what would have happened if the Tans had known they were took.'

Opening the cover gingerly, Hanna looked at the first page. What she saw made her gasp. The sepia images were as clear as if they'd been taken the previous day. All shot from the same angle, they showed a small farmyard, surrounded by dry-stone sheds and with a high, open-fronted barn. A mud-splashed vehicle crowded with armed men almost filled the yard. The woman squinted sideways. 'Them's Tans there in the Crossley Tender – 1919, it was. It was the day they came to the farm to fire the barn.' Though Hanna recognised the uniforms by the distinctive black berets, she'd forgotten the name of the armoured vehicle, which had a long bonnet, an open front and a high-sided rear. Of course, she thought. A Crossley Tender. I've heard the name in songs.

Owen had approached and was staring at the photographs. 'These are amazing.'

The woman nodded vigorously. 'That's what my husband said. No point in keeping them stuck in the attic, he told me. Not when the word is out that the library's looking for this class of thing.' She began her story again, this time for Owen's benefit. 'The Black and Tans had us all in fear of our lives around these parts. There was a barracks in Carrick back then. Our own boys were up in the mountains fighting for independence – girls and women too, though I've never heard anyone give them much credit for it – and families were burned out or shot for any bit of support. Churchill recruited the Tans over in England. Young fellas out of the trenches after the First World War. By all accounts, half were drunk and the rest had lost their marbles. My granddad said you'd run for the ditch if you heard the sound of the Tenders on the road.' She pointed to another photo. 'Lewis guns, he told me those were called.'

Several men in the photograph were holding a woman and three children at gunpoint, while others were hustling a man and a teenage boy towards a wall. The rest of the photos on the page appeared to have been taken in quick succession. The man and the boy spreadeagled with their faces against the wall. An officer giving orders. Men with guns balanced on their shoulders, carrying flaming sods of turf on a pitchfork and a shovel. Then a close-up of the officer's face as he shouted a command. Mrs O'Carroll screwed up her eyes. 'I can't remember that fella's name, though my grandfather told it to me. I know they got the sods from the fire where his mam had been cooking the dinner. She had just put it on the table when they came.' Turning to the next page, she revealed another sequence of photos. There was image after image of the barn burning. The mother holding her apron out to protect the screaming children. A little boy who'd escaped his mother being threatened by a Lewis gun.

Owen took a deep breath. 'You do know that these are exceptional?'

'Well, I thought they might be. There weren't many cameras round these parts back then. By rights we shouldn't have them pictures, you know. My granddad's father smashed the camera as soon as he heard that they'd been taken but, sure, God help him, he knew nothing about how cameras worked. Granddad had hidden the film. It was years before he developed it, he told me.'

Owen took a deep breath. 'Well, we'd like to have the album here for a while, Mrs O'Carroll. We'd take a better look at it and make copies of the photos. Would that be all right?'

Hanna, whose mind had been racing, intervened. 'Let's not get ahead of ourselves. There'll be a form we'll get you to fill in, Mrs O'Carroll. That way we'll have an accurate record of what you leave us, and everyone will understand what's involved.' She caught Owen's eye. Tim was an ass but she didn't intend to discuss him before a member of the public.

Getting the message, Owen agreed. 'Of course. If you give us a contact number, we can phone you. Do keep it carefully in the meantime, though, Mrs O'Carroll.' He threw Hanna a sidelong glance. 'It really should be conserved as soon as possible.'

Unaware of these undercurrents, the woman nodded. 'Ah, sure, we've minded it for a hundred years. We'll manage a small bit longer.'

Still loath to let the album go, Owen asked another question. 'Are they dated? Is anything written on the reverse of the photos?'

'God, no. My granddad had more sense. "No names, no pack

drill", that was his motto. It was my mother stuck them into the book. She wanted writing under them but he wouldn't have it. Not under those ones. Old ways die hard. The other photos, yes, but not them.'

Owen goggled at her. 'There's more?'

'Pages of them. Taken before his dad whipped the camera. He had a great eye, my granddad. A great interest in farming and history and that. If he'd had the education, he would have worked for the newspapers.'

'And the others are dated?'

'Didn't I say they were?' She turned a page with a flourish. 'There you are!'

By a desperate effort, Hanna managed not to laugh. Each photo was a close-up of a cow. Dated from January to July 1919, they filled dozens of pages, with 'Daisy', 'Moll' or 'Fodhla' written beneath them in careful italic script. Owen remarked in a strangled voice that those images might throw light on the others. He bent over the album. 'If the camera was smashed immediately after he took the farmyard shots, and if the farmyard shots were taken after the last cow photo ... and since, judging by the clusters of dates, he used the camera, on average, about once a week ...' Owen glanced up at Hanna '. . . then the burning of the barn must have happened sometime in late July.'

Mrs O'Carroll turned the pages back to the images of the farmyard. 'It's plain as the nose on your face, now I come to look at it.'

Owen smiled at her kindly. 'Well, we can't be certain, but it's what we call extrapolating from internal evidence.'

'If it was me, though, I wouldn't be going from the writing.' Observing his blank expression, the woman turned to Hanna. 'Amn't I right? I mean, look at the barn stacked up to the rafters. That's your internal evidence. It must have been late July.' Turning to Owen, she spoke slowly, as if explaining to a child. 'It can't have been earlier, can it? Hadn't the family got all their hay saved?'

She departed with the album in her plastic bag, leaving Owen looking sheepish. 'So much for my special training! And, look, I'm sorry, I should have considered protocol before I asked her to leave us the album.'

'Don't beat yourself up. Protocol should have been on last week's agenda.' Hanna laughed. 'Having said that, I didn't think to ask about it myself. That's the effect of Tim's three-hour meetings. They rot your brain.'

A cough from the doorway made her turn round. Fury O'Shea was standing on the threshold with The Divil under his arm. 'I suppose you're going to tell me I can't bring this fella in.'

'Would it make any difference if I did?'

'Not a pick.' Fury strolled in, carrying the elderly terrier. 'I passed Pats O'Carroll's wife in the courtyard.'

'And no doubt you know why she was here.'

'I do, of course. Half the peninsula does.' He leaned his bony behind against Hanna's desk and looked down at her. 'She had a full bag in her hand and she coming out, though. What's the story? I thought you wanted people to bring things in.'

'Tim Slattery's put the cart before the horse again, as usual. But we'll get procedures in place to receive material. I'm not worried.'

Fury raised a sardonic eyebrow. 'Is that so? Because, if you ask me, you should be.'

'Why?'

The Divil growled deep in his throat and Fury took hold of the little dog's muzzle. 'Because procedures and protocol will be the least of your troubles. One thing in life leads to another, Miss Casey, and you're about to open a can of worms.'

Chapter Five

Jazz lifted her face to the sun, stretched out her legs and rested her feet on a cushion of sea pinks. The wiry flowers tickled her bare toes. She was sitting on a peeling, painted bench with her shoulders against the dry-stone wall that bounded her clifftop garden. The bench, which stood about eight foot back from the sheer cliff's edge, gave a view of the Atlantic stretching away to a shimmering horizon. Few people took the grassy path that followed the cliff's winding contours so, having scrambled over the low wall, Jazz could sunbathe as if she sat alone on the edge of the world. Far below, sluggish breakers crashed against the rocks and, high above her, seabirds were gleaming dots in the blue sky. She could tell the cries of the herring gulls from the piping of oystercatchers, and from the long call of a black-backed bird whose name she didn't know. Only a year ago, she wouldn't have noticed the distinctions but, since coming to live at Maggie's place, she'd discovered the joys of solitude, one of which was a heightened awareness of other lives coexisting round hers.

Hanna had inherited the little house from her great-aunt Maggie when she was a child. By the time she'd returned to Ireland with Jazz, it had been derelict, and she'd never have thought of living there if she hadn't been desperate to get out of Mary's bungalow. Isolated and off the beaten track, it had provided a refuge in which to accept that she was no longer Mrs Malcolm Turner, and to rediscover herself as Hanna Casey. And now, thought Jazz, cheerfully, it's a refuge for me.

Maggie's place felt like heaven to her after months of life in a studio flat in Lissbeg. Rented accommodation being scarce, her landlord had squeezed every possible cent out of his property, justifying his greed by calling the cramped spaces 'designer living'. Jazz had lived with a shower so small she could hardly turn around in it, a fold-up bed and a kitchen composed of a two-ring hob, a minute sink and a microwave, inadequately concealed by a screen of fairy lights. In Maggie's place, her bed was cream-enamelled, with a brass ball on each of its four tall bedposts, and the kitchen, instead of being tucked away, was the heart of the house. Fury, who'd done the restoration for Hanna, had installed cupboards, appliances and thick slate worktops at one end of the sunny living space, and retained the hearth and fireplace at the other, with Maggie's painted dresser standing next to the chimney breast. It was open-plan living with all the charm of a period country cottage, and a little extension at the back, which replaced a tumbledown lean-to, provided utility space and a proper bathroom.

Leaving the bench, Jazz crossed the wall, and approached the house along a roughly scythed pathway between tasselled grasses starred with clover and poppies. It was Saturday afternoon and Hanna was coming over for tea. The undergrowth hummed with the drone of bees and insects, and an iridescent damsel-fly flashed past Jazz's face, soaring up the garden and over the roof. The house, built of whitewashed stone, stood with its back to the road and had a half-door facing the ocean. Ash trees grew crookedly at one gable end, stunted by the wind and seeking the shelter of the wall. Little grew in the garden now, besides the wildflowers and grasses, but Hanna could remember hours spent spreading seaweed to fertilise the thin clifftop soil. 'In all weathers. I used to hate it but Maggie was old, and she still grew spuds, so they'd send me round to help her.' No one farmed on the seaward side of the winding road now, and Jazz's home was the only remaining house facing the ocean. Yet, in Maggie's childhood, so Hanna had told her, the clifftop had been a patchwork of fields, and whole households, often composed of three generations, were fed with the produce of the salt-scoured land.

Jazz's offer to make apple tart for Mary had been a tease: most of her time was claimed by her job, so her cakes generally came from HabberDashery. In the sunny kitchen, she tumbled scones from a paper bag and put two slices of walnut cake on a plate. Even in calm weather the sound of the ocean filled the house. She was accustomed to it but, unconsciously, it soothed her. At work she often felt pressured and tried to do several things at once, but here she found she moved slowly and focused on small pleasures, like the rich colour of gooseberry jam spooned into a yellow bowl, or the faint scent of the wild roses she'd placed in a glass on the deep windowsill. She was lifting cups down from the dresser when Hanna appeared at the door. 'Am I early? Usually I get stuck behind a tractor but there wasn't a soul on the road.'

'No, you're fine. I was just about to make sandwiches.'

'Gosh, this is a serious spread.'

'Proper afternoon tea with all the trimmings.'

'Can I help?'

'Nope. Sit down and tell me some gossip.'

Hanna sat in a fireside chair and admired the basket of furze that Jazz had set on the stone hearth, where the golden flowers echoed the effect of firelight. 'I'm not sure I've a word of gossip to offer. I'm great. Brian's fine. Your grandmother is impossible.'

'What's she done now?'

'Just the usual bout of serial texting.'

'I gave her a lift last week and she seemed in good form.'

'The texts are getting madder, though. The other day I dropped in some shopping, and she'd either forgotten she'd asked for it or else she's started to stockpile.'

'It wasn't just that you'd got her the wrong kind of cloves?'

'Oh, you heard about that?'

'She wasn't happy.'

'No. This was something else, though. Dishwasher tablets. Six consecutive texts about having to wash up by hand, and when I went round, she had a full box under the sink, unopened.'

'Maybe she just wanted a bit of company. I ought to drop in more often.'

'Oh, darling, don't start worrying. You're busy.'

'Yes, but so are you. We all are.'

Later, as they sat eating cake at the table by the window, Jazz raised her eyebrows. 'So, what's this they're saying about the library?'

'What have you heard?'

'Something about a call going out for material.'

Hanna pulled a face. Since Tim's meeting, nothing had been done about procedure. With no guidelines, and interest spreading like wildfire, the branch librarians had begun to dread the arrival of yet another boxful of photos or letters, often belonging to completely the wrong period. But, despite phone calls and emails from his colleagues, Tim had apparently gone to ground.

Jazz licked coffee icing off a walnut. 'So what's the actual period you'll cover?'

'1919 to 1923. The War of Independence to the end of the Civil War.'

'I've never really understood what the Civil War was about.'

Hanna looked amused. 'You could always come and look it up in the library.'

'Stop being a bore. Tell me.'

'Well, some of those who fought for Irish independence from Britain couldn't accept a treaty that was made. It was supposed to be a compromise that might lead to something better but, to them, it was betrayal of the cause. So they carried on the struggle and ended up fighting their former comrades.'

'Diehards. Okay. Heavy stuff. What kind of material are you after?'

'Letters, journals, photographs. Ephemera, like posters or, say, train tickets.'

'Ephemera?'

'Printed things you wouldn't expect to survive. Day-to-day bits and pieces. Letters are a case in point. People put them in books as markers, or tuck them away out of sentiment. Sometimes things survive because they get put away so carefully that they're forgotten.'

'Like Maggie's book?'

The casual question stopped Hanna in her tracks. Not noticing, Jazz got to her feet. 'The tin's still in the dresser.' She crossed the room, carrying a chair to allow her to reach the top shelf, lifted down a shabby biscuit tin and came back to the table. Hanna watched in silence. Of course, she thought. Maggie's book. How come I didn't think of it? When she'd moved into the house, she'd found the biscuit tin in a shed, and opened it to discover pages from an old school copybook stitched together and bound in cardboard with a brown paper cover. Now, as Jazz took it out of the tin, the sight of the neat rows of stitching reminded Hanna that Maggie had owned a treadle sewing machine. Its cast-iron base, painted and fitted with a flat timber top, now stood in the garden, piled with stones and shells and feathers Jazz had collected from the beach. Jazz moved the teacups and pushed the makeshift book towards her. 'Hadn't you remembered it?'

'Yes, of course. Of course I remember. I hadn't forgotten it exists. How could I? It sheds so much light on this house, and the family and what happened here. I suppose I just didn't think of it as material. It's … I don't know … private, I suppose.' She was aware that she was trying to explain to herself as much as to Jazz, whose nose wrinkled.

'How d'you mean?'

'It's a kind of diary. I don't think Maggie intended people to see it.'

'But isn't that why people keep diaries? To leave a record for other people to read?'

'Perhaps.'

'But you don't think so.'

Hanna looked down at the book, trying to imagine that she was Owen assessing something that had been brought in for inspection. Though some of the pages were dated, others weren't, and while some entries were notes, such as you'd find in a diary, others read more like a journal, or even a story. Some were no more than shopping lists. The first entry had been composed on an emigrant boat to Liverpool, and the round, childish handwriting wandered between the ruled lines, as if Maggie had sat braced against the rolling of the waves.

July 20th, 1920. I never thought that I'd have to leave Finfarran. I suppose I won't be the first or the last who's had to go this way. I'm worried about Mam even though I know the neighbours will mind her. Mrs Donovan will anyway, she's always been good to us, though these days you wouldn't be sure of anyone. When there's a price on a neighbour's head people do be sorely tempted, and every family on the peninsula with someone out in the hills does be all the time frightened of informers. All we can do is pray Liam will be safe.

Liam was my grandfather, thought Hanna. Dad's father, who died before I was born. In 1920, Liam couldn't have been more than nineteen, and Maggie was younger than he was, years younger than Jazz is now. Jazz was still pursuing her point: 'It's exactly the sort of thing you're looking for, isn't it? That extract would be brilliant. From a marketing point of view, it's pure gold.'

'From a marketing point of view?'

'Don't look at me like I'm crass. I'm a marketing manager. And you do see what I mean about that paragraph? It's immediate and condensed. Draws you in, makes you want to know more.

Isn't that the point of having your display boards? To inform, educate, stimulate discussion? What's the phrase – "the library as a community living room"?'

'Where did you find that?'

'It's on the county library website. I thought it was rather good.' Jazz was amused by Hanna's evident distaste. 'There's nothing actually wrong with soundbites, Mum.'

'I never said there was. It's just that most things in life are more nuanced than a soundbite can convey.'

'And *that* is what us marketing people like to call "the challenge".'

Maggie could have talked to me, thought Hanna. I was twelve when I was sent round to spread seaweed for her spuds. She was in her eighties. If she'd wanted to share her story, she could have sat me down and talked. I might never have found her book. It could have been lost in a pile of stones in a muddy field on a cliff. Suddenly she remembered asking her father why Maggie had left her the house. 'Why me? What would I want it for?'

They'd been driving to Maggie's funeral and her father had shushed her and smiled. 'Life is long, pet. You might have a use for the house when you grow up.'

And I did, thought Hanna. This house kept me sane. I couldn't have recovered from my divorce living in my mother's back bedroom, and, without this isolated setting, Brian and I could never have had our slow, unobserved wooing. With a start, she realised Jazz was staring at her. 'I'm sorry, sweetheart, it's just that this has taken me by surprise.'

'I still don't see why.'

'Well, do you remember the entry Maggie added just before she died?'

'In the 1970s?'

'1975. It was one of the ones she wrote on scraps of paper and slipped between the cardboard and the cover.'

Hanna found the page and read aloud: '*Hanna hardly opens her mouth and I say little enough. She's a great worker. I went to Lissbeg the other day and got an appointment with the solicitor. I want her to have this house and the field when I'm gone. Maybe one day she'll need a place where she can feel safe and be happy. If she does and she has this place, I think Mam would be glad.*' She looked at Jazz. 'That was about me.'

'So? What are you saying? Obviously an entry from 1975 doesn't fit the period. But you don't have to use it.'

'It's about me.'

'Well, don't use it if you don't want to. But surely the 1920s stuff is important.'

'Are you saying the 1970s stuff isn't?'

'All I'm saying is that I don't think you're being rational.'

I'm not, thought Hanna. I'm being emotional. Jazz sees this as history, but I see Maggie as the person I knew. Maybe it's because she straddles the gap between history and lived experience. This is what Fury meant. It's a can of worms.

Jazz had gone to the kettle and made another pot of tea. She poured it and sat down again, facing Hanna. 'Mum, there's no pressure. It's your choice. It'll be the same for everyone who has stuff tucked away. They can all choose whether or not to bring it into their library.'

'Will they understand the implications of putting it on display, though?'

'Well, that's their problem, isn't it?'

Hanna stabbed her cake with her fork. No, it's not, she thought. I'm the one with the job of explaining the implications to them, and I'm not sure I understand them myself. But there was no point in arguing, so she smiled and said she supposed Jazz was right. Later, as she was leaving, she picked up the book. 'Do you mind if I hang on to this? I'd like to read it again.'

Jazz hugged her goodbye. 'Of course I don't mind if you take it. And it wouldn't matter if I did. You own it.'

Driving between the scrubby clifftop and the lush farmland that stretched away on the opposite side of the road, Hanna considered that parting remark. It's the central issue, she thought. Owen and I have been focused on how to catalogue all this material, but keeping a record of physical ownership is just the start. Maybe the real questions will be about ownership of the hidden stories behind the bits and pieces that people entrust to us.

Chapter Six

Ronan kicked his legs in his blue denim sling. He was strapped
to Conor's chest, facing outwards, and on his head was a white
beanie hat with puppy dog ears, two round black buttons for eyes
and another for a nose. Having carefully tightened the straps,
Conor climbed out of the jeep. As he'd pulled into the timber
yard he'd seen Fury and The Divil emerging from a doorway and
now they were ambling towards him. Conor was dressed in work
boots, jeans and a faded shirt, and Fury, wearing his corduroys
and torn waxed jacket, had his own woolly hat pulled low above
his nose. At the sight of The Divil, Ronan flailed his arms and
legs and began to squeal. As they got closer, Fury raised his voice.
'How's it going, Conor?'

'Grand. I'm here for fence posts.'

'Well, so long as it's not windows. I've an order in for a week
and they haven't arrived.'

'Is that for the place you're working on up behind Cafferkys'
smokehouse?'

'Another feckin' holiday home. You wouldn't mind them coming but you'd wish they wouldn't destroy decent houses. There's nothing wrong with the windows that's in it, but they have to have triple glazing.'

The Divil reared up and placed his front paws against Conor's knees. Ronan gurgled, struggling to reach him. Fury looked down thoughtfully. 'See now, normally that fella can't abide a baby. Stick-throwing age, that's when he likes a child. Old enough to play and young enough not to get bored too quickly. Babies would be no use to him at all.'

'It'll be a while before this lad starts throwing sticks.'

'Isn't that what I'm saying? Yet there's yer man, up on the back legs, with the tongue hanging out of him. If you'd told me that, I wouldn't have credited it.' Still on his hind legs, The Divil danced backwards and Ronan kept his eyes on him, wriggling with delight. Conor blew on the fluff of hair on top of the baby's head. 'He's never shown any interest in the old dog back at the farm. But babies change every day, don't they? My mam says Ronan's been trying to crawl lately. Aideen was kind of upset because she'd missed his first go.'

'There'll be plenty of firsts yet. She'll end up sick of them.'

It was inconceivable to Conor that any stage of his son's development could be less than enchanting. He and Aideen had agreed to wait before starting a family but, secretly, he'd been glad when Fate had intervened in the form of a burst condom. He adored Aideen, and when she'd agreed to marry him it had felt like a dream come true. He'd worried that she might balk at moving in with his parents, so when she'd said she'd love to live on the farm, he'd thought he'd reached the pinnacle of his ambitions but, as he'd told his dad, Ronan's birth had taken things to a whole new level. Paddy had clapped him on the shoulder. 'I was the same way when Joe was born.'

'Oh, right. Not when I came along?'

'Ah, don't be a fool, boy, you know what I mean.'

Fury was still considering The Divil, who remained fixated on Ronan. 'I'm telling you, this is phenomenal. Wait – that child hasn't a custard cream in his fist?'

'Of course not. We're weaning him, but not onto custard creams.'

'Because The Divil can scent one of them at fifty paces. A custard cream is that fella's biscuit of choice.'

'I thought he was mad for Tayto?'

'In a pub, yes. He'd have a sup of a pint and a packet of salt and vinegar. But the Jack Russell's an abstemious breed. He wouldn't be looking for pints and crisps at four in the afternoon.'

'I'd say poor Ronan can forget the crisps and custard creams till he's older. Aideen's pretty fierce about what he eats.'

'Ah, they all start off that way. I was the same with The Divil. Mind you, if you don't stay focused, you're apt to let your guard down. There was a while there when your man was big into pester power and I only got sense and drew the line when it came to demands for sushi at football matches.'

'Does he still follow the county team?'

'He does and he doesn't. He got the hump when they wouldn't let him in to see last year's final.' Often it was hard to know whether Fury was saving face or joking. In this instance, the truth was that he'd found out embarrassingly late that dogs were banned from the stadium. But his statements, however far-fetched, were seldom challenged. Though he was famously discreet, a word from him could mean that no other tradesman on the peninsula would work for you, and that was a risk few people were willing to take. Fury was just Fury. His age and his firm belief that knowledge was power had combined to make him an expert on all that happened in Finfarran, and his resultant sense of stewardship both irritated and reassured his neighbours. But irritation got you nowhere with Fury. You had to accept that he viewed himself as a fixer of lives, as well as of planning permissions, leaking roofs and boilers, and that, in his world, fixing required convolution and manipulation.

Conor returned to the incomers who'd insisted on triple glazing. 'Where are they from, the crowd who bought the place behind Cafferkys' smokehouse?'

'It's a fella from Australia. Says his people came from round here.'

'And did they?'

'Of course they didn't. His name's Whelan. There was never a Whelan in Finfarran.'

'Except for that crowd with the paint shop in Carrick.'

Fury's sniff contained all the scorn of a man whose family had lived in Finfarran from time immemorial. 'That Whelan in Carrick had a father came from Cork.' He bent down and scratched The Divil, who was still staring fixedly at Ronan. 'I wouldn't say a word against his shop, mind, he does good deals on brushes. I don't like the cut of this other Whelan, though. Do you know what he did the first day I met him? Opened the door of my van and left a bottle of whiskey on the seat.'

'Was it good stuff?'

'Mighty. But would you credit that behaviour? No price named and no deal done, but he lays his hand on my van door like he owns it.'

'I'd say you named a high price, so.'

'I did, and I told him straight he could take it or leave it.'

This was a serious matter since much of Fury's pleasure in a deal lay in haggling. The Divil growled sympathetically, causing Ronan's wide eyes to grow round in wonder. Feeling rather sorry for Mr Whelan from Australia, Conor said he ought to be getting on. 'I brought this fella out so's Aideen could have a bit of a break. Una's at home but she's trying to get a grip on the farm paperwork. He'll be due a feed, though, and I've got these fence posts to pick up.'

Fury nodded. 'No bother. I'll see you round. Give my respects to your mam.'

Since Paddy's death, many people had been sending respects to Una. She was well liked. Everyone knew that Paddy hadn't always been easy to live with, but Una had given no sign when things were tough. She had a rare ability to see both the good and the bad in the people she loved, and to preserve a sense of proportion under stress. After his accident Paddy had been unable for heavy lifting, so he'd holed up in the poky little room they called 'the office', and tackled the vital admin work that went with running a farm. He'd hated it but, as Una had said, it gave him a reason to keep on keeping on. Now the admin had become Una's province, while Conor worked the farm with the hired labourer and Aideen divided her time between the deli and minding Ronan. Even in the short time since the funeral, they'd become adept at filling gaps and covering for each other, but childcare, farm work and computers are all inherently prone to glitches and, every so often, their schedules went adrift.

Today the chat with Fury had taken longer than Conor intended and, by the time the fence posts were loaded, Ronan was beginning to demand his feed. As the jeep bowled along the last stretch of the road home to the farm, Conor chanted a litany of field names, hoping to avert a full-scale tantrum. 'Look, Ronan, look out there. See the green field? See the yellow one this side? The Calf Field, the Long Field, the Top Strip, Old Acre, the Back Meadow, Tom's Meadow ...' He glanced round at the baby, who was strapped in the car seat behind him. 'Good boy. Look. No, this side. Look there.' Ronan's lower lip was out, but his head turned to follow the pointing finger. Conor swung the wheel and headed up the hill towards the yard. 'The Fort

Field, the Bog Field, Skeenarinky, the Hill Field, the High Field, Moineenbeg ...' Some of the names he chanted weren't of fields he could see from the jeep but they were visible in his mind's eye, stretching away for miles, and now, lulled by his voice, Ronan was gurgling, not pouting. Turning into the yard, Conor heaved a sigh of relief. The last thing he wanted was to hand over a screaming baby to Aideen who, he knew, would have spent this respite from childcare coping with household tasks.

He found her in the scullery off the kitchen, loading the tumble drier. 'I bet you haven't sat down since I've been gone.'

Aideen looked up at him, pushing her curls off her forehead. 'No, but I've got masses done. This is the last load, and I've sheets out on the lines.'

'This fella's ready to be fed.'

'Was he good?'

'Not a bother on him. We counted the fence posts, didn't we, Ronan? And we named all the fields on the farm as we came home.' Handing her the baby, Conor went through to the office, where Una was sitting at Paddy's desk frowning at the computer screen. Conor looked over her shoulder. 'Is that the Reactor Milk Record form?'

'Yes. Don't tell me it doesn't need filling in yet, because I know. I'm working my way through all the forms on the Department of Agriculture's website.'

'You won't need to read them all. Paddy set up a checklist and linked it to the calendar.'

'I know. I'm just trying to get my head round the whole picture. I can see why he hated being stuck here when he wanted to be out farming.'

'We could get someone in to do the online stuff.'

'No, we couldn't. It'd cost a fortune and, anyway, you'd be looking over his shoulder.' Una gave Conor a gentle push. 'Or hers. And it's really annoying, so back off and leave me at it.'

'Aideen's feeding Ronan. She says dinner's in half an hour.'

'Perfect. Now go away.'

After dinner Aideen took Ronan up to the orchard. It was a blustery day, perfect for drying laundry, and Ronan squealed happily when he saw the swinging sheets and muslin squares. She thought of the house where she'd grown up, in St Finian's Close in Lissbeg, where washing was draped on a plastic rotary drier in the backyard. Here on the farm, lines were stretched between poles high enough to take double sheets and duvets, and a cord was strung between two gnarled apple trees, so that kitchen cloths could be dried close to the house. The sky was a cloudless blue above the green, rustling orchard, and when Aideen tested the laundry, she found it was dry. A gust of wind caught the sheet she had taken hold of and, whipping it away, made a billowing white canopy over her head. Looking up, she could see sunlight through the fine weave of the cotton. The sheet swung down, enveloping her and Ronan, and she felt him lean back in her arms. Then, as the wind whirled the fabric back into the air, she stepped away from the clothesline, thinking Ronan had been scared by the disappearance of his world. Instead, he laughed up at her, his fists bunched in excitement, and her heart turned over in a sudden spasm of love.

Holding him tightly, she carried him to the seat that Paddy had built beneath Conor's tree. Close by, in the hedge, was a clump of foxgloves. A few purple flowers still nodded at the top of each fleshy stalk and, lower down, clustering pods contained next year's seeds. Aideen sat on the wooden seat and looked deep into Ronan's eyes. When Conor had proposed, he'd given her a ring set with chips of lapis lazuli because, he said, they matched the colour of her eyes. Aideen preferred it to the huge diamond ring Joe had bought for his fiancée. It was unexpected and typical of Conor, whose practical approach to life concealed a romantic streak.

When Ronan was born she'd thought his eyes were going to be blue, like her own, but the nurse had shaken her head. 'Sometimes they can appear blue and it's only lack of pigment. They mightn't establish their true colour for months.' Shortly afterwards, in textbook fashion, Ronan's eyes had begun to darken. Aideen had tried to ignore the change but it seemed that their colour had now been established as brown. Turning him round on her knee, so he could see the flapping laundry, she bit her lip. The textbooks had also told her to expect mood swings, which the nurse, who was English, had dismissed as 'Something and nothing. It'll just be your hormones, pet. You'll find they'll pass.' But this isn't just hormones, thought Aideen. It's how things will be for the rest of Ronan's life. Hugging him, she felt her eyes fill with tears. It had been bad enough dealing with the forms they'd given her at the clinic, asking questions about her family's medical history. How could she parry neighbours' questions and cope with the awkward silences? She couldn't face endless conversations with people like Mary Casey. Why couldn't his eyes stay blue, and not go changing colour, so everybody would just smile and say that he took after his mum?

Chapter Seven

Dan's family's shop and smokehouse were by the road above the pier at Couneen. Further up the hill, a straggling group of deserted cottages had once been home to a thriving fishing community. Among them was the house on which Fury was working for the Australian and, at the top of the row, facing the little pier, Dan's grandfather's cottage, now a shed piled with products sold in the shop. Everything he knew about the ocean he'd learned from his late granddad whose cottage had been a haven when he was a boy. Charm and good looks had made Dan popular with his schoolmates, but none of them had lived close to Couneen. In comparison with his, Bríd's childhood had been easy. Her parents were comfortably off and, living in town, she'd been able to hang out with friends. On the far side of the peninsula, Dan's equally hardworking parents had struggled to make a living in an isolated, depleted community with no public-transport links. He probably would have rejected the thought that he'd grown up lonely with a massive chip on his shoulder, but Bríd had always known and understood.

Somehow, they'd hit it off from the beginning and, mooching around the schoolyard, he'd talked to her about things he'd never mentioned to anyone else. She found him fascinating. Part idealist and part cynic, he came alive only when describing his dream of having an eco-marine tour business, or when castigating those he called 'the bloody powers-that-be'. Even now, although he owned a boat, and increasing numbers of tourists were arriving each year in Finfarran, his sense of being hard done by was still acute. 'Look at my mum and dad, still scraping a living. They had to put in an internet café to keep the grocery viable, and now they've added the smokehouse out the back. That's three businesses in one and they're only treading water. And here's me, trying to sell whale-watching trips when holidaymakers can hardly find their way out to Couneen.'

Bríd's instinct was always to seek a practical solution. 'Maybe you need a website or an online presence. You could ask the tourist board for some advice.'

'The only ones they'll give a hand to are the crowd back in Ballyfin.' Dan scowled as he spoke. 'And that's just Disneyfication. They get subsidies chucked at them and the rest of us can go hang.'

There was no evidence for this, and Bríd was tired of hearing him say it. 'Listen, we're all paying taxes. If you don't ask you don't get.'

'And half the time, if you ask, you get sod-all.'

'All right, be a misery-guts, I don't care. And, actually, I retract that statement. Because when was the last time you paid a penny in tax?'

'Isn't that what I'm saying? I can't make a living wage.'

'What about those cash jobs you do on the side?'

'My granddad worked his arse off every day since he was nine. And look at the hours my mum and dad put in. What has the government ever done for us that they want to cream off our profits? Anyway, the odd day's labour is more honest than shuffling along in a queue for the bloody dole.'

It was a familiar, circular conversation, though lately they'd had it less frequently. Since he'd moved to St Finian's Close, Dan had lost much of his moodiness and Bríd had been happy to relax and enjoy what, secretly, she admitted to herself, amounted to playing house. While she couldn't imagine life without his presence, she wasn't sure that she wanted a deeper commitment, at least not yet. But neither was she untouched by the desolate beauty of Couneen, or the romantic image of Dan as a free seafaring spirit, unconfined by landlubberly rules.

Though Dan's father had never worked as a fisherman, he had grown up among them and retained family contacts, and Dan had been badgering Bríd for weeks to stock Cafferkys' smoked salmon at the deli. 'It's all produce of Finfarran and there's no nitrates or artificial preservatives. It absolutely fits HabberDashery's brand.'

'Yes, it probably does, but I'd need to talk to Aideen.'

'Well, what's stopping you?'

'Nothing. It's just that she's had a lot on her mind lately, what with the baby and Paddy's death.'

'It's only a matter of putting in an order.'

'No, it isn't. If it's going to be a regular order, there are implications. I don't want to sign a contract with your parents and then find our customers won't buy. They might not. It's expensive stuff.'

'We do mackerel too. It's cheaper.'

'I know. And I'll talk to Aideen.'

'We don't need a contract. Not at first. Dad's not going to force you to take it if we find it won't sell.'

'Look, you can't speak for your mam and dad any more than I can for Aideen. You're right, it's a good idea but—'

'But I'm just the go-between.'

'Don't be daft. I want to do this right, that's all. So let's not get ahead of ourselves.'

She still hadn't broached the subject with Aideen when Dan relayed an invitation to visit his parents on their half-day off. He drove her there on a sleepy Sunday morning when an onshore wind was blowing and the sky was a pearly grey. There weren't many sandy bathing beaches on this side of the peninsula but the cliffs were full of charming, half-hidden inlets, like Couneen, and the deserted hills were a paradise for walkers. Dan's mum, who had made lunch, proudly produced a platter of fish from the smokehouse. 'We're serving it here now in the internet café. Cyclists come in to use the Wi-Fi connection, which is great because they stop for a sandwich or something to take on a picnic.' Nothing in her manner suggested that this was a sales pitch, though Bríd was beginning to wonder if Dan was equally guileless. He wasn't above using a social occasion to further his ends. But it was too late to worry, so she smiled and accepted a crusty bread roll stuffed with salmon and watercress. 'Gosh, you've a stunning view of the pier, and this salmon's delicious.'

'Try some of the mackerel on a cracker.'

The picture of innocence, Dan held out the crackers and Bríd resisted an urge to say that she'd hardly begun on her roll. Clumsy though his behaviour was, she sympathised with his impulse to support his parents and, besides, he was looking spectacularly handsome, his dark hair blown in the wind and his tan showing to advantage against his white T-shirt. He had the longest eyelashes Bríd had ever seen on a guy, and deep creases at the corners of his eyes from squinting against sunlight on the ocean. To relieve the moment of tension, she laughed and took a cracker. 'This is pure luxury! I'm lining up the treats.'

Fidelma, Dan's mum, smiled at them both. 'It's great that you had time to come over to visit, and it's nice to sit down once in a while with Dan.'

Dan's father agreed. 'It is. We don't see you back here enough, these days, son.'

Bríd saw Dan stiffen. Comments on his whereabouts always made him defensive, something she'd learned when they'd been dating at school. Half the girls had fancied him, but it wasn't in Dan's nature to cheat, and Bríd had assumed he'd known she trusted him. Yet one day, when she'd casually asked how he'd spent the previous evening, he'd accused her of interrogating him, and stormed off in a huff. Now she glanced at him covertly, vaguely irritated but, before she could pin the sensation down, Dan had relaxed and laughed across at his dad. 'You mean you don't see me lounging around with a can of beer and a sandwich. I'm down at the pier all hours, working on that boat. And I'd be here a lot more if I could raise the money to do eco-tours full time.'

Fidelma smiled at him affectionately. 'You'll manage it, never fear. Aren't we a family of entrepreneurs?'

'God knows, we've had to be.' Downing his drink, Dan stood up to fetch another. 'Does anyone fancy a walk when we're finished here?'

His mother pushed back her chair. 'Sit down, I'll get your beer and bring out the pudding. When we're finished, you two love-birds can go walking. I'm going to put my feet up for the first time this week.'

So Bríd and Dan walked up the hill to the old row of cottages, where crows nesting in a tumbledown chimney cawed at their approach. When they came to the end of the one-track road, they continued upwards on sheep paths, carved knee-deep through the friable turf by sharp, pointed hoofs. It was hard to follow the narrow ways among the purple heather and, as she edged along, Bríd almost turned her ankle. Dad steadied her from behind. 'You okay?'

'Fine. I stood on a stone that rolled.' Turning to face him, Bríd looked back down the hill. 'You get spectacular height pretty quickly, don't you?' They stood looking down at the sagging row of cottages, each of which stood in its own small plot. Below the houses, the corrugated roof of the smokehouse gleamed in the fitful sunlight, and Bríd could see pallets of goods stacked in the yard behind the shop. Dan had parked on the slope that led down to the inlet, where the wind was driving the incoming tide against the stone pier, and the undertow as the waves surged back produced a deep, sucking sound, audible from the side of the hill where they stood. He pointed to a flat boulder. 'Let's sit for a while. I'm still digesting that humungous lunch.'

Bríd scrambled towards the boulder, scratching her knee in the process, and sat on it cross-legged, looking at the view. Dan, who was taller, waded more successfully through the heather and stretched out beside her on the flat, sun-warmed stone. Linking his hands behind his head, he stared up at the sky. 'There's a storm coming.'

'Should we be getting back to the car?'

'No. I'd say it's hours away. We'll be home before it hits.'

Bríd looked down at the derelict houses, which seemed very small from this bird's eye viewpoint. 'It must have been rough living there in the teeth of the winter gales.'

Dan pushed himself into a sitting position. 'They're in a dip of the land. Can't you see? I remember being in my granddad's place in a force-ten gale, and the windows hardly rattled. They were tiny, of course, and the walls are thick. We blocked the windows when he died and the house got turned into a shed. Dad said he didn't want passers-by seeing stuff and breaking in. Which was a laugh, because nobody ever came here.'

'Back then, maybe, but things are different now. I mean, you get tourists, and there's walkers, and your mum said cyclists come by. And now people drive out to buy from the smokehouse.'

Dan gave her a sideways look under his curling lashes. 'And you know why? Because the produce is brilliant.'

'Stop it, Dan.'

'Stop what?'

'Pushing. I've said I'll talk to Aideen.'

He lay back again with his dark head on her thigh. 'It is brilliant, though. Tell me you loved your lunch.'

'I did. It was delicious.'

'Now tell me you love me.'

Laughing, Bríd looked down at him. 'This is business, Dan. I'm not going to succumb to your evil wiles.'

Placing his hand on the back of her head, he drew her face down to his. 'Evil wiles sound terribly interesting.'

'Just stop!' Bríd kissed him and pulled away, still laughing. 'Shut up about the smokery. I want to hear what's happening with your boat.'

He shrugged. 'You know what's happening. Dad deals with anyone who turns up when I'm working with you.'

'Look, Aideen and I have been talking about this. It's great to have you at the Garden Café, but you shouldn't jeopardise your own business by helping us.'

'A hundred euros a week or so, and that's when the weather is decent. I'd hardly call it a business.'

'Well, it won't be if you don't put your back into it.'

'Are you saying you don't want me helping out in Lissbeg?'

'Of course not. I've just said it's great to have you. But you've got your own dream, Dan.'

Dan's face hardened. 'Don't keep on about the eco-tours thing, okay? I'm getting nowhere with it and I don't need you to remind me.'

'But that's what I'm trying to say. You have to engage with an enterprise if you want it to succeed.'

'I don't need a lecture on how to succeed either. I'm not a total gawm, Bríd. I do know what I'm at. Eco-marine stuff is a growing market. If I wanted to, I could feck off and work somewhere else. I could be doing tours in glass-bottomed boats, or taking people out looking for dolphins. I'd make good money, and be at sea, and I wouldn't have all the feckin' pressures of running my own business. But that's the point, isn't it? I'd be in Dublin or West Cork, or off in Australia.' Dan's voice cracked and, alarmed, Bríd looked down at him. He gave her a crooked smile and muttered, 'I wouldn't be here.' For a moment she thought he meant that they wouldn't be together. Then he sat up abruptly and stared down at the pier. 'I wouldn't be in Couneen.'

Glad that she hadn't betrayed her mistake, Bríd kept her voice level. 'And that's what matters?'

'It always has been.' With his eyes on the grey-blue horizon, Dan reached out and took her hand. 'I wish you'd known my granddad. He was a legend. I don't just mean an amazing guy, I mean everyone looked up to him. There was nothing he didn't know about boats and sailing. He could name you every creature that swam in the ocean, and every rock and current for miles around. He started fishing in a tarred currach when he was thirteen, and before that he'd been gutting the catch and mending his dad's lobster pots. He was his own man, Bríd. This was his place. The powers-that-be might have paid for that pier, but men back here built it, and they did it for starvation wages. Mighty men who were ground down by the crowd that was in charge. They knew this place and they loved it. So did he. '

Bríd's fingers were reddened where he'd crushed them and, when he turned to her fiercely, she moved her hand to conceal it. But his eyes seemed to be looking at something else. 'You know something? There's no one but you understands this shit. No one.' He slipped his arm around her waist and laid his head on her shoulder. 'He never made me promise to stay, but I know it's what he'd have wanted. You can't break faith with the past, can you? Not if you've got any pride. He made me see that.'

Chapter Eight

One day a week Mary Casey volunteered in a charity shop in Lissbeg. There were three of them almost cheek by jowl in Sheep Street, surviving on short leases and peppercorn rents. Before deciding which to approach, Mary had assessed their respective window displays. One, which supported an animal shelter, featured a poster of a kitten wearing a baby's bonnet. In her view, that was unacceptably mawkish. The second had a nativity scene at Christmas and three crosses surrounded by flowers at Easter: this she rejected on the grounds that you couldn't trust priests or nuns with money. 'I'm not saying a word against them, and they do great work for the poor, but the highest court in the land couldn't get them to open up their accounts.' The third shop, run by a children's charity, had a mixture of clothing and bric-a-brac in its window. This, according to Mary, was both straightforward and canny because people liked to see what was on sale before they went in.

Having made her choice, she'd presented herself, expecting a warm welcome. Before their retirement, she explained, she and her late husband had kept a village post office. 'Back in Crossarra. We were the only shop there. Thirty years and more of sound retail experience. We sold household goods and groceries too, and ours was the first electric bacon slicer west of Carrick. That's what I have to offer, and I doubt if you could do better.'

The manager had assured her drily that experience wasn't required. 'We're always looking for volunteers and we offer a half-day's training.' Mary's first instinct had been to take umbrage, but the brightly painted interior was attractive and the jumble of varied items for sale had intrigued her, so she'd said that she'd be happy to lend a hand.

Secretly, she'd been glad of the training, and remained slightly daunted by the shop's electronic till, but, once settled in, she'd established herself as an asset. Clothes delighted her almost as much as opportunities to criticise and advise, and she had an eagle eye for customers looking for bargains describable as 'vintage' or 'upcycled chic'. More often than not, she bullied and flattered them into successful purchases with the result that they returned time and again. Occasionally, however, she identified someone as what she called 'a chancer' and made it her business to ensure that they'd never come back. Today she had her eye on a lady who'd spotted a designer camisole among a collection of cheap Penney's blouses. Mary could tell by her shifty manner that she thought she was unobserved. After much overtly casual browsing, the woman concealed her prize in an armful of miscellaneous tops and, assuming a hearty manner, came and dumped them on the counter. 'Well, Mrs Casey, I didn't know this was your day in the shop.'

'Do you tell me that? No, I'm always here on Wednesdays. But I suppose we all get forgetful at our age.' As the customer was a good twenty years younger than Mary, this remark didn't go down well. Caught off guard, she stammered, giving Mary an opportunity to deal her another shrewd blow. 'Did you want to try those on? Because I'd say you have several different sizes there.'

'Well, no, actually, size doesn't matter. I'm, er, planning to paint the shed and I want a few to wear and just chuck away.' Unwisely, given Mary's demeanour, the woman kept going. 'A job lot I could give you a fiver for?'

Expertly, Mary fanned out the clothes on the counter, exposing the wisp of chartreuse silk with its crimson ribbons and lace. In ominous silence the customer blushed from her neck to her hairline. Had she held her ground she might have got away with it. Mary had a soft spot for a true connoisseur of fashion, and the camisole was a truly beautiful find. But an opponent's loss of confidence always brought out her killer streak. 'Well, the sight of you up a ladder in this might disconcert the neighbours. Wouldn't you say?'

As the woman scuttled out and Mary returned the garments to their hangers, an elderly man who'd been browsing the bookshelves wandered across to the till. He was wearing a zip-up windcheater and carrying a large suitcase. Mary eyed him judicially, deciding the suitcase was old but expensive. Transferring her attention to his face, she recognised the owner of Carrick's medieval castle. He gave her a sweet, conspiratorial smile. 'Well, that was a pleasure to watch. I see you take no prisoners.' Partly gratified and partly suspecting that she was being laughed at, Mary asked what she could do for him. Charles Aukin placed the case on the counter and, opening it, revealed that it was packed full of clothes. 'I wondered if you might have a use for these.' He looked at Mary over his round, gold-rimmed glasses. 'They're not exactly fashionable, but I think they're what's known as good.'

One glance told Mary that this was an understatement. The fine wool jackets, tweed skirts and piqué cotton shirts were timeless classics, evidently belonging to a middle-aged woman of medium height and average figure, to whom money was no object. Along with the silk headscarves, a quilted gilet and a lightweight Burberry, they amounted to a wardrobe straight out of the *Lady* magazine. Charles looked at them affectionately. 'She always dressed the part, my wife. You wouldn't catch her in things like this in Manhattan, but wherever we went she'd swan out in advance and get herself suitably attired. This was her Castle Lancy gear.' He sighed. 'Poor Isobel.'

Lady Isobel de Lancy's death a few years previously had been the talk of the peninsula for months. Born and raised in New York, she'd never been in Ireland before what had been her first and only visit to her ancestral home. Unheralded, she and Charles had appeared, apparently for a holiday, and remained at the castle because, as it turned out, Isobel had been ill. As time passed she'd become worse, and Mary could remember much gossip about her desire to be buried in the family crypt. Somehow this fact had emerged and been passed around the grapevine, producing universal disbelief. Why, with all her money, didn't she fly back to the States and find some doctor to cure her? Mary had tossed her head over coffee with a friend in the Garden Café. It was pure self-indulgence, she'd said. Or proof that, whatever the illness was, it had softened the woman's brain. 'I mean, what sort of eejit comes out with stuff about breathing her last in the Dear Old Country and sleeping among her forefathers' bones?'

Pat Fitz, Mary's friend, had spread butter on a scone. 'Sick people can get awfully stubborn.'

'What's wrong with her anyway?'

'I don't know. I haven't heard. It could be that she's had it a while. Maybe they gave out that they came here on a holiday but the poor woman knew she had something incurable.'

If that was the case, thought Mary, lifting a skirt and finding cashmere cardigans, she spent a hell of a lot of money on clothes she didn't have much time to wear. Looking up, she caught Charles Aukin's eye and remembered another thing Pat had said in the café. 'It's her husband I feel sorry for, Mary. What's he going to do when Lady Isobel's gone? Shut up the castle, go back to New York, and leave his wife buried there in the crypt? It wouldn't be decent. You want a grave you can visit now and again with the odd bunch of flowers. And, however rich the man is, he can't keep flying back here just to do that.'

Charles's voice interrupted Mary's reminiscence. 'So, may I leave you these? Do you think you can sell them?'

'I'd say they'll be snapped up before you get to the end of the street.' This was hyperbole. Donations to the charity shop had to be priced by the manager, who looked after a second branch in Carrick and only came to Lissbeg once a week.

Charles smiled. 'Good. Well, I'll leave them with you. The case is saleable too, right?'

'People want wheelie ones, these days.'

He sighed again. 'I guess so. Isobel was an old-style traveller. The kind that tipped a porter to carry her case.'

It seemed a bit sad to send him away carrying an empty suitcase, and if he'd held on to his wife's clothes this long, parting with them must be a painful wrench. A thought occurred to Mary. 'You won't need the suitcase yourself? I mean, you're not having a clear-out because you're going back to New York?' If he was, it was a prime piece of gossip and she couldn't resist the temptation to find out. Having mentally characterised him as a rather pathetic figure, she was disconcerted to hear him chuckle.

'In the midst of death we're always in life, aren't we?' He gave her a wink, which Mary considered outrageous, and began to repack the clothes they'd taken from the case. 'It's remarkable how we cling to the most unlikely bits of the past. This tweedy persona didn't fit Isobel. She was much more herself on the Orient

Express in a black feather boa, wearing diamond rings over her elbow gloves. But these were the last things she wore and I guess that's meant something. At all events, it's taken me until now to get rid of them.'

Diverted by the mention of gloves, Mary leaned on the counter. 'I know what you mean. You hang on to things you've no use for. When my husband Tom died I had a clear-out, but I couldn't part with his gardening gloves. He was a great man for the flowers. I can't be doing with gardening myself, not with these knees. Anyway, you'd hate the worms. But I kept the gloves, and what for? God knows.'

'I'm sorry for your loss.'

'Ah, well, it was a good while back. Before you lost your lady. I miss him still.'

Charles reached over and snapped the locks on the suitcase. 'I guess it's the people around us who keep us rooted in the present. Without them, time slips about. At least, that's what I find.'

'I know. There's times it's easier to recall something from years ago than to remember what happened only yesterday. Not always, mind, but now and again. It annoys me.' Wondering why she'd told him that, Mary returned to business. 'I'll take these through to the back and we'll have them priced up by tomorrow.'

Charles took a baseball cap from his pocket, apparently for the sole purpose of putting it on in order to raise to her as he left. As he prepared to go, Mary considered asking if he'd seen a piece she'd read that morning in the *Inquirer*. It was about short- and long-term memory. One of those *Ask the Doctor* columns with a pen-and-ink sketch at the top of a man with a stethoscope round his neck and a big toothy smile. You could bet your bottom dollar that whoever had written the piece looked nothing like the picture. Chances were it was a woman, or the editor, or an intern, and that the whole thing was lifted off the internet. It was interesting, though, and she wouldn't mind chatting with someone about it. But the moment had passed, and when Charles was gone, she was glad she'd kept her mouth shut. You couldn't be talking to people when, half the time, they were making a game of you and, indubitably, that was what Charles Aukin had done. Pausing on the threshold before leaving, he'd winked at her again. 'I'm not going back to the States, by the way, so feel free to pass the word along.'

Having left the charity shop, Charles continued along Sheep Street, turned into Broad Street and, pausing to admire the geraniums in the horse trough, crossed the road and went into the library. Hanna was at her desk and got up to greet him. 'Owen's gone to lunch. Come through.' It was part of her job to turn over a new page of the psalter at intervals, and she loved the occasions when Charles phoned and suggested he might drop by. Meticulous though he was in insisting that she was now its custodian, Hanna understood how much he missed the pleasure of having the book to hand in his home.

Having locked the outer door, she led him into the dimly lit exhibition space where screens on the walls gave access to digitised images, with options to zoom in on details, and explanations and translations of the text in several languages. In the centre of the room, in a toughened-glass display case, the psalter lay open on a gilded lectern. Written in Latin, the little book of psalms had been created in a monastery near Carrick sometime in the eighth century. No larger than a novel you might buy in an airport, its illustrations combined depictions of Finfarran's rural landscape with the wildest excesses of medieval fantasy, in inks and paints that remained as bright as if they'd been ground and applied only yesterday. Hanna knew the manuscript well, having been involved in its digitisation process, yet the moments when she touched it still felt magical. No matter how often she looked at it, she always found something new. A previously unseen face would leer from behind trailing whorls of foliage, a line of text would leap out at her, enhanced by tiny spots of blue or ochre, or a turreted city would appear within the elaborate curves of a capital letter. Turning the pages always sent a tingle down her spine, giving a sense of being in touch with the skilled hands that had created it, and those that had kept it safe for a thousand years. The de Lancys had acquired it by what Fury asserted was 'double dealing at the dissolution of the monasteries'. Hanna took that to be one of his more extravagant inventions but, as generations of de Lancys had shared the habit of keeping records of their possessions, there was no doubt that, before coming to the library, the psalter had been in Castle Lancy since 1547.

With Charles beside her, she unlocked the display case, lifted the Perspex bars that held the book open on its lectern and, reaching out, carefully turned the page. Charles bent forward in recognition. 'Hey, here he is! I've always loved this little guy.' Running across a double-page spread, within a border cross-hatched in green and yellow, was a single illustration of a room hung with tapestries. Hanna remembered her own pleasure in examining them in close-up and finding a depiction of Belshazzar's feast in the incongruous setting of a sumptuous palace in the mountains above Ballyfin. The room in the illustration was unfurnished except for a desk, at which a woman in a wimple and a blue robe was standing, and a stool on which the man at whom Charles had pointed crouched. The man held an open book on his knee and flourished a large quill pen. The woman appeared to be dictating. Her mouth was open and her hand raised, and the scribe, who was dressed in a monk's robe, had his eyes fixed on her face. Above the two figures was a cloud of birds of all sizes and colours, so delicately painted you could almost hear the sound of their fluttering wings. Though the woman and the man appeared unaware of the birds' presence, the viewer was clearly intended to see them as important, because the floor of the room was made up of an intricate pattern of fallen feathers, and the quill in the scribe's hand had been picked out in gold.

Chapter Nine

As usual on the days when Charles came by to visit the psalter, he and Hanna had lunch in the Garden Café. It was an agreeable arrangement to which they both looked forward, Charles because he led a lonely life at the castle and Hanna because she enjoyed his company. Occasionally, she wondered why Charles's mild eccentricities amused her while Tim's posturing annoyed her at work and Mary's behaviour could drive her mad at home. Ultimately, she supposed, the difference was that Charles indulged himself at no cost to others. Beneath his disingenuous appearance was the shrewd, calculating mind that had made him a powerful businessman, but a deep well of kindness underpinned both.

As they crossed the garden he spotted a table for two beside the fountain. 'I'll take that if you want to go place our order.' Hanna made for the café and he sat at the little table, placing his baseball cap on the wide rim of the granite basin.

She came back shortly, carrying coffees on a tray. 'I ordered chicken on rye for us both.'

'That's perfect.' Charles looked across to where Jazz and a group of her workmates were gathered by the herb beds, holding notebooks. 'What a place for a breakout meeting.'

Hanna followed his gaze. 'Her company rents offices in the old convent building. She's a lucky girl.'

'I guess you're pleased that she's settled down in Finfarran.'

'Who knows what'll happen in the future, but I'm glad that she's here now. You never stop worrying about your kids, even when they're adults.'

'Isobel and I didn't have kids. I was too busy making my fortune and she was too busy spending hers. Some de Lancy went to the States in the late eighteen hundreds. Made a packet out of a silver mine. As far as I know, the family left the castle under dust sheets and only came back to Ireland to hunt and fish. Isobel's parents hardly knew they had a place here. She told me she hadn't known herself till she found out from her attorney when her dad died.' Charles smiled. 'We had a whale of a life. Isobel used to get what you Irish call "notions". Ballooning in the Serengeti, opera at La Scala. She'd see some programme on PBS and, next thing you know, we'd be off on a plane or a cruise ship. I was telling your mom at the charity shop this morning.' He chuckled. 'She was all agog. Thought I was planning to pack up and leave Finfarran myself.'

'Oh, Lord, I'm sorry. She does like to know what's happening.'

'No need to apologise. I get a kick out of people like her. She's what my father used to call a feisty old broad.'

'That's one way of putting it!' Hanna took a sip of coffee and, not wishing to appear as inquisitive as Mary, refrained from asking Charles the obvious question.

Stirring his own coffee, he answered it anyway. 'I told her I have no such plans. Well, of course I haven't. I can't leave Isobel buried in a crypt under an empty castle. She was a party girl, hated being alone.' He indicated his surroundings with a wide sweep of his hand. 'Anyway, I like it here. Finfarran's a good place to live. People look after each other – there's a proper sense of community. I doubt Isobel would have fitted in, though, and I'm kind of glad she never found that out. We might have had trouble if she'd started to play lady of the manor.'

'Well, I'm sure ...'

Charles shook his head. 'Poor Isobel hadn't a clue about Ireland. She'd have tried to organise cricket matches and invited Father Cassidy to play bridge.'

'Oh dear.'

'Yep. I'm not sure she could tell the difference between here and Agatha Christie's England, and folks would have been too polite to inform her.' A waitress had arrived with the sandwiches and Charles bit into his chicken on rye. 'Either that or the neighbourhood would have turned up en masse waving pitchforks. I hear it happened before.' Seeing Hanna's startled expression, he laughed. 'I mean back in the day. Wasn't there a siege at the castle during the Civil War?'

'Well, yes, I think there was a skirmish. There was only a

caretaker there at the time. It wasn't an attack on the de Lancys, though. The family was in New York.'

Despite their long presence in Finfarran, there was still a vague sense of the castle as the seat of foreign invaders, and Charles was used to hasty attempts to protect him from this fact. Coming from a country where plain speaking was regarded as a virtue, he found the kindly impulse rather wearing. He grinned at Hanna. 'It won't have been the first skirmish the old place had seen. There's a hell of a lot of history behind those walls.' Then, fearing his joke might have been ill-chosen, he moved to what he assumed would be safer ground. 'I see where the library's planning displays on the War of Independence.'

'And the Civil War. There'll be display boards in all the branches. We're gathering material now.'

'And looking for funding?'

'Actually, no, it's state-funded. A national initiative.'

'I wondered if I might help.'

'I can't imagine the county council refusing a donation. But, really, it isn't necessary.'

'I do have an interest.'

'In local history?'

'That too. I've read up a lot since Isobel's death. But that's not what I mean. If Lissbeg Library's going to have an exhibit, I assume the story of the psalter will be central.'

'I don't quite see ...' Realisation dawned on Hanna. 'You mean that it would have been in the castle during the Civil War.'

Alarm had made her eyes widen but, in his enthusiasm, Charles didn't notice. 'Exactly. Lying in the drawer in the book room, where the family kept it. According to what I read, the guys who broke into Castle Lancy planned to blow it up if they couldn't hold it. It's a fantastic story. After all those centuries, that would have been the end of the Carrick Psalter. Nothing more than collateral damage in a war between neighbours who'd once fought as allies. Think about it. A national treasure with real local significance. A unique book, nearly blown to smithereens. If that's not the perfect hook for a display board in a library, what the heck is?'

'And the thing is, he's absolutely right!' Wearing the hoodie and sweatpants into which she'd changed after work, Hanna was striding up the Hag's Glen beside Brian. It was their regular evening walk up the tapering valley to a rocky cleft where a peat-brown river fell as a slender waterfall. No dwelling or road could be seen from the site that Brian had chosen to build on and, except for birdsong and falling water, there was no sound to be heard. Pausing to take a deep breath of the clear air, Brian looked at Hanna. 'That's impressive. A unique link between your library and the commemoration.'

'I know.'

'So why are you looking doubtful?'

'I'm not.'

'Oh, come on, Hanna.'

'Well, okay, maybe I am. Let's forget it for now and enjoy our walk.'

Later, having eaten in the kitchen, they climbed the internal staircase that led to the garden on the flat roof. It was what Hanna described to herself as an architect's garden, as unlike Maggie's wild, sloping field as it could be. Birch trees in pots and tall, formal ornamental grasses made a setting for seating that faced down the glen and across the distant forest to the ocean. With a wine bottle on the table and glasses in their hands, they relaxed and watched a scarlet sunset sky fade to pink and gold and darken to purple. Brian lay back and stretched out his legs, cradling his glass on his chest. With his head tipped back, he could see the evening star glimmer above a drifting cloud. Soon, thousands of other tiny pinpricks of light would appear. Turning his head, he looked at Hanna and saw that her mind was elsewhere. 'You've been moody since you came home. Is something wrong?'

'What? No, of course not. I'm sorry. I'm still brooding about these display boards.'

'I thought Tim had come up with the forms at last.'

'It's not that. I was thinking of my conversation with Charles.'

'You've lost me.'

'Wait, hang on, I'll be back.' Hanna disappeared downstairs and returned a few minutes later, carrying Maggie's makeshift book. 'I told you about this when I found it. It's my great-aunt Maggie's.'

'I've never seen it.'

'No. I left it at Maggie's place when I moved here. I suppose I thought it belonged there. Jazz produced it the other day and suggested we might use it in the Lissbeg Library display.'

'Are the dates relevant?'

'Some of them. It starts during the War of Independence. Maggie's brother Liam was out fighting.'

'Her brother?'

'Yep. Maggie was my dad's aunt. Liam, her brother, was Dad's father.'

'Liam survived the war, then?'

'Yes. Dad was born in the 1940s.' Hanna opened the book. 'Liam was lucky to survive. He came down to visit his mother one night and there was a Black and Tan raid. Liam escaped but it ended in tragedy. Listen to this.' She turned the pages and found the entry.

'When Dad looked up and saw them passing the window, he knocked the lamp off the table, then, as the door smashed in, he was out between them like a bull at a gate and made it over the ditch. The officer and a couple of the Tans turned back to fire at him and I think the one that was left in the house with us didn't know what to do. Anyway, he did nothing for a minute. Then he must have realised that Dad running out was a diversion, because he went for the door of the room where Liam was. Mam and I tried to stop

him, though I'd say Liam was out the back and gone as soon he heard the row. I was listening out and I heard shots fired up on the road.

'But Hannie heard the Tans firing at Dad and she ran out the front door after him. I don't think the one who hit her knew she was only a child. She came up behind him in the dark and he swung round and got her on the side of the head with the butt end of his gun. I was on the threshold by then but I couldn't get to her in time.

'It was black as the hob of hell outside so I thought Dad might have got away. When the officer saw what they'd done to Hannie, and the men he'd left guarding the road came down without Liam, he swore and ordered them back up to the lorry. The neighbours found Dad in the morning. He'd got most of the way to the far ditch when a bullet hit him in the neck. Hannie lasted till the next day but the doctor said her skull was fractured and she died.'

Brian winced. 'God, that's brutal.'

'I knew nothing about it before I found Maggie's book. Maybe my dad wasn't told. I've wondered if Liam felt guilty. I mean, he risked coming down from the mountains that night to visit his sick mother, and the result was that his father and sister were killed.'

'Have you talked to Mary about it?'

'No. She's never had a good word for Maggie. It sounds

daft, but I think she was jealous of her. By the time my dad was growing up, Maggie had come back from England and was living on the cliff again, all on her own. Dad used to drop in to give her a hand and, I guess, when he married, Mary resented him spending his time there. I've always assumed that that was why I got the job of going round to help Maggie. Anyway, it was way back in my childhood. Not something I'd want to rake over with Mam.'

'Talk about a can of worms.'

Hanna screwed up her face. 'That's what Fury said when he heard that Tim is planning these displays. I wasn't sure what he meant at first, but I realise now. They were complicated times, Brian. Mine's not the only family with stuff that doesn't get talked about.'

'You don't have to mention Maggie's book, though. It's not in the public domain and you can choose to keep it that way.'

'But now Charles has pointed out the link between the Civil War and the psalter, and you've just said yourself that he's right – there could hardly be a better focus for the exhibit in Lissbeg Library.'

'But, darling, what you want is to keep your family out of the picture. I can't see the harm in focusing on the psalter.'

'That's because you don't know what I didn't tell Charles at lunchtime.' Closing the book on her knee, Hanna hunched her shoulders. 'When I found Maggie's book in the tin, I did a bit of research on my granddad Liam. I'd known nothing about him, so I was curious. It turns out he was one of the diehards who fought in the Civil War.'

'I still don't see the problem with Charles's suggestion.'

'Don't you? Well, try this for size. Liam led the lads who made their last stand in Castle Lancy. He was the one who nearly blew the psalter to smithereens.'

Chapter Ten

Aideen put Ronan into his cot and sat down to watch him sleeping. This was the time of day she liked best, when everyone and everything on the farm was folded in. She savoured the concept, loving the idea that the term for the pens in which Conor kept sheep had the same root as the word she used for wrapping Ronan in his blanket. I enfold him, she thought. Sitting on the side of the bed, she considered the baby's tender mouth and delicate eyelids. He lay on his back in his sleeping suit, as the district nurse and the baby books had prescribed. A fleecy blanket, knitted by Una, lay on the changing table. Nevertheless, he's folded in, thought Aideen. Each night I enfold him in loving care. Even in prayer, though I'm not sure who I pray to.

She bent closer to listen to Ronan's breathing. In his first few weeks she'd been worried by how it would change from fast to slow. Una had smiled. 'Conor used to stop breathing altogether. Total silence. Then he'd start up again with a snort and put the heart across me. But he was grand, he grew out of it. They all do.' Una's reassurance made all the difference to Aideen, to whom parenthood still felt mysterious. Growing up without her own mother hadn't bothered her. Life in St Finian's Close was quiet, but Gran and Gran's elderly cousin, whom Aideen had called Aunt Bridge, were the kindest of guardians. Like most children whose time was spent in the company of adults, Aideen had developed a keen sense of what was expected of her, and, early on, she'd learned that mention of her mother made Gran sad. Aunt Bridge had explained that this was because her mum had died so young. 'She wasn't yet twenty, pet, and no one expected it.'

Aideen's favourite book at the time had been a collection of fairy tales. 'But people do die having babies. Snow White's mother did.'

'Sometimes they do. Not nowadays, though. Not often.'

So she'd accepted the idea that the subject should be avoided, for fear of upsetting Gran and giving Aunt Bridge that troubled look. She wasn't sure when she'd grasped that her mum had been unmarried, and she still found it strange that, when she was small, she hadn't missed her father. As soon as she'd gone to school she'd encountered questions in the playground, but instinct had told her not to take them home to St Finian's Close. Instead, she'd asked her Aunt Carol, Bríd's mum. 'Did my dad die too? Am I an orphan?' By then she'd moved on from fairy tales to *The BFG* and *Harry Potter* and the idea of being an orphan had felt important and impressive. But again there'd been a frisson that she'd been quick to recognise. Carol, her late mum's sister, had fobbed her off with a choc ice. Recognising that this was yet another unwelcome subject, Aideen had eaten the choc ice, played in the back garden with her cousins, and said no more.

When she arrived home, it was evident that Carol had made a phone call and a course of action had been decided upon. Over cake – unusual in St Finian's Close on a weekday – Aunt Bridge had mentioned her father and, to her surprise, Aideen had found that he was alive and well. 'But how come we don't see him?' A swift glance was exchanged between Aunt Bridge and Gran. 'Because we don't need to. We're grand here the three of us, aren't we? Plenty to do, plenty to eat and drink, and a house of our own. We're fine as we are.'

It was clear to Aideen that they wanted her to accept this announcement, but she also knew that it was the simple truth. And no one at school, or anywhere else, had made her feel bad about it. A generation earlier, the child of an unmarried mother and an absent father would have been stigmatised, but the Ireland into which she was born had shaken off many old prejudices and, besides, Aunt Bridge and Gran were held in high regard. Neither had been young when they'd taken responsibility for her, and Gran's health was frail, so the town's impulse was to admire them. Inevitably there'd been gossip but none was malicious, and Aideen had grown up unaware of it. For a while in her adolescence, still influenced by books, she'd imagined her father turning up to claim her; or that, for some reason, he'd need her so badly that life would take a new and exciting course.

But the fantasy hadn't survived the prosaic discovery that his name was Murphy, and was now married and ran a garden centre somewhere in Cork.

The loss of Aunt Bridge and Gran, who'd died within a year of each other, had cast Aideen adrift for a while. Left alone in her final school year, she'd moved in with Aunt Carol while Bríd was in Dublin doing her culinary course. After that, the hard work of building the deli's business had absorbed her and, having married Conor and given birth to Ronan, she'd thought of her life as complete. She hadn't even considered getting in touch with her dad to invite him to her wedding. What she'd been told in her childhood still made sense to her: why should she look for him when she had no need of him? Yet lately she'd begun to feel less certain. I'm still fine, she thought. I know who I am and where I fit into my world. I've never missed having a father and I don't feel the lack of him now. Staring intently into the cot, she watched a frown, like a dreaming puppy's, pucker Ronan's forehead. But, dammit, she thought, things change when you have a baby. There's far more to this than the easy stuff about nappy rash and wind.

There were two wedding photos on the windowsill above the changing table, one taken in Italy, the other in Carrick. The first was a selfie. The angle was crazy because they'd been dancing on a table outside a trattoria, high in the hills above Florence. It was sunset and the loggia in front of the restaurant was smothered with vines and roses. Aideen wore daisies in her hair, they were holding glasses of wine, and a group of locals was sitting around the table, laughing and singing. She smiled at the memory of that impromptu celebration, and the sight of her own radiant face dappled with golden sunlight.

For months before that photo was taken she'd been swept along in plans for a double wedding with Joe and Eileen. But in the midst of those lavish preparations, something inside her had snapped and, without telling anyone, she and Conor had taken a plane to Florence and made their vows in a cypress grove, with neither celebrant nor witnesses. On their return, sheepish but unrepentant, they'd had a registry office wedding in Carrick, at which Conor's parents were the only guests. Joe hadn't been bothered, and Eileen had found the whole thing exciting, but it was Paddy's support that had mattered most to Aideen. He'd been the first to tell her she'd been right to follow her gut instinct. 'If the big, fancy church thing felt wrong, then why go through with it?'

She remembered the anguish she'd suffered in coming to that decision, and the relief she'd felt when she'd brought herself to tell Conor. His response had made up for all her soul-searching. 'I'd go to the moon with you, if that's where you wanted to marry me. This is about us and nobody else.' In the first photo Conor, too, was wearing a crown of daisies, which she'd dropped on his head just before he'd taken the laughing selfie. In the second, wearing his good suit and tie, he stood on the registry office steps on a rainy Irish day. And in both shots he only had eyes for her.

That's your dad, she told the sleeping baby. He loves me like we both love you, more than anything else in the world. Touching Ronan gently with one finger, she wondered if Aunt Bridge and Gran had hovered over her cot in St Finian's Close. She wished they could have seen her happily married, though she knew that, if they'd been there, she'd have had to marry in church. When you owe so much to people, she thought, you can't ignore their feelings, and she was honest enough to recognise that her joyful Italian wedding couldn't have happened if those two staunch Catholic women had still been alive.

Downstairs in the kitchen, Conor was sitting in an easy chair by the range. Having hosed his boots in the yard, he'd left them outside on the doorstep, and he sat gazing unseeingly at his outstretched stockinged feet. Una was setting the table for the evening meal. 'If you don't get yourself upstairs to that shower, I'll have to keep everything hot and it'll spoil.'

'I know, but I'm dead. Give me five minutes.'

'If I give you five, you'll fall asleep and it'll end up being an hour.'

Conor shut his eyes and yawned widely. 'You could feed me intravenously. Pump it into my veins when I'm snoring away.'

Una sat down opposite him. 'Five minutes, and I'm going to talk to you to keep you awake.'

He opened one eye and looked at her. 'There isn't anything wrong?'

'Not a thing. Don't be twitching.'

'It's lonely for you here in the house without Paddy.'

'It is, but you're missing him, too, out on the farm.'

Conor pushed himself upright. 'I suppose. Well, I am, of course. But with everything to do, there's no time to brood.'

Una laughed. 'Are you saying there's nothing to do here in the house?'

'No, but—'

'Don't worry. I know what you mean. I'm fine, really. Ronan's a great distraction. He keeps me on my toes.'

'Aideen's looking forward to him walking.'

'Everyone's that way with their first. I'll have my work cut out for me when he starts that.'

'I don't like you having the pressure of looking after him.'

'Conor, I'm his granny! Don't be daft. We're in this together and we're all doing our bit. Anyway, I don't have all the pressure. You and Aideen mind him too.'

'But when you're not minding him, or making meals, you're stuck in the office.'

'Which is absolutely fine. It all keeps me from feeling lonely.' Una linked her hands round her knee. 'What's the real problem, love?'

Conor shook himself vigorously. 'Nothing. It's just that I'm tired. There's times it feels like we work like the devil and still we're not making a profit.'

'We're keeping ourselves afloat, though, and things are getting better. There's many a farming family can't say that.' Una's voice softened. 'Paddy was very proud of his sons, you know. You and Joe pulled together after your dad had his accident, and Joe did the decent thing about money when he and Eileen got married. He may have no yen for farm work but he worried about leaving you and Paddy to cope.'

Conor controlled the sceptical look he could feel forming on his face. It was true that, to compensate for his absence on the farm, Joe now paid the hired labourer's wage. But neither Conor nor Paddy had been as impressed by this gesture as Una was. For all his genial charm, Joe was lazy and, in Conor's view, his salesman's job for Eileen's father suited him. Much hearty back-slapping, long lunches, a fat salary, and an office door he could shut each day at precisely 5.30 p.m.

All the same, Conor couldn't deny that Joe's marriage had been a game-changer for the farm. When Paddy and both his sons had worked it together, the place hadn't yielded enough to provide a living wage for all three. This was why Conor had taken a part-time job at Lissbeg Library, and why Paddy's accident had tipped the McCarthys dangerously close to bankruptcy. But now the hired man, whose wages Joe paid, did three times more work than Joe had ever done, and old Dawson, Eileen's dad, had offered to upgrade the farm's ageing machinery. It was a generous gesture from a rich man who owned an agriprovision company, and who'd brushed aside Paddy's doubts by saying they were now part of his family. This statement, though well meant, had made Paddy uncomfortable and he'd insisted that the investment should be a loan, not a gift. Neither old Dawson, Eileen nor Joe had understood the extent to which the acceptance, even as a loan, had wounded his pride. But Conor did and, while grateful to old Dawson, he harboured a slight resentment towards Joe, who'd laughed when their dad had demurred.

Una gave Conor a gentle smile. 'Credit where credit's due, love. Joe is work-shy, I'll grant you that, and he hasn't more than a grain of sensitivity, but his heart's in the right place.'

'I wish I could pay off that damn debt to old Dawson, though.'

'You will. We're edging towards profit, and that's down to you and Aideen. I've gone back through last year's accounts. What she's bringing in from the deli, and the fact that you're now supplying them, is making a real difference to the bottom line. And the hours you're putting in are tipping the balance. We'll get there yet. Paddy knew that and, like I said, he was proud of you.' Una looked at Conor thoughtfully. 'You don't miss your work in the library? It was a grand, cosy desk job, like Joe's.'

Conor grinned, acknowledging the gibe. 'Easy seeing you've never worked in a library. It might have been nine to five but it was full-on. God, there were times when coping with the public was worse than driving a flock of sheep. Half the crowd in

Lissbeg could hardly remember to carry their library cards, and the other half only came in to get out of the rain.' He leaned back in his chair again, his hands behind his head. 'I do miss the books, though. I loved the smell of them. Did you know there's an actual word for it? Bibliosmia. It's caused by the chemical breakdown of compounds in paper. Actually, it's just the process of paper rotting, but it gives off a kind of vanilla smell.'

'That sounds disgusting.'

'It's not. It's great. I used to go round sniffing the books like a junkie. Not the stock, the old ones that got left behind by the nuns.' Conor closed his eyes reminiscently. 'The bindings were brilliant too. The leather-bound ones are calfskin or goatskin. Actually, really old books are written on parchment, and that's made of calfskin too. Or sheepskin. There's a line about it in Shakespeare's play *Hamlet*. His dad made leather gloves, so he knew about skins.'

'You should go on a TV quiz. Where did you pick all that up?'

'YouTube mainly. I used to mess around on the library computers.'

'And you don't miss having the time to do that sort of thing?'

'I told you. There wasn't a lot of time to be messing. A librarian's work is as full-on as a farmer's. It's just that there's less mud.'

Chapter Eleven

The mums' book club at the library was due to begin in half an hour. When Aideen arrived, Hanna was going through the post. 'Morning. How's my favourite godson?'

'Thriving.' Aideen sat on the chair by the desk. 'Sorry, I'm crazy early. Conor drove me in and took Ronan with him to the supplier's. He's going to pick me up when I'm finished here.'

'Libraries are perfect for killing time. The papers have come if you want to sit down at your leisure.'

'I'm not sure I could concentrate. I was awake half the night.'

'What was the matter?'

In fact, Aideen had lain awake thinking about her father but, still bound by the silence that had surrounded him in her childhood, she shrugged and said Ronan had kept her up. 'Just a tummy-ache. But then he was too tired to go back to sleep. He's right as rain this morning. It's me and Conor who are whacked. I know I could have grabbed some sleep if I gave the book club a miss, but I didn't want to. It's great to get a break from baby stuff and sandwich fillings.' She yawned. 'Incidentally, we're stocking Cafferkys' smoked salmon now. People are saying it's pricy, but it's gorgeous.'

'Give me a shout if you ever want me to babysit. It probably counts as part of what I signed up to, and it might compensate for the fact that I'm pretty lax on the religious side.'

'Oh, you know that wasn't what mattered to us. You were top of the list when it came to choosing his godmother.'

Hanna smiled affectionately. 'Well, you can always rely on me to come up with a book token on his birthday, and I do have a special bottle of wine laid down for his twenty-first.'

'You see, Eileen, who was angling for the job, just wouldn't have been up to it.' Aideen's second yawn turned into a giggle. 'I shouldn't sound ungrateful but, God, her idea of baby gifts! She keeps sending Gucci Gucci Goo stuff.'

'Gucci does baby clothes?'

'Smothered with logos. Conor thinks it's hilarious.'

'I hope they wash well.'

'Don't ask! And God help the poor scrap if she's still at it when he's older. He'll be dying for football boots and she'll produce a pair of designer loafers.'

Through the glass wall behind Hanna's desk, Aideen could see a group of tourists being shown the psalter. Most were listening to the guide respectfully but one woman was evidently argumentative. Following Aideen's gaze, Hanna looked round. The woman, trailed by what looked like twin adolescent daughters, had badly dyed hair, tartan trousers and a sweatshirt with a university crest on the back. From where Aideen stood, her shoulder blades appeared as sharp as knives, and the scarlet-tipped finger with which she punctuated her remarks resembled an eagle's talon. Oliver, the short, owlish guide, seemed unfazed by her, and the two girls wore identical bored expressions, as if they'd long been resigned to their mother making scenes in public.

Hanna pulled a face. 'Oh, Lord! Still, she won't shake Oliver. Once he starts listing facts he can't be stopped.'

Aideen saw Oliver glance down at his watch. Each of the guides recruited from Lissbeg's local-history society brought a personal flavour to the psalter tours, but they all worked to a standard script timed to allow browsing in the gift shop before the next group arrived. Through the glass Aideen could see Oliver's mouth opening and shutting as he summed up salient points and ignored the woman's apparent aggression. Cold looks from the rest of the group did nothing to deter her and, as soon as he'd finished, she was first to leave, doubling back the way she'd come and paying no attention to the large signs for the shop. Aideen made big amused eyes at Hanna when, moments later, a dyed head appeared round the library door.

'Are you the librarian? Because I assume that the exhibition in there falls under the library's auspices?'

With no witness but Aideen to consider, Hanna decided to model her response on Oliver's deadpan recital of bald facts.

'This building is owned by the county council, and nationwide library services fall under local-government management. But, essentially, the answer to both questions is yes. Is there anything else you wanted to know?'

'There most certainly is. I want to know why, when I pay good money to see what is called "The Carrick Psalter Exhibition", I find myself looking at two pages completely devoid of text.'

Hanna frowned. 'I'm sorry, Mrs ... ?'

'Foley.'

'I'm not sure what you were expecting?'

'I assume you know the definition of a psalter?'

Out of the corner of her eye, Hanna could see Aideen suppressing a giggle. Still channelling Oliver, she replied that the definition of a psalter was 'a copy of the Biblical psalms'.

'And you know what a psalm is?'

'A psalm is a sacred song or hymn, used in Christian and Jewish worship.'

The woman opened her mouth again and, as the interrogation was getting irritating, Hanna cut to the chase. 'Can you tell me what your problem is, Mrs Foley?' With a stab of her scarlet talon, Mrs Foley approached the desk. 'A psalter is a collection of psalms. You've admitted it. And a collection of psalms is what I expected to see when we came here today. Not a picture. Texts. The written word. I particularly wanted my girls to see an authentic example of Irish Minuscule script.'

'Well, as the guide will have told you, we turn a new page of the book at regular intervals and, as it happens, the current spread consists of illustration. But a digitised version of each page is accessible via the wall screens.'

'Nonsense!' Mrs Foley advanced even closer. Behind her mother's razor-sharp shoulder, one of the girls remarked that she couldn't be arsed about Irish Minuscule. 'Be quiet, Astrid!' The woman came closer still and glowered at Hanna. 'If I'd wanted to see the text on a screen, I'd have looked it up on the internet. I paid to see the real thing and I won't be fobbed off with a cartoon version.'

'I assure you—'

'I want my money back.'

So this was where it was going. Taking a deep breath, Hanna eyeballed her. 'You would not see the text of the Carrick Psalter on the internet. Our digital images are copyright. You've just been looking at a unique manuscript, preserved for centuries in the locality where it was composed. A guide was present to answer your questions and give you information. If you don't feel that was worth the admission fee—'

'I've told you I don't.'

'Then I'm sorry. But I'm afraid there's no question of a refund.'

'That sign outside this building is misrepresentation!'

One of the girls yawned widely, setting Aideen off in the background. 'Oh, come *on*, Mum, it was just a few euros.'

'It's six euros for an adult, Astrid, and three for a child under twelve.'

'Well, you're lucky nobody asked you to prove what age me and Ingrid are.' Linking her twin, Astrid looked at Hanna. 'She tries this kind of thing on all the time and it's boring. If I were you, I'd stick to my guns. The British Library woman did. She called Security.'

'Astrid!'

'Oh, give it a rest, Mum.' Still linking her sister, Astrid slouched to the door. Her mother shot a last volley of fake outrage at Hanna. 'You haven't heard the last of this. I shall write to the *Irish Times*.'

The door slammed behind them and Hanna grimaced at Aideen. 'Thank heavens you were the only person here.'

Aideen grinned. 'I thought you were brilliant.'

'These things do happen occasionally, but I'd rather not have an audience.'

'So what was she on about?'

'You mean besides trying to get a refund?'

'I mean why do some of the pages have no writing?'

Hanna laughed. 'It's kind of ironic, given her line of attack. Only two spreads in the book have illustrations and no words, and both show images of a scribe writing. So it's likely they're there to draw attention to the importance of the texts.'

'Psalms are the word of God the Father or something, aren't they?'

'Well, they address God. They're supposed to have been divinely inspired, though. In the monastic tradition, the written word carries huge weight. You get it in the gospels. *In the beginning was the Word, and the Word was with God, and the Word was God.* People still argue about what that means but, when the psalter was created, the scribes probably took it literally. Words written in sacred books were sacred.'

Aideen stifled another yawn and apologised. 'Sorry, I'm interested really. So, is that why the capital letters in the psalter are decorated in gold? Conor says the inks and paints cost a fortune, so the more expensive ones got used for the most important bits. The blue paint came from ground-up bits of lapis lazuli.' She held up her left hand. 'Like the stone in my ring.'

'And the lapis lazuli came from a single region of Afghanistan. Imagine the cost of transporting it on camels across deserts, and over the seas to Ireland in boats. In each of the psalter's double-page spreads there's a figure wearing blue robes and a monk holding a quill pen painted in gold. People at the time would have recognised the importance of those colours. And, overhead, there are circling birds dropping feathers, linking the scribes' pens with the concept of God's word descending from above.'

'You're awfully well informed for someone who says she's not religious.'

'Well, I do adore the psalter.' Hanna laughed again, this time at her own choice of words. 'That verb says something about my subconscious! Can a sacred book be sacred to someone who doesn't practise the religion that inspired it? I think it can.'

Aideen's brow wrinkled. 'But what does that mean? Would you die to protect it? Would you kill?'

'That's a bit of a leap.'

'But it's logic, isn't it? Like, if a monk believed that the Word was God, and that that made a book sacred, wouldn't he be ready to die for it? Isn't that what martyrs do? Die for what they believe in?'

The door opened and several of the mums' book club came in. As Aideen got up to join them, Hanna glanced through the glass to where a new group of tourists had gathered around the psalter. A couple of nuns were bent over the showcase, as if at an altar, and a student was rapidly sketching in a notebook. Though hardly aware of each other's presence, the boy in his T-shirt and cut-off shorts and the nuns in their frumpy, modern version of their order's medieval habit shared a look of rapt concentration. I recognise that look, thought Hanna. It's been on my own face when I've touched those pages. That's the magic of the psalter. What makes it a sacred book for me is not its religious associations, or even its age or its beauty. It's the way that the pictures and words speak to each other, layering up possible meanings and offering contradictions. It lies there unchanged and perfect, like an insect suspended in amber. Yet its meaning is fluid. It expresses all the rigidity of a patriarchal mindset and intersperses it with so much that flows.

Three hours later, Hanna was in her car on the road to Carrick, resigned to the prospect of another of Tim's top-secret meetings.

When she crossed the car park to the central library, she saw Owen lingering on the steps. Quickening her pace, she caught up with him, and they went in together. 'Have you seen the agenda?'

Owen rolled his eyes. 'Just now. It came through in an email when I was driving. Apparently the importance level is HIGH.'

'Suit him better if he'd pulled his finger out and organised those forms.' Typically, Tim had left it to his assistant to devise and circulate the forms required to log the incoming material. Opening her phone, Hanna found the agenda, which was headed 'COMMUNICATION' and consisted of the word 'PRESS' followed by two bullet points: *Print* and *Broadcast*. 'Well, isn't *that* a surprise.' As she made this scathing remark, she noticed a junior colleague nearby and, instinctively, found herself lowering her voice. *Though I can't think why,* she thought crossly. *It's pure cowardice. We all tiptoe around Tim's blatant self-promotion as if he might fall apart if the truth were told.*

The gathering in the library's stuffy meeting room was restless. It was a beautiful day and, despite the windows' half-lowered blinds, the sun made their plastic chairs feel uncomfortably hot. Tim appeared to have come dressed for cricket. Given that his time was spent at a desk, his white shirt, flannels and natty V-neck pullover were ridiculous, but more than one of his colleagues looked enviously at the broad-brimmed straw hat with which he fanned himself. Tapping the table, he brought the meeting to order. 'Now, I really want today's session to be focused. We need a mean, lean communication strategy from the outset.'

No one mentioned the initial lack of communication with the public. That ship had sailed and, anyhow, systems were now in place. Nevertheless, hot though it was, and eager though everyone was to be done with the meeting, several hands were raised. A colleague opposite Hanna and Owen managed to get in first. 'I'd like a sense of the format before we go further. Does each branch library focus on a theme? And how local do we want our material to be? For example, if Mrs X arrives with something relating specifically to Lissbeg or Carrick, do I include it in my exhibit or pass it on to Hanna or to you, as the case may be? Because, if it's the latter, Mrs X won't like it. She'll want to see it taking pride of place close to her home.'

The girl beside him chipped in: 'And is this to be an information trail? I mean, do we send people from place to place to accumulate information? Because some branches don't have much display space.'

'But then there'd be the issue of duplication.'

'If we go for themes, would each branch cover the whole period?'

'That point about locality struck me, too.'

Listening to this cacophony of voices, Hanna sat back to see how Tim would cope. As usual, he was shrewd enough to let them talk until they ran out of steam. Then he joined the tips of his fingers. 'In my view, we need to begin by taking a broad approach.'

The man who'd first spoken asked what that meant.

'When we meet again, I'd like each of you to make a pitch for why your branch should focus on a specific. A theme.' Tim waved his hat, suggesting a world of possibility. 'A striking theme or, indeed, an object, which will really pack a punch.'

'Yes, but—'

'I'll want you to knock my socks off. I'll want to know that the thought of complaining won't even enter Mrs X's head. She'll be gripped. Drawn in. She'll be on board. Because that's what we need. We need buy-in so, most of all, we're looking for sensational narratives.'

Hanna's heart sank. The psalter's presence in Castle Lancy during Finfarran's final Civil War skirmish was exactly the sort of narrative Tim meant, and provided a new twist to a story that, only a few years ago, had brought national and international papers and TV crews to Lissbeg. She cringed at the thought of how a tabloid might cover it. *Lissbeg's Explosive Civil War Legacy. Whodunnit, Hanna? Librarian's Family in Priceless Book Plot.* The voices around her rose and fell and, though much of the reaction ranged from irritation to resignation, some of her younger colleagues looked eager to rise to Tim's challenge. Listening, Hanna said nothing. She could control whether or not Maggie's book would feature in the libraries' commemorations, but the psalter's story belonged to the nation, not her. So, even if the tabloid headlines she'd imagined were unlikely, she needed time to consider this very personal can of worms.

Chapter Twelve

Dew was falling after the hot, humid day. White moths fluttered round the citron-scented candle on the table, and bats zigzagged up the glen through the gathering dusk. Brian, who was sitting by Hanna in the roof garden, reached out and took her hand. 'You're worried, so you might as well tell me about it.'

'Oh, it's just that I'm still conflicted about Maggie's book. Today's meeting was another demonstration of the lack of sensitivity Tim's bringing to this commemoration.' The book was on Hanna's knee and she looked down at its dingy cover. 'I can hear Owen say that this has significance – I mean, that's what he'd say if I showed it to him. But, except for that raid by the Black and Tans in which Hannie and her father were killed, Maggie writes mostly about her time in England. Looking for work, places she stayed, that kind of thing. It's not as though she describes what was going on here. There's a friend called Lizzie Keogh she hears from occasionally but, otherwise, she seems to have been cut off.'

'Darling, what are you trying to talk yourself into?'

Ignoring Brian's question, Hanna opened the book. 'And there's an entry I'm not sure I'd want Charles Aukin to read. Here it is, September 7th, 1920.'

The de Lancys are gone out of the castle. They do hardly be here anyway much now but to go fishing and I suppose you couldn't expect them to stay and be burned out or worse. That's the thing about the rich, they can always run away and find a welcome. I remember Dad saying that was all changing and Liam stamping round saying change couldn't come fast enough. Dad took me to see the castle one time when the family was abroad. It's not really a castle, just a big house, but Dad said the walls around it are Norman, so that means they've been in it for hundreds of years. Liam says they plundered Finfarran from the first day they arrived. I'd say they had plenty of money always, and where did they get it but out of the mouths of the people? It was no different over here in England. I met a girl in a tea shop whose granny was put to work in a cotton mill when she was seven, and the mill owner lived in a big house and rented out slums to his workers. I don't know what the de Lancys will own if the lads free Ireland. They got out fast enough anyway at the first sign of danger.

There was a big room in the castle with books in it. The caretaker's wife took us up to it. She was a cousin of Dad's on his mother's side or I'd say we'd never have got in. There were shelves of books reaching round the room and right up to the ceiling. They had red leather backs to them and a gold stamp on the front that Dad said was the family arms. The woman had to keep the light off them, and put a fire in the grate each week so they wouldn't get damp. She said there were papers and books locked away in drawers as well.

The family employed a power of servants always. When Dad was small he worked there himself, cleaning boots. The de Lancys leased him the farm of land when he and Mam got married. Liam says they were damn lucky to get such an honest tenant. At least that's what he used to say to Dad's face. Behind his back I've heard him call him a lackey.

I don't know why I'm sitting here on the bed writing down all this rubbish. I suppose it takes me home again to be writing about Finfarran. I do think of it all times. I do dream of the forest. The other night I dreamed I was climbing Knockinver and Dad was with me, and Liam, and the dog was behind us. It was a grand day with the clouds flying and the sun shining on the mountain. When I woke I was thinking of Mam. I do worry about her all the time when she's only the dog for company. For all Dad used to say the de Lancys cared for the people, they haven't come next, nigh nor near the castle since the fighting began. I had a card from Lizzie Keogh the other day that said she'd heard from her brother. She made no mention of Liam and she didn't call her brother by name. I'd say that means they're still on the run in the mountains. I know the fight is going on, for you'd see it here in the papers.

Brian looked perplexed. 'You really think Charles Aukin would worry about that?'

'I don't think he'd welcome public discussion about the de Lancys' behaviour.'

'But, darling, that was written a hundred years ago.'

'It's a record of what people thought of his wife's family. I don't want Charles to be hurt.' Hanna stood up and went to lean on the steel rail that surrounded the roof garden. She had showered on coming home from work and, too tired to get dressed again, was wearing her kimono. The heavy pale-yellow silk, woven with white and jade-green chrysanthemums, glimmered in the dusk, like the moths' wings. After a moment she spoke again. 'You know that I was christened Hanna-Mariah? Mariah was Dad's mother's name, and I used to think that Hanna was something my parents came up with themselves. Then I read this.' Her voice faltered as she quoted the final words in Maggie's book. '*It's right that the child should be called after Tom's mother, but I'm glad that he named her Hanna as well. She's twelve years old and her hair and eyes are just like Hannie's.*' There was a pause and, turning her back to the rail, she looked across at Brian. 'Okay, you're right. This isn't about Charles Aukin.'

'I didn't say so.'

'You didn't have to. Mind you, I truly don't know how Charles might react to that entry. He misses his wife badly. But that's not what I'm struggling with. Not really.' She came back to the table in a swirl of rustling silk and slumped crossly into the chair beside

Brian. Splashing wine into a glass she glowered down the glen at the darting bats. 'I've been dreading this, but there's no help for it. I'm going to have to sit down and talk to my mother.' Brian smothered a laugh and, reluctantly, she grinned. 'Okay, I know how that sounds but, honestly, Brian, I dread it. We don't sit down and talk about things, Mam and I. We never have.'

That conversation, and the dinner they ate later, ended in laughter but the following weekend, when Hanna approached the bungalow, she felt tense. Having watched her gentle father's efforts to please her difficult mother, she'd spent most of her life cultivating emotional distance from Mary. Unwilling and unable to cajole her, and aware that to confront her would upset Tom, she'd avoided conflict and, consciously, felt proud of her restraint. Unconsciously, though, she told herself wryly, it was passive aggression. I cut her out and, probably, that was cruel. But what other weapon did I have? She was neurotic, I was at her mercy, and children protect themselves as best they can.

Tom was the only child of a late marriage so, as Mary always said proudly, he'd fallen in for the family shop when most lads his age were still scratching for work. Hardly out of their teens, they'd had a big wedding at which Mary, wearing American stilettos, had waltzed to the local showband's cover of 'Walking the Streets in the Rain'. Hanna was born and had grown up above the shop, five miles from Lissbeg. She could remember the grocery counter and the post-office grille, and the bench by the two petrol pumps where kids used to gather to eat Tayto and drink red lemonade.

When cars drew up, Mary would take Tom's place selling stamps and postal orders, and Hanna would be called to slice bacon while her dad worked the pumps. Casey's kept a little of everything: flour and tea and vegetables, baking powder, apples and mouse traps, packets of biscuits and biros, soda bread made to order by Mary and jars of Fruitfield Old Time Irish Marmalade. In the 1980s, when Hanna married and settled in London, her dad sold up and built Mary her dream retirement home. The bungalow, a box on a concrete plinth on the main road linking Ballyfin to Carrick, had fitted wardrobes, double glazing, a kitchen with a pull-out larder, and a bright light in the middle of every ceiling. Hanna disliked it heartily, although, as she frequently reminded herself, it must have been heaven to a couple accustomed to steep stairs and dark, poky rooms. Now, when she walked around the house and tapped on the kitchen door, Mary was standing at the sink wearing a pair of yellow Marigolds.

'Did you get my texts?'

'Yes. Both of them.' Hanna came in and put her bag on a chair. The texts, requesting teabags and a Mr Kipling Battenberg, had come when she was on the road and required a detour to a shop. Removing her rubber gloves, Mary reached for her apron strings. 'I would have made a cake myself if you'd given me decent notice.'

'Is the Battenberg for us to eat now? Oh, Mam, there was no need for it. I brought a packet of biscuits, we'd have been fine.'

Mary pursed her lips. 'Well, I wanted the tea, and you always bring biscuits with chocolate that's way too thick.'

Hanna took the teabags to the cupboard where they were kept. As she opened it, Mary planted her hands on her hips. 'You needn't be checking up on me. You can see for yourself I have only a few bags left.'

'Why would I be checking up on you?'

'What else were you doing a while back when you were foosthering under the sink? You were counting my dishwasher tablets. You thought I didn't notice, but I did.'

Hanna decided not to be drawn on the subject of dishwasher tablets. Infuriating though Mary could be, it was sad to see her struggling on her own. Not, thought Hanna, that she'd ever come clean and admit it's a struggle. She'd rather plague the lot of us, and leave us increasingly worried, than simply say she's lonely and ask for help. Though, if I'm honest, in her place I'd probably be no different. I'd hate it if I ever became a burden for Jazz.

As Mary made tea, Hanna took down the rose-patterned cups and saucers she remembered from her childhood. 'Bone china', she reminded herself. Mary's possessions always came with impressive adjectives. Her pans were 'original Le Creuset', her steak knives 'ebony-handled', and her pin in the shape of a lovers' knot was known from the day she'd received it from Tom as 'my filigree, nine-carat brooch'. Seeing it now, pinned to her mother's cardigan, Hanna thought of her dad and prayed that she'd handle this meeting well.

She'd tried to explain to Brian why she thought it was so important. 'Whether or not I choose to keep Maggie's book private, Castle Lancy will feature in the library displays. It's inevitable. And one thing leads to another. Owen, if nobody else, will spot that the psalter must have been in the castle during the fighting, and it's a matter of public record that Liam commanded those diehards. I can't leave Mam out of the loop. My family is part of the story and we need to talk about it before the rest of Finfarran joins in.'

'She may not want to.'

'I know, but I've got to try.'

But she'd seen that Brian hadn't really understood. His family were city-dwellers with no sense of the underlying currents of rural life.

Setting out the bone china and unwrapping the Battenberg, Hanna hoped that she wasn't about to do the wrong thing. If only, she thought, I were better equipped to deal with this, able to challenge her, like Jazz does, or calm her the way Dad could. She was reaching for the cake slice when Mary forestalled her. 'I can still use a knife in my own kitchen, thank you. The best day you ever lived, you could never cut cake straight.' This was nonsense but Hanna said nothing. Cutting the cake in precise slices, Mary demanded what she called her 'silver-plate strainer'. 'And don't try to tell me it's not needed with teabags. There's dust comes out of them when you're down to the last few in the box.' Hanna fetched the strainer and its shell-shaped holder and set it on the table. Having got her way, Mary poured tea. 'So to what do I owe the honour of this visit?'

'I wanted to talk.'

'Did you, indeed?' Mary put down her cup and squared her shoulders. 'I've made my will, you know.'

'What? Mam, don't be ridiculous. I haven't come to find out about your will.'

'Well, you might as well know, now you have come, that I'm leaving this house to Jazz.'

'I'm sure she'll be grateful, but you're not going to die yet.'

'Damn right I'm not. I've no intention of it. I just like things tidy.'

Hanna took a bite of cake and immediately wished she hadn't. Now they'd begun to talk, her mouth had gone dry. Reaching for her cup, she thought wryly that tea was the Irish cure-all on every tense occasion, from weddings to births and funerals and, of course, the reading of wills. 'Actually, I wanted to talk about Maggie.'

Mary's lips tightened. 'Oh, for God's sake, Hanna, I hardly knew Maggie Casey. Why would I want to be talking about her now?'

'Fury O'Shea did the work on Maggie's house for me, remember?'

'I do, of course.'

'There were lots of bits and pieces that got thrown into a skip. But I did go through everything and I found a biscuit tin.'

'A what?'

'An old tin. Maggie had put a book in it.'

Mary picked at the marzipan on her plate. 'She was always wanting books, your great-aunt Maggie. Your father had to trudge down to the library to pick them out.'

Hanna recalled that the only books Maggie had owned were an *Old Moore's Almanac* and a dusty family Bible. 'I remember she liked detective novels. She used to want me to sit and read them aloud to her.'

'Ay, that would be Maggie. Always wanting something.'

'I think she was half blind by then, Mam.'

Mary snorted. 'And always making the poor mouth for attention.' So far, thought Hanna, this is not a success. But she kept going. 'Anyway, there was this tin. With a book in it. A sort of diary.'

Suddenly Mary leaned forward and stared fiercely at the cake. 'What's that there?' Thinking a fly might have landed on it, Hanna moved the plate. 'Nothing. What did you see?'

'I mean what's that cake?'

'Mam, it's a Battenberg. The one you said you wanted.'

A look of consternation flitted across Mary's face. 'Well, I know that. I'm not stupid.' She poured more tea without using the strainer, then struck the table hard with the flat of her hand. 'There now! Look what you made me do! No one could drink that tea and it full of bits!'

'Mam, are you all right?'

'Of course I am. You've never liked that strainer. What's all this nonsense about a biscuit tin?'

Unsure of what had just happened, Hanna said that it didn't matter. 'It was something I found when I moved into Maggie's. It had some old papers in it, that's all.'

'You said a diary.'

'Well, a kind of journal she kept when she went to England.'

Mary's eyes slewed sideways. 'And did it say why she had to go there?'

Hanna chose her words. 'She'd had an affair of some kind. I reread that bit last night.' One line had stayed with her, echoing now in her mind, though she didn't speak it aloud. *'I'll never go into a church again. I never thought a priest could be so bad as to drive a girl out of a place when her mam had no one left but her to depend on.'* There was a pause in which she became aware that she and Mary were eyeing each other across the table, like wrestlers. Then, with a toss of her head, Mary looked away.

'Mam.'

'What?'

'You know we're collecting material to display in Finfarran's libraries? It's a national initiative and we're taking part.'

'I know. The charity shop has a stack of leaflets by the till.'

'How do you feel about it?'

'What do you mean, how do I feel? It's nothing to do with me.'

'It covers the time when Maggie was writing her journal and Dad's father was out fighting.'

'Liam was dead long before I met Tom.'

'But Dad must have talked about him.'

Mary looked mutinous. 'Why would he? He was only a child when his father died.'

Oh, Lord, thought Hanna. She knows she's let something slip that she hadn't intended, but, now we're here, there's no going back. Taking a breath, she looked straight at her mother. 'Well, if you didn't hear it from Dad, and you hardly knew Maggie, how do you know why Maggie went to England?'

Mary reached for the teapot. 'I never said I knew. I asked if you did. And I'm sick to death of talking about Maggie Casey. Leave it be.'

Chapter Thirteen

At breakfast Conor said he'd bring Ronan up to the field. Aideen, who'd intended to stay at home, told him he didn't need to

'I know, but it's a fine day. The air will do him good.'

She laughed. 'There's plenty of fresh air down here in the garden.'

'Look, do you want me to take him out of your way, or what? I'm not bothered.' Seeing Aideen and Una's expressions, Conor, who'd spoken gruffly, looked embarrassed. 'I like having him with me when I'm working. If I can't carry him up to the fields much longer, I want to while I still can.'

'But why would you have to stop?'

'He's kicking a bit at the sling now he's started trying to walk.'

Una smiled as she scraped remnants from the breakfast plates for the hens. 'Ah, it's only a phase. He'll be roaring to be carried again, wait and see. You'll be reading books about how to get him to stop.' Conor made a face at her. 'Don't sneer at baby books.

They teach you a lot of stuff. The never-again thing is a recognised syndrome.'

Aideen had Ronan sitting on her knee, fed and changed and playing with a crust of toast. 'Take him if you want to. I think it's nice.' Conor shot her a grateful look. 'It's weird, when he's so little, to be thinking "never again".'

Una ruffled his hair as she passed with the bowl of scraps for the hens. 'Now you're making a meal of things. Don't be daft.'

Aideen didn't want to contradict Una, who, she knew, was probably right. She still sympathised with Conor, though, and touched his hand under the table as she asked what his plans for the day were. 'I have to go up to the out farm. We'll be sitting up in the tractor. Ronan likes that.' Aideen tossed him the sling, which was hanging on a chair, and he went whistling into the yard with Ronan strapped to his chest.

Una, who was planning to tackle some form-filling, suggested that Aideen take advantage of her unexpected freedom. 'Why not go off and have yourself a wander round the shops?' So, with no other plan than that in mind, Aideen changed into cleaner jeans and pulled on a sweatshirt, wheeled her Vespa out of the shed and set off on the road for Carrick.

It was another fine day, though cool enough to make her glad of the sweatshirt. Bowling along on the Vespa was something she'd missed since she'd had Ronan. The car and the tractor, with its safety cab, were okay for a baby, but she wouldn't take him with her on the bike. Travelling Finfarran's little back roads was a particular pleasure. Bordered by ditches and fences of furze, they wound between fields with names that Aideen suspected she'd never learn. There are too many, she thought, and it's too late for me to absorb them, and that's what it's like to be married into a farm. It pleased her to think that it wouldn't be like that for Ronan. He'd belong properly. The names of the McCarthy fields would be rooted in his memory, a litany learned from Conor that he would chant to his own kids. Assuming, of course, that he'd stay on the land and feel part of it. Una had warned her not to make assumptions about Ronan's future. 'Every child raised on a farm grows up pitching in. It's good for them, but it's all the more reason to make sure they know they can choose what to do with their own lives.' It seemed impossible to imagine Ronan making career choices, but everyone said that kids grew up faster than you expected. Look at him now, thought Aideen. Already he's making Conor think 'never again'.

Her sleeves billowed as the Vespa sped between the flowering hedgerows. Conor had had a bike when they'd started dating and she'd bought one after their trip to Florence. His was now scratched and knocked about from muddy trips to bring down the cows for milking, but hers remained shiny and gave her a secret sense of sophistication. The girls who rode Vespas in Italy didn't look anything like farm wives or nursing mothers. They belonged to the world Aideen felt she'd entered when she and Bríd had first opened the deli. Life had felt edgy then, and full of promise in a way that had changed after she'd got married. Not that I'd want to go back to that, she told herself, but it's nice just to be me now and then, instead of a mum or a wife.

No matter where you were on the narrow peninsula, the presence of the ocean was always with you. Even where the shoulders of mountains obscured the sight of it, there was a salt tang in the air and a sense of dragging and thrusting currents driving waves onto beaches and carving the jagged shapes of the towering cliffs. The Atlantic winds were never absent either, carrying gulls' cries and the scent of seaweed from east and west and sudden violent cloudbursts from the north. Yet growth flourished. Finfarran's winter gales could rip roofs from barns and sheds and snap tree trunks but, in the stony earth heaped by the roadsides, curling briars and the roots of low-growing bushes gave cover to a myriad of flowers. They delighted Aideen. As children, she and Bríd had picked them on roads leading down to the sandy beach near Lissbeg. Now, with the wind catching the curls that fluttered at the edges of her helmet, she sang their names aloud above the sound of the Vespa's engine in a joyous private litany of her own. 'Cuckoo flower. Starry saxifrage. Fox's cabbage. Meadowsweet.' She swerved to avoid a pothole and raised her voice to a shout. 'Red clover. Rosebay willowherb. Dog violets. Moneywort and Robin-run-the-hedge.' Like the other kids in Finfarran, she and Bríd had called that by its local name 'sticky Bob', but 'Robin-run-the-hedge' seemed more in tune with the speed of her moving bike. In Latin, the plant, which had tiny hooked bristles, was called *Galium aparine*, something

Aideen had learned by looking it up. People called it cleavers too, and stickyweed, and goosegrass. Swerving, she admired a huge cloud of it, which had cast itself, like a green net, over a patch of hemlock. She continued turning the country names over in her mind. Mine is book-learning, she thought, not bone-learning, like Conor's knowledge of field names, but it's something I can give Ronan. Conor can teach him the average oat yield in a well-tilled acre, and I'll tell him about things that grow up on their own.

She'd acquired her knowledge of wildflowers on the internet and in the school library, while Conor, as a teenager, had been walking the land with Paddy. Neither Aunt Bridge nor Gran had welcomed the drooping bunches she'd carried home from her walks. Unlike the supermarket flowers arranged in a vase on the polished hall table, hers had scattered frail petals on the kitchen lino and wilted in jars of water that had soon turned scummy and green. But their educational value had been acknowledged and, for a year or two, she'd immersed herself in an interest of which Gran and Aunt Bridge had approved. After a while, the botanical names neatly entered in her notebook had, for the most part, slipped from her mind, but the country names still added to her pleasure in flowers that were frequently ignored or dismissed as weeds. She loved their leaves and seed heads, often more striking than their blossoms, and delighted each year in their reappearance on the wind-ravaged ditches, from the first gleam of pale-yellow primroses to the spiralling briars and umbelliferous hemlock.

Soon she was on the main road, passing Mary Casey's bright pink bungalow, and, within fifteen minutes, approaching the outskirts of Carrick. The day was heating up and the town was crowded. Its high street, where painted Victorian shopfronts were lost behind chain-store façades, was thronged with chattering tourists and busy shoppers. The park was swamped by what looked like several coach parties, and even the backstreets, where Aideen found parking for the Vespa, had holidaymakers crammed around pavement tables. Wriggling out of her sweatshirt and slinging it over her shoulders, she wandered about for a while, looking for somewhere less busy to have coffee. She had vaguely imagined she might browse for a new summer dress, but now the thought of stuffy fitting rooms defeated her. All the pleasant cafés were full, several with queues outside them, and increasingly the bustle and heat felt stifling. So, returning to the bike, she put on her helmet and rode back to the ring-road where Castle Lancy stood on a crag above a roundabout.

Circling the castle roundabout, she took the exit to the east. It felt silly to go home so early, so she told herself she'd travel on and find a quiet village where, even if there were tourists about, there wouldn't be coach parties. The exit she'd taken was the main route to Cork, and she was looking out for a side road into the countryside when, up ahead, she saw a sign saying 'Coffee'. It was hooked under a larger sign that read Honeybee Garden Centre. On impulse, Aideen glanced in her mirror, indicated, and swung across to the entrance, where two large urns spilled trailing begonias.

The garden centre was a large modern structure surrounded by outdoor areas where plants and shrubs were ranged on steel shelving, and trees with their roots in hessian bags stood marshalled in railed enclosures. Wire baskets and heavier trolleys were lined up by the entrance, which was reached from the car park via a covered walkway. Swinging her helmet, Aideen approached it between wooden posts festooned with clematis. The automatic entrance doors sprang open as she reached them and inside, beyond displays of tools and garden furniture, she could see a conservatory coffee shop where one or two people were sitting. More chairs and tables stood in a paved garden area onto which the conservatory opened. Though none of this was what she'd had in mind when she'd set off from Carrick, she decided it was attractive and that now she was definitely thirsty. So she bought a coffee, which came in a little cafetière with a shortbread biscuit, and carried her tray out to the pretty garden.

It was evident that this place belonged in a different league from the Garden Café. Aideen sat down and, with a professional eye, admired the tables and seating, an assortment of the retail area's expensive garden furniture. She could tell that the customers here wouldn't find it extortionate. They were well-dressed ladies who lunched, probably with a glass of prosecco, and who'd driven here from Cork or Carrick to pick up cushions for their garden rooms or plants for their barbecue areas. Aideen tried and failed to imagine Ann Flood from Lissbeg Pharmacy, or Pat from Fitzgerald's butcher's shop, or any of Jazz Turner's colleagues, willing to sit in a glorified warehouse drinking coffee at almost ten euros a throw. All the same, the coffee was delicious, and the buttery, crumbly shortbread melted in the mouth. Telling herself she'd saved a fortune by not going shopping, she sat back in the elegant chair and decided that, now she was here, she'd enjoy herself.

Somewhere in the distance a water feature gurgled. Aideen spun out the coffee as long as she could, sipping it slowly and stirring brown sugar into the last half-inch. In fairness, she thought, you do end up with two decent cupfuls. Idly wondering where the coffee beans were sourced, she reached for the menu but, before she could read it, was interrupted by an accusatory bark. Directly across from her table, The Divil had appeared in front of a panel of woven willow fencing, his paws squarely planted and his curved nails black against the granite paving slabs. Keeping his eyes on Aideen's face, he barked again and sank back on his haunches, motionless except for the furry folds that waved like bunting at the tips of his half-pricked ears. Fury stepped out from behind the fence, hands in his torn pockets and his waxed jacket drooping to the tops of his wellington boots. His face was as expressionless as The Divil's was alert. 'There you are, so. I didn't expect to find you here.'

Aideen explained that it wasn't her normal hangout. 'Actually, I've never been before. I came across it by accident.'

'Do you tell me that?' Fury didn't show a great deal of interest. 'I wouldn't be here myself if my Couneen client didn't have notions. A paved patio is what he wants and nothing will do only Valencia slate.'

'Is that expensive?'

'Arm-and-a-leg time, girl. Mind, I'm not complaining. The money rubs off all the way down the line.' The Divil's intense gaze was making Aideen slightly uncomfortable. Seeing her reaction, Fury laughed. 'Where's the little fella?'

'What?'

'The baby. Is he not with you?'

'No. Conor has him this morning. Why?'

Fury clicked his fingers at The Divil. 'Stop staring, you. Mind your manners!' Discomfited, The Divil wriggled and flattened himself on the granite, his muzzle resting on his extended forepaws. Though he rolled his eyes sideways at Fury, his black nose still pointed at Aideen. Fury pushed him with his boot. 'He's got a thing for your little lad, and God alone knows why. I told Conor I've never seen the likes of it.' He lounged over, sat down at the table and, chasing the crumbs round Aideen's saucer with a long, bony finger, looked at her from under his woolly hat. 'I'd say you've had Paddy's month's mind.'

Aideen took a spoonful of coffee that was mostly brown sugar. The month's mind was the requiem Mass traditionally held a month after a funeral, and she wasn't certain whether or not Fury would disapprove if it hadn't been held. 'We didn't have one in the end. Una said she felt bad because the priest seemed to expect it, but Paddy wasn't a churchgoer so it would have been a bit weird. It must be pretty hard to be a priest these days. I mean, people still roll up for weddings and funerals but they back off from a lot of the other stuff.' She looked at Fury. 'Would you have come if we'd had one?'

'I'd say I would. I'm not one for the holy stuff but, shur, month's minds began as drinking sessions.'

'They did?'

'The "mind" bit comes from a Norse word that meant ceremonial drinking to the dead.' Fury grinned at her. 'Now so! I learned that in sixth class in Lissbeg. There was a lot of things taught then that you won't find kids learning now.'

'You mean it just used to be a big party?'

'That's it. Everyone sitting round in their hats with horns on, knocking back cups of mead.'

Aideen looked down at The Divil, who was scratching a crumb from his whiskers. 'Actually, we had wine at dinner and raised a glass to Paddy.'

'Well, there you are. Same difference. If you'd had a few of the neighbours round, they could have worn horned hats. Though they tell me that's wrong too. Ahistorical.' Fury got to his feet and clicked his fingers at The Divil. 'We'd better get back to work before the Australian starts checking up on me.' Before turning away, he gave Aideen a sharp look. 'Births and deaths, those are the times when people come up with rituals. It's human nature, girl. We're just trying to make sense of things.' He scratched his unshaven chin. 'Maybe we feel that contact with the past will help us deal with the future.'

'Do you think it doesn't?'

'Christ, I don't know, I just lay feckin' slate patios.'

He left, with The Divil trotting at his heels, and Aideen sat back, wishing he hadn't reminded her of Paddy. Today had felt like an in-between day, a time when she could step out of her life and play at being a lady of leisure with no one to worry or think about but herself. Trying to recapture the moment before The Divil had appeared round the fence, she picked up the menu to see if the coffee suppliers were listed on the back. Then she sat stock-still, staring at the name of the garden centre's proprietor. It was her dad's.

Chapter Fourteen

Removing a half-smoked roll-up from behind his left ear, Fury ambled out of the garden centre. The Divil followed, ears pricked and alert, as if he supposed that Ronan might be somewhere in the vicinity. When they reached the battered red van, incongruously parked among Volvos and Range Rovers, Fury lit the cigarette and looked down severely. 'She told you he's at home, so you might as well get in and stop making a fool of yourself. Wouldn't you smell him if he was anywhere hereabouts?' The Divil gave up and, leaping onto the passenger seat, sat with his forepaws braced against the dashboard. With the cigarette dangling from his lower lip, Fury went to the other side of the van and got in. He reversed out of the parking space with great skill and assumed carelessness, causing a woman with a Chanel handbag to point aggressively at an area signed Lorries/ Vans/Commercial Vehicles. Ignoring her, Fury swung the wheel and, entering the No Entry lane, cruised towards the exit. The woman glared after him as, edging into the westbound stream of traffic, he set off with The Divil curled up beside him, his black nose tucked under his tail.

Crossing the roundabout below Castle Lancy, the van skirted Carrick and was travelling down the main road in the direction of Lissbeg when Mary Casey, emerging from her bungalow, recognised Fury and stopped him with an imperious wave of her hand. She was wearing a coat and had an oilcloth shopping bag hooked over her arm. Fury pulled in and leaned across to open The Divil's window. 'Is it Lissbeg?'

'It is. The bus is woeful these days. You'd never know when it'd come.'

Scooping The Divil over the seat back, Fury opened the door. 'Climb up, so, and don't be saying it's hairy.'

Mary pushed her bag onto the seat and mounted the step majestically. 'Matter a damn what I say or I don't say, that dog sheds.'

'You can wait for the bus if you'd rather.'

'Don't be annoying me.' Settling herself beside him, Mary sniffed as he drove on. 'And this van stinks to high heaven of linseed oil.' She placed her shopping bag on the floor and announced that her shift at the charity shop had been changed at short notice. 'Mrs Commisky's been taken in with her feet.'

'Is it bad?'

'Only bunions. She told them it was her heart, and I don't blame her. They won't see you at all if you're not at death's door.'

'How's your own health?'

'Ah, sure, lookit.' Mary shrugged. 'We're none of us getting younger.'

'That's a fact.'

She eyed him sideways, apparently uncertain of whether to say what was in her mind. Observing the look, Fury said nothing and appeared to be concentrating on the road. Mary came to a decision. 'You knew my Tom's aunt Maggie when you were a young fella, didn't you?'

'I did jobs for her for a month or so before I went off to England. I wouldn't say I knew her. I was only a lad. That was a good while before you and Tom were married.'

'What did you think of her?'

'She paid on the nail, anyway. There weren't many in them days who did.'

Mary looked straight ahead through the windscreen. 'I never liked her.'

'Ay, well, I can't say that I did. She wasn't exactly what you'd call convivial.'

'She was what I'd call demanding. And she never had any sense of the fitness of things.'

'Sure, the fitness of things is a matter of opinion. What you'd think was perfectly fine might be anathema to me.'

Mary snorted. 'Like what?'

Fury threw her a sly glance. 'Paint colours, maybe.'

She gave an appreciative hoot of laughter as the van turned off for Lissbeg. 'You'd have every house on the peninsula painted grey if you had your choice.' Then, like a dog with a bone, she reverted to Maggie. 'I suppose you're like Tom, you fell for her poor-me act.'

'I never saw sign of any act. If you ask me, Maggie just didn't care what people thought of her. She went her own way and kept herself to herself.'

'Did she talk to you about why she went to England?'

'Sure, that was fifty years before I worked for her. To me she was old, we wouldn't have been chatting.'

'What did you do for her, anyway?'

'Built walls round her field.' Fury cocked an eye at Mary. 'Why do you want to know?'

'Hanna started talking about her a while back. I don't know was she trying to test my memory.'

'What call would she have to do that?'

'I'd say she has a notion I'm going ga-ga.'

Fury grinned. 'And are you?'

She tossed her head. 'You'd think the young never forgot to turn off a bathroom light.'

'Was that it?'

'Ay, maybe. And a few other things.' Mary sniffed. 'Is it bullseyes I'm smelling as well as linseed oil?'

'Silvermints. I keep a few in the glove compartment for The Divil.'

'God forgive you, Fury O'Shea, they're pure sugar. The poor dog will end up with no teeth.' There was a low growl from the back of the van, where The Divil was sitting in a box of timber offcuts. Ignoring it, Mary frowned. 'So Maggie never said why she took herself off to England?'

'She did not. Mind, she gave me a bit of advice about how to cope when I got there myself. Some things don't change, no matter how much time passes. I'd say there's lads from Eastern Europe now facing the same things in England that Maggie knew in the nineteen twenties and thirties and I went through in the nineteen seventies. Sleeping six to a room in damp digs run by a blood-sucking landlord, and putting up with all kinds of abuse.' Fury looked sideways at Mary again. 'Nobody takes the emigrant boat with hardly a penny in their pocket unless they've a damn good reason to leave home. My dad had died and left everything to my wastrel of a brother, so there was feck-all reason for me to stay. I don't know what Maggie's reason for going was.'

They'd reached Lissbeg and Mary was silent while Fury drove past the Old Convent Centre and turned the van into Sheep Street. When he pulled up outside the charity shop, she spoke as she opened the door. 'I suppose you'll tell me the old are always demanding.'

Fury chuckled. 'I wouldn't have the nerve.' As she slid down to the pavement, he leaned over to shut the door, and The Divil leaped from the back of the van onto the passenger seat. Mary made a show of brushing dog hairs from her coat, then, nodding her thanks for the lift, she disappeared into the shop.

After Aideen left the farm on the Vespa, Una had continued to clear away the breakfast things. Then she went into the office to work at the computer. The task she'd taken on since Paddy's death had become easier and now she felt less stupid and frightened when she sat down at the desk. Recently, she'd even begun to change some of Paddy's systems, laying out information more accessibly and coming up with a way of colour-coding important dates. At first the thought of changing things had made her feel disloyal and she'd been tempted to turn to Conor for approval. But that hadn't seemed fair. Like herself, he'd only begun to come to grips with things without Paddy in the background, and he couldn't absolve her from a sense of guilt, which, in any case, was inappropriate. So why saddle him with it?

Having struggled alone, Una felt proud of herself, though now, with the immediate pressure lifted, she had more free time in which to assess her loss. With the ghost of a smile, she told herself that the idea of being a granny had been hard enough to adjust to without having to get to grips with being a widow. Paddy had been astonished when Conor and Aideen had announced that they were going to have a baby. Later, in their own room, after the hugs and exclamations, he'd told Una it made him feel ancient. 'I mean, for God's sake, you and I are only spring chickens yet.'

They hadn't made love for ages, what with the state of Paddy's back and his depression, but that night it had happened and, afterwards, Paddy had started to laugh. 'How are we going to face the kids if we've gone and got you pregnant? We'll have to buy twice the nappies and invest in a double buggy.' It was nonsense, of course, since Una had been through the menopause ten years earlier, but they'd giggled so much, and added so many details to Paddy's fantasy that they'd ended up with their heads under the pillows, fearful that Conor and Aideen might hear them through the wall.

Una rested her chin on her hands and stared at her screen. She was glad Paddy had lived to see Ronan born. Sometimes, when he'd been terribly low and suffering chronic pain, she'd half wished him out of his misery. Yet when, once or twice, he'd told her that he'd seen no point in living, the twist of her heart had banished the thought that, for his sake, she could perhaps be happy to let him go. The fact is, she thought, we were made for one another, and if our time had to be short, at least we knew how lucky we were.

In her youth she'd been a romantic, hitchhiking halfway across Europe as soon as she left school, and taking a job in a taverna on Mykonos instead of coming home and finding what her mum had called proper work. The taverna was where she'd met Paddy, who'd arrived on a lads' long weekend with a crowd from his local GAA club. He was huge, with a thatch of fair hair, and not noticeably handsome, and his lack of small-talk had made for a few uncomfortable dates. But here, unsought and unheralded, was love. The strength of the feeling had shaken her, and Paddy's impulsive proposal, made on a beach at sunset, had been unexpectedly poetic. God alone knows, thought Una, where he'd picked up a quotation from Yeats. We'd probably both been taught it at school, and he'd been listening while I'd been dreaming of travelling the world. The skin on Paddy's ears had been pink and peeling, and his eyes were narrow from squinting against rain and wind in the fields. They'd sat side by side watching millions of stars begin to prick the night as the sun drowned itself in the 'wine-dark sea'. 'There they are now for you, Una, the "heavens' embroidered cloths".' Raising his arm, he'd held up his hand between her face and the sky, and Una had seen the stars shining between his outspread fingers. Then, in the gathering darkness, his voice had spoken in her ear. '*The blue, the dim and the dark cloths, of night, and light, and the half-light.* I don't know what Yeats was talking about, saying he couldn't give them to that woman because he was poor. Aren't they there for rich and poor alike? And, anyway, she wouldn't need a man to give them to her.' He'd sat up again and Una had run her hand across his back, feeling the grains of sand that clung to his skin. Then, without looking at her, he'd made his proposal. 'Tell me this, would you take them from me, Una? If I offered to spread them under your feet, would you walk my world with me?'

The realities of his world had come as a shock to her, not least because the requirements of the farm had meant that Paddy had been reluctant to travel abroad again. Once or twice, when the boys were young, she'd persuaded him to take the family off on a package holiday, but he'd been constantly on the phone, checking up on the land and the animals, and, though he'd tried not to show it, she'd known that he couldn't wait to get home. Eventually she'd given up and accepted things as they were and, with a nagging sense that the price of love had been loss of opportunity, she'd comforted herself with the thought that Conor's unlikely love of Italy was a resurgence of her own romantic streak. And that was so unfair to poor Paddy, she told herself regretfully. Conor, with his love of books and his sensitivity, is just as much Paddy's son as mine.

Conor had fallen for Italy when working in Lissbeg Library, where Hanna had shown him a book about Canaletto. The serene eighteenth-century vistas of Venetian canals had entranced him and afterwards, so he'd told Una, he'd typed 'Images + Italy' into a search engine and been blown away by a mixture of really old paintings and really cool photos, including guys on Vespas whizzing round cathedral squares. As soon as he'd saved enough to buy his own Vespa, he'd taken himself off for a weekend in Florence, the cheapest Italian break he'd been able to find. Paddy had made difficulties when he'd heard about the plan, complaining that Conor was skiving off work. It was the closest Una had ever come to falling out with Paddy and, eventually, she'd won Conor's case by reminding Paddy of Greece. 'Don't you remember what it was like? How can you not remember? Blue skies, grapes and wine, and a different kind of sunshine, the kind that seeps right into your bones. Give him a break, Paddy. He's a hard worker. He deserves to see the world. He might even find his life's love, like you did. Think of that!' So Paddy had laughed and let him go and, though Italy had enthralled him, Conor had found love closer to home.

Joe was different. As soon as he'd got engaged to Eileen, Una had seen what would happen. A wife with a preference for city life, and whose father had plenty of money, offered Joe both an escape from the farm and a chance to play the big man. His desire to help his family was real but, being Joe, his swagger made him insufferable. Inevitably, Conor's life choices had lessened as soon as his brother was no longer there. Though the labourer Joe paid for was reliable, Paddy's declining health had meant that Conor was needed twenty-four/seven, so Aideen's willingness to live on the farm had been a relief. He's lucky, thought Una. She may be shy but she's her own woman, and they're a match. What could be more romantic than that exchange of vows in a cypress grove, with wreaths of daisies in their hair and a couple of hired Vespas parked in the background? Those two will always have that to remember, just as I remember Paddy and me under the stars on that beach in Mykonos. And I won't live in the past, she told herself firmly. I won't brood and, in time, I'll move on and be happy. That's the tribute the living owe to the dead.

Chapter Fifteen

Owen was sitting in the reading room at the library with a poster spread on the table in front of him. It was yellowed, and torn at the edges, and had deep marks showing that it had been folded up for years. The paper was worn away at the joins of the fold marks, leaving a grid of holes that obscured the print in places and pockmarked the smudged features of a young man's face. Hanna looked over his shoulder. 'Did this arrive today?'

'Foxy Dunne came in with it. That guy who's a personal trainer at the gym.'

In the long nose and close-set eyes in the face she was gazing down at, Hanna recognised the features of a lad she'd often seen bounding across the nuns' garden, exuding energy and swinging a Nike gym bag. The poster was headed 'POLICE NOTICE' and announced a reward of a thousand pounds for information leading to the capture of its subject. Beneath his face were the words 'WANTED FOR MURDER IN IRELAND' and he was named as John Dunne, 'also known as Seán O'Dowd', and described as 'looking like a clerk or a small-shopkeeper'. Owen turned it over carefully, revealing what looked like a thin layer of soot covering the back. 'Foxy said it was found in the attic when they cleared out an old family house. It must have been near the chimney – look at the state of it. At least it was folded up, or the front would be filthy as well.'

'Do they know what happened to John?'

'He wasn't caught. He lived through the fighting and then died young of TB.' Owen blew gently on the back of the poster, making no difference at all to the layer of soot. 'It's another piece that should be conserved and the chances are that it won't be. Even the National Library's strapped for cash.'

'At least you can scan it.'

'I know. And I'm wondering if we could have a section on conservation in our display. People haven't much of a clue, and it's pertinent. Half the stuff coming in to us will end up degrading to nothing if it's not stabilised.'

'We could put the idea to Tim.'

'It's not going to knock his socks off, though, is it? Slow, meticulous, skilled work isn't Tim's thing.'

That evening, while Brian was out at a meeting, Hanna returned to Maggie's book. The poster had reminded her of Maggie's description of the first stage of her journey to Liverpool.

One fellow on the train from Carrick was singing in Irish but he shut up when the soldiers got on. I put my head down and moved away from him because there'd been a poster on the platform with a photo of Liam on it. It said he was a known dissident who'd shot a policeman in Crossarra. That was the night of the raid. We heard the shooting up on the road after Liam got out at the back, but mostly we were thinking of Dad and Hannie. The poster called him a murderer, and the photo was the one that was printed in The Inquirer *the time Liam won the prize for his poem. I don't know how the police could have got hold of it because John Joe Quinn the editor of* The Inquirer *had word last year to destroy all photos of lads that are on the run. Mam had one cut from the paper but Dad burned that on the fire. But they got hold of a copy some way and it's up there on posters with five hundred pounds on Liam's head. It turned my stomach. I was afraid that the soldiers on the train would ask me questions when they saw my name. But there's plenty of Caseys in Ireland and the soldier who looked at my passport only glanced at it. I'd say he was dying to get home to his tea.*

Hanna imagined the shock of fear Maggie had felt when she saw Liam's face. It was evident that such posters had been run off on presses owned by local newspapers, and clear that the *Inquirer*'s editor had been pressured both by the Black and Tans, who acted as auxiliaries to the police force, and by the freedom-fighters who were his close neighbours. Though his press had been commandeered, he'd destroyed photos that could have been used on police posters. But how many homes had been raided for family albums, and how many mothers like Maggie's had kept photos of sons and daughters out fighting or spying? Remembering the poster in the library, Hanna wondered how it had survived. Had the Dunne family risked tearing down posters, in the hope that if fewer were on display there'd be less chance that somebody would be tempted by the reward? Did someone at the time simply have a sense of history? Or might it have been pride in the size of the bounty on John Dunne's head?

Her own first response to the poster Owen had shown her had been unedifying. Though she'd hastily concealed it, what she'd felt had been indignation. If John Dunne was worth a thousand pounds to the authorities, why had Liam merited only half that amount? It was a shameful thought, suggesting, as it did, a hierarchy of sacrifice, as if courage and grief and loss could be assessed in terms of money, and public approval of those who'd suffered be measured accordingly. And yet, thought Hanna, isn't that what happened? The veterans of the War of Independence came home as heroes and, complicated though things were by the horrors of the Civil War, a veteran in the family was a source of pride, and the bigger the price that had been on his head, the greater the family's prestige. And look at me now, a hundred years later, she told herself wryly. Apparently I, too, subscribe to that dubious scheme of values, which isn't just unedifying, it's daft. Because, while I don't know why my grandfather's story wasn't passed down in the family, judging by what's in Maggie's book, there wasn't much about him to like or be proud of.

I'm writing this up on deck. Every bit of timber and iron up here is wet with the spray, but it's better than being down below in the cabin. I've found a place between two benches. The cold would strike up if you'd sit on the deck but I have my suitcase under me. It's a good leather one I borrowed from Lizzie Keogh. God knows when she'll ever see it again but I said if I met someone who'd take it over I'd send it back to her.

Lizzie said there's always someone on the boat that'll tell you where to find digs. Maybe in a while, if the sea gets calmer, I'll go back down and ask. Paud Donovan sold the cows for us anyway. He's taken the grazing too at a fair rent. Mam couldn't cope with the cows on her own, and I have ten pounds out of the money that Paud got for them. I don't know if Mam understood when I said I was taking it. I left the rest under the clock and I said she'd have money regular when I get a job in Liverpool. The priest said to send my wages home care of the presbytery, and he'll make sure she has all she needs. Mrs Donovan will look in on her. I don't think Liam would want me to leave Mam, and I'm sure Dad wouldn't. But I was given a choice that was no choice, so what would they have me do?

I don't know why I'm writing this really. There's so much I can't and I won't say. I don't know what's ahead of me and I've no way of letting Liam know that I'm going. Maybe Lizzie Keogh will manage it for me. She has a brother is in the same brigade.

I got up this morning early and was looking away towards the forest. You can't see it from the cliff but I knew the trees were there with the fallen leaves still deep underneath them. There'd be birds singing on the bog too, where we left the turf drying. I never thought I wouldn't draw it home myself for Mam.

The entry ended there. Between the pages, a memorandum was dated the previous day.

<u>To Buy</u>
Stockings
Soap
Notepaper. Envelopes
Bootlaces
Bullseyes for Mam

<u>To Do</u>
Lizzie's for suitcase
Pay account at Cathcarts
Ask Mrs D to send round 'The Inquirer' to Mam each week

Leaning back, Hanna stared down the glen. Fury had told her that the Donovans had moved away while Maggie was in England. 'She didn't come home to Finfarran until her mam died in the 1930s.'

'Had her mother been living alone?'

'I don't know.'

Though Fury had become a friend, and had been told when she'd found Maggie's book, Hanna had never offered to let him read it. Neither had he asked. Knowledge was his stock-in-trade but so was discretion. Nor had she told him when she'd found the answer to her question, on one of the pages slipped between the book's jacket and cover. It was dated July 1938, and the cold anger with which Maggie had written had made it seem far too private to share.

Liam has gone away out of this house. He's been living here with Mam, and the place like a shed by him. There was no comfort in it. I've told him he's no longer welcome. He's been itching to marry Mariah Keane from the post office back in Crossarra these last fifteen years. He can go there and be done with it, now that Mam's dead and buried. I said nothing at all when I came in the door, nor in the burial ground. I stood while the priest squeezed out his prayers and the neighbours shifted and snuffled. I couldn't have a one of them back to the house for shame at the state it was in.

And when Liam came home after dark I knew he'd been off drinking with his cronies. I'd seen the lot of them at the back of the church with their black suits. They were all out like himself in the past, fighting the British and standing against the Treaty. Some of the men at the funeral today spent months in prison with Liam, and I'd say one or two are touched in the head after what they went through. Not Liam, though. There's nothing wrong with him and no excuse for his behaviour.

Mam never said a word against me, I know that much. She never had a bad word for him either, but when she wrote and told me she'd left me the house, she thanked me for sending her money. She'd had nothing from the bould Liam in all those years. Not a lick of paint on the house by him, nor a clean sheet to a bed. And Mam's ware, that was always clean, thrown up in a heap on the dresser.

And then to stand with his back to the fire and say I'd deserted my duty. He was half drunk with his bloodshot eyes and he roaring out that, when he'd come home from prison, poor Mam was sitting here like a shadow. I wouldn't doubt him. Why wouldn't she be with her husband dead and her heart grieving for her daughters? I told Liam it wasn't me that first brought trouble to her. I said that I'd never have gone away if I'd had any choice in the matter. In my own mind I was screaming, though I kept my voice quiet. I didn't say it was because of him that my own trouble followed.

I told him to go to Mariah Keane. The house and the field are mine now. I won't go back to England. He can seek his bit of a pension if Dublin will let him have it. He can write up and send them a list of his medals. I suppose he deserves recompense. It's true to say that he offered his life up for Ireland. The truth no one admits is that he sacrificed our lives too. Mam seems never to have blamed him. But I do. I'll blame him till the day I die. Not for doing what he saw as his duty, but for standing here on the night our mother was buried and telling me that I deserted her.

Chapter Sixteen

The kitchen in St Finian's Close was full of the aromatic smells of spices as Bríd prepared a curry for dinner, and Dan sat on the table drinking beer. Turning to fill a pan with water, she flicked a tea-towel from her shoulder and threw it across the room at him. 'If you're going to do nothing but swing your legs, you can open a beer for me.'

'Consider it done.' Dan went to the fridge and fetched a beer, pouring it into a glass and setting it down by the hob. Leaning over the bubbling pot of curry, he breathed in deeply. 'That smells amazing. You've made enough to feed the five thousand.'

'I've never known you and Conor to say no to second helpings. I bet there won't be a spoonful left by ten o'clock tonight.' Dan hitched himself back onto the table, crumpled the tea-towel into a ball and chucked it at her. Bríd caught it one-handed. 'They'll be here in half an hour. Get off your arse and set the table.'

'Can't a man finish his drink?'

'And, while you're at it, for God's sake, would you go and have a shower? You stink of engine oil.'

'It adds depth to the turmeric.'

'Just go, will you? You'll have to clean that table now you've been sitting on it.'

'I've a perfectly clean arse.' Dan slid off the table. 'Anyway, you have to eat a peck of dirt before you die.'

'Well, I'm not having any deaths here because of poor hygiene.'

He caught her from behind in a bear-hug and planted a kiss on her neck. 'God, you're a terrible bully. Lighten up, Bríd.' He frequently told her to lighten up and, depending on her mood and the circumstances, it either annoyed or amused her. Early in their relationship, he'd said that his granddad had taught him to roll with life's punches. 'You can't control the weather, so making plans is pointless. You have to be ready to think on your feet.' This was a different approach from Bríd's, whose life was based on forward planning. Having located a culinary-science course in Dublin, she'd set about achieving the required Leaving Cert points to secure her a place and, getting there, had worked to gain the highest possible grade. Most of the others who'd trained with her had had plans to go abroad as soon as they qualified, but Bríd's ambition was to return to Lissbeg. Her married siblings were settled there, and her parents' house was the hub to which everyone came for dinner on Sundays, and gathered at Christmas and Easter to enact well-loved rituals. So she'd planned to find work in a local hotel and build a career in catering in Finfarran. But, though driven, she wasn't inflexible. When Aideen's inheritance had offered the prospect of a partnership, Bríd had embraced the opportunity, confident that what they could each bring to the table would produce the perfect recipe for success.

Dan was the single element in her life that didn't fit in. The relationship they'd had at school had ended in a bust-up after which they hadn't spoken for months. While she'd been in Dublin he'd taken off for Australia but, typically, had discovered too late that you had to be a graduate to get a working-holiday visa. So he'd travelled as a tourist and, unable to work legally, had slept on beaches and taken jobs for cash. Later, he'd made fun of his situation, saying that having your pecs oiled while you posed in designer beachwear for a fashion shoot wasn't all bad. But, in fact, he'd been too embarrassed to admit, even to himself, that he'd made a mistake. And then, just before his visa ran out, he'd met a guy who'd offered to invest in his dream of running marine eco-tours from Couneen pier. Had Bríd been with him, she'd have asked pertinent questions, but to Dan it had felt that, at last, he'd found a fair wind.

Inevitably, things had gone wrong when he got home to Ireland. The investor turned out to be crooked, Dan came close to arrest, and only the fact that Bríd was back, and they'd picked up where they'd left off, had made him believe he might make a new start. But the underlying dynamic between them had changed. He was a month or two older than Bríd, and at school she'd looked up to him, yet, so far, his attempts to establish himself had all been failures, while her business was going from strength to strength. Bríd was perceptive enough to see that this could be disastrous. For all Dan's arrogance, it was hard to make him believe that she needed him. Occasionally, he'd let his guard down and cling to her unexpectedly, as on the day they'd visited Couneen, but when she tried to tell him how much she loved the spice of danger he brought to her ordered existence, he always made a joke or put himself down. Or else, as now, he'd kiss her and tell her she needed to lighten up. Badinage and sex were his default settings for deflecting introspection, and he had long practice in using either, or both, as a defence. Sometimes she wished he required less emotional input and, now and then, without warning, her patience would suddenly snap

Released from the bear-hug, she turned round and he held out his hand. 'There's half an hour before they arrive. Let's not waste this shower. Come up and join me.'

'Dan, I'm trying to make dinner.'

'The curry is simmering gently …'

'I have to get the rice on.'

'And it's far too early to start cooking the rice …'

'Stop it, okay? There isn't time. I have to get things sorted.'

He backed away with a conspiratorial smile. 'You so want to.'

'I *so* do. And it doesn't make any difference. Because I've got stuff to do here.'

'Lighten up, Bríd.'

'Feck off, Dan.'

She could hear him laughing as he crossed the hall and clattered up the staircase and, smiling, she went to clean the table and set out the cutlery. At school he'd had only to look at her under those coal-black lashes and every inch of her skin had felt as if it were on fire. There was a game he'd played from the far side of the classroom, fixing his eyes on her bent head and concentrating until the force of his gaze had made her look up. Once, he'd teased her from a distance throughout an entire chemistry class and, during the next break, they'd made love behind the sports hall. She'd said the same thing then – we can't, there isn't time, we'll be caught – and he'd just laughed. Now, suddenly, her whole body ached for him, and she was halfway to the foot of the stairs before she realised she'd left the kitchen. He hadn't closed the bedroom door and she heard him kick off his trainers before crossing the landing to the bathroom. But there really wasn't time for this, and the thought that Conor and Aideen might arrive early made her turn back. She and Dan weren't at school now, she told herself. They lived together, were adults and shared a bedroom, and delayed gratification never did anyone any harm.

Before deciding what to wear to dinner, Aideen had fed Ronan and put him down. Conor was lying on the bed, half asleep. He'd had a long day and tomorrow would be the herd's first TB test without Paddy on the sidelines. It'd be great, thought Aideen, to curl up beside him and give dinner with Bríd and Dan a miss. Still, it might do him the world of good to get out and have a curry and a few beers. She couldn't drink because she was feeding Ronan, so he wouldn't feel bad about having a few and leaving the driving to her.

Opening her wardrobe, Aideen considered her options. She hadn't put on much weight during her pregnancy and, since Ronan's birth, had gone back to her normal size eight. But, these days, she didn't feel like dressing up for a night out. It's only St Finian's Close, she thought, not a restaurant. All the same, it seemed rude not to make an effort. Conor, she knew, would struggle into a shirt and decent jeans, as would Dan, but if a dinner involved an actual invitation, she and Bríd usually tried to look good. Having held up various garments and rejected them, she selected a dress that she'd bought the previous year. It had been one of those shopping days when she'd needed an outfit for a party and had come away having spent too much on something she wasn't even sure she liked. But it was suitably summery, with a tight bodice and a pattern of flowers that reminded her of paintings she'd seen in Florence, and now, as she held it out, the swing of the skirt made her feel energised. She took it off its hanger and laid it on the bed beside Conor, who had fallen asleep and was snoring gently.

In a way, she thought, it's just as well that I didn't splash out on a new dress the other day. Not on top of my expensive coffee and dinky shortbread biscuit. She hadn't told Conor about her visit to the garden centre. Ronan had needed attention as soon as she'd come through the door, and Conor hadn't got in for his evening meal until after dark. Una, who'd spent most of her day at the computer screen, had simply asked if she'd had a good time. With Ronan fussing in her arms, Aideen had nodded. 'Great. Listen, I'm going to take this fellow up. Will you want a hand with the dinner?' When she'd come back downstairs, she'd set about tasks in the kitchen and, by the time they'd eaten and cleared up, Conor and Una had been focused on plans for the following day.

Aideen told herself that she'd needed time to process what had happened. As she'd sped home on the Vespa, her mind had been in a whirl. It was weird to think that her dad could have been somewhere round the corner while she sat there drinking her pricy coffee. Like The Divil, he might have stepped out and confronted her. Though that, of course, was nonsense because, if he had appeared, he wouldn't have recognised her, and she wouldn't have had a clue who he was.

That night, she'd taken her phone and keyed in a LinkedIn search, wondering why she'd never done so before. He seemed to be there but, because she wasn't a member, she couldn't get in and see any detail. So she'd tried the About Us section of the garden centre's website, and found his photo and bio at once. Derek Murphy, an ordinary-looking businessman, posed at a desk with greenery in the background and the kind of lighting that showed he'd paid to get his image right. It turned out that he'd acquired the place on the outskirts of Carrick recently, having begun, as

Aunt Bridge had said, with an outlet in Cork. At the top of each page of the website there was a honeybee logo and a line in fancy script that read *Making Your Garden Bloom for Three Generations.* Reading the bio, Aideen had found that his great-granddad had been a seed merchant, and that the place in Cork had begun as a small shop. It had all felt too much to deal with, so she hadn't searched any further. Instead she'd turned off her phone and gone to bed.

Now, as she looked at Conor, whose face was half buried in the duvet, she wished that she'd told him what had happened. Not having done so made it feel like some kind of big deal. And it's not, she told herself firmly, slipping into her shoes. We've always known my father was out there. It's never been a secret. It's just that his name on the menu came at me out of left field. Ronan whimpered in his cot and Conor rolled over. 'I've got to get up and get dressed, right? Is Ronan waking up?'

Aideen went to the cot. 'No, I think he's dreaming. Are you sure you're okay to go out?'

'Of course I am and, anyway, we couldn't cancel at this stage. Bríd will be over there cooking up a storm.'

They arrived on time and Dan opened the door and ushered them in. He was shaved and looking tidy, and when Bríd emerged from the kitchen Aideen saw she was wearing a new silk shirt. Pleased by the glimpse of her own dress, caught in the hall mirror, Aideen kissed her, said she looked great, and followed her into the front room where dips and chapatis were set on the coffee-table. It was so easy to relax with old friends that she hoped, once Conor sat down, he wouldn't drop off to sleep. But instead he seemed to have got his second wind. Happily slouched on the sofa, he praised Bríd's raita and told her about his plans for the following year. 'I'd say we could cover most of the basic fresh stuff you'll need for the deli. Salad leaves. Things like that. We should sit down and talk about veg that need storing too, like onions. Aideen said you were thinking of making preserves yourself, to sell.'

Bríd said she was. 'We haven't costed anything yet, but it feels like a no-brainer, especially if we're getting the produce from the farm.'

Aideen chipped in from the armchair where she was sitting. 'I'll be more hands-on again by next year, so we won't have to keep falling back on poor Dan.' To her surprise, she saw Bríd throw an anxious look at Dan. Wondering if she'd said something wrong, Aideen took a chapati, as Dan, who seemed to her to be fine, sank onto the sofa.

Accepting a bottle of beer, Conor asked him how he was doing. 'How's the business? Are you getting many tourists out in the boat?'

Dan shrugged. 'Tipping along. You know yourself. The boat's fighting back a bit.'

'What's the matter with her?'

'Nothing I can't fix. It just takes time.'

Eager to atone for whatever faux pas she'd unintentionally made, Aideen explained that this was what she'd been saying. 'You don't want to be wasting your time lending a hand to us at the Garden Café.'

Bríd cut in quickly, 'Don't go putting him off. It's brilliant to have him.' She laughed as she spoke, but Aideen thought she could feel an undercurrent of tension, though Dan was lying back, necking a beer. He put away two more before they went through to the kitchen and, as they laughed and chatted through the meal, Aideen could see he was drinking more than the others. By now Conor had had several beers, and the combination of alcohol and tiredness was clearly catching up on him, but it was good to see him looking so relaxed. At the end of a good-humoured row about something they'd all seen on Netflix, the conversation drifted back to work. Aideen watched Dan's expression change as Conor returned to the subject of the boat. 'I suppose what you need is investment. Would you try going to the bank?' Once more, Bríd seemed tense, and Dan's eyes appeared to glaze over.

'What makes you think that would help?'

Conor looked confused. 'A loan would give you a kick-start, wouldn't it?'

'Yeah, well, banks tend to be less obliging than filthy-rich relations like old Dawson.'

Aideen and Bríd opened their mouths simultaneously but, before they spoke, Conor suddenly seemed to sober up. 'Ah, shit, don't listen to me. What do I know?' Dan tilted his chair, raised his beer to his lips, and said nothing.

Aideen looked at her watch. 'You know, we really ought to be hitting the road, Bríd. Una's sitting with Ronan, and Conor's up with the lark tomorrow.'

'You won't have tea or a coffee?'

'No, honest. We ought to be going.' She got to her feet, then looked at the smeared and empty dishes on the table. 'Can I give you a hand with all this?'

'No, you're grand. Dan and I can sort it.'

As Bríd came round the table to kiss Aideen, Dan lounged to his feet. 'No problem at all. I'm a great hand at scouring pots. Shur, what else am I good for?' He laughed as he held out his hand to Conor and gave Aideen a hug, but Aideen could see Bríd looking tight-lipped. Clearly, however, this was not the moment to start asking questions, so they left with smiles and repeated expressions of thanks for the lovely meal.

When the door closed behind them, Bríd turned to Dan who was standing in the hallway, a beer bottle dangling from his hand. He met her gaze and raised his eyebrows. 'What?'

'Jesus, Dan, Conor's your friend, could you not even be civil?'

He swung the bottle to and fro, saying nothing, and Bríd's patience snapped. 'And if you wouldn't be decent for Conor's sake, you might think about Aideen. After all, you're living rent-free in her house.' She stopped, horrified by what she'd said, and took a step towards him, but his eyes warned her not to get too close.

For a moment neither of them spoke. Then Dan took a swig of beer and looked at her mockingly. 'Lighten up, Bríd. I'm sure that if Aideen wants me evicted, she'll send Conor round to chuck me out.'

Unable to trust herself to speak, Bríd pushed past him into the kitchen and, furiously, began filling the dishwasher. For a moment Dan stayed where he was before turning away and going into the front room. Half an hour later, when she went in to clear the remains of the starters, he was lying on the sofa, fast asleep. Biting her lip, Bríd fetched a spare duvet, tucked it round him, turned off the lights and went upstairs to bed.

Chapter Seventeen

A strong wind, blowing all night, had become a soft breeze at dawn. When Jazz got up around 7 a.m., she opened the seaward windows and let salt-laden air sweep into the house. Already the grass was warm underfoot. Wearing PJ bottoms and a T-shirt, she strolled down the garden with a mug of tea in one hand and an orange in the other, climbed the stile and sat on the clifftop bench to have her breakfast. It was Saturday and she'd offered to pick up Mary and drive her into Lissbeg at ten o'clock.

The ocean was as smooth as a millpond, the horizon a silver streak dividing dark water from pale blue sky. At first light Jazz had been woken by the sound of seabirds calling on the wind. Now she could hear nothing but the rhythmic pulse of the waves, endlessly striking and drawing back from the cliff. She peeled her orange and divided it into segments, idly wondering if anyone else had ever done the same, sitting on that particular spot on a morning in late summer. The thought of other lives lived here intrigued her. The eyes that had opened and seen sunlight dappling her bedroom wall. The hands that had wielded a broom in the kitchen, knowing exactly how many strokes it took to reach the corners and to follow the fall of the floor to the half-door. According to Fury, the original earth floor had had an incline, so the woman of the house could throw soapy water on the hearthstone, then sweep the suds down through the room and out the open doorway. The stone tiles he'd installed for Hanna retained that gentle slope, hardly perceptible until you came to brush them or to use a mop.

None of this would have interested Jazz before she'd moved in but, now that she had a house to keep, she enjoyed the thought of Maggie, Hannie and their mother moving through the rooms she cared for, washing and wringing, and baking bread on the hearthstone, with firelight catching their bare arms and tumbled hair falling into their eyes. She'd imagined them like figures in a period TV drama, scrubbing the table and boiling pots of food for the pig or the hens. But when she'd told her mum, Hanna had grinned. 'I doubt if there was anything attractive about boiling up kitchen scraps for animal feed. The smell must have been horrible, for starters. And, when I knew Maggie, her hens were a constant torment. They were always getting into the house, and I was the one who had to chase them out and clean up their droppings.'

'Did she have a pig?'

'Not then. I suppose the family did when she was young.'

Relishing the sweet juice as she swallowed a segment of orange, Jazz reminded herself that Maggie's family had been poor. Oranges, if they'd had them at all, were probably a treat at Christmastime, eaten by the fire with frost glowing on the windowpanes and their animals bedded in straw outside in the shed. 'So, did you have hens too when you were a kid?' she'd asked Hanna, who'd thrown back her head and laughed.

'God, no, your nan couldn't have coped! She likes her eggs to come from a supermarket, equally sized and stamped Class A.'

'But you had a village shop.'

'We never sold farm eggs or butter, and practically everything came shrink-wrapped in plastic. Mary took pride in keeping up with the times.'

Flicking the orange peel over the cliff, Jazz prepared to go back to the house and get dressed. Unlike Mary, it seemed that Maggie had been a throwback, determined to live in old age as she had when she was a child. And, actually, when you removed the romantic filter conjured by TV dramas, it was hard to visualise her moving from room to room, and bizarre to think that Hanna could remember the house with an earth floor, smoke-stained walls and the smell of Maggie's leaky paraffin lamp.

Mary was waiting by the gate when Jazz pulled up at the bungalow. Easing herself into the passenger seat, she looked pointedly at her watch. 'It was ten we said, wasn't it?'

'I take it you're implying I'm late.'

'Nothing of the kind! I'm just checking my watch.'

'And what does it say?'

'It says five past ten. But I've no doubt you'll tell me it's wrong.'

Jazz pulled into the stream of traffic and set off for Lissbeg. 'Actually, Nan, you're lucky I'm not even later. It's such a gorgeous day that I didn't want to leave the cliff.'

'I can see that you didn't spend much time getting dressed up for town.'

'Damn right I didn't. It's the weekend.' Jazz grinned at her. 'You're looking wonderfully spruce, though. What are your plans?'

'D'you mean am I going to be asking for a lift home?'

'I mean that it looks like you're going on a spree.'

Mary, who was wearing a navy blue skirt with a matching jacket and pearls, said she planned to return an unfinished library book. 'Hanna made me borrow a daft thing called *Bread Matters*. I've no patience with it, I'm taking it back.'

Jazz knew that Hanna and Brian were due to have lunch with Mary the following day, when Hanna could easily have taken the book and returned it on Mary's behalf. But to say so seemed unkind. If this was her grandmother's only reason for a trip to Lissbeg, the text demanding a lift into town must have been prompted by boredom and, if that was so, the pearls and navy suit, worn with patent leather shoes, were rather sad. She asked if there was anything else Mary needed to do.

'My God, you're fierce inquisitive, aren't you? Did your mam never teach you to mind your own business?'

'Of course she did. Mum's a stickler for privacy. I'm more like you. Shamelessly nosy.'

Mary emitted a hoot of laughter. 'I don't have any specific plans, as it happens. I'm going to look round the shops.'

'How about seeing if Pat Fitz is up for a cup of coffee?'

'Don't you start trying to organise my life for me. I've plenty of places to go and people to see.'

They had reached Lissbeg and Jazz was about to offer to take Mary home later, when a thought crossed her mind. 'How about if I pick you up when you're ready, and we go back to my place for a coffee? You still haven't seen what I've done with the house.'

Mary hesitated. 'I daresay you've got plenty to do without making coffee for me.' They both knew that Jazz's morning was committed to her anyway as, regardless of how long Mary spent wandering round Lissbeg, she'd still need a lift home to the bungalow afterwards. Seeing the thought on Jazz's face, Mary bridled. 'Hanna can drive me home when she's finished work.'

'Don't be daft. You'll be sitting round till lunchtime. I'll wait here while you drop in the book, and we can go straight out to Maggie's. You don't want to go round the shops on a Saturday, Nan, they'll be packed. Come on, indulge me, I want to show off my bockety old shed.'

Mary snorted appreciatively. 'I suppose you won't be happy until you get your own way.'

'How well you know me. Look, while you nip into the library I'll get us a couple of cakes from the deli. What do you fancy?'

'Oh, don't ask me. I wouldn't know what's fashionable.'

'Nan, this is cake we're talking about.'

'I know well what we're talking about. What I'm saying is that people's idea of food these days is wojeous and the claptrap that's written about it is even worse.' Mary produced the library book and brandished it in outrage. 'I mean, Holy God Almighty, look at this *Bread Matters* yoke! According to Hanna it had rave reviews.'

'Sounds great.'

'It sounds like your mother's decided I'm entering my second childhood.' Mary glowered at the book. '"Changing the way we think about bread". Dear God, the cheek of them! It had me awake half the night, I was that cross.'

In the deli, Jazz decided to play safe and hedge her bets. Having chosen a couple of sugary rum babas, she added two plain scones, which Bríd told her had just come out of the oven. Then, as the spiced pear conserve she had at home was likely to be deemed wojeous, she selected a pot of blackcurrant jam. Returning to the car just as Mary emerged from the library, she handed her the cake box to hold while she found her key. Mary fastened her seatbelt and, with the box balanced on her knees, remarked that she always enjoyed a decent rum baba. A few moments later, as they sat in gridlock in Broad Street's weekend traffic, Jazz's phone pinged, announcing a text. 'It's from Mum, asking if you're with me. I'll tell her I'll take you home later.' The traffic had freed up by the time she'd replied and, by cutting through Sheep Street, she soon picked up speed.

Once on her way, she was tempted to ask what had been said in the library but, remembering Hanna's recent concern about Mary's erratic behaviour, she decided that winding her nan up would be irresponsible. So, instead of provoking what she assumed would be another stream of outrage, she drew Mary's attention to the countryside, lush and green on either side of the one-track road she'd turned onto beyond the town. 'I love living so near to Lissbeg and yet being way out in the country.'

'At your age, I would have thought you'd want a bit of life. Not to be stuck out in the middle of nowhere with no one around.'

'But that's the point. I've got the best of both worlds. I can hang out with my friends in Lissbeg or Carrick and be back here in the middle of nowhere in less than half an hour. Look, Nan, isn't it glorious?' Jazz lowered the car window and took a deep breath of fresh air. Black and wine-red berries were clustered on brambles in the hedgerows where, in places, the palest of purple flowers still showed among the thorns. At the foot of the ditches, neon-bright montbretia was beginning to scatter its orange flowers as its leaves turned rust-red. The broad fields had been harvested for silage, leaving them striped in gold and green and studded with rolled bales. Mary pursed her lips and declared that flooding on the roads got worse every year. 'What can they expect when they block decent drains and pull out every wall? Fine big fields, that's what the farmers call them. Ranches is what they have, and the country ruined by them.'

'I didn't know you were into farm management.'

'I've eyes in me head, girl, haven't I, and I grew up in the countryside. I know more than enough about it, thank you, and I'm happy living where I am.'

When they reached Maggie's place, Jazz parked the car at the pull-in by the gate, and led the way along the gable end towards the front of the house. As ever, the view as she turned the corner made her heart sing. Mary observed the huge sky above the shimmering ocean without comment. Her lip curled as they approached the half-door and, when they went inside, she stood impassively just beyond the threshold, considering the slate worktop, Fury's cream-painted cupboards, and the comfortable chairs by the hearth at the end of the low-ceilinged room. Having made her initial examination, she marched to the fireside and sat down heavily, drawing her navy skirt over her knees. Jazz had left the top of the half-door open, and the cries of gulls rising from the waves could be heard above the chirping of birds in the ash trees outside.

Ensconced in her chair, Mary continued to scrutinise the room. There was little that Jazz had brought with her. Hanna had carefully chosen the furniture for its setting and, as it wasn't suited to Brian's house, had left it in place when she'd moved to the Hag's Glen. Jazz's additions consisted mainly of coloured throws, a few pictures and photographs, and bits and pieces for the kitchen, including her beloved Delonghi coffee maker and a scarlet Le Creuset casserole dish in which she did most of her cooking. Now, while she made coffee, she watched Mary's overt inspection. In anyone else, she'd have found it offensive, but Mary had brought disparagement to an art form. Opening the cake box, Jazz called across to her. 'So, what do you think?'

'You keep it clean enough, I'll say that for you.' With a toss of her head, Mary indicated the closed bedroom door. 'Though I dare say you'd rather I didn't go in and check the state of your bed.'

'You don't need to. I'll tell you. It looks like a bomb hit it.'

'Not much change there, so.'

'You try living in a studio flat where you can't even eat breakfast till you've folded your bed away. I'm still luxuriating in liberation.'

'Is that what you call it?' Mary cast an appraising look at the *súgán* chairs by the table, and at Maggie's dresser, which Hanna had left piled with blue and white plates. 'Well, if living like a hippie is what you want, I suppose you've found the right place.'

'A hippie? Honestly, Nan! This place is pure *Country Living* magazine. Mum could probably rent it out for photo shoots.' Coming over, Jazz hunkered down and, setting a cup by Mary's chair, glanced up at her. 'Do you remember the house in Maggie's day?'

'Ah, you're talking about years ago. I don't know that I ever came here.' Mary's face had assumed the blank look she wore when she found a conversation tedious.

'She writes about it in her book. There's not much description, though.' As soon as she'd said this, Jazz remembered that, according to her mum, Maggie and Mary hadn't really got on. Unsure if her nan even knew about the existence of Maggie's book, she decided she'd better talk about something else. 'What do you think of my coffee?'

Mary said it wasn't bad at all. 'I'd have one like that with Pat Fitz sometimes, inside in Lissbeg.'

'Shame she wasn't around today, we could have asked her to join us.' Jazz stopped abruptly. 'Doesn't she teach a computer class in the library on Saturday mornings? I thought you'd signed up to that.'

'Ay, well, I went to a few sessions. Then I missed one and, when I came back, they were all going on about Twitter and Facebook and social-media nonsense. I couldn't follow one word in ten.'

'Oh, Nan! You dropped out because you'd missed a single session!'

'No, I didn't.'

At this point, Hanna would have faltered, fearful of upsetting Mary, who was now very pink in the face. But Jazz was made of sterner stuff. 'Yes, you did. You freaked because you couldn't keep up with the others. But there's nothing to it, Nan. Hang on, look at this.' Scrambling to her feet, she went and flipped open her laptop. 'Here, check out my socials.'

'You see, that's the sort of stupid language I can't be doing with.'

'No, wait. Listen. You don't have a Facebook page, so we can just forget that bit. Are they all doing Insta?' Seeing the look on

Mary's face, Jazz giggled. 'Okay, forget Insta. Just let me show you how Twitter works, I bet you'll really love it.'

'No, I won't. And if you haven't the manners to carry me over a bite to eat with this coffee, I suppose I'll have to stand up and fetch my own.' Laughing, Jazz came and joined her, carrying the cakes on a plate. 'Stop it, Nan. Let me show you Twitter. It's practically made for you.' She hunkered down beside Mary and gave her an affectionate hug. 'Basically, it's just loads of people having a bit of a gossip and being judgemental. Plenty of kittens in bonnets too, so lots for you to dislike.'

Chapter Eighteen

When Mary got home she went to her bedroom and took off her navy blue suit. Smoothing it onto a quilted satin hanger, she covered it with a dry-cleaner's polythene bag. With the suit safely hanging in the wardrobe, she removed her blouse and folded it into the laundry basket before unclasping what she always referred to as her 'single-strand freshwater pearls'. The necklace had been a birthday present from Tom. Returning it to its velvet nest in her jewellery box, Mary put on an everyday dress to which she transferred the little love knot she'd worn on the suit's lapel. Then, having tidied her hair at the mirror, she went into the kitchen and enveloped herself in an apron before making an egg mayo sandwich.

Generally, she liked to eat lunch promptly at one o'clock, but she and Jazz had ended up surfing the internet for hours. From the outset, Mary had announced that she wanted no messing about with her phone. 'You're not downloading or uploading any apps to that, I'm telling you straight. I make phone calls with it, I send texts, and that's my lot.'

'But there's all sorts of apps preloaded here, Nan. You just have to click on them.'

'If there is, it's only because the young fella in the shop told me he couldn't delete them. I said I didn't want them and he spouted out all sorts of rubbish about how they came with the contract.'

'Well, yes …'

'So I told him straight that if he left them there I wouldn't go next, nigh nor near them. And I won't.'

Jazz had placed her laptop on the table. 'Okay, let's stick with this. Come on over and look.'

Now, shelling a hardboiled egg with great efficiency, Mary marvelled at the willingness with which she'd gone and sat beside Jazz. When anyone else gave her instructions her instinct was to resist them, but Jazz's good-humoured hectoring never bothered her. This was odd, she thought, given that Jazz was the spitting image of the pup of a husband Hanna had gone and married. Mary disliked Malcolm Turner heartily and felt that, if everyone had their rights, Jazz should have taken after the Caseys, not the pup. But no. Tom's skin had been fair as translucent porcelain, and Mary, born a brunette, still retained a pink and white complexion. Jazz had sallow Turner skin, a feminine version of her dad's handsome features, and jet-black hair, which, unlike the Caseys', wouldn't curl even on the dampest day. At times, her resemblance to Malcolm was uncanny yet, while the thought of him still made Mary furious, she couldn't think of Jazz without a smile.

Placing two slices of bread on the breadboard, she spread them with mayonnaise and began to assemble her egg sandwich, adding sprigs of watercress and a sprinkling of grated cheese. She was hungry for something more substantial than she'd had over coffee with Jazz. After half an hour of the intricacies of Twitter, they'd paused for rum babas and returned to the table to scroll through Instagram photos on Jazz's phone. A selfie of Jazz and Hanna had led them to Facebook, at which point Mary had sniffed. 'Pat Fitz is forever sticking up photos for her family in Toronto. I tell her they'll have no interest but she won't listen.'

'That's daft. I bet they love them.'

'Ah, who wants to see the geraniums in the old horse trough in Broad Street?'

'Someone who grew up in Finfarran and went away? They might feel nostalgic.'

'There's far too much thinking about the past going on these days.'

'Well, I think sharing family stuff is lovely. Oh, wait, look at this.' Jazz had swiped back to Instagram and found another photo of herself and Hanna, perched on the edge of the horse trough with the scarlet geraniums blooming in the background. 'Doesn't Mum look great?'

Mary had affected a lack of interest but now, as she reached for the breadknife, she thought that, in fairness, Hanna had looked all right. You could see when they sat next to each other that she and Jazz were clearly mother and daughter. Perhaps this was because, instead of the artful, mobile curves that surmounted her dad's melting eyes, Jazz had inherited Hanna's straight, uncompromising eyebrows, which, thought Mary, with a pang of loss, were just like Tom's. And in more than just appearance, Hanna and Tom had been two of a kind. They shared a love of books and an instinct to avoid conflict and, in the face of this affinity, Mary had often felt patronised and left out. She adored Tom and resented any claims on his time but her own but, at the back of her mind, she'd felt that to be jealous of her own daughter was ridiculous so, up to now, she'd avoided thinking too hard about her relationship with Hanna. But the fact is, she told herself, that I always saw her as an interloper. Someone who stole Tom from me, the way his aunt Maggie did. Someone he talked to about things he never discussed with me.

With her sandwich cut into four perfect triangles, Mary removed her apron and took her plate to the kitchen table, her mind still grappling with the past. She'd always wondered if Hanna had realised why she'd been packed off to Maggie's, and if she'd known her mother was trying to kill several birds with one stone. It had seemed to Mary to be a foolproof plan. With Hanna round at Maggie's place, no one could say that the Caseys had failed to care for an elderly relative, but Tom's time would be spent at home, focused, as was proper in Mary's view, on his wife, not his daughter. Inevitably, when she'd talked to Tom, his first thought had been for Hanna. 'I'm not sure a child would want to be cooped up with a grumpy old lady. Maybe we could pay someone to drop in to Maggie now and again?' He'd backed down when Mary had replied that, if Hanna wasn't happy, she could stand up and speak her own mind. Later, she'd wished she hadn't said that, because of the look Tom gave her, and because she'd suspected that he and Hanna would discuss her behind her back. Though, knowing them both, it was more likely that they wouldn't, because nothing that passed between them ever seemed to be said aloud. Which, as far as she could tell, was exactly what had happened. Hanna had taken over day-to-day responsibility for Maggie, Tom had spent more time at home, yet their unspoken bond had seemed stronger than ever.

And that, Mary told herself crossly, biting her egg sandwich, had meant that her plan, although it had proved practical, had only increased her sense of being left out. The memory annoyed her. Before Tom died, she thought, I'd never have sat around brooding on things like this. Maybe it's because, when he was here, he was always looking after me and coming up with ways to keep me happy. And why wouldn't he? Wasn't that what he promised to do when we were wed? She knew people thought that Tom had spoiled her and, perhaps, she told herself grudgingly, he had. But she also knew that he'd needed her, and that the day she'd agreed to marry him had been the happiest day of his life. That was the last thing he'd said to her in the cubicle in the hospital and no one, alive or dead, could take that away.

Having started to brood, she found she couldn't stop. The morning spent in Maggie's house with Jazz had been disturbing. Mary had been inside it only once before, soon after she was married, when Tom had apparently thought that his wife and his aunt would become great friends. Possibly he'd known better and was indulging in wishful thinking. One way or the other, that visit had not gone well. The earthy smell of the house had alarmed Mary, who'd dressed to impress and was unable to contain a shudder when a hen was shooed off a chair so she could sit down. Fearful for her polished, two-tone shoes, she'd surreptitiously hitched her high heels over the wooden chair-rail and caught a malicious gleam in Maggie's eye, as if the old lady could see right through her. Behind Maggie's offhand manner, Mary had recognised a will as indomitable as her own. It wasn't a situation conducive to polite conversation and, though seldom at a loss for words, Mary couldn't think what to say. Maggie had sat in a broken-bottomed chair with her bare feet in unlaced shoes planted on the earth floor, as Tom had chatted easily, sweeping the hearth, making up the fire and boiling the kettle. They'd drunk strong tea from blue-banded mugs, and the taste of turf smoke in the milk had made Mary want to gag. Today, as she'd sipped coffee with Jazz, the fact that the house still retained Maggie's hearth had seemed almost uncanny. She'd been glad when they'd moved to the table to look at the laptop and Jazz's phone, though that, too, had felt strange and out of place. It was as if the present and the past were overlaid on one another as her eyes constantly strained to make sense of complex shapes.

The scrolling images on Jazz's screens had added to her confusion. Twitter, it appeared, consisted of people talking about hundreds of different subjects all at once. Fingers racing, Jazz had dipped in and out of dozens of conversations, none of which appeared to have any conclusion. Occasionally, she'd added a comment or retweeted, which was another term Mary found irritating. 'Why can't you speak plain English like anybody else?'

'Oh, come on, Nan, it's not complicated. A tweet is a statement, an image, or a reply. A retweet is when you repeat it, so that it spreads.'

'And you've just spread a picture of a cow wearing a rugby shirt.'

'Well, you have to admit it looked good on her. Anyway, there's no harm in it. That's an account that just puts up cute stuff, for entertainment. The ones to ignore are the nerds and trolls and the people who go in for shouty capitals.'

'Shouty capitals', Jazz had explained, were tweets that were typed in all capital letters. 'Basically, it means you're shouting to try to drown other people out.' There'd been a pregnant pause after the explanation, followed by a moment when Jazz had caught Mary's eye. 'Or it could be when somebody hasn't *quite* grasped how to use her keyboard.'

'We're talking about my texts now, aren't we? I've told Hanna I can't be doing with the size of things on that screen, not with my arthritis.'

To do Jazz justice, she hadn't laughed out loud. 'Don't worry, Nan. You're not tweeting to the world at large, you're sending texts to your family. And, anyway, it doesn't matter because—'

'What?'

'We're kind of used to you being shouty.'

Giggling, Jazz had gone to make more coffee and, with her eyes on a spider spinning a web at the corner of Maggie's window, Mary had heard her own voice echoing round the walls of Hanna's library. There hadn't been many people there when she'd gone in with her rejected library book. Hanna was at her desk doing something official. Owen was at the far end of the room. Through the glass wall behind Hanna's head, Mary could see a group of tourists being shown round the psalter exhibition. To begin with, all she'd intended to do was to hand back the book and perhaps borrow something else. But, as she'd put it on the desk, she'd remembered that Hanna had said one critic had called it 'perfect bedtime reading'. Suddenly, all the anger she'd felt as she'd lain in bed the previous night had consumed her. It was as if the critic, and Hanna, and the whole world had combined to make her look stupid. Giving her a book with a daft title, about nothing but bread! Was that how the lot of them rated her intelligence?

Did they honestly think she'd want the likes of that for bedtime reading? Had they no notion of how hard it was to sleep in a bed by yourself when your husband of more than fifty years was gone? And the look that had been on Hanna's face when she'd gone and picked it out for her! 'Here's something you should enjoy, Mam.' Just because somebody baked decent bread didn't mean that bread was the only thing they were interested in. Just because she'd kept a village shop didn't mean that she couldn't even read a proper book!

It had taken a moment to realise she was shouting and, as the rage built up inside her, she'd discovered she couldn't stop. Hanna's face was white and her mouth was half open. A woman holding a newspaper was looking at her in alarm and, from the other end of the room, Owen was coming towards her quickly. Before he reached the desk, Mary had clenched her fists and mastered herself and, setting down the book, had said in a voice she was glad to hear sounding normal that, as Jazz had gone to the deli and would be waiting for her outside, she wouldn't wait to select another title. Then, inclining her head to Owen, she'd turned and walked out briskly, leaving Hanna looking shell-shocked. Part of Mary's mind had pitied her, but by the time she'd crossed the library courtyard, she'd felt it had served her right. Anyway, she thought, pushing away her half-eaten sandwich, there's no point in dwelling on what happened. I wasn't to blame. Why wouldn't I hold my ground and defend myself? Jazz never drives me to do things that make me feel bad when I've done them, so it stands to reason that it was all Hanna's fault.

Chapter Nineteen

It was a balmy day with a stiff wind and a hint of autumn in the air. On the pier at Couneen, Dan was whistling as he worked on his boat. There wasn't much that could go wrong with an engine that he couldn't fix and, with a bit of ingenuity and lateral thinking, he reckoned he should have the *Shearwater* back at sea in no time. Or, at least, before he risked losing the only booking he'd had for several weeks. He was cleaning his hands on a rag before pausing to smoke a cigarette when he saw Fury and The Divil descending the slipway. When they reached him, Dan was sitting on a fish box with his back against the stone wall. Extending a foot, he pushed another box in Fury's direction. 'How's the Australian's palace coming along?'

'Oh, no expense spared. Though, fair dos, he pays the bills as they come.' Fury set the plastic fish box on end and lowered himself onto it gingerly, reaching behind his ear for a half-smoked roll-up. The Divil observed a pile of nets by a bollard and went and turned himself round several times before curling up in the middle of them.

Fury bent forward to take a light from Dan. 'You shouldn't be smoking them coffin nails, you do know that?'

'Talk about the pot calling the kettle black.'

'If these yokes haven't killed me yet, I'm ready to take my chances. But at your age, boy, you ought to have more sense. When did you start?'

'I'd say my granddad had me smoking butts when I was a kid.'

'I suppose he was pouring rum down you as well?'

'He wasn't Captain Haddock, you know.'

'Captain Haddock smokes a pipe.'

'I mean my granddad wasn't a comedy pirate.'

'Not an Hergé reference at all, then.' Dan looked blank and Fury nodded at The Divil. 'Ah, for God's sake, even yer man there has read *Tintin*. Well, I say read, I mean he likes the pictures. Which, of course, is what makes the graphic novel universal. Come here to me, Dan, here's a fact for you. Did you know that, in the French version of the *Tintin* stories, Snowy the dog is called Milou?'

'I don't even know what you're talking about.'

'Well, that's clear if you didn't even know that Captain Haddock's a character created by the late great Belgian cartoonist Hergé. Now there was an artist, if you like. Couldn't beat him with a stick.' Through a haze of tobacco smoke, Fury transferred his attention to the engine. 'Is she kicking?'

'Like a mule. I have her nearly right now, though.'

'You won't need a part?'

'Touch wood.'

'You can give me a shout if you end up finding you need one. I've a fella in Cork.'

'Jesus, Fury, don't put the evil eye on her. Parts cost money.'

'You could do me a bit of labouring and pay it off that way.' Seeing Dan's expression, Fury chuckled. 'There's nothing wrong with honest work. Did your granddad never say that to you?'

Dan grinned. 'Plenty of times. That isn't the point, though.'

They sat in silence for a few minutes. Casually balanced on the upturned box with the roll-up dangling from his lip, Fury looked the picture of relaxation, but his penetrating gaze was making Dan feel uneasy. As if to shield himself, Dan exhaled his own cloud of smoke. He felt that he couldn't explain without sounding arrogant. 'I know I did bits for you in the past, but ...' Unable to find words to finish his sentence, Dan shrugged.

Fury chuckled again. 'Maybe it's different when you're a big businessman.'

'Oh, give me a break. You know that's not what I think.'

Uncharacteristically, Fury stopped teasing him. 'All right, fair enough, I do. No one can say that you're not a hard worker, and there's nothing wrong with wanting to make a go of things here in Couneen.'

The note of sympathy in Fury's voice made Dan drop his guard. 'Yeah, but what's the likelihood? That's the question.

The odds are stacked against me, aren't they?' The memory of a misunderstanding several weeks before still made Dan sweat whenever he thought of it. He'd been on his way to the café and bumped into Mark Browne, Lissbeg's bank manager, who'd asked casually how his business was going. Dan had replied with a laugh, 'I don't suppose you'd like to give me the cost of fixing my boat?' At that stage, he'd thought they were just engaged in ordinary badinage but, to his amazement, Mark had invited him in to discuss a loan. The day had passed in a whirl and, overcome with relief and excitement, he'd over-egged the story when he'd gone home to Bríd. Then, annoyed when she told him he shouldn't count his chickens, he'd heard himself saying it was a done deal. 'Mark Browne knows a good thing when he sees it. He'll set me up and, I'm telling you, Bríd, there'll be no holding me then.' Far worse than the agony of embarrassment in Mark's office had been the horror of having to reveal the outcome of the meeting.

Bríd's face had taken on a look of controlled resignation. 'It doesn't matter.'

'They're all the same, aren't they? The bloody powers-that-be. They grind you down.'

'Honestly, Dan, it doesn't matter.'

'Telling you one thing and then changing their mind.' He hadn't been sure who he hated more that evening, himself for having got carried away or Bríd for not calling out his lie. Of course the bank would never have loaned him a penny without collateral. How could he have imagined such a thing? And of course Bríd wouldn't hit him when he was down. But, God, he thought, it would've been so much better if she'd turned on me. The look on her face, and the way she'd reacted when Conor mentioned a bank loan at the dinner party, had made him feel that she saw him as a pathetic problem child.

Stubbing out his cigarette, he looked Fury in the face. 'Do you believe I can make a go of things here?'

'Would it make any difference if I told you I didn't?'

'Probably not. My mum and dad never give up, do they? They keep bashing on.'

'They're twice your age, son. You've got your whole life ahead of you.'

'My granddad wouldn't have given up. He kept working out of this pier when every other fisherman in Couneen had fecked off to America.'

'There's a lot to be said for sticking to your guns.' Pinching out his roll-up, Fury replaced the stub behind his ear. 'On the other hand, there's something to be said for knowing when to quit.'

'Yeah, well, I'm not a quitter.'

'That's plain to see.' Fury shifted his weight on the box and, immediately, The Divil raised his head from his nest of nets. Squinting down at the little dog thoughtfully, Fury banged his hand on his knee. 'Holy God, I've just had a light-bulb moment.'

'A what?'

'You know, like in a cartoon when they draw a light-bulb over a character's head.'

'Are we back to *Tintin*?'

'Yes, we are. Exactly that. It didn't strike me before, but I'd say it must be the answer.'

'Okay, just so you know, we're also back to me not having a clue what you're on about.'

'Your man The Divil has been acting strange lately. It's something that's been weighing on my mind. I was telling Conor the other day at the timber yard. You see, normally that dog can't abide a baby. Turns his back when he sees one, can't be doing with them at all. But Conor and Aideen's little fella, Ronan? Totally different. Your man sees him and, straight away, it's like he's been hypnotised.'

'Honestly, Fury, you've lost me.'

'No, wait now, hold your horses and try this for a theory. The baby's there strapped to Conor's chest in a blue sling. Handy for taking your son round to the timber yard, says you.'

'No, I don't.'

'Stick with me. There he is and The Divil looking up at him. What does he have on his head?'

'The Divil?'

'The baby. I said stick with me. *A white fluffy hat with two cocked ears, black buttons for eyes and a round black nose.* That's what he has on his head. And what does he look like?'

The Divil was now on his feet wagging his tail furiously. Dan sighed. 'I don't know what the baby looks like, but I know you're going to tell me, so could you get on with it? Some of us have honest work to do.'

Triumphantly, Fury spread his hands. '*The baby looks like Snowy!* Milou. Tintin's sidekick. And aren't them books The Divil's first pick? Show him any graphic novels you like, and *Tintin's* the one he'll go for. And for why? Because he identifies with Snowy, also known as Milou.'

Dan looked sceptical. 'Really?'

'Absolutely. Readers respond to books in which there's a central character they can identify with.'

'And you're saying you think that The Divil reads books?'

'Holy God Almighty, are you out of your mind or what? He's a dog, he can't read. Get a grip, man. I told you. He looks at the pictures. And pictures have a narrative force that transcends the written word.'

'Do they?'

'Well, of course they do. Graphic novels were inspired by the medieval woodcut tradition.' Pushing himself off the fish box, Fury shook his head. 'Everyone knows that. It's common knowledge. The trouble with the likes of you, Dan, is that you don't understand the genre.'

While it was easy to find summer staff in a tourist town as charming as Lissbeg, the students who turned up looking for a job tended to call in sick in kite-surfing weather and, today, Bríd had taken a familiar and wholly unconvincing call. She'd phoned Aideen immediately afterwards. 'Karen's pulled a sickie.'

'Oh, for God's sake! Or is there actually something wrong with her?'

'She sounded like a dying duck, but I'd say she's down at the beach. Will you be okay on your own in the deli if I'm at the café with Pavel? Dan's in Couneen.'

'No problem.'

So, while Bríd worked in the Garden Café, Aideen had coped alone with HabberDashery's midday rush. It had been no worse than in the early days when each had often held the fort while the other was at the cash-and-carry but, being out of the swing of it, Aideen was glad of a breather when lunchtime was over. People rushing to grab something to eat at their desks could often be demanding, and she'd been serving for two hours non-stop. When the last of the office workers was gone, she cleared away the things she hadn't had time to deal with sooner, and poured herself a well-earned coffee. For the next ten minutes she was undisturbed, except for a man who wanted some bread and a salad box, so she took the opportunity to give Una a call. 'How's Ronan?'

'Mighty. We had a bit of a wobbly when he wanted the cats to take a nap with him, but he's fine.'

'Did Conor get time for lunch?'

'No, but I've made a steak pie for dinner. He can gorge himself then.'

'Do you want me to bring anything home? I might have some smoked salmon going begging.'

'Perfect. We could have it as a starter.'

'Right, I'll bring it along if it's not sold by the time we close.'

Though there was an established rule that any food taken home must be accounted for, exceptions were made for stock that would otherwise have to be thrown out. In the early days, when the girls had hardly made enough to pay themselves wages, dinner in St Finian's Close had often consisted of unsold coleslaw, eaten with heels of cheese and the crusty ends of French bread. Things were better now but, even so, they remained meticulous about paying for saleable stock. The surplus of Cafferkys' smoked salmon had caught Aideen's eye when she was checking on sell-by dates in the fridge. Now, as the door opened and Bríd came in, she decided to mention it. Two unopened packages would have to be disposed of, which put the fish in a different class from the bits and pieces that would normally be left over at closing time.

Putting her bag behind the counter, Bríd asked how lunchtime had gone.

'I never stopped serving. How were things at the café?'

'Crowded. I reckon Dan and Pavel are becoming a team. They've got a system in place that's moving the queue much faster.' Bríd paused and flushed awkwardly. The girls hadn't had a chance to talk face to face since the dinner party, and Dan's name had conjured up the difficult conversation about the boat. 'Listen, I'm sorry about the other night.'

'God, no, why would you be? It was a lovely meal.'

'I don't mean the meal, I mean Dan behaving like an utter plank.'

'He didn't, really.'

'Look, shut up, will you, and let me apologise. You know what Dan's like and, anyway, he'd been drinking, but he shouldn't have gone for Conor like that.'

'Conor was pretty pissed himself. Well, actually, he was exhausted.' Aideen, who'd spent the drive home from the dinner party worrying, rushed on: 'He wasn't exactly sensitive, but he didn't mean any harm.'

Bríd went behind the counter and poured herself a coffee. 'Why should he need to be sensitive? If I go tiptoeing round on eggshells, that's my choice. But when Dan decides to get all neurotic, it shouldn't be your problem. And you were our guests.' She stopped, took a breath, and looked squarely at Aideen. 'Look, that's another thing I've been meaning to talk about. We've never discussed the fact that he should really be paying you rent.'

Dan's moving into St Finian's Close had happened by degrees. At first, when the girls had been sharing, he'd simply slept over on nights when he and Bríd had been out on a date. Conor had done the same back then and though, nominally, the lads still lived with their respective parents, it had almost felt like a four-way house share. Then, when Conor and Aideen married, and she was focused on her pregnancy, Dan had become a fixture. Now she shook her head. 'No, why should Dan pay rent? I mean he sleeps in your bedroom. It's not like he's taking up a room that I – well, that we could let out.'

'You've said it just now, though, haven't you? It's your house, not mine.'

'It's part of the business.'

'Yeah, but Dan complicates things.'

It hadn't occurred to either of them to set up a formal partnership. Though Aideen's inheritance had provided the start-up funding, without Bríd's know-how they couldn't have opened the deli. Anyway, they were family, and everything had been done on a wing and a prayer. The spare rooms at St Finian's Close had become storerooms and office space, so the thought that the house might have rental value simply hadn't arisen. Bríd was looking at Aideen over the rim of her coffee mug. 'I'm right, aren't I? He does complicate things.'

'But he's practically family.'

'Except that he isn't. You and I are and, now that you're married, so's Conor. But Dan's just someone I happen to sleep with.'

'No, he isn't!'

'Okay, someone I'm in love with, who now sleeps in St Finian's Close, treats it as his home and hosts dinner parties there. Really, really badly, I might add.'

'You guys had a row after Conor and I were gone, didn't you?'

Bríd leaned against the counter. 'Yes, we did. Which was daft, given how drunk Dan was.'

'Oh, Bríd. What did you say?'

'This and that. I may have mentioned non-payment of rent.'

'But I never said I wanted it!'

'I know, and it's fine, he knows that. We patched things up the next day, so you don't have to worry.'

'Conor shouldn't have said that about the boat.'

'No, Aideen, that's bollocks. Conor wasn't prying. He cares. It was a perfectly fair question and, anyway, Dan didn't have to come out with that low crack about you having rich relations.'

Aideen sighed. 'To be honest, it was a bit close to the bone. Conor's desperate to pay old Dawson back. He hates owing money, and the fact that Joe set the loan up for him makes it even worse.'

'Christ, we've really got ourselves a pair of neurotic males!' Bríd frowned. 'No, I'm only joking. Conor's nothing like Dan. Was he very upset?'

'Don't worry, I'd say he was far too tired to take it in. And, listen, you've got to forget all this about Dan paying rent. He's not family, but he's kind of part of the business. He's doing great things at the café and he's not even on the payroll.'

'Yes, and that's something else that isn't on a proper professional footing. Okay, you could call it helping out, but you might call it muscling in.'

'Oh, God, you didn't say that to Dan?'

'No. It's true, though. Like the way he moved into St Finian's Close, it just happened. Bit by bit.'

Aideen took her mug behind the counter to rinse it out. 'You're not thinking you want to break up with him?'

Bríd laughed unsteadily. 'Of course not. I'm smitten, you know that.'

'Okay, so look at it this way. You could end up married. That would make him one of the family.'

'I don't think Dan and I are the marrying kind.'

'So what do you think will happen?'

'I don't know but, whatever it is, I don't want us messing things up for you and Conor.'

'You won't. And if I think you are, I promise to say so. Okay?'

Coming to join her at the sink, Bríd gave her a one-arm hug. 'Okay, partner. Onwards and upwards, then?'

'Yep.'

Aideen watched Bríd wash her mug and put it in the drainer. It no longer seemed an appropriate time to mention the sell-by date on the Cafferkys' salmon. She couldn't remember how they'd come to stock it and, looking back, she suspected that no decision had been taken. Yet, somehow, an order had gone in and, on the very reasonable grounds that it was a practical arrangement, Dan had offered to deliver the salmon from Couneen to Lissbeg. And here we are, thought Aideen, overstocked and not selling. Sooner or later, this would have to be talked about, but now, having heard that unsteady laugh, and seen Bríd look so worried, she hadn't the heart to broach a subject that might make matters worse.

Chapter Twenty

Hanna was propped up by pillows in bed with Maggie's book against her up-drawn knees. Next to her, on a bedside table, a shaded lamp cast a pool of light on the page.

Liverpool, December 1921

I've had no word from Lizzie. This isn't a bad place to work. Mrs Carr has a sharp tongue in her head but she pays what she owes you. My room's no bigger than a prison cell but it's warm because it's right beside the kitchen, and the eating isn't bad. I get the same food that the lodgers get, and they have to pay through the nose for it. You'd have sausages and rashers and eggs for your breakfast, though she calls the rashers bacon. The tea's weak and the milk is skim but she cuts the bread thick. The work's not the worst either, though your back would be bad with the stairs. Scrubbing and cleaning's no bother to me, the trouble is that there's nobody here to talk to. There's a rule that I'm not to go standing around joking with the lodgers and Mrs Carr wouldn't demean herself to be chatting with a skivvy. I'll stick it out though for the time being, for fear I'd find nothing better.

All the time I do be thinking of home. I missed the cows when they were gone. I didn't know what else to do only ask Paud D to sell them. I couldn't leave Mam alone long enough for me to go up to milk them. I couldn't tell what would happen to us and Mam wouldn't stop crying.

The neighbours buried Dad and Hannie the day after Dad was shot. I wanted to go to the funeral but Mam got worse when the coffins were being carried out of the house. She screamed till I took off my coat and said I'd stay home with her. I was afraid Liam would go to the burial ground, but he didn't. Mrs Donovan said the word was that he was back in the mountains. I prayed he'd stay there.

I think Mam had always accepted that Liam might be killed. Two lads that joined the Volunteers with him died in an ambush in April, and the Tans pulled another behind a lorry for miles before they shot him. Liam is Mam's only son but if the news that he was killed had come I think she could have taken it. He was ready to die for Ireland and she'd have said it was God's will. What she never expected was that Hannie and Dad would go first. Afterwards she kept saying that Liam would never have come home that night if he hadn't heard she was sick. It was only a cough that was troubling her but someone had told Liam that she was bad. They'd been up in the hills beyond in Cork for ages so he couldn't have come home then, even if he'd wanted to, but in April the lads got ordered back to Finfarran and that brought him closer to us.

His crowd had only been back in Finfarran a day when he turned up. He was dead tired when he came in the door and we'd only chatted a small while when he went down to the room to sleep. Mam made tea and boiled eggs. He hadn't a pick of fat on him. He hadn't seen Hannie for more than a year and he couldn't get over how big she'd got. He had barley sugar in his pocket for her twelfth birthday and she said he'd missed Christmas and my birthday too, so where were the presents for them? Mam said that just seeing him was a tonic.

He was in good spirits that night and he said he had a good commandant, so he reckoned if the lads had enough bullets they could hold out for months. He said the English were running scared and they'd soon want a treaty. He was right too. A treaty's been signed. But it's come too late for Hannie and Dad and me and Mam and the cows.

In the sleek, modern room, the book's homemade appearance was incongruous. Hanna sat staring at the black expanse of the window. Out there, although double glazing muted their cries of pain and triumph, she knew that creatures were moving through the glen. Twisting through heather and lurking by rocks, furred shapes with pricked ears were in pursuit of prey and, in the distant forest, trees were stirring and murmuring in the salt wind. There was a full moon and Hanna was aware of reflected light from the shimmering silver ocean beyond her view. Beside her, Brian moved, and spoke without opening his eyes. 'You're not asleep.'

'No, sorry, I'm reading. Did I wake you?'

'Are you okay?'

'Fine. I woke and couldn't settle. I thought if I browsed through Maggie's book I might fall back to sleep. Not my brightest ever idea, though.' Hanna's eyes pricked with tears. 'I wish I'd been able to talk to her about what she went through, Brian. I know that's daft because, even if I'd been old enough, she wasn't the confiding sort.' Brian, who had an early meeting scheduled for the next morning, moved to avoid the spill of light from the bedside lamp. His voice was blurred with sleep. 'You said that she'd had an affair?'

'Yes. She was seventeen when she went away because of it.' Hanna turned the pages. 'I think she found work in various places. This was Liverpool.

'The first day I was here Mrs Carr had a laugh at me. I was down on my knees in the hall doing the bottom step. What I should have done was start at the top and work my way down, and I'd have seen my mistake soon enough when I came to kneel on the wet step I'd just scrubbed. But your one went past when I'd only begun and she stopped and called me a fool. What kind of a place had I come out of, she said, that I didn't know how to do stairs? I was hard put not to tell her I'd come out of a house far cleaner than hers is. But I didn't want her throwing me out so I shut my beak and took the

pail and went up to the first landing. I hate her stairs. They've got ugly red and black oilcloth on them and you have to scrub it down with yellow soap.'

Hanna looked across at Brian. 'Are you asleep?'

'No, go on.'

'I wasn't thinking that day because my mind was on the mountain. I was thinking of the day James drove over in the cart and offered to help with the turf. It was a long drive for him, and Mam said he was very good. She was still in no state to be working on the bog herself, so I'd been up and down on my own all that week with the jennet. It'd be easier driving in the cart, James said, and two of us cutting and footing would do the work quicker. He has great strength in his arms. He works in his dad's forge. His dad was able to spare him, he said, because we were neighbours in trouble. Now the neighbours will have to draw home the turf he and I cut for Mam.

'We went up the first time with the sun on our backs and the high sky shining. We had a bottle of tea along with us, and a cake of bread I'd made the night before. When we'd a few hours' work behind us we stopped for a drink of the tea, and for James to smoke a gasper. I sat back against the cart with the sun on my face. There was bog cotton moving in the wind all around, and white butterflies dancing. If you look at them close you can see they've got pale green veins. We didn't talk much that day because I didn't know him.

I'd only seen him a few times going to Mass. I don't know is there a church here near Mrs Carr's house. I wouldn't go in if there was because the sight of a priest would sicken me but a church always smells nice inside.

'I've got this book here on my knee and I sitting on the bed. If I was at home, there might still be light on the mountain but in England it gets dark sooner and the houses are taller and crowded so it's hard to see the sky. There's great colour and light here in all the shop windows, only I'm afraid to go walking the streets. There's always fellows wanting you to go down the alleyways with them.

'The priest crept up on us when me and James were together in the forest. I'd say he'd been peeping and prying round us for weeks. We'd gone to a place where James and his wife used to go before they were married. I knew well myself what I was doing. James said his wife hadn't been out much lately because of the baby. And I said to myself when I heard that, What matter? What she didn't know couldn't hurt her. And by then James was saying it would kill him if he couldn't see me. That's what a man will always say so I didn't take much notice. I knew it would kill me, though, to be sitting all day in the house seeing Mam.'

Hanna's voice faltered. Brian, who'd been drifting off to sleep, pushed himself upright and registered interest. She looked at him ruefully. 'Darling, I'm sorry, it's the middle of the night.'

'No, it's not. There's light in the sky, see? I'll have to get up soon, anyway.'

'That is so not true.'

'Hanna, I'm way too sleepy to be reassuring. Keep going. You need to. Finish the story and maybe we'll both get some sleep.'

'The priest turned on me when James was gone and I didn't know what he'd say to me. My mind went off sideways. I wondered if James came offering help when we buried Dad and Hannie because he'd had his eye on me and was just waiting for his chance. Then I thought that, whatever else happened, Mam had the turf cut anyway. And then the priest told me he'd give me a choice. I could get on a boat and go away off to England or he'd preach against me from the pulpit and shame me before the world. He stood there with the birds singing all around him and asked me how could I let that happen to Mam? She'd lost all she had and Liam mightn't live to come back to her. How could I do it, he said, and he spitting the words at me. How could I rob my mother of her good name?'

'Shit.' Brian kicked back the duvet and sat on the edge of the bed rubbing sleep out of his eyes. 'That's foul. And this fellow James just walked away?'

'Seemingly. She doesn't write about him again.'

'I see what you mean when you say it feels private.'

'Yes, but when does private pain become history? It's more than just one exploited teenager's story, it's an insight into the norms of the time.'

'Except that you couldn't call that period normal. Liam was out fighting for independence. A completely new order with reimagined norms.'

'You think so?'

'Well, I guess so. It was something he and his comrades were ready to die for, so the aspirations must have been pretty huge.'

'Okay, so it's an insight into life on the cusp of change. Or the starting point of an analysis of how nothing changed really. You could argue that things got worse, not better, for Irish women after independence.'

Brian yawned and gave her an apologetic smile. 'You could but, you know what, darling, I really don't want to. Not right now. I've a huge day's work ahead of me and, now I'm awake, I probably ought to go and prepare for this meeting.'

'No, don't. Go back to sleep.' Knowing how unrealistic that instruction was, Hanna groaned. 'I'm sorry, really I am. I don't suppose it would help if I made tea?'

'Not even slightly. There's no point in us both wandering about in the pale dawn. Why don't you get some sleep yourself if you're able?' That suggestion was equally unrealistic, but Hanna waited till he'd gone downstairs wearing his towelling bathrobe before she got out of bed and wrapped herself in her kimono. Leaving the book behind her on the duvet, she crossed the room, drawn by the grey light filling the sky. She had said nothing to Brian or Jazz about Mary's meltdown in the library but, on waking and reaching for Maggie's book, she'd known it was concern for her mother that had disturbed her sleep. The sudden bizarre rage had been over in less than a minute, leaving her half wondering if she'd imagined it. From the corner of her eye she'd seen a couple of the library's browsers exchanging amused glances, and by the time Owen had reached the desk Mary had assumed an air of dignified calm. By day, Hanna had managed to tell herself that the rant had hardly been more than a slight increase in Mary's customary aggression, but now, after a troubled night, her mind was racing again.

I didn't imagine it, she thought. It feels as if she's sort of coming unstuck. With her forehead against the cool windowpane, she attempted to marshal her thoughts. Logically, it might be sensible to suggest a visit to the doctor but the likelihood was that, if she did so, Mary would take offence. Besides, people inevitably grew tetchy as they got older and, since outrage could almost be described as Mary's default setting, perhaps this was just how things would be from now on. But that's not what I'm scared of, thought Hanna. I'm afraid things will get worse. That there'll come a time when she won't be able to cope alone in the bungalow and I'll have to face living with her again.

Far in the distance, wreaths of mist were gathering over the forest, stained pale pink by the rising sun. A hundred years ago, thought Hanna, Maggie and James were down there when the priest crept up on them, tracking them through the undergrowth, like a fox. Did my dad know Maggie's story? If he did, would he have felt ashamed of her? Would he have felt it shamed him too?

It seemed impossible that Tom, so gentle and so concerned about Maggie, would think that what had happened to her could have robbed the Casey family of its good name. And it hardly seemed likely either, thought Hanna, that Maggie had ever sat down and confided in Mary. Yet it was clear that Mary knew something about why Maggie had gone away. Frowning, Hanna recalled the stilted conversation they'd had in her mother's kitchen, cut off so decisively by Mary's refusal to talk. Could Mary have been upset because her memory was failing and she couldn't recall something she once knew? Or did she know all about Maggie's affair and see it as something the neighbours would call shameful? But surely someone as brash and assertive as Mary wouldn't care what people might say?

Watching the mist disperse and the pink sky darken to crimson, Hanna reminded herself that her parents, born in the 1940s, had grown up in a very different Ireland from her own. And even when I was a child, she thought, the norms I lived with were different from those of Jazz's generation. Which poses a question. What good would it do to use Maggie's story as a talking point to explain that priest-ridden past to Jazz, or Conor, or Aideen, or to any of the young mums or schoolkids who passed though Lissbeg Library? They have their own lives to live, thought Hanna, and all of today's pressures to contend with, and if that particular aspect of history is irrelevant to them, was Mary right to tell me to leave it be?

Chapter Twenty-One

Brian and Hanna's house was so far from any other dwelling that its windows could remain uncurtained and reveal spectacular views of the glen. The site hadn't been chosen because of an obsessive desire for privacy. Brian simply loved the dominance of the landscape, and the challenge of designing a home that would blend into its surroundings. Yet a sense of privacy hadn't been unimportant, because behind that professional challenge lay the fact that the house was a personal labour of love. In order to persuade Hanna to come and live with him, he'd reasoned that the Hag's Glen house must offer all that she'd valued in Maggie's place and more. The back hills might lack the majesty of her windswept clifftop, but the mountains that loomed at the head of the glen had all of the cliffs' drama, and the distant shimmer of the ocean beyond the forest completed the view. Above all, the remote glen offered the sense of freedom he knew she'd prized when she lived in Maggie's house.

He knew now that he'd loved Hanna from the day she'd appeared in his office, frantic because Fury had begun work at Maggie's without seeking planning permission, but the relationship had got off to a rocky start. Having lost a young wife to cancer, Brian hadn't been looking for love, or even companionship, while Hanna, bruised by her divorce, had been stressed out and irritable. Yet they'd shared a dry sense of humour, which had slowly brought them together, and now he couldn't imagine a life without her.

Having given up on getting back to sleep, he was downstairs preparing for his meeting when Hanna appeared, still in her kimono and carrying a tray. 'I know you said tea wouldn't help.'

'Oh, come on, then. Chuck it over.' Brian swivelled his chair away from his desk, which commanded views both up and down the glen. Hanna perched on the windowsill with her teacup in her hand. She had poured his tea into a mug, which was how he preferred it, but her cup was a shallow porcelain bowl with a curved handle, a deep saucer, and a gilded design that echoed the chrysanthemums on her kimono. An eighteenth-century find in a London antiques shop, it had seemed to Hanna appropriate for use on this opalescent Finfarran morning. Brian looked at her affectionately. 'You didn't get back to sleep?'

'No, but I'm fine. Not the worst thing to be up early either. While Tim's focused on his vanity project, there's still day-to-day stuff to contend with. Like Learning Technology.'

'Is it you doing the learning or is Learning Technology a thing?'

'Both. We're supposed to keep up to speed with stuff like online learning resources.' Balancing her cup with one hand, she made air quotes with the other. '"Engaging and satisfying, with quality content and game dynamics that maintain learners' attention." We offer a portal to hundreds of courses, so you've got to have some kind of notion of what's involved.'

'You and game dynamics? Seriously?'

'I said some kind of notion, not in-depth knowledge. Still, it all takes time and Tim doesn't care. He prefers to focus on flashy stuff.'

'Is that how you see this commemorative project?'

'No. I mean that's the extent of Tim's interest in it. It's not just me, Brian. Okay, I've got personal pressure because of the pros and cons of offering up my family story, but each branch librarian in the county is having to think this project through with damn-all leadership. We can't even discuss it sensibly in a meeting because Tim's agendas always come down to how we can big ourselves up.' Brian raised his eyebrows at her and she laughed. 'Sorry, that's a revolting phrase. Proper Tim-speak.' Transferring her fingers from the handle to the bowl of the cup, she felt the warmth of its contents through the eggshell-thin china. 'It's a national commemoration, but the truth is that each display in libraries all over the country will be made up of little individual stories. Thousands of different memories, probably contradictory, all deeply important to the families who retain them and containing dormant seeds of animosity and grief – buried things that could sprout and provoke division in communities. If Tim couldn't even be arsed to deal with basic stuff, like setting up systems for catalogues and permissions, he's certainly not going to engage with the implications of that.'

'All you can do is your best.'

'Oh, Brian!'

'Sorry. I know that's pathetic.'

'No, I'm the one who's been pathetic but, look, I've made a decision.'

'When?'

'Just now, upstairs, when I was watching the sunrise. Right from the start I've been reluctant to put Maggie's book on display. Now I know why. Jazz quoted a line from the council's website to me a while back, about libraries having a function as community living rooms. Well, how can I offer up Maggie's life for public discussion if Mam won't even talk about her at home? I don't think my dad would have wanted me to, not with Mam like she is. If there's going to be discussion, it ought to begin in our own living rooms.'

'Are you going to say that to Mary?'

'I dunno. Maybe I'll just listen to her for once, and leave it be.' She smiled at Brian over her cup. 'Sometimes I wish I got on with her like you do.'

'Oh, she and I just flirt with each other.'

Hanna laughed. 'And you're trying to prepare for a meeting, so I'll shut up.' Turning away, she settled herself on the windowsill and gazed down the glen to where smoke was beginning to curl from a distant farm chimney.

The previous day, Owen had turned up at her desk, looking anxious. 'Well, we've had our first withdrawal.' Briefly, Hanna had been confused and, seeing her reaction, he'd explained. 'A lad from Ballyfin came in a while ago with a letter. Remember? Sent home from prison by a guy who'd been captured during the Civil War?' Hanna remembered that the lad had explained he'd heard chat about the commemorations and asked his mother if he could bring in the letter. Hanna had asked if his whole family was in agreement.

'How d'you mean?'

'Well, you say your mother was happy for you to bring this into the library. But who wrote it?'

'My great-granddad. I think. Or maybe it was an uncle. On my dad's side of the family. Dad and Mum split up, so I'm not sure.'

'Okay. Well, maybe you ought to touch base with your dad about bringing it in.'

The boy, a stocky, cheerful lad about Conor's age, worked in one of the offices in the Old Convent Centre. He'd looked perplexed by Hanna's caution. 'I don't really see Dad much. I suppose I could email.'

'I think you should. We need permission from the people who

actually own each piece of material before we can put anything on display.'

'Okay.' The boy had returned the half-page of notepaper to its envelope, catching its edge on the flap as he pushed it in. 'Do you want to hang onto it then, till I hear from my dad?' Unable to bear the careless way the letter was being handled, Owen had issued an interim receipt and said that they'd keep it, pending further instructions. And yesterday the boy had returned, looking sheepish, and left with the envelope and its contents stuffed into his back pocket. Instead of replying to his son's email, it appeared that the man had phoned his ex-wife in a rage, and the outcome had been a demand for the letter, the existence of which the father had barely remembered, to be sent to him with its envelope forthwith. It was evident that its content, and the context in which it was written, had hardly arisen. Now, remembering what it said, Hanna felt close to tears. It had been sent from a Dublin gaol on the morning of its author's execution. A death notice, cut from a newspaper, which had also been in the envelope, revealed that he had been shot at 7 a.m. on his eighteenth birthday. The few lines were written in a neat, schoolboy hand.

My Dear Mother, you must bear this and be brave because I am going to die for Ireland. I have no bad word to say for my comrades or for the men who will shoot me. You must pray for us all and for all mothers. I am going to a happier place and we will meet again in Heaven. There will be a priest with me and I have asked him to pray for you. God save Ireland and God bless you and my father. I send you my love and you must not fret only think of me tomorrow at seven o'clock. My love to you Mother and I will think of you. Pray to the Sacred Heart for me, whose heart was crowned with thorns. Your loving son, Paul

Usually Hanna wore jeans and a T-shirt for work but today required something more formal. A cruise line selling holidays to the 'Culturally Curious' had offered to pay an enhanced entry fee for the psalter exhibition if their groups' visits could be marketed as Personally Attended by the Librarian. The council, eager for the income, had been unable to resist and agreed that Hanna would turn a new page of the psalter especially for the passengers, who arrived by coach from Ballyfin, where their ship berthed overnight, and travelled on to have tea in a hotel in Carrick. Today's charming mainly middle-aged group was Scandinavian, four women and two men, dressed in expensive casual clothes and wearing sunhats. They gathered in the courtyard, where she greeted them from the library's steps before leading them into the exhibition space and, having given her own version of the guides' standard script, collected them at the glass case and prepared to open the psalter. They crowded round, suitably impressed and speaking in low voices, as she opened the case and inserted a finger under a page, loving, as always, the velvet touch of the vellum. 'Vellum is made from calfskin. It would have been prepared in an alkaline bath, not tanned like leather. This is early medieval and, as you see, in beautiful condition.'

The Culturally Curious made notes on their iPads as she continued: 'By the nineteenth century, chemicals were being used to speed up production. This often weakened the vellum so, paradoxically, later manuscripts are more vulnerable to disintegration. Earlier ones, if they've been safely kept, are more likely to remain in good condition.' Hanna looked down at the newly revealed double-page spread. It was one on which the text of the psalm had been confined to just a few lines, allowing the illustrator to run riot. 'So, these are the four opening verses of what appears in the King James Bible as Psalm Ninety-One. They're written in Latin, but you can access the translation on our wall screens.' As usual, one or two in the group turned away, distracted from what they had come to see by the prospect of scrolling through interactive menus. Hanna raised her voice slightly. 'I'd suggest that you concentrate on the book itself first, and allow yourselves to appreciate the layout. We don't know how these things were designed. They might have been the result of the medieval equivalent of committee meetings, or influenced by the requirements of a patron. You can see, though, that the artist must have been given some freedom of expression.'

A short blonde woman with her hair cut in a fringe asked if the text and the images would have been done by the same person.

'That's another thing we don't know. We can't even be sure if the artwork was done by a man or a woman or, indeed, by several people at different stages. And all sorts of things will have affected each artistic decision. Look at the first verse.' Hanna pointed at the flowing script, translating it from memory. '*He that dwelleth in the secret place of the most High shall abide under the shadow of the Almighty.* Do you see how the word "High" is lifted above the others on the line?'

The women nodded. 'Because the positioning demonstrates the meaning?'

'Well, yes, it does, but it also deals with a practical problem. If you look closely, you can see there's a slightly rough patch just below the word. The function of the alkaline bath when the vellum was being prepared was to remove hair from the calfskin. But if follicles were too embedded they got left behind, leaving patches like that one. And when a scribe came upon one, he or she had to write around it.'

As the group moved in to peer at the verse, Hanna stepped back to make room. Seen from this slight distance, the text and its illustrations melded, producing the effect of a single picture. At the top of the left-hand page, above a capital Q, a hawk hovered with outstretched wings that extended beyond the text into the margins. It was painted in broad strokes of brown ink and its beak and talons were gilded. Within the frame of the capital letter, gorgeously coloured in scarlet and green, a group of figures on horseback, carrying hooded birds on their wrists, was trotting towards a white, pinnacled castle. A fragment of the King James translation echoed in Hanna's mind: *I will say of the Lord, He is my refuge and my fortress.* Further down the page, as if drifting between the verses, other birds of prey appeared, painted so precisely that a falconer could tell which was a goshawk and which a kestrel or a peregrine. On the facing page, groups of armed men were depicted as solid oblongs, like many-headed pantomime horses. Leading the armies were more birds, carrying streaming pennants and round shields in their curved talons. They were tramping up through the text as though climbing a steep mountain and, here and there, responding to imperfections in the vellum, the artist had drawn outcrops of rock, and patches of prickly furze with grotesquely large thorns, like scimitars.

Hanna's eye travelled back up the page to the huge hawk that hovered above the illuminated capital. Beneath its wings, women and children stood with their arms around each other, bound together by garlands. Their heads were thrown back and their flowing robes were made of coloured feathers. One of the tourists had crossed to a wall screen and found the English translation of the psalm. Adjusting her glasses, she read it aloud to the others. '*Verse four. In scapulis suis obumbrabit tibi et sub alis eius sperabis. He shall cover thee with his feathers, and under his wings shalt thou trust: his truth shall be thy shield and buckler.*' Automatically, Hanna's mind capped it with the next verse. *Thou shalt not be afraid for the terror by night; nor for the arrow that flieth by day.*

'And, look!' exclaimed one of the men, pointing at the psalter. 'There are the archers.' A file of figures pranced across the bottom of both pages: foxes, mice, bears, and small birds riding on antlered deer, all with bows slung across their backs and quivers of feathered arrows. The women beneath the hawk's wings were open-mouthed, as if they were singing God's praises or screaming in terror. But the archers were dancing. With their knees raised and their headgear at jaunty angles, they were led by a bear with a huge paunch, who was drinking from a bottle. And at the rear of the file, a couple of mice were pushing a wooden wagon loaded with books and piled with gold coins.

When the tourists had left, with expressions of delight and a flurry of last-minute questions, Hanna returned to her desk. Owen was tidying up after a toddlers' show-and-tell session, sponging the covers of picture books and packing toys into a plastic basket. As Hanna came in, he looked up and said that there'd been a call for her. 'It was Charles Aukin.'

'Any idea what he wanted?'

Owen shook his head. 'Nope. He said he'd been up to Dublin. Oh, and he sounded kind of excited.'

'How do you mean?'

'I don't know. He's usually rather contained, isn't he? Sort of quiet and assured. But he seemed really animated, and he said would you call him back.'

Chapter Twenty-Two

The first of the year's autumn gales had hurled itself at Finfarran from the Atlantic. It struck overnight and, warned by forecasts and their own inherited knowledge of wind and weather, householders in the towns had tied down garden trampolines, stacked away patio furniture and furled or dismantled rotary clothes driers. In seaside villages and on the hill farms, anxious eyes had been cast on roofs, trees and power lines, while boats and animals were safely secured and sheltered. After a night of shrieking wind and horizontal rain, the sun rose on a soaked landscape scattered with blown debris, and to the sound of chainsaws opening roads blocked by fallen branches.

To Aideen's relief, Ronan had slept through everything and Conor had returned, dripping but safe, from two excursions into the night to check on the barns. She didn't know what he could do if the wind got under the corrugated-iron roofs and lifted them, and she had a strong suspicion that he didn't either, but she understood his impulse to check, rather than lie in bed imagining all kinds of disaster. Now, in the grey-washed morning, it could be seen that nothing bad had happened to the farm buildings close to the house. Conor, who'd fallen deeply asleep after his second foray, struggled into consciousness as soon as the room lightened and, pulling on the clothes he'd dropped on the floor a few hours earlier, went to drink tea while Una cooked breakfast. He'd disappeared by the time Aideen brought Ronan down to the kitchen. Una looked up and smiled as they came in. 'What a commotion! Did the little fella sleep?'

'Like a log. I don't suppose we'll see Conor for the rest of the day.'

'I did a big bag of rasher sandwiches to keep him going. He's got coffee in a flask too. He won't die of hunger or thirst.' Una poured a mug of tea for Aideen. 'It's just as well we got plenty of apples picked before the storm. D'you want to give me a hand today making chutney?'

'Sure. When would you want to begin? I've a few things to get done for Ronan.'

'There's no rush. I'll clear up and organise myself first.'

'Are the trees okay?'

'There's not a leaf left on them. Whatever fruit there was is gone too.'

'Could we gather windfalls?'

'No point going looking, love, they'll be in the next parish. I wouldn't worry anyway. We've most of the crop saved. The worms and the crows can have the rest, and welcome.'

Out in the yard, the tattered heads of crimson and purple hydrangeas were being tossed about by what was now a stiff breeze. Having fed Ronan, Aideen went through to the washing-machine and filled a basket with a load of laundry she'd done the night before. She left the baby with Una and carried the basket up to the orchard, treading carefully over slippery clumps of sodden leaves. As Una had said, the trees hadn't fared badly and, since the wide plot was enclosed by thick hedges, the poles that held up the washing lines were fine.

Placing her basket on the wooden seat beneath Conor's apple tree, Aideen considered the ruin caused by the wind. There wasn't an apple or a leaf left, but the spreading branches had withstood the night's destruction. None of the fruit trees in the orchard was tall. In springtime, chill winds from the north often blasted their topmost blossoms, leaving them shrivelled and blackened, as if burned. In response, the trees grew low, largely sheltered by the hedges, and harvesting the fruit was a matter of shaking, not climbing. Una had done most of the picking this year, though Aideen had joined her one sunny day, collecting the fruit that rained down from the branches, and keeping an eye on Ronan, who'd begun by admiring butterflies and ended by rocking a wicker basket so riotously that the apples cascaded onto the grass again. Looking at Conor's leafless tree, it was hard to believe that this had been only a week ago and, suddenly, Aideen wondered if Ronan's own little tree had survived. Unaccountably, she found herself starting to panic, unable to locate the slender sapling among the long grass. Then, with a thumping heart, she saw it swaying in the breeze, a few golden leaves lifting like bunting on branches that were hardly thicker than twigs.

When she'd hung out the washing, she returned to the house, where Una was doing the dishes, and said she'd go up and make the bed and tidy things upstairs.

'Do, love. Leave Ronan with me, he's fine in his playpen. It'll keep him from under your feet.'

So Aideen went up and applied herself to housework. When she and Conor had decided they'd live at the farm after they were married, Paddy and Una had insisted that newlyweds needed private space. An en-suite bathroom had been installed off Conor and Aideen's bedroom, and the room next door, which had once been Joe's, had become their own living room. It had a sofa and chairs, a TV, and an alcove fitted with a little fridge, a countertop and kettle, like a kitchenette in a posh hotel suite. Since Ronan's birth, the alcove had proved its worth for brewing midnight tea when she was up with him but, except when they'd watched films that would have bored Una and Paddy, the living space hadn't seen much use. While Paddy was alive, the farm kitchen, with its chairs by the range, flagged stone floor and scrubbed wooden table, had remained the heart of the household and, since his death, it continued to be the family sitting room. Having space to yourself was great, thought Aideen, but nothing could be better than the welcoming kitchen, full of the fragrant smells of cooking and baking, and lit from two sides by windows facing the garden and the yard.

She smiled, remembering Bríd's first reaction to the farm. Though careful to conceal it, Bríd had obviously been disappointed – apparently she'd expected something that looked like a picture on an old-fashioned chocolate box, complete with thatch and roses round the door. There was nothing quaint about the McCarthys' farmhouse, which was a two-storey building with grey cement render and a mossy slate roof. Aideen loved the workmanlike building. Its spare, clean interior was relieved by oases of spacious comfort, which, after St Finian's Close, felt like luxury: the deep chairs by the glowing range, the generous tiled scullery, and the utility room, where one washing-machine dealt with muddy work clothes and another had slatted shelves and a worktop above it, for airing and folding household laundry.

All the same, she thought, as she made the bed and began on Ronan's cot, there was something to be said for privacy. When she'd seen her dad's name at the Honeybee Garden Centre, her instinct had been to find out more before telling anyone else. The obvious starting point had been the garden centre's website so, when she'd had a free moment at home, she'd gone upstairs and done some research on her phone. The website must have been put together by a professional. It was labyrinthine but admirably easy to navigate.

Delving into the About Us section, she'd realised that each staff member had their own photo with a few lines under it, saying what they did and why they'd chosen to work for Honeybee. This meant that the company's brand was constantly reinforced throughout the website. Its reputation for sustainability came across loudly, as did its image as a business that treated employees like family and was interested in their lives outside work. Tapping the various links, Aideen had read about warehouse staff who ran quiz nights in their local community centres and horticultural students who did holiday work in the garden centre each year, having learned their love of flowers from childhood trips to it with their parents. A floor supervisor in the Cork branch was interested in fly fishing, and one of the waitresses in Carrick was hoping to go to India to teach in a home for the deaf. From the waitress's bio Aideen had accessed a section about the coffee shop and, scrolling through it, had come upon the name of its manageress. It was Yvonne Murphy and appeared on the screen as a bright blue hyperlink.

Assuring herself that Murphy was a very common name, Aideen had waited a full minute before hitting the link, which had brought her back to the About Us section and a photo of a girl's smiling face. Here, the text told her chattily, was evidence that the company really was a family business. Yvonne was 'the only child of Derek Murphy, our esteemed owner', and 'as well as being passionate about food' she was 'mad about music and always up for a night out with the girls'. According to her bio, she was five years younger than Aideen, who'd closed the website immediately, knowing that she'd return to it but needing time to process what she'd seen. Yvonne was dark-haired and pretty, with curls like Aideen's own. She had a sleek, assured air about her, as befitted the boss's daughter, but her smile extended to her eyes, which were wide-spaced and brown as polished conkers.

Now, having made up Ronan's cot and tidied the living room, Aideen sat on the sofa, opened her phone and returned to the website for what felt like the millionth time. Underneath Yvonne Murphy's photo was a CONTACT ME link that produced her email address. Having copied and pasted the address into her contacts list, Aideen took a deep breath and slowly began to compose an email, biting her lip as she wrote. But, unable to get beyond 'Dear Yvonne' without endlessly hitting delete, she closed the phone, thrust it under a cushion, and linked her hands tightly on her knee. The email address was VonnieM@Honeybee.com. How could one be certain that it was private? Possibly, anything sent to the company's server disappeared into a central pool. But, no, that would be inefficient. Surely the point of putting up a manager's email address was to ensure quick, informed replies to her customers' enquiries? So the chances were that Yvonne Murphy opened her emails herself. Of course, it could be that everyone on her team had access to them. But that, too, seemed unlikely. Aideen had reckoned that most of the coffee shop's staff had been students doing holiday work, and the bios she'd read on the website had confirmed this impression. Access to company emails would be well above their pay grade.

She was still struggling with the ramifications of whether, and how, she ought to draft an email to her unknown half-sister when she heard Una calling from downstairs. Fishing the phone from under the cushion, she shoved it into her back pocket and, secretly glad to give up on both privacy and the problem, ran down to the kitchen to help make chutney.

Aideen loved the seasonal rituals by which the days in the farm kitchen were measured. Nettle soup was made with February's first green shoots, and the new-laid eggs that were plentiful at Easter time resulted in sponge cakes, omelettes and frittatas, followed by all the bounty of summer fruits and vegetables, and autumn's jam, jelly and chutney-making marathons. Each season produced its own recipes, preserved on scraps of paper between the pages of old family cookery books or passed on by Una, who retained dozens in her head.

Like the cellophane-wrapped flowers Aunt Bridge had bought in the supermarket, food in Aideen's childhood had been most prized for an appearance of uniformity. At St Finian's Close, mushrooms had come scrubbed and spotless in neat plastic boxes, eggs never needed to have specks of chicken shit washed from their shells, and vegetables arrived identical in size and shape and without blemish, with no suggestion of the soil they'd been grown in. On the farm, mushrooms were picked in the fields with dew on their crinkled edges, eggs came warm from the nest with downy fluff stuck to their shells, and onions, carrots and potatoes grew in the garden. Soil and occasional tiny snails were scrubbed away under the yard tap, and the peelings and skins were thrown onto the compost heap to help feed the following year's crop.

Una's chutneys were made with whatever constituted a glut. She altered her recipes accordingly, so one year the labels on her jars might read 'Pear' and another 'Green Tomatoes' but the heady smell of brown sugar, vinegar and spices was unchanging, and conjured other early autumn rituals and scents. Running downstairs, Aideen found herself thinking of smoky bonfires, the swelling husks of dark brown chestnuts, and of wasps settling on the honey-dark skin of overripe pears. But the thought of chestnuts brought her back to those eyes as brown as polished conkers, so she pushed it away, resenting its intrusion.

In the kitchen Una was shaking her finger at Ronan, telling him he must never touch the range. 'Hot! See, pet? Very hot! That's dangerous. You must never touch it. You might get burned.' When Ronan had first begun to stagger about they'd put up a fireguard and, at the moment, he was in his playpen at the far side of the room, peering solemnly over the rail at the warning finger. Una laughed as Aideen came in. 'I know he's as safe as houses there, but my granny was always scared of letting a child near the fire. It seems to have been passed down to me in the genes.'

'Do you want me to start chopping?'

'If you'll begin on the onions, I'll get the rest of the jars heated.'

The onions had been lifted weeks ago and laid on the earth to dry. Afterwards they'd been tied in bunches and hung from a rafter in one of the farm sheds, where they'd gleamed like clusters of bronze balls when touched by the evening sunlight. Ronan had loved it when Conor had held him up to make them swing. 'You have to go gently at them, now. They're not toys. They're for eating.' Responding to Conor's tone of voice, Ronan had pushed the swinging clusters carefully with one finger, his eyes round with wonder and delight. Now he squealed reminiscently as Aideen began to strip the onions' papery skins and chop them. Whatever else went into Una's chutneys, onions and apples were always the starting point. Many of the apples were windfalls, which had dropped from the branches early and been pecked by birds and invaded by worms before they'd been collected. Cutting away the blemished parts, Aideen steadily chopped the fruit and swept it into a pan she'd already half-filled with onions. Una joined her at the table to dice peppers and carrots and crush garlic, their two knives sounding in counterpoint against their chopping boards.

Marmalade, one of the ginger cats, strolled in from the yard and, ignoring Ronan's excited reaction, leaped onto one of the chairs by the range. Marmite, the elder of the two cats, seldom deigned to come indoors, preferring to sun himself on the step or patrol the hayshed for mice, but Marmalade enjoyed his creature comforts and had even been known to yowl when given the wrong brand of cat food. Paddy, who'd secretly doted on him, had had a set speech about how this was a sad metaphor for the times. 'Each generation softer than the one that came before it! The time will come when the sight of a mouse will give cats a nervous breakdown!' Watching Marmalade wind himself into a sinuous knot, Aideen felt a lump in her throat at the thought of Paddy's absence. This, she thought, was the downside of seasonal rituals – the inevitable sense of loss you felt when part of the pattern was broken. Paddy had drawn such strength from what he'd called 'ordinary life going on'. The trouble is, Aideen told herself, that the timelessness of the endless rhythms of planting, growing and saving just demonstrates the shortness of human life.

Before Ronan was born, the smallest thing she'd taken care of was a lamb. Life on the farm had been very new to her then. One of the ewes had produced a squirming reject with huge ears, a gaping pink mouth and sharp black feet. Within a few hours of its birth, Conor had carried it in from the field to the farmhouse and Una had settled it into a cardboard box under the range. Wrapped in an old towel, and panting as if it had run a marathon, the lamb had seemed to Aideen to be far too small to survive. But Una had taken the whole thing in her stride. Producing a bottle of feed, she'd shown Aideen how to encourage the pink mouth to close on the sterilised rubber nipple and, gently rubbing the lamb's woolly back, had coaxed the little creature to begin to suck. 'There's a place just above the tail where the ewes nuzzle the lambs when they're feeding. Instinct will make them suck if you do the same.' At first Aideen had been almost afraid of the responsibility but, within twenty-four hours, she was making up bottles and taking delight in the growing strength of the lamb's plaintive cries. Now she remembered her conversation with Paddy in the orchard, when he'd told her how the rhythms of the seasons had helped him ward off depression. By then she'd got past the stage of seeing farm life through rose-coloured spectacles. 'But they die, don't they? The lambs. We raise sheep for slaughter.'

'Everything dies, girl. Lambs and flowers and grain that's cut down to make bread. Whatever lives dies eventually. That's Nature's way.'

Aideen looked over at Una who was weighing currants. 'Were you born on a farm?'

Una shook her head. 'No, I married in, like you did. But my granddad was a farmer, so it wasn't completely new.'

Aideen wished that she'd arrived with the same level of competence, but Gran's late husband had worked in an office in Lissbeg. Under lowered eyelashes, she watched Una cutting up sticks of fennel and shaking seeds from the heads onto a plate. If my mum hadn't died in childbirth, she thought, Ronan would have had two grannies, like most kids, and, if Paddy had lived, he would have had a granddad on Conor's side. No one can help it when people die, but my dad's alive and Ronan has a right to have a relationship with him. Just to be ordinary. To be able to say that his mum's dad lives in Cork and owns garden centres. To hear at first hand that, on my side, three generations of his granddad's family were seed merchants. To be able to mention it casually, and not feel people around him stiffening. As the thought crossed Aideen's mind, her hand slackened on the chopping knife. Why, she wondered, had no one made any comment when she'd said she wanted only Paddy and Una at her registry office wedding? She'd never thought much about that because, in her mind, her real wedding had taken place in the olive grove above Florence, where anyone else's presence would have felt superfluous. But, now that she came to think of it, wasn't it strange that everyone, even Bríd, had said nothing? Could they all have been treating her in the way that she'd treated Aunt Bridge and Gran? Maybe they'd thought that any mention of her dead mum and missing dad disturbed her. And, okay, if she was honest, maybe it did. And that wasn't something she wanted to pass on to Ronan. He deserved better. He deserved a future that wasn't overshadowed by the past.

Chapter Twenty-Three

Hanna had phoned Charles Aukin and, to her surprise, was invited to come for a drink the following evening. She'd intended to look in on Mary after work but, as Owen had said, it was evident that Charles was eager to talk, so she'd accepted his invitation, thanking her stars that she hadn't told Mary she'd come by.

When she arrived at the castle she was greeted by Fury, who threw open the door and stood back, as if he'd been transformed into a butler. Except for its turreted gateway and formidable curtain walls, most of Castle Lancy had been knocked down and rebuilt over the centuries, and the fortified keep, which had once bristled with medieval spears, was now a slightly run-down Georgian manor. The hall was floored with a checkerboard of black and white tiles, and a central staircase branched left and right to an elegant railed gallery. Looking up, Hanna saw The Divil at the top of the first flight of stairs, crouched under a marble bust of a de Lancy in a wig. Surprised by her reception, she faltered. Fury took her by the elbow. 'In the name of God, will you come on in before we all die of cold!' He slammed the door behind her and jerked his head towards the staircase. 'The man of the house is above in his book room.' Looking up, he fixed a compelling eye on the crouching Divil. 'And, yes, I know he keeps a packet of custard creams up there for you, but we're going back to the cellar, so hard luck.' With that, he stalked off, a fantastic, lanky figure, his waxed jacket flapping and a wrench sticking out of his torn pocket. The Divil leaped down to follow at his heels and they disappeared in the direction of a green baize door.

The hall was certainly chilly and Hanna remembered that the castle's boiler was said to be so temperamental that no one but Fury could coax it to behave. Turning left when she got to the half-landing, she made her way up to the book room, the thought of which made her inclined to laugh. It was fitted out with glazed cases surmounted by busts of Plato and Aristotle, and had a writing desk complete with brass inkwells and a lamp. There were high-backed leather armchairs, a fireplace with imposing caryatids, and a sense that everything, even the books, had been bought from a London catalogue in the early 1800s. Hanna could imagine the de Lancys perusing it over the breakfast table, and approving the option for their family crest to appear on the books' calfskin binding, which was fashionably finished with a wine-coloured, ribbed spine. On lower shelves there were bound volumes of *Punch*, the *Illustrated London News* and *Horse & Hound* but, while these were well thumbed, she guessed that few of the books had ever been read by the room's intended occupants, and thought it unlikely that this had changed since Charles had arrived. As far as she knew, his taste in reading ran to financial journals and the *Times* crossword, so she couldn't imagine him enjoying the poems of Catullus or an uncut, beige-bound copy of *Tristram Shandy*.

Now, however, as she entered the room and Charles came to greet her, she saw that every flat surface was piled with open books, most of which appeared to have been bought recently. They were bristling with paper markers, as if he'd been doing some kind of research. She had been here only once before, when Charles had first shown her the psalter, which he'd produced from a shallow drawer in the large mahogany desk. His expression as he'd opened the drawer had been quizzical, like a conjuror's at a children's party. That first sight of the psalter had left Hanna speechless, and the stipulation that it must be housed in her library would, in itself, have made her grateful to Charles Aukin for life, but in getting to know him better, she'd come to feel affection for him, as well as gratitude.

Now he looked excited as he moved about, pouring wine, settling her in an armchair, and sitting down at the lamplit desk. His genial presence was very different from that of the man he'd appeared to be at the meeting a few years previously, when the gift of the psalter had been discussed with Tim. Arriving at the county library in full boardroom mode, Charles had shaken hands briskly and made his position known. 'For me, the bottom line is that the monks created a psalter that reflects the surroundings shown in its illustrations. That's why I want it in Lissbeg.'

Tim's response had been unctuous, eager to press a point but careful not to lose a donor. 'Of course, it's called the Carrick Psalter so perhaps the County Library in Carrick would be a better fit. Just a thought. You may feel otherwise.'

Charles had remarked in a level voice that he'd thought he'd made himself clear. 'It's Lissbeg Library or nothing. That's the deal. I don't change my mind without good reason.' He'd looked at Tim over his gold-rimmed glasses. 'And I do like to get my own way.' Tim had withdrawn his suggestion instantly, and Hanna, who'd been in the background, had had to struggle to keep a straight face.

Now, fizzing with energy, Charles beamed at her across the book-strewn desk. 'I don't know if you recall our conversation about my wife's family? In the Garden Café over chicken on rye?'

'Of course. You'd given some of her clothes to the charity shop.'

'And you and I had been looking at the psalter. That double-page spread of the little guy working away with the big gold feather.' Charles sipped his wine and rubbed his hands. 'So, here's the thing. I made a couple of cracks that day about people's attitude towards Castle Lancy. Local folks. Remember?' Unable to think where this was going, Hanna nodded. Charles leaned back in his chair and continued, 'I've been thinking about it a lot since then. Reading up on local history. Figuring out a plan.' He looked at her earnestly. 'I've no real claim to the place except by chance, Hanna, but, you know what, I really want to feel part of this community. Everyone's been so good to me since I've been here.'

'So what's your plan?'

'Remember what I said about the psalter? That it must have been here in this very room when the castle was under siege? And how it could have been blown to bits with nobody any the wiser? It's not like anyone knew it was here. With due respect to my wife, the de Lancys were always acquisitive. You could say opportunist.' Charles waved his hand at one of the books on the desk, which had *A History of the de Lancy Family of the Province of Munster in Ireland* stamped in gilt on its wine-coloured spine. The author's name appeared beneath the title in smaller letters, *Henry Forbes-Lancy, Fellow of All Souls College, Oxon.* 'That was privately printed in the eighteenth century. Compiled by a poor relation, kind of a hanger-on, they called the family librarian. Seems the de Lancys picked up the psalter in 1547, when the monastery here was dissolved by royal decree. But the chances were that, if people had known they'd bought it, the family would have been taxed or forced to present it to the Crown, so they squirrelled it away and kept schtum. Henry puts it less bluntly but that's the reality.'

Charles interrupted himself with a laugh. 'Sorry, I know I'm rambling. I've just got really involved in this local-history stuff. The point is that I couldn't stop thinking about that idea of mine.' Rubbing his hands again, he went on, full of enthusiasm, 'No matter which way I kicked it about, it still seemed pretty damn good. A national treasure with real local significance. A unique book that nearly went up in smoke. I mean, that's a story, right? So why not raise this thing to a whole 'nother level? What if Castle Lancy were part of the information trail? Loop me in, so that people going from library to library could visit the castle too, and hear the story of the siege and the psalter right here on site.'

Hanna's mind was racing. Though she'd heard nothing more from Charles in the weeks that had followed their lunch in the nuns' garden, she'd spent much of that time on tenterhooks, expecting that Owen would make the connection between the siege and the psalter. If it happens, she'd told herself, I won't try to divert him, but there's no onus on me to draw his attention to it. After all, the story's just one of many that could be chosen to frame Lissbeg Library's narrative. As time passed, and having salved her professional conscience, she'd begun to relax and hope that Charles had forgotten his suggestion, and that the siege would end up as nothing more than a marker on a timeline – a date and a caption, perhaps, maybe a graphic. No need for mention of Liam Casey's involvement, and no fear that she'd have to respond to questions from reporters. But here was Charles talking about the kind of exposure she hadn't even considered.

His eyes sparkling, he thumped the desk decisively. 'Looping the castle in was a no-brainer, but I knew there was still a missing piece in the jigsaw. And then, the other day, I was up in Dublin for a meeting. An arts funding thing with the great and the good. I bumped into a woman there who's a television producer. Magazine show, goes out three times weekly on RTÉ. I watch it a lot.'

Cold certainty swept over Hanna. 'Would that be *Nationwide*?'

'That's the one! I gave her the whole shtick and she really loved it. So I put her on to Tim Slattery, and it seems we're good to go.'

As she attempted to retain an impassive expression, Hanna's mind was frantically joining dots. Before leaving work for the evening, she'd done a final check for emails and found yet another summons to a meeting at the County Library. It was Tim at his most pompous, suppressed elation larded with portent and marked 'IMPORTANCE HIGH', and the attached agenda had simply read '*Nationwide*'. With an effort, she smiled at Charles. 'You don't waste time, do you?'

'Nope. Never have. See an opportunity, scope it out and, if it ticks the boxes, go for it. That's always been my way.' He was so pleased with himself that Hanna hadn't the heart to deflate him, and anyway, she thought, what would be the point? What could I say that wouldn't sound weird or neurotic? Or disloyal to Tim, who, after all, is my colleague as well as my boss? Fury was right. One thing in life always leads to another, and it's pointless to imagine that you can keep it all under control.

The following morning Hanna arrived in Carrick after a sleepless night. Once again, she encountered Owen on the steps to the library and they took the lift up to the staff room together. It was already full of their colleagues, chatting and slinging bags on the backs of chairs. Tim, of course, had yet to arrive. Feeling obscurely guilty for knowing more about what was coming than the others did, Hanna sat down and remembered the moment when Charles had mentioned Liam. They'd been on their second glass of wine by then and the desk was scattered with papers as well as books. 'This kind of research is new to me, not what I'm used to, but I'm really enjoying it. Nothing that occurred in Finfarran was of national significance, except in the sense that what happened here was happening in every other county in Ireland. But I dug around on the internet and came up with local references, and I printed out a couple of journal pieces.'

Moving a copy of Margaret Ward's *Fearless Woman*, and stacking Tom Barry's *Guerilla Days in Ireland* on top of Fintan O'Toole's *Enough Is Enough*, Charles had picked up a sheaf of pages and looked at Hanna over his gold-rimmed glasses. 'Did you know that the commander of the boys who made their last stand here in the castle was a guy called Liam Casey? How about that?'

Hanna's first instinct had been to avoid revealing her relationship with Liam, exactly as Maggie's had been a hundred years previously on seeing his poster in the railway station. Over the course of her sleepless night, she'd told herself that was ridiculous. Far better to have owned the connection immediately than to have made a show of dabbing at a splash of wine on her knee. But her impulse had been to cause a diversion and, having gained time by going to the bathroom to put water on the stain, she'd contrived to restart the conversation with a comment on

Barry's book. 'He was writing about his own experience of making raids on the British forces and dodging back into the hills. It's an iconic book, and a unique eyewitness record. What did you think of it?' As she'd hoped, Charles had launched into an enthusiastic critique of *Guerilla Days in Ireland* and Liam's name hadn't come up again.

Tim arrived ten minutes late for the meeting, wearing autumnal tweed and sporting his gold pocket watch, this time with a fob dangling from its chain. Oh, no, thought Hanna. He's being a country-house gent suitably attired for addressing a camera on the steps of Castle Lancy. She had an absurd vision of Tim stepping back to allow a tracking shot to draw the viewers into the castle, the door being opened by Fury in his disreputable woolly hat, and The Divil wearing a black tuxedo jacket.

Taking a seat at the head of the table, Tim joined the tips of his fingers and was about to speak when he was interrupted by Arthur, the librarian from Ballyfin. A cadaverous, balding man in a suit that was rather too big for him, he was older than Tim and evidently ready to use age to pull rank. 'Sorry to butt in, Tim, but I see that, once again, we have a single-item agenda, and I'd like to raise some practical matters first.' Tim didn't look happy but conceded the floor with a lordly wave of his hand. Arthur consulted his notebook. 'At our last meeting you asked us to "pitch" themes to you that would "really pack a punch" and "knock people's socks off". I understood that these "pitches" would be the subject matter of our gathering today.'

Tim, who'd clearly forgotten what he'd demanded, gave a bland smile. 'Indeed, but as you know yourself, Arthur, things move on. What I'd like to discuss today is something that will allow us, as a county, to punch well above our weight.' He paused, pleased with his turn of phrase, unwisely giving Arthur a chance to reply.

Arthur seized it. 'It's this question of packing a punch that concerns me. You'll remember that I had reservations about it at our last meeting and, since then, my concerns have grown more acute.' Hanna could feel a frisson around the table and was pretty sure that Arthur felt it too. Encouraged by the expressions on his colleagues' faces, he squared his shoulders and placed a pencil on the first point on his list. 'Nothing that's come into my branch could be described as likely to knock anyone's socks off. Nor, in my opinion, should we be looking for sensational material. The fact is, however, that my opinion is irrelevant. The project is intended to be a community endeavour and our business is to respond to the public, not the other way round.'

A colleague opposite Hanna cleared her throat. 'This is exactly what I'm finding in my branch. I had a lady come in to me with a half-finished cardigan. A little girl's size, hand-knitted with a Fair Isle pattern. Some woman in her family had sat by a window with it for weeks, keeping lookout while her husband was receiving stolen army rifles and hiding them in the turf stack till the boys came to pick them up. By the look of the cardigan, somebody else had cast it onto the needles and the poor woman herself could hardly knit. It's just a mess, really, nothing to look at. But I think it's a great kick-off for discussion.'

Owen chimed in: 'Personally, I'm still concerned about conservation.'

'Which brings me to my next point.' Arthur stabbed his pencil at his notebook. 'We haven't discussed the logistics of this project sufficiently. Some objects simply aren't suitable for display boards. As it happens, I have tables I can use along with boards, but others haven't. It's a point that was raised tangentially at our last meeting, Tim, and I *have* emailed you more than once since then.' Murmurs around the room indicated that others had sent Tim similar emails.

He raised his hands, palms outward, and embraced the room with a smile. '*Mea culpa*, you're perfectly right. I have got behind with my emails. But I'm very excited to tell you that I've been forging ahead on other fronts, and I've achieved a new dimension for Finfarran, which I think you'll agree will put us ahead of the pack.'

Arthur bristled. 'But this is precisely the issue. It's not a competition.'

Tim's own shoulders squared under his expensive tweed jacket. 'On the other hand, to take a *balanced* view, I think there's a certain amount to be said for healthy competitiveness.'

'But in this instance—'

'If nothing else, I expect you'll agree that it stimulates hard work.'

The inference was so offensive that Arthur's jaw dropped and, before he could recover, Tim raised his voice. 'Which is why I know that this news will make us redouble our efforts to be better than the best!' Lifting the agenda, he held it up facing outwards, as if displaying a signed treaty or contract of vast importance. 'This hasn't been easy, but I've pulled some strings and managed to up the ante.' Hanna watched him rise to his feet, as if he anticipated a round of applause. Having regained the meeting's focus, he held a long, dramatic pause before gesturing towards the single line on the agenda. 'Remember I said that Finfarran's library system was about to appear, front and centre, on the national stage? Well, you can forget the stage because I've come up with something much better. I'm talking about the nation's TV screens.'

Chapter Twenty-Four

'OMG! Tim Slattery's absolutely shameless!' Jazz was listening with mounting indignation as Hanna described what had happened at the meeting.

Hanna shrugged. 'He's always run the county's library service as a personal fiefdom. Appropriating Charles's idea is just par for the course.' She and Jazz were drinking coffee in Maggie's place. A blustery wind spattered the windows with raindrops and, though the house wasn't cold, Jazz had lit the first fire of the year. The basket of golden furze flowers had been replaced by driftwood, and light was painting the wide stone hearth. Worn smooth by the waves and impregnated with salt from the ocean, the driftwood hissed occasionally, throwing up green tongues of flame that died in showers of sparks. Hanna pushed a piece with her foot, causing another flurry. 'Maggie called these spurts of flame "fire fairies".'

'That sounds a bit whimsical for Maggie.'

'Irish fairies aren't whimsical. They're dangerous and need careful propitiation.'

'Such as?'

'You put out food for them at Halloween.'

'Seriously? Maggie did that?'

'A saucer of milk on the doorstep every year till the day she died.'

'Because she was afraid of fairies? Or, wait, isn't it ghosts at Halloween?'

'She never showed any fear of the supernatural.' Hanna pushed the piece of wood deeper into the flames. 'Maybe that was because she'd experienced real danger and malice. This house was like her snail shell. It protected her. If she thought there were dangerous spirits about, she had charms to make sure they stayed outside her door. Besides, there are different levels of belief. I'd say that, as much as anything, the saucer of milk was a tribute to the women who'd lived here before her. It's an ancient ritual. She wouldn't have wanted to be the one to break faith with the past.'

'And back then people really believed in fairies?'

'You can't just say "back then", it's simplistic. It's like the lazy idea that everybody in her generation was either a slave to the British or ready to die for Ireland's freedom. Life's more complicated than that.'

After a moment, Jazz held out her hand to the leaping flames. 'You're not okay about this *Nationwide* thing, are you?'

'I just wish I'd told Charles that Liam Casey was my grandfather.'

'What? You didn't?'

'I wanted time to think.'

'Oh, Mum! Honestly! This is a thing you do and it's so dumb. Look at how you tried to hide stuff from me when you and Dad were divorced.'

Half laughing, Hanna pushed her hand through her hair. 'Well, there's an example of something that really was complex! Most divorces are, I suppose.' Jazz looked unconvinced and Hanna raised her eyebrows at her. 'Well, what would you have done in my place?' It was something they'd made their peace with a long time ago, and could talk about now as water under the bridge.

Jazz grinned. 'Told the truth, maybe? Or, okay, maybe not. I admit it was complicated. And I still can't believe I was naïve enough to believe Dad when he said the divorce was amicable.'

'Your dad's an accomplished manipulator.'

There was a residue of bitterness in Jazz's voice. 'And I was Daddy's little princess, so I fell for it hook, line and sinker.'

Hanna gave her a loving smile. 'Most fathers are heroes to their daughters. That was the problem. How could I tell you he'd sat you down and told you a bare-faced lie?'

'I coped okay when I did find out.'

'You were older by then and you'd had time to settle down in Finfarran.' Hanna shrugged. 'Besides, your dad adores you. I knew he was scared of losing you and I didn't want that to happen, so he'd got me between a rock and a hard place. I was never sure I was doing the right thing, though, and your nan was always issuing dire warnings. She kept saying that, one day, you'd find out that both your parents were liars.'

'That is *so* Nan, and it's absolute bullshit. You didn't lie. You went silent. Or, if I pushed, you rabbited madly on about something else.'

'It's the default Irish reaction. "Whatever you say, say nothing."'

'And you think you'll get away with saying nothing to Charles about Liam?'

'We're way past that point. This thing's got legs of its own. I can't control it.' Hanna leaned forward and poked the fire vigorously. 'But, look, I came here today to ask you something. I wondered if you'd come with me to your nan's.'

'When?'

'Now, if you're free. When I went round before, she refused to discuss Maggie. Which is rich, by the way, coming from someone who normally can't keep her mouth shut. She's aware of the library project, though, so I think she should know I've decided not to submit Maggie's book as an artefact. And I ought to prepare her if Liam's name is going to come up on TV.'

'Have you discussed all this with Brian?'

Hanna sighed. 'He's been listening and I've been going round in circles. Anyway, this is a Casey-family thing.' Looking up, she encountered an enigmatic look from Jazz. 'What? What are you thinking?'

'Nothing. Of course I'll come if you want me there. It's just that I've never known you to go in for confrontation with Nan.'

'It's not about confrontation. She's been a bit erratic lately. I don't want her upset.' Hanna poked the fire again, making the green sparks fly. 'The truth is that, if you're there, she's less likely to bite my head off, and there's a chance she'll listen even if she won't talk.'

Mary's eyebrows went up when she saw them appear at the back door of the bungalow, but she welcomed them in and gave them each a perfunctory peck on the cheek. 'How well you wouldn't text and say you were coming! Here am I with my apron on, in the middle of my work!' Jazz gave her a hug and filched a carrot from the table, where Mary was engaged in creating a cottage pie. The vegetable peelings were piled on outspread pages of the *Inquirer* and, pushing them aside, Jazz sat down and put her elbows on the table. Mary flapped a tea-towel irritably. 'Will you leave things alone!'

Biting into the carrot, Jazz made a cheerful grab at the tea-towel. 'You know I always graze when I'm in your kitchen. I can't help myself.'

Hanna went round to the other side of the table and drew up a chair. Having come without so much as a bar of chocolate for her mother, she had a feeling she'd got off on the wrong foot. Mary was scathing when people arrived with 'one arm as long as the other', even though she always announced that she'd more than enough food in her cupboards already. It was a throwback to a time when open-handedness was the supreme virtue yet few households ever had much to spare. To shame a neighbour by exposing her poverty would have been disgraceful, so the custom of bringing a gift of food when you dropped in unexpectedly had allowed both guest and host to save face. These days, the offerings were seldom opened during the visit, and elderly people living alone frequently found them difficult to dispose of. As a result, packets of biscuits or cake would be brought to the GP's surgery or the library with the suggestion that the staff might enjoy them with coffee. At work, Hanna had grown adept at pretending to know nothing of their provenance but, by that stage in the pointless, guilt-ridden game of pass the parcel, the gifts were often well past their sell-by date, and became crumbs for the birds in the nuns' garden. Generally, Mary was first to condemn what she called wanton food waste. Nevertheless, Hanna could tell that today's failure to honour established convention had been noted.

Jazz and Mary were still sparring amicably. As Hanna attempted to marshal her thoughts, her eye fell on a framed religious picture that had dominated the hallway of the house where she was born. It now hung in its ebony frame above her mother's fridge-freezer. The lugubrious image of Christ, which had a red vigil light under it, gazed reproachfully at Mary's microwave, his wounded hands pointing to the flaming heart on his chest. The heart, picked out in tarnished red sequins, was circled with thorns and pierced by a bloody spear. Standing below it was a small statue of the Virgin Mary, dressed in white with a blue sash covering her pregnant stomach. Hanna remembered it high on a shelf in her parents' shop in Crossarra, from which it was lifted down each year to be washed. The Sacred Heart, she'd been told, had belonged to a family member who'd 'gone into the nuns'. In those days, if asked, she would have said that she hardly noticed the garish picture. All the same, she thought, it was part of my childhood, ever-present like the plaster virgin mother with her upturned eyes and pious, simpering smile. Though less common than they used to be, images like these still permeated Finfarran's day-to-day landscape and, looking at them after so many years in different surroundings, Hanna found them repellent. She was aware that her love for the psalter made her position hard to defend, and recently, over dinner, she'd tried to discuss her misgivings with Jazz. 'This is the danger of powerful iconography. It's most effective when it works on an unconscious level.'

Picking an olive from her pizza, Jazz had flipped it neatly into her mouth. 'I know.'

'The psalter comes from the same starting point, of course, but it's different. There's nothing sentimental about its images. If anything, they're a secular comment on the religious text.' Jazz had shrugged and selected another olive and, with a feeling that she was losing her audience, Hanna had tried harder to explain. 'I didn't want you influenced by repressive religious concepts. Guilt and blood sacrifice and weird, twisted attitudes to sex.'

'I wasn't.'

'But how can you tell?'

'It's my job to know how to quantify the effectiveness of a message. And it's totally quantifiable, Mum. It's not complex. There's no need to waste time wondering what people might think or feel. You can tell just by exposing them to it and looking at what they do.' Hanna had accepted this answer with relief. It might have felt trite but, at least, it suggested that Jazz's unconscious was untroubled by bloodstained crowns of thorns.

Mary rapped smartly on the kitchen table. 'Is either of you going to tell me why you've turned up at my door?'

'Oh, shut up, Nan, we just came by. Though, wait, I've got something for you.' Jazz finished the last of her carrot and rummaged in her bag. 'I've been carrying it round for ages thinking I might see you in town.' Looking gratified, Mary sat down and Jazz held out a screwtop jar. 'The finished product comes in a box. This is just a sample.'

'Oh, I see. A factory reject.' Taking the jar, Mary unscrewed the lid and sniffed the contents. 'In fairness, I suppose it doesn't smell too bad.'

'It's a beautiful marigold night cream and you're going to love using it. I picked it out specially for you, so stop being ungrateful.'

'I thought you were threatening to bring me a marigold facemask.'

'Well, if you like the scent, and you find this is right for your skin, maybe I will.'

Hanna was determined not to lose sight of the purpose of their visit but now she felt like the spectre at the feast. Jazz was dabbing cream on the back of her nan's hand, extolling its lightness, and to introduce an unwelcome subject seemed crass. Mary held out her hand to show her the cream and looked at her sharply. 'What are you doing sitting there with a face on you?'

'I was just thinking I'm sorry we didn't bring something over for tea.'

'If that's a hint, you might as well put the kettle on. God knows, it's seldom enough you come by.'

'Let me do it.' Jazz made for the sink, crossing her eyes at Hanna behind Mary's back. 'Mum wants to talk about this project she's doing in the library, don't you, Mum?'

Hanna took a deep breath. 'Well, yes. The thing is, Mam, it's not just going to happen in the libraries. Charles Aukin has offered to have a display at the castle as well. You know there was a stand-off there during the Civil War?'

'So I heard.'

'When I read Maggie's book, I did some research and, apparently, Dad's father was involved there. Well, actually, he commanded the group of diehards.'

'D'you tell me that?'

Mary's face was folded in deep curves of disapproval and, thinking she understood why, Hanna kept going. 'Look, Mam, I know you didn't want to discuss Maggie's book. I know you feel it's better not to talk about her at all. So I'm not going to be putting bits of the book up in the library. Mind, I don't think that, these days, people would really be bothered about the fact that she had an affair. But I do agree it's a family thing. I mean I know what you mean.'

Mary was massaging the night cream into the back of her wrinkled hand. 'What do you know, exactly?'

Hanna plunged on. 'That the affair was with a married man. And, the way I see it, he was as much to blame as poor Maggie. More, really. She was young and traumatised. But I know the priests were practically all-powerful back then.' Over Mary's shoulder, she saw Jazz grinning at her use of 'back then'. Inwardly cursing her daughter's sense of humour, and reflecting that at least some of it had been inherited from herself, Hanna took another breath. 'Well, obviously not everyone. But Maggie believed that a word from the priest could shame her whole family.'

'They were hard times.'

'Anyway, the point is that I know you don't want Maggie talked about, so I wanted to reassure you. That's all.'

'Is that the way of it?'

'And, Mam, there's something else as well. It's kind of exciting.' Hanna had decided to say nothing about the book's revelations that Liam had been an unpleasant drunk who'd sponged off his sister. Better to focus on the romantic image of a daring freedom fighter, and the reflected glory in which Mary could bask. '*Nationwide* is coming to film at the castle.' Watching her mother's face, Hanna mentally crossed her fingers. In the background, Jazz had turned to fill the kettle.

Mary's expression gave nothing away, and silence filled the kitchen. Then, tossing her head, she opened her pursed lips and spoke. 'I never had any call to care what a priest might say about me. My mother had a cousin a bishop. Once removed, mind you, but he knew what was owed to family.'

The moral complexities inherent in this were too much for Hanna, so she smiled encouragingly. 'The telly thing will be something to talk about, won't it? How Dad's father fought for Ireland's freedom.'

There was a long pause before Mary folded her hands across the bib of her flowered apron. She fixed her eyes on the red lamp above the fridge-freezer. 'Hartnett was the name of the pup that took Maggie into the forest. James Hartnett. His father had a forge. The priest told James that the way to wipe out his sin was to join the fighting. To leave his poor wife that he'd cheated on, and whatever death he died at least he'd be in a state of grace. I never blamed Maggie for what happened to her. She was only a child and the times were strange. But I'll tell you this, I disliked her from the first moment we met, and I never forgave her for what she told Tom.' Mary's voice rose dangerously. 'By the time the Treaty was signed, God had wreaked no revenge on James. Of course he hadn't. Only a fool of a priest would come up with a stupid idea like that. And when the fighting went on, with Liam's lot on one side and the Treaty lads on the other, James ended up in command of the crowd that laid siege to Castle Lancy. It was over in half an hour with one man dead.'

'Who was it?' Jazz spoke from the far side of the kitchen with the kettle in her hand, halfway to the tap.

Mary turned to her heavily. 'It was James. Liam killed him. Years later, he told Maggie he knew what James had done to her. People had whispered. They always do. He boasted to her that he'd shot the man who'd brought shame on the Casey family. And years after that, when my poor Tom was hardly a teenager, Maggie sat him down and told him his dad was a cold-blooded murderer.'

'But, Nan, there was a war on. If Liam shot James it was in a fair fight.'

Mary jerked her head dismissively. 'Ah, for God's sake, did nobody ever teach you right from wrong? It's what a person is feeling and thinking when they do something that matters. Maggie said nothing but the truth. It was murder. But I don't want to hear a word about all she suffered. What kind of woman would tell a young lad that his dead father did that?'

Chapter Twenty-Five

Aideen woke to the sound of Ronan babbling. The voice from the cot was no more than a drowsy murmur, so she wriggled closer to Conor, who hadn't woken, kept her eyes closed and hoped Ronan would go back to sleep. Outside, the sky was beginning to lighten and shrill birdsong was greeting the chilly dawn. As always, Aideen had carefully opened the window a crack before going to bed. According to the books she'd read, and to the nurse at the clinic, ventilation was vital for building a strong immune system and banishing any bugs that might manage to sneak into the house.

Parenting still felt perilous to Aideen. You based your decisions on instinct and the voices of experience and tried to back them up with expert advice, but half the time you were sure you were making mistakes. Everyone told her that things were different after the first baby: you'd be so distracted by the time you'd had several that there wouldn't be time to worry, and no baby was ever the worse for a bit of healthy neglect. Bríd, who had brothers and sisters, claimed that middle children had the best deal. The youngest was never allowed to grow up and the eldest was weighed down by impossible hopes and expectations, but in-between children could just get on with living their own lives. Aideen couldn't imagine herself having that many kids. Perhaps, she thought, that's because Ronan wasn't planned. I hadn't got further than seeing me and Conor living here with Una and Paddy, a family in ourselves and different from anything I'd known. Now Paddy's gone and I'm a mum and nothing feels sure or certain any more.

The little voice from the cot beside her became a rhythmic snuffle and she knew Ronan was drifting back to sleep. People said she should thank her stars that he was a placid baby and, having heard horror stories at her book club at the library, Aideen reckoned they were right. So far, Ronan seemed charmed by the world. He was able to stand and walk a few steps, though liable to sit down suddenly, and he seemed neither headstrong nor clingy. Although, apparently, this could change overnight. According to Una, babies could get frustrated as they grew more independent. 'Conor used to get furious when he was learning to walk and fell over, plus Joe was an awful tease and used to run off and leave him behind.' Aideen could just see Joe doing it. Her heart had gone out to baby Conor, clinging on to chair legs and feeling that he wasn't making the grade.

It had taken ages to draft an email to Yvonne Murphy. In the end, Aideen had pinged it off in a panic and realised later that she'd signed off with 'Beset' instead of 'Best'. But the response had arrived within half an hour. They'd to-ed and fro-ed several times since, in diffident emails that revealed nothing beyond the facts that Yvonne hadn't known of Aideen's existence and that each seemed well-disposed towards the other. Aideen had been relieved when, eventually, they'd arranged to meet. Talking had seemed preferable to writing, though now the day had arrived, she was less sure. It felt ridiculous to fixate on clothes, as if she were planning a date, but the options kept flapping round in her head in a jumble of colours and shapes. Ten minutes later, having mentally chosen an outfit, she slipped out of bed to assemble it, and discovered the jacket she'd had in mind was at the dry cleaner's. Missing her warmth beside him, Conor stirred. 'You okay?'

'Fine.'

'Is Ronan awake?'

'No, not yet. He was talking to himself earlier, but he's gone back to sleep.' Aideen padded back to the bed and climbed in.

'God, you're chilly. Come over here.' Having woken, Conor was warm and relaxed and ready to make love, but Aideen's mind was flitting between the jacket at the dry cleaner's and the fact that she hadn't told him about Yvonne. She'd intended to, but the right moment hadn't presented itself and, anyway, when she'd drafted her first email she'd thought she might get no reply and that that would be that. Briefly, she tried to find words to explain this to Conor, but his kiss was insistent and she wasn't sure what to say, so she gave up.

In the end, her choice of outfit was a pair of trousers she'd been given by Eileen, who'd bought them online and been too lazy to return them when she'd found she'd ordered the wrong size. They were heavy brown cord with a high waist and a cut that made you look taller than you actually were. Aideen teamed them with biker boots and a leather bomber jacket, partly because the ensemble felt cool and casual but mostly because it was practical. Conor had taken the jeep to Lissbeg, which meant she would have to use her Vespa to get to Carrick. She and Yvonne had arranged to meet in the garden centre's coffee shop, and Yvonne's email had tactfully mentioned that her father was based in Cork, indicating that there was no danger that he'd appear, like The Divil, and find them chatting. Aideen had been relieved to hear that Yvonne needed to work the lunch service: the meeting felt less daunting with a definite finish time and, besides, she had to get back to the farm by midday, when Una, with whom she was leaving Ronan, was off to visit a neighbour. Ever-careful not to infringe on Aideen and Conor's privacy, Una asked no questions about her plans for a morning in Carrick, and she smiled when Aideen came into the kitchen to kiss Ronan goodbye. 'Don't you look nice! Have a good time, now.'

'I will. I'll be back by twelve.'

'Don't be breaking your neck on the bike. I'm not running a tight schedule. We won't fret if you're ten minutes late, will we, Ronan?'

Today's trip was less euphoric than Aideen's previous outing on the Vespa, when she'd laughed out loud and chanted the names of wildflowers. The hedgerows were different, too, beaten back by the stormy weather. The night before Halloween, she had taken Ronan in search of something spooky to put in a vase in the porch. They'd come home with rattling seedpods on tall skeletal stalks, and now the last of the blood-red fuchsia flowers had been washed away into the gurgling ditches. Glad of her quilted leather jacket, and the sweater she wore under it, Aideen came to the main road and sped on.

When she reached the garden centre she found it decked out for Christmas, as if there weren't weeks of shopping days to be got through yet. The urns at the entrance had been replanted with trailing ivy and cyclamen and flanked by reindeer sculptures made of willow. As Aideen approached the building, she shook her red-gold curls out of their scrunchie, took out her mobile phone and switched it off. Beyond the automatic doors she saw a fibreglass nativity scene with a garden shed for a stable and horticultural gift suggestions casually grouped among the kings and shepherds. The side aisles still displayed ordinary items, like potting compost and pesticide, but carols were playing discreetly, and Aideen detected a strong odour of cinnamon from the coffee shop. In the deli or the Garden Café, this early riot of festivity would be sure to produce tart comments, but it appeared that the Murphys positioned themselves to be ahead of the game. Peering into the conservatory, she could see that one of the outdoor tables for two was occupied. The girl who was sitting there had her back to the entrance and all Aideen could see of her was the turned-up collar of a jacket and a mass of dark curls tied up in a scrunchie.

Back at the farm, with the breakfast things cleared and the dishwasher stacked, Una took Ronan up to collect eggs. He had learned to take them gently and place them in the basket and, while his presence made the job last three times longer than necessary, it entertained him and gave Una great pleasure. Recently, she'd realised that much of what she'd loved about having a baby in the house again was how it had lifted Paddy out of his depression. I know that now, she thought, because it's doing the same for me. If I'd been told a couple of years ago that so much in my life would change, I'm not sure I could have coped with the prospect. Yet here I am, carrying on because I've got no option, and some of the things that give me strength are as fragile as these eggs. Little moments of happiness in a great well of misery, and no assurance, when each one ends, that there'll ever be another. I suppose that's what being around babies teaches you. Like Conor says, watching them grow is all about never-again moments, so you have to take each as it comes and enjoy it while you can.

They'd collected the eggs from the empty nests and moved on to where some of the hens were still roosting. One or two tended to flap their wings when approached, and Ronan pressed close to Una and hid behind her legs. Instinctively, Una made clucking sounds, to soothe both the hens and the baby and, as a ball of irate wattles and feathers scrambled away towards the door, she reached back and put her hand gently on Ronan's head. 'She's grand, love, she just doesn't like us disturbing her. She'll go out now for a scratch and a peck around and she'll be fine.' Una could feel Ronan nodding, his face still pressed against the backs of her knees. Picking him up, she swung him onto her hip. 'Would we look to see what she was sitting on? Will I show you the nest and you'll give the egg to Granny?'

There was a shadow in the doorway and Conor looked in. His back was to the sunlight, so Una couldn't see his face. 'I ran into Jim Hickson outside his office, Mum. Probate's through. I said we'd come by to see him next week.'

Una's response was a measure of how far she'd come since Paddy's death. Back then, numbness had fogged her mind and, in the week after the funeral, when she'd driven to see the solicitor with Aideen, she'd hardly been aware of the box of files and papers on her lap. Now, though saddened by the memory, she was quick to sense Conor's suppressed excitement. 'What's the story?'

'Jim says Paddy had some little dormant life-insurance policy. He calls it peanuts. He says he only went looking because of due diligence. If you ask me, he was clocking up extra hours he could charge us for.' Conor bent his head and stepped through the shed door. 'But that's what he found and, okay, it's small but it's taken a load off my shoulders. With this in the pot, we can break the back of what we owe to old Dawson.' Una could think of several other things on which such a windfall might usefully be spent. But the look on Conor's face kept her silent. The debt, with its implications of dependence on his brother, had clearly been undermining his self-confidence, and it was evident that the effect of this news was immense. Ronan was kicking on her hip, unfazed by the scuttling hens now he was safely in her arms. Abruptly, Conor took a step forward and caught hold of his son's flailing foot in its little wellington boot. 'Jesus, Mum, I wish I could tell Paddy.'

'I know you do, love. Here, have you told Aideen?'

'I tried, but maybe she hasn't a signal in Carrick. I couldn't get through to her phone.'

Yvonne looked sleek, assured and friendly, exactly like her photo. She jumped up and pulled out the other chair that stood at the table. 'Is this okay? To sit here? It should be pretty quiet.'

'It's fine. Perfect. Thanks for saying you'd meet me.'

'You haven't brought the baby.'

'Ronan? No, well, we couldn't really have talked if I had. Not properly.' Aideen hesitated. Yvonne appeared to be feeling as tentative as herself. Perhaps having Ronan as a distraction would have been a good thing.

Tilting her chair, Yvonne signalled to the guy behind the counter. 'I said we'd have coffee when you arrived. Is that okay? Would you rather I got you some tea?'

Aideen assured her that coffee was fine. When the guy brought it, several minutes were taken up by pouring it out and commenting on the scones that came with it.

'We bake our own daily.'

'Do you? Bríd does the same at the deli. We make them for the Garden Café as well.'

'Sounds like a big enterprise.'

'God, no. Not compared to this. We've only been in business a while. Like I told you, Bríd's my cousin.' Aideen faltered, realising that, somehow, Bríd, too, must be related to this dark-eyed girl whose coffee came in fancy cafetières.

Suddenly Yvonne put her cup down. 'My dad was crazy about your mother, you know.'

Aideen blinked. 'Really?'

'I haven't told him you got in touch, but I spoke to my auntie Jessie. Actually, I didn't tell her either. I just said I'd heard rumours and she came out with the whole story. She's my dad's older sister. He's got several. He's the only boy and they all adore him. Jessie's a terrible talker once she gets going.' Yvonne blushed. 'You're probably thinking that I am too.'

'No. I just … I don't really know anything about them. My mum and your dad.'

'Jessie said they were going out. She said they met at a disco when he was doing a holiday job. Your mum was seventeen or something, wasn't she? He'd just left school. The whole family was up in a heap when they heard she'd got pregnant.'

Yvonne coloured again. 'Sorry, yours must have been, too, of course.'

'I guess. Aunt Bridge and Gran never talked about it.'

'They brought you up?'

'Yeah. Aunt Bridge was actually Gran's cousin. They were old. And ... well, they didn't talk about it.'

Yvonne sipped her coffee. 'Dad certainly didn't. I don't even know if he told my mum.'

This remark was made casually, but Aideen's eyes widened. 'Look, I don't want to make trouble.'

'I'm sure. I could tell from the emails. Anyway, I was the one who suggested we meet.'

Aideen swallowed a mouthful of scone and decided she'd better come out with the question she hadn't been able to formulate in an email. 'Why? I mean, why did you want to meet me?'

'I've been trying to work that out and I think it comes down to common or garden curiosity.' Yvonne blushed again. 'Oh, God, that sounds horrible when I say it. I'm sorry.'

'No. Why should you be?'

'Because it's a big deal for you, isn't it?'

'That doesn't mean it has to be a huge deal for you. And I don't want to upset your mum, I just thought ...'

'That Dad will want to meet you.'

'Not me.' Aideen shook her head. 'I thought he might like to meet Ronan.' Even now, faced with the possibility of actually meeting her father, the assumptions of her childhood were unchanged. I've never needed him, she thought, and I don't really want him around. I just want some form of contact so Ronan will know he's there. So we can all talk about things as if they're normal. But if his wife doesn't know, was I wrong to go reaching out to his daughter? Oh, God, she thought, looking helplessly across the table at Yvonne. I'm just adding another layer of deceit and potential hurt.

Yvonne was eating a scone and jam briskly. Reading Aideen's mind from her face, she put down the scone. 'Look, I didn't say my mum doesn't know. I just said I've no idea whether she does or not. And, for God's sake, it happened ages before she met Dad. She can't complain, can she?'

'Not about him and my mum, maybe. But if he didn't tell her, she could be upset about that.'

'Okay, but now's his chance to. I can't see him sneaking off and meeting you and Ronan behind her back. And it all happened so long ago, how could it possibly hurt her?'

'Do you know what he and my mum planned to do if she hadn't died having me?'

'Auntie Jess said they were all for getting married. But the families would never have let them do that, would they? Dad had a place got in uni. He was due to go up to Dublin.'

And then to work in the family business, thought Aideen. He had no choice. The Murphys would never have let him get married when he was just out of school. I bet Gran wouldn't have allowed it either. God, I was lucky to have her. Somebody else might have had me put up for adoption. But, of course, she'd just lost her daughter. If I'd been in her position, I wouldn't have let me go either. I couldn't have.

At the far side of the table, Yvonne was spreading cream on her last piece of scone. She's nice, thought Aideen, really nice, but she's got no idea of what it's like to be pregnant and have a baby. For her, this is like second-guessing the next twist in a TV drama. Something that happened ages ago when people went to discos. For her, it's not real, because it happened way before she was born. And I've just been thinking of my point of view, and Ronan's, but what if my dad's like me and just never needed me around? Do I have a right to complicate things for him now? Somehow, she'd felt that this affluent girl with the managerial manner would be competent to advise her on the next step she should take. She'd thought Yvonne would come along with an attitude and a plan, and that, between them, they'd work out when and how to bring Derek Murphy into the picture. But none of that seemed to be happening, and now she wondered why she'd ever imagined that it would.

Chapter Twenty-Six

Fury disdained purpose-made overalls. Instead of going to the Homebase outlet in the mall in Carrick, he had the habit of buying his work clothes at boot sales and charity shops and wearing them until they were fit for nothing but the bin. It was a Wednesday when he and The Divil ambled along to the shop in Sheep Street and found Mary sitting behind the counter.

'That's a grand day out there, Mrs Casey.'

Mary was glaring at the till. 'Ah, don't be coming in here to me with the weather forecast. God be with the days when people ran proper cash books. Money in, money out, a couple of coloured biros and there you were.'

'Are you having trouble with the electronic register?'

'If I am, you needn't go round Lissbeg telling the world my business.'

'Haven't I better things to do? I'm here for a shirt.'

Mary gestured towards the rails of men's clothing. 'Well, you know where they are, though I'm not sure you've come to the right shop. We get a better class of item left into us here than you'd find on the average building site.'

'Well, that's where you're wrong. Half the lads on the London sites wear Christian Dior polo shirts. Grand bit of stretch in the shoulders and the cotton lasts for years.' Having made this lordly, and probably fictional, statement, Fury disappeared among the rails. The Divil pattered round to Mary's side of the counter, his ears pricked and his head on one side. She looked down, flapped her hand and called across the shop, 'In God's name, Fury, would you take this animal out of here? I'll have people complaining the merchandise is hairy!'

Fury's voice came from behind a display of winter-weight anoraks. 'He's nowhere near the merchandise. And I'll tell you this and tell you no more, ten euro is an extortionate price to put on a second-hand shirt.'

He emerged carrying a lumberjack shirt in plaid flannel, and Mary reared up, ready for a fight. 'I'll have you know that shirt's Kenzo! Look at the logo.'

'Well, that's no justification for the price tag. What kind of man wants to go round wearing logos?'

'It's fleece lined!'

'It's not, you know. It's padded.'

'And isn't that twice as good?'

Fury removed the shirt from its hanger and turned it inside out. 'I'll tell you something else. It's not Kenzo. It's knock-off. Look at the finish. You could be had up for peddling fakes.'

Thrusting The Divil aside, Mary surged from behind the counter. 'If you're going to start messing about with that shirt, you can pay for it. Give it here to me before you have it torn.'

'We'll call it a fiver.'

'We will not.'

'Oh, fair enough, say six euro, so.'

'You can say what you like, I'm not here to haggle. Have you no shame? This is a charity shop!'

'Show a bit of charity, then.' Fury cocked his head at her and Mary swelled with outrage.

'A *children's* charity shop! There's families out there dependent on food banks and you're here trying to rob them blind.'

'D'you know what it is, you're no fun at all.' Reaching into his back pocket, Fury produced a thick roll of banknotes. 'There you are. Six for the shirt, so you can't go round saying you got the best of me in a bargain, and ten more for the collection box. Will that satisfy you?' He folded the ten-euro note, pushed it into the box that stood on the counter and flicked a euro coin onto the fiver he'd laid by the till.

Mary threw up her hands with such violence that The Divil yelped in surprise. 'Ara, for God's sake, you're making things worse! The feckin' till knows the prices on the tickets. What do I do when the manager does the tot and the takings are wrong?'

'You tell her to look in the collection box. She'll have ten extra euro in there.'

'How is she going to know *why* it's there, though?'

'You've a tongue in your head. Can't you tell her?'

'I could try. Do you think she'd believe me? That one's checking up on me all the time.'

'God, Mary Casey, you must have a fierce bad reputation.'

The Divil appeared to decide that, at this point, Fury had gone too far. With the air of a subaltern standing up to an officer, he placed himself in front of Mary and sat down on her feet. After a moment's stand-off, Fury shrugged. 'Right so, but I've no more change on me. Take four euro out of the box and stick it into the till.' Seeing Mary's blank expression, he counted it out on his fingers. 'The fiver, the one euro coin, plus four coins out of the box, make a tenner.'

'I'm not going fiddling with that box. Yer one would accuse me of stealing.'

'She's not here, woman. How would she know you'd touched it?'

Mary looked at him darkly. 'Have you never heard of cameras?'

'I have, of course, and I've eyes in me head. There's no CCTV here.'

She folded her arms and glowered at him. 'I'm not touching that box.'

'Oh, Name of God! Fair enough. Here's another fiver. Give me back me euro coin.'

Mary swiped the price tag and thrust the two notes into the till.

Then, instead of returning the coin to Fury, she dropped it into the collection box and began to fold the shirt, which had now cost him twenty-one euro. He shook his head admiringly. 'At this rate, I might as well fly to London and pick up my work shirts in Savile Row.'

Thrusting the shirt into a bag, Mary propped herself against the counter, ready to be magnanimous in victory. 'I'd say it's a while since you were in London, is it?'

'Long enough. It's a young fella's game over there.'

'I've never been.'

'I'd say I won't see it again myself. But, God, when I was there I worked on great buildings. There was one at Piccadilly Circus, opposite that statue of the fellow with the bow and arrow. If you were up on the top stage of scaffolding and you looked back down along Regent Street, you'd see a big grey curve of Portland stone buildings and the traffic, jammed together, streaming away. It was like standing on a cliff above the ocean back there in Couneen and looking down at a massive shoal of mackerel. Not that you had much time to go rubbernecking off the scaffold. The foreman we had on that site was a fecker.'

'I'd say it was hard work.'

'It was brutal. And, Holy God Almighty, you lived hard. I've seen digs in Kentish Town with whole villages crammed into them. Lads that came over one by one and ended up bunking together. The only address they had was the brother's or the neighbour's or the cousin's so, when they got to London, they found their way there. And there they stuck. Twenty or more, sharing bedrooms and shaving themselves in the one tin basin. God, the state of them digs would sicken you. And bedbugs!'

'No!'

'Big as the buttons you'd have on your coat.'

Mary shook her head. 'That's fierce altogether.'

Fury hitched his skinny hip onto the counter beside her. 'I was up at the top of St Paul's Cathedral once, cleaning stonework. It'd all be done by specialist lads these days, but back then you went where you were sent. Jaysus, you wouldn't believe the size of them statues up close. Twelve foot and more looming over you, like they were hanging in the sky. They're only meant to be seen from the ground, but the men who carved them put in all the detail. St Peter with the cockerel crowing beside him and your other man with his eagle and his book.'

'Do you believe in it?'

'What?'

'Peter at the gates of Heaven with a key, and all the people who've died living inside, singing hymns.'

Fury snorted. 'Six to a room and three to a bed, like the lads in Kentish Town?'

'Ah, you know what I mean.'

The Divil had stretched out on the floor with his nose between his paws. Fury scratched him absently with the heel of his battered boot. 'I don't waste my time thinking about it. One thing's certain, at our age we'll be finding out soon enough.'

'I'll have you know I've no intention of turning me toes up yet.'

'None of us ever has, girl.' Fury clicked his fingers at The Divil. 'I should go. I've a meeting with my Australian. God, when I think of the buildings I've worked on, and look at me now installing a feckin' hot tub back in Couneen.'

'Is he going to live there?'

'Two weeks in summer, I'd say, till he finds the sun doesn't always shine on the west coast of Ireland. Then he'll be globetrotting off somewhere else. Small blame to him. If I had his youth and his money, I might do the same.'

Mary looked at him shrewdly. 'No, you wouldn't. Not if you had the choice.'

'Well, I wouldn't go making a hames of a grand little house before I left.'

'Is it not looking good?'

'He thinks it's champion. I think it looks like a right pile of shite.' Fury went to the door and looked back at Mary with a grin. 'But I've just forked out twenty-one euro for a fake Kenzo shirt, so what do I know?'

Mary spent the next half-hour dealing with customers, most of whom browsed and bought nothing. In the lull that followed, she went around with a duster, straightening books and polishing finger marks off the bric-a-brac. Suspecting that The Divil had spread hairs on the floor, she brought out the vacuum cleaner and wielded it energetically before returning it to its place in the back. Then she sat on the high stool behind the counter again. From the corner of her eye, she could see the edge of the window display, which was changed each week by the manager on her visits to Lissbeg. There was a strict rule that nothing in it could be sold without her permission, and a notice saying that staff were forbidden to remove items for closer inspection or fitting. Nervously, Mary turned her stool to face away from the window. An incident the previous week had unsettled her, even though, in the end, it had been passed off with a laugh. A customer who'd been trying on shoes had brought a pair to the counter and Mary had taken the money and found her a suitable carrier bag. Then, when the woman was ready to leave, it had struck Mary that a pair of ankle boots had gone from the rack. Sure that she'd seen them there not ten minutes earlier, she'd demanded to know if the woman had taken them. After all, she'd told herself later, it wasn't unknown for such things to happen. People's behaviour was scandalous sometimes. Look, for example, at yer one who'd tried to sneak off with the camisole. But this woman had pointed out that she hadn't so much as a handbag to put the boots into. She'd come in with just her purse in her hand and Mary had had to give her a bag for the shoes she bought. At that point, Mary had seen that the boots were in the window, conspicuously displayed on a large pile of books. Luckily, the woman had laughed and told her she wasn't to worry. It could happen to a bishop, she said, and, look, there were no bones broken. She'd left with a smile but Mary had been mortified. It wasn't as if she hadn't known that the boots were in the window. She'd noticed them as she'd come in to work. So how, she asked herself, had she forgotten? It was the sort of thing that, these days, caused Hanna to look at her sideways, and, having detected a note of concerned condescension in the woman's response, Mary feared the story might be passed on. Determined not to dwell on this possibility, she assured herself that she'd got the better of Fury anyway. She'd extracted the full price of the shirt plus an eleven-euro donation, so no one could say that she wasn't up to her job.

Perched on her stool, she thought about Fury's description of Regent Street, and of the huge weathered saints hanging high in the air above St Paul's Cathedral. He'd brought something to mind, which, at the time, she couldn't catch hold of, and, now that the shop was quiet again, she realised what it was. In her childhood, the wall that had enclosed Lissbeg's convent had run the full length of Broad Street, as grey and forbidding as a granite cliff.

One night in the year they'd left school, she and Tom had scaled it. They'd arranged a double date with her friend Pat and Pat's boyfriend, Ger Fitz, but, at the last minute, Ger's dad had insisted he work late in the butcher's shop. So Mary and Tom had gone for a drink on their own and, before leaving the pub, Tom had got the barman to open him a bottle of wine to take out. It was Blue Nun, which was what all the girls drank in those days, and Mary had thought he might take her down to the dunes on the bar of his bike. Instead, when they'd got to a shadowy part of Broad Street, he'd hooshed her up on the wall, where she struggled to get her balance and ended sitting astride the coping stones. With her skirt riding up her thighs, and clutching the bottle that Tom handed up to her, she watched him stand back, take a running jump and swing himself up beside her before dropping to the ground on the other side. 'Give me the bottle first, then jump and I'll catch you.' Half laughing and half terrified, she'd obeyed him and found herself crouched in damp grass between smooth dressed stone and dark, resinous conifers. She could recall the strangeness of that as clearly as if it had happened yesterday. In those days, the nuns' garden had been sacrosanct, as holy and inaccessible as the space beyond the altar rails in the chapel. None of the school's classrooms overlooked it, and the tall conifers planted behind the imposing boundary wall had ensured that no glimpse of what was beyond could be had from upstairs windows in Broad Street.

Sitting on her stool in the charity shop, Mary could see herself giggling in Tom's arms. Excitement and fear of discovery had made her dizzy, and she could hear Tom breathing as if he'd just run a race. Standing between the wall and the shaggy conifers, they strained their eyes as they tried to get their bearings. Then, sticking the bottle of Blue Nun into his jacket pocket, Tom grasped her hand and drew her between the trees onto a path. Directly ahead, at the far side of the fountain, was the wall of the convent building, pierced by pointed stained-glass windows from which shafts of light fell across spiralling herb beds, like spears of bloodstained gold. Mary was wary but, holding her hand, Tom crossed the gravel, moving slowly so that it wouldn't scrunch. When she resisted he stopped and put his mouth to her ear. 'The light doesn't even reach as far as the fountain, we'll be grand.'

'What're we doing?'

'I want to look at the statue there in the middle.'

'Just so long as there's nothing else you want.'

She could tell he was grinning. 'I'm not risking getting caught with my pants down in the nuns' garden, if that's what you're thinking.'

It was exactly what she'd been thinking, though she snorted derisively. 'Chance'd be a fine thing!' Tom gave her ear a nip with his teeth and she stifled a giggle against his shoulder before they moved on. That fountain was just the same then as it is today, thought Mary. The stone is more weathered now but it's just the same. She recalled the water bubbling from the carved flowers at the base of the statue of St Francis in his monk's robe. The saint's outstretched arms and cupped hands were dark against faint starlight and, high above, a north wind drove clouds across the sky. When they reached the basin, Tom hunkered down with his back to it and Mary slid down beside him, trying to get comfortable on the gravel.

'I thought you wanted to look at the statue.'

'I do but let's have a swig of the bottle first.'

They passed the bottle between them, kissing between each warm, sweet mouthful. Looking back, Mary recalled the sound of the water falling from the flowers, and the edge of the stone basin digging into the back of her neck. Relaxed by the wine and the sense of protection afforded by the fountain, she could smell the scents of rosemary and lavender, and hear an owl calling from somewhere beyond the convent's moon-silvered roof. When the bottle was more than half empty, Tom began to take off his shoes and socks.

'What in God's name are you doing?'

'I'm going to give a libation to St Francis.'

'A what?'

'A swig of the wine. The poor fellow deserves it, locked in here with all those holy virgins.'

'Are you out of your mind? If one of them looks out, they'll be sure to see.'

'I told you, the light doesn't reach this far and, anyway, what harm? We'll be back over the wall before they have time to unbolt the doors.'

'Jesus, Tom ...'

But he'd rolled up his trousers, climbed into the basin and begun to wade across to the statue waving the bottle of wine. Mary's heart was in her mouth for fear he'd start singing or shouting. He reached the statue and splashed wine over the saint's sandalled feet and then, bending down, wedged the bottle between the stone flowers. 'Might as well leave him a nun for the night.' Choking with laughter, she'd hung over the edge of the basin and he'd splashed back, grasped her hands, and pulled her in to join him. They'd kissed again, standing in the dark water, while billowing clouds above them embraced the moon and extinguished the stars.

The charity shop's door opened, rattling the sign that hung from a plastic sucker attached to the glass. Startled, Mary turned to see a man pointing at the bookshelves. 'Is it okay if I look and see what you've got?' She nodded but her mind was still in the past. From the day they'd met, she'd known that she'd marry Tom. He was clever at school and played football for the county and, for all his size and strength, was the gentlest lad in town. And, every so often, as on that night, he'd sweep her off her feet and do something crazy and unpredictable, making her feel that, together, they could take on the world and win. That was before she'd had Hanna, when it had seemed to her that Tom's focus had changed overnight. Not content with spending so much time round at his aunt Maggie's, he'd become a doting father as well. Pat, who by then had married Ger, had called Mary an eejit – surely she should be glad of a husband who spent time with his child?

This reaction had made Mary conceal an accumulation of jealousy, which, having simmered for years, had flared up disturbingly when Hanna revealed the existence of Maggie's book. In Mary's opinion, it was just like Maggie to leave behind a time bomb in a biscuit tin, demanding attention even after she'd gone. And yet, she thought, if Maggie hadn't sat down and made that book, I'd never have known what I know now. Silently, with her eye on the shop's stock of second-hand novels, she recalled

Jazz and Hanna's response when she'd found herself recounting what Liam had done. God alone knew why she'd told them. She'd never meant to. It was like someone else was speaking, she thought, and I couldn't get her to stop. The memory made her flinch, just as the thought of the boots in the window had, but, all the same, she hugged it to her in triumph. Anyone could tell from Hanna's face that she'd never heard that story. Not from Maggie's book and, more to the point, not from Tom. I was the one he told it to, thought Mary. I was the one who held him on the night of Maggie's funeral, when he broke down and cried in my arms like a child. Maggie had destroyed his vision of his dad as a hero and, now she was dead, he couldn't work out whether he'd hated or loved her, or even be certain that what she'd told him about Liam was the truth. He'd carried that story inside him for years, thought Mary, and now I know that he never shared it with Hanna. They talked about things they thought I wasn't clever enough to discuss with them, but I was the only one in the world he could talk to about that.

Chapter Twenty-Seven

The little first-floor office at the back of the house in St Finian's Close had once been Aunt Bridge's sewing room. Aideen and Bríd had packed up the threads, pins and ribbons, the treasured scraps and patches of lace and other fabric, the boxes of crochet hooks and knitting needles and, along with Aunt Bridge's sewing machine and piles of patterns and magazines, had given them to Lissbeg Library, which hosted dressmaking classes once a week. Much of what they gave away Aunt Bridge had bought in the town's former haberdashery shop, and it was Aideen's memory of childhood trips to what had then seemed a treasure-house that had inspired them to call their business HabberDashery. When the room was cleared, they'd installed shelves and assembled a flat-pack desk unit from Ikea, and since Bríd's college course had included a business-management module, it was she who'd taken the job of doing the books.

Now, sitting at the Ikea desk, Bríd stretched and shrugged her shoulders to loosen them. Having been more eager than Aideen to grab the chance of expanding into the Garden Café, she was relieved by the slow but steady increase in their monthly returns. Conor's vegetables and salad leaves were making a difference to their running costs and reputation, while local and tourist footfall were increasing at the café, which had had impressive online reviews since they'd taken the lease. The previous week, when Bríd and Aideen had both been at the deli, they'd decided they should consider stocking Una's homemade chutneys. What they hadn't done was mention the matter of Cafferkys' smoked salmon, which had become an elephant in the room.

Pushing her chair away from the desk, Bríd tried to analyse the problem. It was weeks since she'd faced the fact that they were overstocked with Dan's parents' salmon. Two packets that had passed their sell-by dates wasn't a big deal in the grand scheme of things. Nevertheless Bríd had been thrown by the discovery, and more so by the fact that Aideen had hesitated to mention it. Not only that, she thought, but I couldn't bring myself to discuss it with her or with Dan. Instead she'd phoned Dan's mother. 'I'm not sure how many packs Dan said we needed. And is it a regular order or does he come for them as and when?'

Fidelma had sounded worried. 'He wasn't specific. I mean, he said you were getting lots of new customers at the café, and that salmon and watercress bagels were doing brilliantly.'

'The salmon's gorgeous. It's pricy, though, so we do tend to sell more boring egg sandwiches than exciting salmon and watercress bagels. Anyway, I just wanted to flag that, now the tourist season's tailed off, we might not be taking so much.' It had seemed the most tactful way of putting the Cafferkys on notice without seeming too disloyal to Dan. She would have preferred to talk to him before calling Fidelma, but she'd suspected that, if she'd done so, she wouldn't have got a straight answer. That night, she'd raised it with Dan as dispassionately as she could. 'We're going to need to cut down on the salmon, going into the winter. I gave your mother a call.'

He'd looked at her sideways under his dark lashes. 'What's the story?'

'Nothing. I just wanted to flag it to her. But we ought to get ourselves organised at this end too. I know it's been a case of suck it and see to begin with but, by now, we should be reviewing our requirements.'

'Suck it and see? You'd want to watch out for the health and safety inspector.'

'Don't be a dork. You know what I mean. And the fact is, we've been overstocked and we just can't afford that, Dan.'

'Oh, lighten up, Bríd. I've been selling it hand over fist at the café.'

'Yet Aideen discovered packets that were way past their sell-by. We had to chuck them.'

'Jesus, you didn't, did you? Vacuum-packed smoked salmon lasts for ever.'

'The rule is sell-by plus three days when the packet has been unopened in a fridge.'

'Smoke's a preservative.'

'And rules are rules. We don't break them.'

He'd flashed her a dangerous look, then laughed and kissed her lightly. 'We're going to have to get you some dominatrix gear.'

'Shut up. I'm serious.'

'I know you are. Forget it. You've talked to Mum and, anyway, it makes sense for us to cut back. We've got half the trade now the tourists aren't around.'

'That's not actually true. According to the figures, it's not half, it's ...'

The rest of what she'd been going to say had been lost in a huge bear-hug, and there hadn't seemed to be much point in returning to it. And now another, underlying, issue had raised its head. In their brief chat the previous week, Aideen had assumed that Conor would join their discussion about Una's chutney and they'd spoken of having a meeting at the farm. What wasn't discussed was whether or not Dan should be there too. His insistence on going with the flow and keeping things informal had meant that, up to now, his role in the business hadn't been clear. But it ought to be clear, Bríd told herself, and it's not that I'm a control-freak. Leaving things as they are isn't fair to him any more than it is to the rest of us. He won't want to hear that, but it's true.

At the opposite side of the peninsula, Conor was whistling as he drove along the coast road. It was a shining day of bright sunshine and brief sleet showers, reminiscent of summer but bringing warning of icy weather to come. As he approached Couneen, a bevy of seagulls rose above the pier. Conor watched them circle, wings flashing, and dive in ones and twos, scavenging fish. When he reached Cafferkys' shop, he swung the wheel and pulled in at the slipway. Getting out of the jeep, he walked down to where Dan, seated on a bollard, was scraping scales off herring and throwing the heads and guts to the screaming gulls. Dan looked up and saw him. 'How's it going?'

'Good. How's the engine?'

'I have her fixed. Do you want a couple of fish to take home for your dinner?'

'Thanks. That'd be sound.'

'Let me finish them off and I'll stick a couple in a bag for you.'

Conor squatted beside him and sniffed the air. 'God, seaweed smells great when you're used to the smell of slurry.'

Dan nodded at the dozen or so gutted fish at his feet. 'I suppose you won't mind that these weren't caught on the quota.'

'You haven't the boat registered?' Conor kept disapproval out of his voice but, sensing it, Dan grinned.

'I've it registered all right, I just couldn't be arsed to apply for quota allocations. No one's going to come way out here chasing me for catching a fish supper. It's not worth their while.' Standing up, he gathered the fish into a plastic bucket. 'Come up to the shed and I'll stick yours in a bag.'

They walked towards the slipway against a fresh breeze and

paused at Dan's lockup shed. Ducking inside, Dan emerged with the fish bagged up and a couple of cans of Coke. 'I'm doing the lunchtime shift for Bríd but I've half an hour to spare. D'you want one of these?' Conor nodded. If he took a break with Dan now he could eat his sandwiches on the road later and lose no time. They sat slumped in a couple of deckchairs in a sheltered corner where the sun drew a tarry smell from the timber shed. The seagulls had moved on to scavenge elsewhere, and the only sounds came from the waves and the distant rhythmic clink of a hammer on stone.

Conor jerked his head in the direction of the hammering. 'Is that Fury still working on the Australian's place?'

Dan nodded. 'Your man wants a dry-stone wall round the whole site.'

'For security?'

'For the look of it, I reckon. He was down here a while back raving about the colour of the local stone.'

Conor grinned. 'And is it local stone Fury's using?'

'God knows. Wherever it's from, I'd say it probably fell off the back of a lorry.'

Conor stretched his legs, feeling the warmth of the sun through his jeans above his wellington boots. 'What's this Aussie like?'

'Seems a nice enough guy. We talked about some of the places I went to when I was over in Oz. God, they've a great eco-marine industry over there. It's booming. That's what you get when the weather's fine all year round.'

'It isn't, though, is it?'

'It is in the north, and wherever you are, it's a helluva lot better than you'd get here in Couneen.'

'Would you think of going back?'

'With no money and no prospects? No chance. Anyway, what about Bríd?' Dan swallowed a mouthful of Coke and stared out across the ocean. 'Fury says there's something to be said for knowing when to quit. This is my place, though. I'm not giving up on it. Well, you must understand that.' He glanced at Conor. 'How many generations of McCarthys have farmed your land?'

'Five, according to Paddy.'

'My granddad told me there's been Cafferkys in Couneen for centuries. He used to say that every man in our family was born to haul ropes here, and that he was damned if he'd be the fellow to let go of the rope.'

Though Lissbeg was surrounded by new council housing, the scale of the little town was still such that everywhere was within walking distance. After lunch Bríd walked down to the café, taking the same route from St Finian's Close to Broad Street that Aunt Bridge had walked when she'd gone to buy laces and threads. Passing the deli, she put her head round the door to say hi to Pavel. He was serving a group of customers and gave her a cheery thumbs-up. Pausing for a break in the traffic, she ran across to the central island, where the geraniums in the horse trough had been replaced by winter pansies standing in rigid, municipal rows, like soldiers in yellow uniform wearing jaunty purple caps.

As she waited to cross the further stream of traffic, Bríd saw Jazz walk briskly through the entrance to the nuns' garden, swinging a leather briefcase, her long, shiny hair tied in a high ponytail. It occurred to her that she'd never seen Jazz without a salon blow-dry and that, even from a distance, the clothes she wore to work looked expensive. According to the grapevine, Jazz's dad was an investor in the company she worked for, and her English gran, who'd set it up, had given her the job of marketing manager. Admittedly, it sounded as if her parents' divorce had been ghastly, so you couldn't say she'd had an easy life. Still, it must be great never to have to sit sweating in your bank manager's office, or to count every cent before deciding what to spend money on. Conscious of her own Penneys jeans and sweater, Bríd watched the trim figure disappear in the direction of the old convent where, she was sure, Jazz's office was furnished from someplace a lot more expensive than Ikea. On the other hand, she told herself, there's a lot to be said for being independent, and fierce excitement to be had from knowing you're in charge of your own destiny.

When she entered the café, Dan was sweeping the floor. There were no customers and she asked if there'd been many in for lunch.

'It wasn't bad. Far more people wanting to sit inside.'

Bríd nodded. This was an inevitable consequence of the changing of the season but, with fewer tourists looking for tables, there was plenty of room indoors for customers, even during the lunchtime rush. Dan put the brush away and came to kiss her, pushing back her hair and tilting her face with both his hands. 'You look amazing.'

With the image of Jazz still in her mind, Bríd couldn't resist fishing for a compliment. 'As good as Jazz Turner?'

'Jazz? Where did that come from?'

'Oh, I don't know. Just that I saw her walking across the garden looking gorgeous. Legs up to her elbows and great hair.'

Dan laughed. 'Is that so? Well, take it from me that Jazz Turner might have the best bum in Lissbeg—'

'Oh, thanks a million!'

'—but you are the hottest, most beautiful, sexiest, hottest—'

'You already said hottest.'

'And I'll say it again. Hottest. Sexiest. Most gorgeous ...'

Over his shoulder, Bríd could see a couple passing the window. She returned Dan's kiss and pulled away. 'I'll take that as a yes, but let's remember where we are.'

'Bet I could make you forget.'

'I bet you could too. So back off.'

Dan gave her a wicked grin and, walking away, began to push chairs under tables. 'The guy from the cruise line looked in to make a booking. He has a party of eight coming to see the psalter and they want to have hot chocolate here before going shopping in Carrick. I raved about your sachertorte so they're going to have that as well.'

'Great stuff.' Bríd put her bag behind the counter and poured herself a coffee. Coming to join her, Dan said that he planned to cook them dinner. 'I stuck a couple of herring into the fridge. We can have them this evening. Conor came by the pier and I gave a couple to him as well.' This mention of Conor seemed a good cue for the difficult conversation she'd decided they needed to have. She was formulating her opening sentence when the phone by the till rang. Secretly relieved by the interruption, she picked it up.

The voice on the other end asked for Dan. 'Tell him it's Andy Cox about the chairs.'

'Er, okay.' Bríd held the phone out. 'It's some guy for you. Andy Cox.' Dan took it and Bríd felt a flash of irritation. This was exactly the kind of thing that needed to be sorted out. If she'd found that Pavel, or any staff member, had given out the café's number for their private phone calls, she would have put a stop to it at once. But she knew that if she raised it with Dan he'd tell her to lighten up. Annoyed though she was, she felt she should give him privacy, so she went to the door and sipped her coffee looking out at the garden. When he put down the phone she turned and saw him giving a double thumbs-up. 'Good news?'

'You're going to love it.'

'So tell me.'

'That was a guy I met yonks ago, when I was doing bits of jobs for Fury. Andy Cox. He's got an online company in Limerick. Catering supplies.'

'And?'

'And he's only going to do us a brilliant deal on chairs for the café!'

Bríd felt as if he'd thrown a bucket of water at her. 'Who said we need chairs for the café?'

'Oh, come on, Bríd, you know we do. These are just tat left by the crowd that failed to get the place moving. Andy's going to give us a great price.'

A bubble of anger seemed to be expanding in Bríd's chest. 'No, he isn't.'

'What?'

'No, Andy isn't going to give us a great price. You know why? Because we're not going to be buying chairs from him, or anyone else. And you know why? Because we can't afford to! And you know something else, Dan? You had no right, no right at all, to go talking to him as if you were in a position to make that kind of decision!'

The air crackled with tension as they stood glaring across the room at each other. Dan's dark eyes had gone blank and, somewhere behind her anger, Bríd's heart went out to him. It was so clear that he'd assumed she'd be pleased. Why in the name of God, she thought, does he do this sort of thing to us? When is he ever going to learn sense? Then the anger took over again. 'You just don't get it, do you? Aideen and I own this company, Dan. You're not a partner.'

Dan had relaxed dangerously and was leaning against the till.

'Okay, I get it. No need to shout. The funny thing is, Bríd, I thought it was you and me that were partners.'

'Well, yes, of course we are, but not business partners. Can't you see that?' Dan's face was white as paper and she hated him for making her feel so bad. Stricken by his expression, she lashed out. 'Look, you're lousy at business! You haven't a clue. You just can't see that there's no future in playing at being a maverick. Ducking and diving and telling yourself that rules are made to be broken. Going round with a chip a mile high on your shoulder, and claiming the Cafferkys always had a bad rap.'

'Let's leave my family out of this.'

'Well, maybe you ought to ask yourself why they've always been stick-in-the-muds. Striking heroic poses is dramatic, but playing the victim doesn't make for success!' Having delivered this at the top of her voice, Bríd ran out of steam and, appalled by what she'd said, discovered her bottom lip was trembling.

Dan came towards her and, for a second, she thought things would be all right. They'd hug and both say they were sorry and, maybe, having cleared the air, be able to talk things through. She was already seeking an opening line when he stopped directly in front of her with no suggestion of apology in his stance. After a moment she understood and, swallowing a lump in her throat, stepped aside to allow him to open the door. The last things she saw before he walked out were his face, so painfully twisted she couldn't bear it, and the complete lack of expression in his eyes.

Chapter Twenty-Eight

Brian was working at his desk in his office when the phone rang. When he lifted the receiver absently the task at hand was forgotten as he became aware of anxiety in Hanna's voice on the line. 'Hanna? Are you okay?' She had mentioned that morning that she had to be in Carrick for a meeting, but that wasn't an unusual occurrence and, though the planning offices were in the same complex as the County Library, she wouldn't normally ring him simply because she was nearby.

'I'm fine. I'm downstairs, actually.'

'Has something happened?'

'I've just had a conversation with Tim.' Her voice still sounded anxious, so Brian invited her to come up.

Hanna hesitated. 'You're not in the middle of something?'

'No, really, it's fine, come on up.'

When she came into the office, she still appeared hesitant. 'I'm sorry, I didn't mean to interrupt you.'

'You haven't. Sit down and tell me what's going on.'

Hanna sat in the chair at the opposite side of his desk. Her expression reminded Brian of their first meeting when, in the midst of her restoration of Maggie's place, she'd arrived in his office worried about Fury's failure to follow planning procedure. But then she'd been spiky and aggressive, while now she looked strangely lost.

'I didn't realise you had a meeting with Tim today.'

'I didn't. I'm here for a health and safety regulations catch-up thing. Just routine. But Tim turned up and asked if I had time for a word in his office.'

'What did he say?'

'What I've been dreading.' She told him the story with her hands tightly clasped in her lap and, watching, he saw her consciously forcing herself to relax, and heard the strain in her voice as she tried to reassure him. 'But, really, there's no need to worry. I dare say I'm overreacting.'

'Let me get this right. Someone's turned up with a letter that says your granddad Liam had it in for James Hartnett.'

'That's it. A lad from somewhere near Ballyfin. Probably around Jazz's age. Tim showed me the letter. It was written a year or so after the Civil War ended, by one of the men imprisoned after the stand-off in Castle Lancy. You can tell he was still very bitter. Like I told you, there's only one line in it about Liam. "Casey said that Hartnett hadn't a decent bone in his body. If he hadn't shot him then, he'd have hunted him down and put paid to him later." Tim's decided it exemplifies how personal animosity finds fulfilment in ideology.'

'Tim's a twat.'

Hanna grinned. 'Well, yes, that too. But he's right, Brian. The letter supplies a valid and interesting talking point. The thing is, it seems to corroborate the story Maggie told Dad when he was a boy, and I'm worried about the effect it'll have on my mother.' Her hands tightened again. 'Obviously, I didn't mention Maggie to Tim. I just told him I didn't like the prospect of Liam being the centre of speculation.'

'And what did he say?'

Hanna's lips tightened. 'That he hadn't anticipated that my response would be unprofessional.'

'*What?*'

'Tim's been nursing a grudge ever since the psalter ended up in my library, not Carrick. They say revenge is a dish best served cold.'

'But "unprofessional"?'

'Over-emotional. Then he got all smarmy and said he could call a meeting to discuss it, and that, if I wanted to step away from certain aspects of the project, no doubt my colleagues would be happy to cover for me.'

'He's taking the piss.'

'Exactly. Can't you just see the agenda for that meeting? "Single item. Importance high. A discussion of the skeletons in the Casey family's cupboard." I can't imagine anything more embarrassing, and the story would be all over Finfarran ten minutes after we'd finished.'

'Do you really think this is about the psalter being housed in Lissbeg?'

'Partly. If it hadn't been for Charles's stipulation, Tim would have been custodian of a unique national treasure, and the county library would have had your state-of-the-art extension. So, yes, I do think that's part of the story. But the thing is that this letter will beef up his press release. Which is where his main focus is now.' Hanna's eyes widened. 'And, oh, God, if I make a fuss, it gives him a new angle. He can prance around in front of the cameras playing at being sensitive and dropping heavy hints about A Story That Cannot Be Told.'

Brian thrust back his chair and came round the desk. 'If anyone's being unprofessional here, it certainly isn't you.'

'Wait. Where are you going?'

'I'm going over to the library to have a word with Mr Slattery.'

'No, Brian, don't!' To Hanna's dismay, Brian sidestepped her attempt to grab his arm and, taking his jacket, stormed out in a rage. It was completely uncharacteristic of him to lose control of his temper and, as the door from his office led to an open-plan part of the planning department, to run after him would be to cause a scene. Defeated, Hanna sat down again, wondering if she should try to call him. But, having seen the look on his face, she suspected he wouldn't answer his phone. Shocked by her conversation with

Tim, and shaken by Brian's reaction, she sat staring at his empty chair. Then, hearing the door handle turn, she swung round, assuming that Brian had seen sense and come back. Instead, she found herself looking at two faces peering at her around the door. She blinked, recognising the hairy snout at floor level, and the woolly hat and beaky nose six feet above it. Seconds later, Fury had slipped into the room and closed the door behind him, and The Divil had made a flying jump and landed on her lap.

'It's bad enough the authorities have you filling in forms if you want to put up a henhouse, without they're not here when you come in for a meeting.'

Fury's tone was so acerbic that Hanna reacted as if she were Brian's secretary. 'I'm so sorry. What time were you expected? He's just stepped out.'

'I suppose that's one way of putting it. Another would be to say he's taken off like the wrath of God.'

'You saw him.'

'In passing. I doubt if he saw us, though. He looked like a man with a red mist before his eyes.'

Unable to think what to do next, Hanna slumped in her chair. 'You know what? I'm having a terrible day.' Immediately, The Divil wriggled round and placed his chin on her chest.

Fury shook his head in wonder. 'Now, there's empathy for you. And people say Jack Russells care about nothing but rats.' Hanna scratched the wiry hair between the silky ears, praying without much hope that the mist would clear from Brian's eyes before he got as far as Tim's office. Fury cocked his head at her. 'What's the story? You might as well tell me while I'm sitting here waiting.' Still feeling she needed to apologise for Brian's absence, Hanna enquired again about the time of Fury's appointment.

'Ah, we just came by.'

'But you said ...'

Lounging around the desk, Fury sat in Brian's chair. 'I said we'd come for a meeting. I don't do appointments. By the look of things, if I did, it wouldn't have made much difference. I mean, if he'd walk out on you like that, he'd leave The Divil and me in the lurch without so much as a qualm.'

'He didn't walk out on me.' Hanna could think of nothing better to say than that it was complicated. Then, as Fury continued to look at her in silence, she gave up and told him the whole story, finishing with something that sounded to her own embarrassed ears like a wail of despair. 'I came away from Tim's office feeling worried for my mam. Stirring this old story up is going to upset her. And now I'm freaked about Brian too. This is so not like him.'

'Ah, but at this stage, he's not Brian Morton the county architect, he's Sir Galahad riding a big white horse.' Fury swung Brian's chair to and fro to inspect it, raising and lowering the seat and adjusting the headrest. 'God, this is a quare sophisticated yoke he's got himself. Is it standard council issue? Because, if so, we must be paying way too much in rates.' He leaned back as far as the chair would let him and looked disapprovingly across the desk at Hanna. 'I notice the public sits on moulded plastic. Very bad for the back.'

Hanna was about to protest that Brian wasn't responsible for his office furniture when The Divil sighed and appeared to fall asleep. His gentle breathing and the warmth of his furry body were relaxing so, instead of allowing herself to be distracted by Fury's teasing, she focused on what he'd just said about Brian. 'What did you mean by Sir Galahad on a horse?'

'A white horse, I said. It's iconic. Like the white hat the good guys used to wear in the cowboy films.'

'I heard what you said. I don't know what you mean.'

'Well, there's a confession for a well-read woman! Your man's gone galloping off to rescue his lady from a dragon.'

'Me? I don't need rescuing.'

'That's never stopped a man yet. We're programmed for it, girl. Haven't you noticed?' Hanna thought of her urbane, good-humoured Brian. Surely this was just Fury fantasising again, or still teasing. Fury caught her eye and winked. 'You know I'm right, and it's stories and songs are to blame. All that derring-do stuff you peddle in your library.'

'No, I don't.'

'I'm not saying you haven't got other bits and pieces as well. Books about differential calculus, say, or the latest vegan diet. But we all start off with heroes and villains. Fionn Mac Cumhaill and Dan Dare and Sir Galahad and James Bond, swooping in and righting everyone's wrongs. It'll be a cross between the bridge of the Starship *Enterprise* and the Knights of the Round Table over there in the County Library. Tim'll be loving it too.'

Hanna was outraged. 'If Brian thinks I want him to play soldiers …!'

'Ah, it's nothing to do with you now, girl. It's all about him.'

As this was something that seemed to require discussion with Brian, not Fury, Hanna returned to the central issue. 'Did you know that Maggie's brother shot James Hartnett?'

'I'd say I might have heard talk of it years ago. James had a wife and a child. They must have left afterwards. He had no family living hereabouts when I was a boy.'

Hanna phrased her next question carefully. 'Do you remember anyone speculating about it?'

'They didn't if they had sense. Not out loud, anyway.' Fury leaned his elbows on the desk. 'Look, there isn't a household in any country comes out of a civil war without something they'd rather wasn't discussed. It's no different here. If Liam had a personal score to settle, he won't have been the only one. It stands to reason. The neighbours out fighting were the same people who bargained at markets, built each other's houses and came together each year to save crops. They may have taken up arms for an idea, but that doesn't mean they forgot the times they'd been cheated over a bullock, or how the schoolmaster made them feel stupid, or the fact that the lad from across the way had stolen their best girl.' Fury shrugged. 'And some fellows will have discovered they weren't as brave as they'd hoped to be, or that, once they were out in the back hills, without their mammy's eye on them, they were as capable as the next fellow of rape.' He eyed Hanna thoughtfully. 'There was more than one informer around these parts as well. Have you never wondered how the Tans knew where to find Liam the night they raided the house? There was a price on his head, remember.'

Hanna looked at him bleakly. 'Do you think one of the neighbours informed on him?'

'I don't think about it at all. What's the point? Many a house was left hungry when a son or a daughter went off to fight for freedom. And, one way or another, life goes on, girl. People still need to do deals, and build houses, and come together if the weather is shite and hay has to be saved. So, when the fighting's over, they put their heads down and, if they've got sense, they say nothing. It takes more than a generation or two for a civil war to turn into a story, and I told you at the start that you were opening a can of worms.'

The Divil's whiskers twitched and he wriggled in Hanna's arms. Turning, she saw that Brian had come in. Fury swung the desk chair casually. 'Well, here he is. Finally.'

Brian stared at him. 'What are you doing here?'

'Last time I looked, this department was still in the business of implementing and advising on planning policies.'

'Last time I looked, that was my desk.'

Unfazed, Fury lounged to his feet and relinquished it. 'We're here about a boiler.' Hanna was about to get up and leave when he lifted another chair and set it beside her. 'Stay where you are, girl, we won't be a minute.' Sitting down, he cocked his head at Brian. 'The boiler at Castle Lancy. Basically it's banjaxed. I've told Charles Aukin I could have a new one in there in jig time, but he's fussing. The castle's a feckin' protected structure on the register.'

'Well, of course it is.'

'So there's all this stuff about filling in a Section Five Declaration application.'

Listening, Hanna realised that Brian was well accustomed to this sort of exchange with Fury. He had sat down and was leaning back with a quizzical expression. 'You do know that you should be talking to the conservation officer, not me?'

'I've always made it my motto to start at the top.'

'And yet you always end up by having to go through the proper channels.'

'Holy God Almighty, talk about time-wasting! If you'd been at your desk, where you should have been, I'd be sorted and gone by now. Am I right or am I wrong when I say I can fit a new boiler in a protected structure if I follow the existing plumbing and wiring routes?'

'This isn't going to work, Fury. I'm not giving you an answer because, if I do, you'll call it permission.'

'Or, looked at another way, I'll save the council a fortune in feckin' red tape.' As the stand-off continued, Hana saw that The Divil seemed to be following things intently. She could feel his muscles tighten and, with a sneeze that made his tail twitch, he sat up on her knee and jumped lightly to the floor. Fury stood up. 'It's a health and safety risk, you know, that boiler.'

'Well, in that case, you'd better make it safe.' With The Divil at his heels, Fury took himself off with great dignity, leaving Brian and Hanna in a stand-off of their own. Seeing her grim expression, Brian lost his air of amused authority. 'You're fuming, aren't you?'

'What happened?'

'Well, I got to Tim's office.'

'And?'

'And, basically, I made a bit of a fool of myself.' Hastily, Brian kept going. 'But not of you. Honestly. I made it crystal clear that you hadn't sent me.'

Hanna's tone was icy. 'Oh, great. That makes me feel *much* better.'

'Darling, I'm sorry. I just lost my cool.'

'Oh, right. And how did that work out for you?'

'If it's any consolation, Tim was just as idiotic.'

'Fury said he would be.'

'Fury did?'

'He said you'd both behave like a couple of kids playing soldiers.'

This didn't go down well with Brian. 'I see. So you told him the whole story?'

'Yes. Yes, I did. You know why? Because while you were off being macho, he and The Divil were here, willing to talk things through with me sensibly.' Seeing Brian's mouth twitch, Hanna couldn't help but smile. 'Okay, it was mostly Fury who did the talking. The Divil just kept me pinned to my plastic chair.'

'They're an efficient team.'

'What did you actually say to Tim?'

'Stuff about libel.'

'What? About libelling Liam? For heaven's sake, Brian! You can't libel the dead.'

Brian looked rueful. 'And that is something I now know. Tim told me.'

'I take it you didn't come to blows?'

'God, no. He sneered a bit from behind his desk while I made forcible points and waved my arms.'

'Tell me the door was shut and the whole library didn't hear you.'

'It was, and I didn't shout. I sort of hissed at him.'

'That must have been impressive.'

Brian groaned. 'Darling, I'm sorry. Really I am. He's just such an evil, pompous git. And you don't need to say it, I know I was pompous too.'

Suddenly Hanna felt too tired to continue the post-mortem. 'Well, I suppose I should be glad I've got a knight in shining armour.'

Brian stood up and came round the desk to hug her. 'What are you going to do?'

'Go back to work, I suppose, and draft some kind of email to Tim. Do I need to refer to your little altercation? How did it end?'

'Embarrassed stalemate. I absolutely did make an ass of myself, but I got in a few home truths as well.' Brian grinned reminiscently. 'You should've seen his face.'

'Oh, great. That'll make things easier going forward.' There was an edge to Hanna's voice again as she picked up her bag to go and, unwisely, Brian dropped a kiss on her head.

'Darling, stop. I've said I'm sorry. Sarcasm doesn't suit you.'

Suddenly, anger came flooding back and she jerked away from him. 'No? Well, you know something, Brian? You look completely ridiculous up on a big white horse.'

Chapter Twenty-Nine

Wearing waterproof trousers, fisherman's boots and a thick woollen jersey, Dan had just finished swabbing the smokehouse floor. With the bucket and broom in his hands and the hose draped over his shoulder, he went into the yard and bent to coil it round a tap fixed to the wall. Straightening his back, he caught sight of the row of cottages up on the hillside. Fury had removed the last of the scaffolding from the Australian's place where the unfinished perimeter wall now snaked gracefully round the building, enclosing a custom-built barbecue on the Valencia slate patio. It was a windy day with clouds sweeping a pale blue sky and, early that morning, Dan had sat watching a pair of humpback whales feeding in the open sea just beyond the inlet. Rising to the surface to breathe, and spurting plumes of mist from their blowholes, they'd rolled and dived repeatedly, chasing sprat. Though he hadn't been able to see their prey, he'd known they were there deep under the water, a shining shoal moving as one, like a murmuration of swallows, helpless to evade the whales' gaping jaws. He'd watched for almost an hour until the wind had changed direction, causing the sprat and their predators to move further out to sea. For a while the whales' dorsal fins were still visible, but soon Dan had lost sight of them and abandoned his perch on the pier.

Putting away the hose, he told himself savagely that if he and Bríd had to break up they would have done better to do so in high summer, when there might have been a chance of work to distract him from his woes. Tourists wanting to be taken out whale-watching, or cyclists needing to be served in his parents' shop. As it was, he'd spent the days since the row hanging around aimlessly, thinking of nothing but Bríd and mentally rerunning the scene in the Garden Café.

It wasn't that what she'd said had been unforgivable. Neither of them had ever had much control when it came to a fight, and Dan could remember several accusations he'd made in the past of which he'd later been ashamed. And this time he'd known, even as he'd stood waiting for her to move aside in the doorway, that Bríd was as shocked as he was by what she'd said in anger. If he hadn't left, they would probably have gone home together and patched things up by falling into bed. But what am I supposed to do now? he thought bitterly. Turn up with flowers and wine and apologise for storming out?

Somewhere at the back of his mind, he knew he had more than just storming out to apologise for and that, if he went back to St Finian's Close, Bríd would tell him so. But he couldn't admit, even to himself, that he'd been wrong to talk to Andy Cox about the chairs. From the way Bríd got her knickers in a twist, he thought crossly, you'd think I'd planned things, whereas I was just going with the flow. He'd bumped into Andy in a pub in Ballyfin. They hadn't met for ages, and it was only when they'd had a few pints that Andy had mentioned he now worked in catering supplies. By the sound of things he was making a mint, and pleased as Punch about it, and his response when Dan had offered to buy a round had been annoying. 'Not at all. Put your money away. I'll stick it here on the card.'

This had been an obvious ploy to show off the fact that the card in question was platinum but, despite himself, Dan had felt crushed. As a result, he'd overstated his role at the Garden Café and, before he'd known where he was, had agreed to Andy's offer of a deal. 'Mates' rates, of course, Dan. You know me, I'll look after you. Stick your work number into my phone and I'll give you a shout when we're sober.' In fact, Dan had been far from drunk, but the pints had taken the edge off his judgement so, without considering Bríd's reaction, he'd keyed the café's number into Andy's fancy phone. The next day there'd been a text, requesting the number of chairs that were wanted, by which time Dan had convinced himself that he'd snapped up a bargain for which Bríd and Aideen would be grateful and sing his praise. And that was totally stupid, he thought, coiling the hosepipe far too tightly around the dripping tap. I was never anything more than a dogsbody in their blasted café, and hardly more than a sofa-surfer at St Finian's Close.

Miserably, he sat on the wall and lit a cigarette, thinking that if there was any silver lining to this disaster it was that he could now smoke in bed again. But the thought of bed without Bríd made him groan. Even in Australia, where he'd found a girl on each beach on which he'd unrolled his sleeping bag, no one had ever been able to take Bríd's place. He remembered the boring chemistry lesson in the middle of which he'd discovered he could make her turn and look at him. Lots of the other girls in their class had been going through a Goth phase at the time, and the honey-coloured hair falling to Bríd's shoulders had shone among a sea of jet-black, backcombed birds' nests.

Drawing deeply on his cigarette, Dan recalled the moment when he'd consciously tuned out from the lesson and concentrated on willing her to look at him, and how the shock that went through him when she did had been like a lightning bolt. He'd known from her startled reaction that she'd felt exactly the same and, after that morning, he'd kept on doing it, partly for the effect on them both but mostly to prove that he could. The idea that he could cause something to happen by sheer force of will had been amazing, the more so because he'd always felt that, except for his looks, Fate had dealt him a losing hand in life. It had felt empowering to be the guy who could get the class swot to make love behind the sports hall, though he'd soon realised that it was far more than that. The fact was that he'd fallen for her, hook, line and sinker, and not just because of the sex, but because she was Bríd.

For the hundredth time, he reached for his phone, where her

number was on speed dial, and, yet again, shoved it back into his pocket. As long as the call wasn't made, he could tell himself things might come right again, but there was no way he could get in touch with nothing to offer but an apology that Bríd might well reject. Slumped on the wall, he smoked grimly, staring at the house on the hill where Fury, dressed in a padded plaid shirt, had appeared and was wielding his stone hammer. The Divil was poised nearby on a pile of cement sacks, his ears pricked and his stump of a tail erect. Then, as Dan stared uphill absently, the door of the house opened and Fury's Australian came out and began to stroll down towards him, picking his way on the unmade road in unsuitable city shoes.

Aideen was sitting on the side of the bath in which Conor was luxuriating in bubbles. She was holding Ronan on her knee and almost overbalanced when he lurched towards the water. Conor steadied him with a soapy hand. 'Put him in with me.'

'I will not. I've only just changed his nappy and got him dressed. Stop it, Ronan. Those are Daddy's bubbles.'

Conor grinned. 'Daddy's going to stink to high heaven at the solicitor's.'

'Well, you needed something to counter the smell of muck.'

'I was thinking carbolic, not patchouli.'

'It's lemon verbena, and aren't you lucky to have someone to run your bath for you?'

'What are you two going to do while me and Una are out?'

'Go into Lissbeg ourselves later. Ronan has books to return to Hanna and I've a few things to get.'

'You mean he's finally got bored with *Find Spot at the Library*?'

'I'm the one who's bored by it, but I've told him there's other Spot books. Haven't I, Ronan?' She bounced him up and down. '*Spot Goes to the Park. Spot Loves His Mum. Night, Night, Spot.*'

Conor flicked a fleck of foam at her. '*Spot Goes to the Farm.*'

'Really?'

'You can't miss it. Spot's on the cover hugging a smug-looking hen.'

'There you are then, Ronan. We'll find you a new book.'

'Is Bríd in the deli today?'

'She's down for the cash-and-carry run. I offered to do it, and take Ronan, but she's going round like a robot, saying she wants to stick to the schedule. She'd be better to take the morning off. I'd say she hadn't slept a wink when I talked to her. She's in a real state about the break-up with Dan.'

'Okay, enough luxury, I'm getting out.' Conor stood up and looked at the bubbles clinging to his chest. 'God, I need hosing down after that. How do you get rid of these?'

'Don't be an eejit. They disappear when you dry yourself.' Aideen handed him a towel. 'Did you hear what I said about Bríd?'

'Yeah, but it's just another argy-bargy, isn't it? What was this one about?'

'She didn't say, but it feels serious.'

Conor went through to the bedroom, towelling himself. 'When we finish with Jim Hickson, Una's fixed to talk with the bank manager. Had I better wear my suit?'

'Well, you're not going cap in hand, asking for money, so I don't see why you should wear a suit, as long as you're clean and not smelling of muck.'

As she waved them off, Aideen felt light-hearted. Now that Paddy's estate was wound-up, the future was looking clearer, and when she'd come home after meeting Yvonne at the garden centre, she'd decided it was best not to pursue meeting her dad. She and Yvonne had parted with mutual assurances that they'd keep in touch and take matters further but, to Aideen's relief, they'd not been in contact since then. Now that Ronan was becoming what she thought of as his own person, it was as if things had somehow moved on. Initially, it had felt important for him to have a relationship with his granddad, but she'd realised since then that she hadn't considered what that might mean for her father's family. It was also good that now she needn't mention it at home, because here too, she'd realised, were complexities beyond what she'd imagined. She'd seen Conor's relief at the prospect of paying off the debt to Joe's father-in-law so, if she were to tell him she'd tried to contact her own wealthy father, would he think that might put him under a new obligation? And, even if that weren't so, he might see her dad as another encroaching stranger, whose presence he hadn't wanted or bargained for. Worse still, what if Conor and Una were to imagine she'd wanted her father in Ronan's life as a sort of replacement for Paddy? Surely in the year they'd lost him that would be painful for them?

Aideen was still feeling relieved when she went back to the kitchen, and was putting Ronan into his outdoor coat when her phone rang. The first thing that crossed her mind was that Bríd must be calling her from the cash-and-carry. But when she looked at the screen she saw it was Yvonne.

Having driven in a daze to St Finian's Close, Dan walked up the front path and fitted his key in the lock. As he went in, Bríd had just come downstairs. They stood for what felt like an age before Dan opened his mouth to speak. Then she lunged down the hall and he caught her in his arms as she buried her head in his chest. Her voice came to him, muffled by the thick wool of his jersey. 'No, don't. Don't say a word. We'll only make things worse.'

Dan kicked the front door closed behind him and, still locked together, they moved towards the stairs. Buoyed up by what he had to tell her, he tried again to speak, between kisses. 'Listen, Bríd, you've got to hear this.'

'No, I don't. I don't want to talk. I know we must but, God, Dan, I've missed you.'

'I couldn't just come back and say I was sorry.'

'Don't, please. I'm sorry too. I shouldn't have said what I did. But sorry isn't enough.'

'I know it's not. That's what I'm saying.' Dan pushed her against the wall of the stairwell, holding her there, a few steps above him. 'Jesus, I've missed you too. We can't keep doing this to each other. But we won't have to now. Wait till I tell you.'

Pulling him towards her again, Bríd kissed him fiercely. She'd spent long, wakeful hours planning what to say when she next saw him, accepting facts that, before their row, she hadn't been willing to face. But from the moment he'd come through the door, words had become the enemy, and all she wanted now was to get him up the stairs to bed. He moved up to stand level with her, and kissed her more gently. 'I'm not here to say I'm sorry. I've got great news.'

It had seemed to Bríd that her bedroom could be a refuge. With its soft mattress and faint scent of the lavender Aunt Bridge had kept in the linen box on the landing, the bed would gather them in and hold them together. Skin to skin, face to face, bones and sinews straining to incorporate self within self. If they could just get there, she told herself, they needn't talk or listen. They could pull the duvet over their heads and never come out again. But whatever Dan had to say to her, it was clear that she couldn't stop him, so she slid down the wall and sat on the step, leaning against the spindles of the banister. Dan crammed himself beside her, one shoulder jammed against the old-fashioned wallpaper that she and Aideen kept meaning to replace with something less pink. He grabbed her hands and Bríd heard her own voice, sounding weird. 'So what is it?'

'We're going to Australia.'

'What?'

Mentally, Dan cursed himself. 'No, don't look like that. I'm not being pushy. Honestly, Bríd, I'm not making assumptions again, truly. And I'm sorry about the chairs thing. But, listen, this is amazing. You know Fury's Australian who's building back in Couneen? He's giving me a job.'

'Wait. What kind of a job? In Australia?'

'On the Fraser Coast in Queensland. I've been there before. Honestly, Bríd, it's incredible. You're going to love it. Mr Whelan – his name's Whelan – he's got money in eco-marine tours over there. A big company. They'll organise our papers. He came down a while back and saw my boat and I didn't think anything of it, but Fury had told him about me and said he ought to give me a job.'

'Why?'

'Jesus, I don't know, I haven't a clue – you know what Fury's like.' Dan's eyes were shining. 'Bríd, it's my dream! Can you believe it? I won't really be leaving Couneen. I mean, when I've got money, I can build back there, like Whelan has. I can do that. That's what he showed me. I won't be breaking faith with the past, and you and me can have a life in the sun!'

Bríd's lips seemed so stiff that she felt they might crack. 'No, we can't.'

'Yes, we can. We can do anything, you and me, if we want to. It's a proper salary. We'll be fine. I bet Conor and Aideen would buy you out of HabberDashery. Or you could hang on to your share and Aideen could take on more staff.'

Bríd could feel the tension in every muscle jammed against hers on the narrow step. She stared straight ahead, aware of his eyes, only inches away, willing her to look at him and say it would all be fine. Resistance took every ounce of willpower she'd got. 'Dan, listen to me. Listen carefully. I'm not going to Australia with you. I don't want a new life. I've work and friends and family here in Lissbeg. This was my dream. Always. I've built it from the ground up and it's a success.' Having spoken, she turned her head and the look of blank disbelief on Dan's face made her want to weep.

'What? You can't mean it. I love you.'

'I love you too. But I'm not going with you to Australia. My dream matters too. Don't you see? It doesn't involve sun and sand and — I don't know — coral reefs and glass-bottomed boats. But it matters. It's about great food and good produce, and family, and helping to keep the town going. Lissbeg's my place, Dan.' Her voice wobbled. 'Oh, God, I really love you, but you've got to see this.'

Slowly, a look of resolution formed on Dan's face. 'So you're saying you won't come.'

'Yes. I'm sorry.'

His eyes blazed at her. 'Then I won't go.'

'No. Please, you have to, Dan. I've been wanting to tell you.'

'I don't understand.'

'I was going to call, but I couldn't bear to. And then I thought I'd write, but that was just ludicrous.'

'Tell me what?'

'It's over. You and me. I can't do this any more. You've got to go because, if you stay, we'll get back together. We won't be able to keep away from each other – you know what we're like. But we'll never make this work. You'll be getting nowhere in Couneen and, sooner or later, I'll convince Aideen to let you take over the café, or I'll invent some other dumb idea that'll end up crippling the business, just to give you something to make you feel good about yourself. And you'll know, Dan. You'll know exactly what I'm at and you'll hate me for it. We're not Darby and Joan. We're never going to be. We'll end up hating each other, can't you see?'

'But I love you.'

'Oh, in God's name, please, please stop saying that! Please go away, Dan. You've got a chance now. Fury's given it to you. Please just follow your dream and leave me alone.'

Chapter Thirty

In the first few weeks after Ronan was born it had been hard to get him off to sleep, so Paddy had taken him out in the car, which would do the trick when all else had failed. Driving of any kind still delighted Ronan, and simply being strapped in his car seat seemed to give him immense satisfaction. He was sitting contentedly behind Aideen, turning the pages of *Find Spot at the Library*, when Yvonne emerged from the garden centre and came towards them.

Aideen opened the window and Yvonne peered in. 'Thanks for coming. Oh, my God, is that Ronan? Isn't he gorgeous? Hello, dotey little boy, do you know who I am? I'm your aunt!'

Aideen had arrived in the crowded car park feeling as tense as a fiddle string, but the tone of Yvonne's voice was so like Eileen's that she almost giggled. Struggling to keep a straight face at the thought of yet another aunt scrolling though Gucci Gucci Goo's website, she smiled up at Yvonne. 'Sort of half-aunt, really.'

'Yes, but isn't it lovely? I haven't a nephew or niece to my name, so even a half one's exciting.'

Aideen looked at the envelope Yvonne had in her hand. 'Is that the letter you told me about on the phone?'

'Yeah. Like I said, Dad wanted to write to you but I didn't have your address.' Yvonne, who'd been making faces at Ronan, held out the envelope. 'Anyway, he didn't think you'd want a letter turning up in the post.'

'No. Thanks, that was nice of you both.' There was no point in Aideen saying she'd hoped against hope that Yvonne would say nothing to her father. She'd known it was too late for that as soon as she'd seen Yvonne's number appear on her phone.

Yvonne broke what had become an awkward silence. 'Right, I'll just leave it with you, then.'

Aideen was longing to know how Yvonne had broached the subject with her father, and how he'd reacted, but to ask seemed inappropriate, so she just accepted the letter, noticing that he'd addressed it to Mrs A. McCarthy, which felt like a whole new level of weird.

Yvonne smiled. 'Whatever else happens, I hope you and I will see each other again.' This was another potential twist that Aideen hadn't considered. Instinctively, she pushed the letter into the glove compartment, wishing Yvonne would go away and leave her to deal with one thing at a time. Suddenly, Yvonne blushed and said that she didn't want to be pushy.

'No, I know. And you're not. I just … Look, I never said sorry for just turning up in your in-box. I sort of hadn't thought the whole thing through.'

'You needn't apologise. I didn't have to answer your email, did I?' Yvonne nodded at the glove compartment. 'I don't know what he said in the letter but I think he was glad you gave him a chance to write. Anyway, look, I'd better get back to work.' She moved away from the car, waving at Ronan, threaded her way across the car park and disappeared through the garden centre's automatic doors.

Aideen drove back to the castle roundabout and took the exit for Ballyfin. A few minutes after the turn-off for Lissbeg, where the traffic grew lighter, she pulled in at a field gate, opened the glove compartment, and lifted the flap of the envelope as gingerly as if it contained a bomb that might explode in her shaking hand. Inside was a sheet of paper headed with the honeybee logo and the caption *Making Your Garden Bloom for Three Generations.* He had used a black biro and signed himself *Derek Murphy*, though the line immediately above his name said, *I'm happy to be your dad.* Aideen read to the accompaniment of murmurs from the back seat, where Ronan was lifting and dropping the flaps of his book's illustrations in yet another attempt to find Spot the dog. It was warm in the car with the windows closed, and soothing to hear the little voice behind her. Outside, a blackbird was seeking worms in the cold earth where the field had been cut back to stubble. Aideen's cheeks were wet with tears that tasted salty when they touched her lips and she licked them away. When she'd read through the letter a third time, she put it back into the envelope and drove on carefully to Lissbeg.

Hanna was restocking shelves from the returns trolley when Aideen came in with Ronan on her hip. She kissed Aideen's cheek, and offered to take the book from Ronan's hand. 'Are we done with this? Have you come to borrow another?' Ronan, who'd beamed at the sight of her, pouted and pulled away. Aideen shook him gently. 'Remember what we said? You're going to give the book back to Hanna and she'll give you another one, so you can keep trying to find Spot. Will we see if she has *Spot Goes to the Farm*?'

Hanna was about to lead the way to where the library's picture books were displayed on low, brightly coloured shelves, when she saw that Aideen's eyes looked as if she'd been crying. 'Are you okay?'

'Yes. Fine.'

But it was evident that she wasn't and, after a moment's hesitation, Hanna took a decision. Collecting *Spot Goes to the Farm*, she ushered Aideen into the empty reading room, settled Ronan on the floor and, having closed the door, pulled out a couple of chairs. 'Sit down. Has something happened?' Aideen, who had resisted at first, took the letter from her pocket and gave it to her, watching her face anxiously as she read it. Then they sat in silence while Hanna chose her words. 'This must have been a shock.'

'Well, yes and no. I was the one who made the first approach.'

'He seems nice.'

'I know. I'm glad. And, to tell the truth, I'm really pleased that he wants to take things slowly. I'd say, when you read between the lines, that he won't get back in touch with me for ages.' Aideen looked hopeful. 'Or even at all.'

'And that would be good?'

'Well, you can see what he says. His wife doesn't know anything about me.'

'He also says he's going to consider how he ought to tell her.'

'But she won't want him to, will she? I mean, she doesn't need to know. I thought I might write back to him and say that.'

'But what about Yvonne? She knows.'

'Yes, but she could say nothing. She wouldn't want to upset her mum.'

Hanna spoke gently. 'But that's not what you're worried about, is it? Have you told Conor you've got in touch with your dad?'

'No. He doesn't need to know either, though, does he?' Aideen flushed. 'I wish I'd never started all this. I thought I was doing the right thing for Ronan.'

'And what about yourself?'

'Look at all the people who might get hurt.'

Hanna took her hand. 'Okay, that's a consideration. But, just for a minute, think about yourself. Aren't you glad to hear that your dad loved your mother? That he's happy to know you're well, and happy to hear that Ronan exists?'

Aideen looked at the letter lying on the table. 'I guess so. It was nice to see his handwriting.'

'You can tell from this that he's a kind man. I doubt if he'd do anything that you don't want him to. But, Aideen, I wouldn't bank on never hearing from him again. I think he will tell his wife, and I don't think you should try to stop him.'

Aideen looked mulish. 'Aunt Bridge said we didn't need him, and we don't.'

'And I think you ought to tell Conor all about this as soon as you can.'

Aideen pulled her hand away and twisted her engagement ring, feeling the edge of the polished lapis lazuli turn against her plain wedding band. When they'd eloped to Italy, she and Conor hadn't had time to buy wedding rings so, when they made their vows in the olive grove, Conor had picked two blades of grass which they'd tied round each other's fingers. After the registry office wedding, Aideen had framed the selfie they'd taken in Florence and put the grasses between the mount and the image of them dancing on the table, laughing and wearing flowers in their hair. Now, as she sat in silence, Ronan crowed triumphantly. He'd turned a page of his book and found a picture of a washing line with a laundry basket beneath it. Lifting the flap that covered the basket, he revealed a litter of kittens and drummed his heels ecstatically on the floor. Close to tears, Aideen looked at Hanna.

'I don't want Conor to know. We're fine on our own, the three of us, with Una.'

Hanna grasped her hand more firmly. 'You mustn't start building a history of deception. Honestly, Aideen, I know what I'm talking about. I had a husband who lied to me for decades.'

'That was different. He was cheating on you.'

'Yes, and he told me he'd lied about it because he didn't want to hurt me. But you know something? In the end, it wasn't the cheating that was the worst of it. It was the lies. The fact that, when I looked back, every scene in our marriage had to be taken apart, scrutinised and rewritten. Every memory of happiness that I had was potentially false. Do you know what that does to a person's head? And, God help me, it didn't stop there in my case. I went on and did the same thing to Jazz. I perpetuated Malcolm's lies because the truth would have hurt her and, as a result, she was messed up for years.'

Aideen looked down at Ronan. 'I don't want us hurt.'

'Then stop trying to keep this a secret from Conor. You're playing with fire.'

The sliding door behind them opened and Owen put his head in. 'Sorry to interrupt but Charles Aukin's waiting.'

Hanna rose to her feet. 'Of course. I'd forgotten. I'm coming.'

Before Aideen could stand up, Charles appeared behind Owen. 'There's no hurry.' Seeing Ronan, he beamed. 'Who's the little guy?'

Hanna picked Ronan up. 'This is Ronan, my godson, and his mum, Aideen McCarthy.'

Charles offered Ronan a handshake. 'He's going to be a reader, I see.' Both of Ronan's hands were required to clutch his book to his chest, but he gave Charles a shy, enchanting smile.

Hanna turned to Aideen. 'I'm due to turn a page of the psalter and Charles is coming in with me.'

Aideen stood up, saying she'd take Ronan home, but Charles interrupted. 'Why don't you join us? Ronan's a guy who likes picture books. Come and show him his heritage.'

He made for the door and, behind his back, Aideen looked at Hanna. 'Should I?'

'Yes, of course. You're welcome. But, look, we were interrupted and I'm supposed to be lunching with Charles. Do you want to drop back later?'

Aideen shook her head. 'No, I'm fine. You're working and we ought to get home.'

Hanna wasn't sure that their conversation had actually reached a conclusion but, seeing Charles glancing over his shoulder, she followed him with Ronan still in her arms. As they walked down the library she managed another quick word with Aideen. 'Please think about what I said. This country was built on half-truths and lies and secrets that couldn't be told. It's the worst foundation for anything. Seriously, Aideen. Don't let it be the basis for Ronan's relationship with his granddad.'

In the exhibition space Aideen held Ronan when Hanna opened the psalter's glass case. He'd become very quiet since they'd come in, awed by the low light and the shining screens around the walls. As Hanna turned the page, he looked down like the others, his eyes wide and *Spot Goes to the Farm* dangling from his hand. Today's page turn revealed text on the two facing pages, interspersed with flowing illustration and beginning with a magnificent illuminated capital C. The letter enclosed an image of hills against a gilded sky in which the moon and sun hung above a series of mountain peaks. Hanna smiled, recognising their outline. 'See, Ronan, those are the hills way up above Daddy's farm.'

Ronan continued to stare at the page intently. Aideen bent to inspect the text, taking care not to hold him too close to the precious manuscript. 'What does it say?'

Charles Aukin answered her. '"I will up lift mine eyes unto the hills, from whence cometh my help." Further down there's a bit about how neither the sun nor the moon will smite us by day or by night.'

Aideen turned to look at him. 'Is that what people were afraid of back then? That the sun or the moon might crash into the Earth?'

'Who knows? I guess, ultimately, they were afraid of the same things that we are. Catastrophes they knew they couldn't control. That's why they felt they needed powerful help.'

'Why should God be in the hills, though?'

'Can't tell you that either.' Charles looked down at the book in its glass case. 'High places have always been thought of as holy. Hard to reach, beautiful and dangerous. A home for the gods.'

Running down the side of the page, a series of little oblong frames was outlined in coloured dots that shone like jewels and, in each frame, a figure in monk's robes sat at a high desk. Most were little tonsured men with big noses, indistinguishable from one another, except for the curve of an arm, a flower in a pot in the background, or the presence of a cat at one figure's feet. Among them, here and there, robed and working with quill pens, were creatures that could have come down from the hills. Without making a sound, Ronan pointed them out with one finger. A fox, with a russet-coloured snout and inkstained whiskers. An owl, whose large, luminous eyes were turned to face the reader. A brown hare, with long, pink-lined ears. Ronan bounced in Aideen's arms and caught hold of the sleeve of Charles's jacket. Jabbing his finger urgently at the hare, he squealed, 'Oook!' Obediently, they all looked closer, and saw a detail that no one but Ronan had noticed. Painted in the same colour as the monks' brown robes, as if the artist had consciously made it hard to spot, the hare's back leg appeared beneath the skirt of its trailing habit, its curved paw tensed against the leg of its tall stool.

Once again, Charles and Hanna had chicken on rye and drank coffee. It was too cold to sit outdoors and Lissbeg's office workers and shopkeepers were eating lunch in a cheerful, noisy fug. Beyond the condensation that misted the Garden Café's windows, the nuns' garden looked bare and colourless. Having found a corner table for two, Charles sat opposite Hanna. 'Not the best spot for a quiet word.'

'Oh, I don't know. When people are talking, you can be pretty sure they're not listening. Why? Did you have something to say?'

'Just that I had a visitor to the castle the other day. Actually, it was Fury. My boiler's acting up.'

'It's a bad time of the year to be left without heating. Was he able to fix it?'

'Sure. At a price. You know Fury.' Charles looked at Hanna over his gold-rimmed glasses. 'In other news, I gather that there's an issue about this television programme.'

She met his eyes. 'Is there? What's that?'

'I hear you're concerned about the content.' Charles paused for a mouthful of sandwich. 'Don't worry, I had it from Fury. It's not the talk of the town.'

'And what did Fury say?' Hanna could hear the tension in her voice.

'Don't get spiky, Miss Casey. Things are going to be all right. He began by filling me in with some details about the stand-off that happened at Castle Lancy. Then he questioned my judgement of character when it came to Tim Slattery, and ended by pointing out that I'm just a blow-in around these parts. Isn't that what you call it? An outsider likely to bumble about upsetting apple carts. Which, according to Fury and The Divil, is what I've done.' Seeing Hanna's expression, Charles shook his head at her. 'No, you don't need to apologise for Fury and, if you've any sense, you'll forget this conversation ever happened. I'm just here to tell you that I'm the one who'll decide what's on my display board at the castle. Plus you have my word that I'll control what Tim says in front of the *Nationwide* cameras. Or anywhere else.'

'But how?'

'Oh, come now, Hanna, it's not rocket science. You were there when Tim and I discussed the terms on which I gave the psalter to the nation. A permanent loan, remember? It's an arrangement librarians tend to dislike, so they tell me, but the bottom line is that I prefer to keep control where I can. An old banker's habit that dies hard.' Charles picked up his coffee cup and winked at her. 'Anyway, after Fury gave me the nod, I called Tim. I reminded him that I don't change my mind without good reason, but that I do like to get my own way.'

Hanna gaped at him. 'So you're saying that ...'

'Liam Casey and James Hartnett will be listed as having been in command of the respective sides in the action at Castle Lancy. Nothing more. That will be the extent to which their names will appear.'

'I can't believe you just lifted the phone and did that.'

'Like I told you before, the last thing I wanted was to come here and make trouble. Besides, I was strong-armed by Fury. He said that if I didn't fix Tim, he wouldn't fix my boiler.' Chuckling at Hanna's relief, Charles winked at her again. 'That was the clincher. Because, believe me, you've no idea how cold that damn castle can get in winter.'

Chapter Thirty-One

On Saturday nights, Hanna never bothered to set her alarm clock, knowing that on a Sunday she could lie in as long as she liked. This morning she'd slept deeply, having sat up late talking things over with Brian, and the sound of her phone seemed to drag her up from a pit. As she pushed her hair out of her eyes, her first sensation was a wave of relief at the thought of Charles's conversation with Tim. This was followed by a familiar sense of annoyance as her waking brain identified the ping of an incoming text. She rolled over, realising that Brian wasn't beside her, groped for her phone and squinted at the screen. *I CANT BE DOING WITH@ THISW SRF* Groaning, Hanna sat up and awaited the second text. It came at once. *THE GARAGE HAS BP IM DOING SCONES*

As she dropped the phone onto the duvet, Brian came into the room. 'What's the story?'

'Mary wants baking powder. She's making scones.'

'Didn't you buy her self-raising flour last week?'

'She can't be doing with it.' Hanna threw back the duvet and got out of bed. 'It's not a problem. I'll drop in after I've had lunch with Jazz.' Brian drew her across the room to the window and they stood looking down at the russet glen. 'Sleep well?'

'Like a log. God bless Fury.'

'I notice you don't object to *him* turning up on a big white horse.'

'Fury's different.'

'So's Charles Aukin, apparently.'

Hanna made a face at him. 'Don't push your luck. We may have kissed and made up but I'm still cross.'

'Very?'

'Slightly.'

'I'll take that.' Brian gave her a one-armed hug. 'Look, I could pick up the baking powder and nip over to Mary if you like. You don't want her texting again while you're chilling with Jazz.'

'No, it's okay. Why should you have to cope with my mam on a Sunday?' Hanna turned and laid her cheek briefly against his chest. 'Tell you what, how about you make us dinner? I won't be late.'

A bright fire was burning on the hearth when Jazz opened the door. Waves beating against the cliff were hurling flecks of foam so high that they drifted into the field. 'They look like flowers, don't they?' Jazz stood admiring them for a moment before ushering

Hanna in and indicating a fireside chair. 'Sit down. I'm toasting.' There was a plate on the hearthstone, covered by an upturned bowl. Tilting it, Hanna discovered a pile of crumpets dripping with butter. 'Crumpets for lunch?'

'Don't be hidebound. I got cheese, and quince jam too, so we can call them savoury bites and make them acceptable. Don't you love how the butter oozes into all the little holes?'

Having slipped off her jacket, Hanna sat down and warmed her hands at the flames. 'Crumpets are perfect any time of day. Remember the crab-apple jelly we used to have them with when you were little?'

'Nursery teas. All my friends were going to McDonald's after school and you were giving me crumpets by the fire.'

'I may have been slightly influenced by reading *Brideshead Revisited*.'

'Or Enid Blyton – oh, dammit!' Jazz had burned her fingers by attempting to lift the bowl. 'What happened to that thing we used to have in London, a plate with a cover that had a handle on top?'

'That was a proper crumpet dish, bought in an antiques shop. I've no idea where it got to.' The dish was among the many possessions that had been lost in the wreckage of Hanna's marriage. Every so often, the lack of one would produce a pang that far outweighed the object's practical loss. To take her mind off the blue-patterned plate with its insulated cloche, she said that Jazz's makeshift cover was far more suited to Maggie's place. 'Not that Maggie ever had crumpets. These are probably the first the house has seen.'

'Nobody here seems to have ever made anything but scones.'

Remembering Mary's texts, Hanna laughed. 'Scones are part of the Irish DNA. Maggie made other things too, though, and all on the open fire. Apple cake that she topped with sugar and spices. Potato farls we ate with country butter and chopped scallions. You could see the salt crystals in Maggie's butter. She churned it herself.'

'What else?'

'Colcannon, made with shredded cabbage and seasoned with white pepper. I loved that. Your nan disapproved. She couldn't believe that pots could be properly washed in a galvanised bucket. But I had the best time eating those meals here with Maggie. They were liberating.'

Jazz sat back on her heels, holding the toasting fork. 'You always say she was grumpy.'

'Well, she was old and alone, and when I look back, I think she was frightened. I know I told you she wasn't scared of fairies, and she never locked the door so she can't have been afraid of burglars, but she must have wondered what was going to happen to her in the end. She'd have hated to be prised out of her snail shell, and I remember talk about putting her in a home.'

'What did happen to her in the end?'

'I found her in the garden.'

'*You* did?'

'I'd come round on my bike after school, as usual. She was down by the potato ridges. She must have gone out to dig some for her dinner. There was an enamel basin beside her, full of the little spuds she called poreens.'

'God, Mum, that must have been awful.'

'And we'd no mobile phones in those days, remember. I had to go rushing off to Lissbeg for the doctor. But I knew when I saw her that she was already dead. I worried a bit afterwards that she might have been lying there for hours, calling. The doctor said death would have been instantaneous, though.' Hanna shook herself. 'It was probably what she'd have wanted. She'd have fought like a steer if they'd tried to put her in a home.'

The cheese Jazz had bought was made with herbs and caraway seed, and tasted delicious on crumpets with quince jam. Hanna ate sparingly, mindful of her planned dinner with Brian, but Jazz managed several crumpets, sitting on the floor with her plate on her lap, as she'd done at teatime in London when she was small. When she finished, and was licking her fingers, she glanced up at Hanna and caught her checking her watch. 'What's the problem?'

'Nothing. Just that your nan texted me this morning. She needs something picked up from the shop.'

'I was going to make coffee.'

'That would be nice but I really ought to go soon.'

Jazz began to gather the plates together and, getting up to help her, Hanna remarked that Brian had offered to do Mary's errand. 'It didn't seem fair to dump it on him, though.'

'Why not?'

The question was so blunt that Hanna found herself at a loss. 'It's just she's my problem, isn't she? Not his.'

Jazz put her hands on her hips, looking for a moment exactly like Mary. 'This is so you, Mum, and it's really unfair to Brian.'

'What?'

'Seriously, I've been wanting to say this. Brian's pretty much family now, and you shouldn't treat him as if he's an outsider. It's not kind. And you absolutely shouldn't go round thinking of Nan as nothing more than a problem.'

'But I don't.'

'Yes, you do. You're scared of the future. You won't face it. You ward Brian off when he tries to give you a hand with her, and I bet you imagine you need to protect me. Look, the bottom line is that Nan's getting older, and the chances are that, as time goes on, she's going to get even more batty than she is now.'

'Darling, that's horrible. She's not batty.'

'Okay. Difficult. Stroppy. Hard to manage. And maybe a time will come when a doctor uses a scarier word, like dementia. But, Mum, if that happens, it won't be the end of the world. Anyway, there's no point in getting screwed up about the future, because nobody knows for certain what's going to happen next. You've just told me what happened to Maggie, and that came out of the blue.'

'But ...'

'You have to let people help you, Mum. It's only sensible. And you've got to stop feeling guilty about the fact that you can't stand Nan.'

'Jazz! That's simply not true.'

'Oh, give me a break! Neither of you can bear the other for long. That's just a fact. You don't get on, you never have, and you're not likely to start now when she's being more Nan-like than ever. It doesn't mean you don't love her, we all know that. And can't you see how frustrating it is to know that you're worried and not to be able to help? Look, I'm the one Nan gets on with. I can be your back-up. I'm talking about ordinary stuff, not big dramatic family confrontations. Right now, all she needs is a helping hand and a bit of entertainment. We could get her to fire her texts at me sometimes, instead of at you. And you know she fancies the hell out of Brian, so why not let him carry a bit of the load?' Jazz stopped in full flight and giggled at Hanna's gobsmacked reaction. 'You're not going to say that she doesn't flirt with Brian?'

Defeated, Hanna sat down. 'No, I'm not.'

'Well, there you are. I'm right about the rest of it too. Brian's as frustrated as I am because you won't let him help. Really, Mum. There's no point in looking back or second-guessing the future. What we've got to do is pull together and make the best of things now.'

When Hanna arrived at the bungalow with the baking powder, Mary waved a reproachful hand at a batch of a dozen scones. 'I couldn't be waiting all day so I went ahead and made those. Take them home to Brian, he likes my baking.'

Hanna put the redundant purchase on the table. 'I told you I'd be coming, Mam. I was having lunch with Jazz.'

Mary brightened. 'How is she?'

Taking a deep breath, Hanna sat down. 'She's fine. Actually, she suggested you might text her sometimes. When you want something bought. She could get it and bring it over here, instead of me. Would you do that?'

'Oh, I see. So I'm a burden.'

'That's not what I said and you can't think Jazz did. You know her better than that.'

Mary pursed her lips. 'A child doesn't want to be hanging around a grumpy old woman.' She shot a shrewd look at Hanna. 'You didn't.'

'Jazz isn't a child. And you're not Maggie.'

Mary fiddled with the lovers' knot pinned to her cardigan. It struck Hanna that, since her father's death, she'd seldom seen her mother without her filigree nine-carat brooch. There was a long silence before Mary spoke again. 'You hated being sent round to fetch and carry for her.'

'You're years younger than Maggie was. You don't need someone to fetch and carry for you. You just need a bit of help now and then.'

'I could tweet Jazz, I suppose.' Seeing Hanna's surprise, Mary assumed an expression of smug satisfaction. 'Now so! You didn't know I've a Twitter account.'

'No, I didn't.'

'Which goes to show, doesn't it, that you don't know it all? It was Pat Fitz that got me up to speed in the twittersphere.'

'But you stopped doing her computer class.'

'I'll have you know that what goes on in your library isn't the be-all and end-all in Lissbeg. I went round to Pat's with my phone and she set me up in decent privacy, sitting above the butcher's by the fire. I'm @MaryFromLissbeg. I've a rake of followers.' Mary frowned. 'Actually, I'd be better to DM Jazz. If you put something up on your feed, the world and his wife retweets it. You might as well be plucking a goose in a gale.' Distracted by a vision of her mother trending in Ireland, Hanna said that this had been kind of Pat. Mary shoved the wire tray of scones across the table. 'Go on now, take these home to your man.'

Recognising that she'd been dismissed, Hanna got to her feet. Then, putting her hands on the table top, she looked Mary in the eye. 'Mam. You don't have to worry that people will be talking about James Hartnett and Liam. They won't.' There was a pause in which she wondered if Mary might announce that she'd no idea who James and Liam were.

Instead, lowering her voice, Mary glanced over her shoulder. 'Did you fix it?'

Thrown by this unaccustomed air of furtiveness, Hanna sought for a way to explain what had happened. 'Charles Aukin spoke to Tim at the County Library in Carrick. And, yes, Fury was part of the discussion.'

Suddenly Mary reassumed her usual air of assurance. 'Fury

fixed it. You had your head screwed on right when you thought of going to him.'

'I didn't. Well, I told him I was worried.' Hanna's throat tightened. 'I was worried about you.' For a moment Mary seemed to be staring straight through her into the past. Then she got up, found a paper bag and, bundling the scones into it, held it out to Hanna at arm's length. 'Well, thank you.'

'You're welcome.'

'Right so.'

Hanna took the scones and they stood there, unable to touch yet closer than they'd ever been before. Deciding it was now or never, she cleared her throat again. 'Look, Mam, I've never said that I'm grateful to you. For taking me and Jazz in when I upped and left Malcolm.'

'Blood is thicker than water.'

'I do want to say thank you, though.'

'You're welcome, child.'

It was dusk and crows were creaking homeward when Hanna, on her way back to the glen, took the route that skirted the forest. Fury, whose house was set beside the road, surrounded by oaks and conifers, was chopping wood in his front yard. Quivering with anticipation, The Divil was crouched nearby, alert for flying splinters for which he leaped like a twisting salmon and caught neatly in his snapping jaws. Seeing Hanna's car slowing, Fury strolled down to greet her, taking a cigarette from behind his ear. 'Not a bad day.'

'I've been round to visit my mam.'

'How's she doing?'

'She's better for what you did.'

Fury's entire attention seemed to be focused on lighting his roll-up and, recognising that what she'd just said had been both unnecessary and unwanted, Hanna moved to safer ground. 'Pat Fitz has set her up on Twitter.'

'That'll keep her going for a while.'

There was an awkward pause in which Hanna was inspired to reach for the bag of scones on the passenger seat. 'Would you take a few of these? My mam baked them for Brian but we're never going to get through them.'

Fury indicated gracious acceptance. 'I don't mind. I'm heart-scalded trying to wean The Divil off the custard creams.' He flicked away his spent match, his tone indicating that the subject of his intervention on the Caseys' behalf was now closed. 'How's the collecting going in the library?'

'Things are still coming in but it's tailing off. That always happens with a project like this one, and it's good because it leaves time to assess what you've got.'

'Is that so?'

'And we're going to have plenty.'

With little attention and less help from Tim, the branch librarians had liaised and made practical decisions. Much of what had been brought in was to be displayed in the form of captioned photographs. Someone was designing a timeline, which would appear in each library, to give an overview, and they'd agreed that the branches would feature material that was as local to each as it could be. So the photos taken secretly by Mrs O'Carroll's granddad would go on display in Ballyfin, close to his family's farm, while Lissbeg would feature the story of a nun who'd hidden medicine in the convent garden, from which it was picked up at night and taken into the hills. Having outlined these arrangements to Fury, Hanna finished with a glancing reference to what had been left unspoken. 'And Owen's drafting a leaflet explaining that, at the time, the psalter would have been in Castle Lancy.'

Fury remarked that the library must have a power of books relating to the period in question. 'As far as I can see, you were hardly let fight if you hadn't got something in print. God knows how any of the leaders ever had time to drill with a gun, when they were all writing poems and pamphlets listing Ireland's wrongs. Not to mention setting the record straight for future generations. Sure, didn't one of the women in the GPO during the Easter Rising say Pádraig Pearse spent most of the time with a fountain pen in a corner, writing the official version of the fight?'

'I haven't heard that.'

'Ay, well, you'd want to read a history book.' Fury pinched out his roll-up and replaced it behind his ear. 'Though just because something's in a book doesn't mean it's the truth.' He straightened his back and looked up at the sky. 'The nights will be getting shorter soon and, before we know it, we'll be gearing up for next year's tourists. Did you hear that young Dan Cafferky's giving up on the boat in Couneen?'

'I heard he's off to Australia.'

'There's a lot to be said for sticking to your guns and, God knows, it takes courage. On the other hand, there's much to be said for knowing it's time to quit.'

Night had fallen by the time Hanna reached the Hag's Glen. As the lights in the farm buildings dropped behind her, she could see the running river by moonlight. The gauge on her dashboard showed a steady fall in the outside temperature and, by the time she approached the house, there was hoar frost on thorn and grass. What must it have been like, she thought, living a life on the run in those hills? To risk death because you believed so fiercely in a dream? Smoke by day and flame by night would have advertised their presence, but they must have needed fires to keep warm and to heat food. Did they build shelters? Or find caves in which to huddle together against the cold? How did it feel to know that, by taking up arms, you'd endangered your family? To be certain, each time you went into action, that there would be vicious reprisals? What was it like to lie in the heather and look down at burning farms and shops and little businesses, and to hear gunfire and know your unarmed neighbours were being shot? And what did it do to your head to find yourself pitted against men and women who, only a few months before, had stood with you shoulder to shoulder?

Stopping the car by the river, Hanna got out, huddling her jacket around her and drawing its collar above her ears. Before the Civil War ended there had been executions and atrocities that, despite the passage of time, her mother's generation still spoke about in lowered voices. And which was worse? Hanna asked herself. The silence that leaves wounds unhealed or the shouting prompted by Tim's brand of self-serving sensationalism? Up at the house, where the lights were on in the kitchen, Brian could be seen pouring wine and moving from the fridge to the stove. Hanna leaned against the car and watched him. The only sound came from the rushing water, and in the distance, the mountain range was blue-black against the sky. Just before she'd left the bungalow, Mary had handed her a piece of paper. 'You might as well take this away with you too. Then you'll have the whole story. I don't know if I'd do better to leave it where I found it, or put a match to it. Still, here it is.' It was a letter in Maggie's handwriting, dated June 1947. Turning it over, Hanna had seen it began *Dear Lizzie*.

'Where did this come from?'

'It was inside in the family Bible your dad brought home from Maggie's place when she died. I suppose Maggie was going to post it and didn't.'

Now, with the letter in her hand and the night wind blowing, Hanna wondered if Maggie had decided to talk to her friend

Lizzie instead of writing, or if, in the end, what she'd put down on the sheet of pale blue notepaper had just been too difficult to share.

I didn't see you to speak to at the graveyard. I was glad you came. It was hard to believe it took ten men to carry Liam's coffin. He'd put a great belly on him since he married Mariah Kane. I didn't set foot in the church but I watched the volley by the graveside. Men grown as bulky as he was, with their coat collars up and their hats down over their faces, as if it mattered who they were or if they'd be seen. They knew damn well that the guards have more sense than to take any notice. Soon there'll be none of them left to go round firing guns in the air any more. Liam hadn't a pick of fat on him when he went out fighting. He'd had his seventeenth birthday that week and he said he'd wait no longer. Mam made him a big feed of rashers and eggs before he left, and he stood up in front of the fire and read a poem out of a book.

Maggie had written the verse without quotation marks or line breaks.

O wise men, riddle me this. What if the dream come true? What if the dream come true? and if millions unborn shall dwell in the house that I shaped in my heart, the noble house of my thought?

Hanna recalled two more lines of that poem by Pádraig Pearse, known to every schoolchild of her own generation.

Lord, I have staked my soul, I have staked the lives of my kin
On the truth of Thy dreadful word.

Tears filled her eyes at the thought of how Maggie's letter had continued.

Liam told Mam that that inspired the poem he wrote himself for the competition in the Inquirer. *The one they printed alongside the photo the Tans found for his poster. I might forgive him for staking our lives, and I won't deny he had courage, but I'll never forgive Liam for shooting James Hartnett. He had no call to go strutting around talking about my honour and God's word. Not when I never said a word myself. I never spoke. I never opened my beak, Lizzie. I never told you my trouble when I wrote. I coped on my own in Liverpool with no one there to help. I lived in exile when I knew my mother would die lonely without me. That was my fate because Liam chose to go out and fight for Ireland. I've never denied that he suffered. But I was near twenty years scrubbing floors in a foreign country and sending most of my wages across the sea. My money kept Liam in drink as much as it fed my poor mother. And then he turned round on the night that she was buried and told me he'd killed the father of my still-born child.*

Pulling her jacket closer, Hanna shivered. It's all water under the bridge, she told herself. Jazz is right. The past is gone and we can't control the future. All we can do is look after each other now. Overhead, there was a rush of wings as a bird swept up the valley. The distant mountains had begun to merge with the darkening sky. Then a second light streamed from the house and she knew, with a rush of pleasure, that Brian had turned it on to welcome her home.

Chapter Thirty-Two

Aideen finished telling Conor her story. 'I didn't want anyone hurt.'

'It doesn't matter.'

'No, but Hanna's right.'

'Look, I know now, don't I? It's now that matters.'

'Will you mind if my father does get in touch again?'

'Do you think he will?'

'Hanna thinks so. I dunno. And, really, Conor, I'm fine either way. Whatever happens, we'll tell Ronan the truth and we'll be grand.'

It was early morning after a night of storm. Ronan had woken them, whimpering at the pain of a new tooth, and they'd carried him down to the kitchen to make tea. Distracted from the tooth by the attention, he was sitting on the floor annoying the cats, which, for once, were curled up together. 'Come here before they lose patience with you and scratch!' Conor swung him into the air, swooping him round and making aeroplane noises.

Ronan squealed with excitement and Aideen caught Conor's arm. 'Don't, he's dribbling on your head!'

'A bit of spit never hurt. Anyway, it's magic. Think of the way we spat in the earth when we planted this fellow's tree.'

'Did Una and Paddy do that when they planted yours?'

'Why do you think it gives such a good yield?'

'Did your great-granny do it too when she planted the crab-apple tree?'

'I'd say she did. It's always been a good-luck charm.'

Aideen took Ronan in her arms. 'Let's go up to the orchard.'

'It's freezing out there.'

'No, it's not. The sun's up. Come and see.' She wriggled into a coat and, keeping Ronan warm under it, took Conor's hand and pulled him into the yard. Together they walked up to the orchard, where skeleton branches reared against the sky. 'Look at the spiders' webs!' Aideen pointed at the gossamer network, which stretched between the branches and linked the trees. The morning light streaming through the dew-spangled webs made them shimmer. 'See, Ronan!' With a patch on his cheek as red as an apple, Ronan put his head out from under her coat.

Conor put his arm around Aideen and hugged them both. 'Paddy used to call those webs the heavens' embroidered cloths.'

Standing in wet grass, Aideen considered the glittering orchard. 'Isn't that from a poem? Blue, dim, dark things, wasn't it? I thought it was about the night sky.' Conor gave her another hug and grinned. 'That's what Una used to tell him and Paddy always laughed at her. He said that a halfway decent poem could stand up to a bit of kicking, and that he preferred the morning to the night.'

Acknowledgements

When I began *The Year of Lost and Found* I hadn't decided how the story would end. I think this departure from my normal process when writing a Finfarran novel arose from the strangeness of 2020, as did the book's eventual ending with its focus on the idea that no one can foresee the future, and on an image of sunrise after a night of storm. I didn't know how resonant the title would prove to be either: that's something that has emerged as the months have passed. In a global pandemic few people escape without losses, yet it seems to me that we can also find – or, maybe, rediscover – things that are precious. I was writing during a year of uncertainty and, as I type these words, I've no idea what lies ahead, but during this time of loss and isolation I've been heartened by friends and strangers all over the world. With your support I've found loving-kindness, reasons to cultivate patience, and ways to imagine a future that won't just take us back to the world we knew before lockdown but will move us on to embrace something better, more balanced and more sustainable.

I'm grateful to old friends who've kept in touch by phone, online and, when regulations permitted, over socially distanced cups of coffee. You know who you are and how much I've relied on your strength and comfort, whether in the form of shared laughter, a virtual shoulder to cry on, or a sympathetic ear when the broadband went down. I'm particularly indebted to the friends who helped me to understand what it might mean to Hanna to face Mary's incipient dementia; and I'd like to acknowledge my late mother's insights into, and lived experience of, the silence and pain surrounding the role of women in Ireland's struggle for independence.

I'd like to thank my neighbours too, in Bermondsey and on the west coast of Ireland, the people who wave and call greetings across roads and beaches, have taken in deliveries, left cake or soup on the doorstep, or lent me carefully sanitised scissors to keep my fringe out of my eyes. Thank you, Maev, Dan and Monica, Noel and Caitríona, Seán, Stephen and Jo, and so many others. And *mo cheol sibh* Nikki and Colm in Siopa an Bhuailtín, Baile 'n Fheirtéaraigh, who kept us supplied with food when we were in quarantine, and Helen Ní Shé who sent photos of our Irish garden when we were stuck in London without so much as a window box.

I'm grateful to the many strangers I've met on Twitter and other social media platforms, whose mutual support and kindness are simply phenomenal. The readers and authors who flooded my timeline when I launched *The Heart of Summer* during lockdown and cheered from the virtual sidelines while I've been writing this seventh Finfarran novel. The Instagrammers and web- and podcasters who distract and entertain me. The medievalists, librarians, politicians and activists who make me raise my head and enlarge my mind. And the regulars and newcomers who comment, chat and send messages to me on Facebook, share little nuggets of happiness and contentment, and offer generous insights into your lives. Once again, you know who you are, and I hope you know how glad I am that you're out there. What you may not know is how much you've helped in the making of this book.

I'm deeply grateful, as always, to my publisher, Hachette Books Ireland, my editor Ciara Doorley, Joanna Smyth, Ruth Shern, Elaine Egan, everyone else on Breda Purdue's brilliant team, and to Hazel Orme, my copy-editor, and Mark Walsh at Plunkett PR. I'd also like to give a huge shout-out to the booksellers, independent and otherwise, who've continued to work behind closed doors, by phone, online, and by click and collect, to get books to readers despite the challenges of Covid-19. The same goes for librarians, literary festivals and all the unstoppable book clubs who've got in touch and asked me to come and talk to them via Zoom; and, of course, for the webcasters and interviewers who've beamed me across the world online and on radio, frequently while I panicked about camera settings and headsets in full make-up and furry bedroom slippers. You've been unflappable and I'm very grateful.

Finally, my love and thanks go to my husband, Wilf Judd, and to my stellar agent, Gaia Banks at Sheil Land Associates, UK. Without you both to steady the boat during this troubled year, *The Year of Lost and Found* would never have reached safe harbour.